INTERCEPTOR CITY

By the same author

DOUBLE EAGLE
A novel by Dan Abnett

• GAUNT'S GHOSTS •
Dan Abnett

THE FOUNDING
BOOK 1: FIRST AND ONLY
BOOK 2: GHOSTMAKER
BOOK 3: NECROPOLIS

THE SAINT
BOOK 4: HONOUR GUARD
BOOK 5: THE GUNS OF TANITH
BOOK 6: STRAIGHT SILVER
BOOK 7: SABBAT MARTYR

THE LOST
BOOK 8: TRAITOR GENERAL
BOOK 9: HIS LAST COMMAND
BOOK 10: THE ARMOUR OF CONTEMPT
BOOK 11: ONLY IN DEATH

THE VICTORY
BOOK 12: BLOOD PACT
BOOK 13: SALVATION'S REACH
BOOK 14: THE WARMASTER
BOOK 15: ANARCH

More tales from the Sabbat Worlds

VOLPONE GLORY
A novel by Nick Kyme

URDESH: THE SERPENT AND THE SAINT
A novel by Matthew Farrer

URDESH: THE MAGISTER AND THE MARTYR
A novel by Matthew Farrer

BROTHERS OF THE SNAKE
A novel by Dan Abnett

TITANICUS
A novel by Dan Abnett

INTERCEPTOR CITY

DAN ABNETT

A BLACK LIBRARY PUBLICATION

First published in 2024.
This edition published in Great Britain in 2025 by
Black Library, Games Workshop Ltd., Willow Road,
Nottingham, NG7 2WS, UK.

Represented by: Games Workshop Limited – Irish branch,
Unit 3, Lower Liffey Street, Dublin 1,
D01 K199, Ireland.

10 9 8 7 6 5 4 3 2 1

Produced by Games Workshop in Nottingham.
Cover illustration by Rostyslav Zagornov.

A CIP record for this book is available from the British Library.

ISBN 13: 978-1-83609-198-1

Printed and bound in the UK.

In memory of my father, who would have liked this one too.

For more than a hundred centuries the Emperor has sat immobile on the Golden Throne of Earth. He is the Master of Mankind. By the might of his inexhaustible armies a million worlds stand against the dark.

Yet, he is a rotting carcass, the Carrion Lord of the Imperium held in life by marvels from the Dark Age of Technology and the thousand souls sacrificed each day so his may continue to burn.

To be a man in such times is to be one amongst untold billions. It is to live in the cruelest and most bloody regime imaginable. It is to suffer an eternity of carnage and slaughter. It is to have cries of anguish and sorrow drowned by the thirsting laughter of dark gods.

This is a dark and terrible era where you will find little comfort or hope. Forget the power of technology and science. Forget the promise of progress and advancement. Forget any notion of common humanity or compassion.

There is no peace amongst the stars, for in the grim darkness of the far future, there is only war.

'Death rides in the seat behind you.'

– Old Aeronautica saying

'For Orison to prevail, indeed for Lysander to remain free, Great Haven must be denied. This is the focus of our efforts. I am told the Archenemy is using indirect routes to strike at Orison Hive, accessing airspace via dead zones. I direct the Aeronautica to interdict these routes at once, especially those that run the line via Vesperus. We've killed that hive once. It will not come back from the dead to bite at us. You will fill the tomb-streets of Vesperus with hunters, with killers. Without delay, make that dead place a city of interceptors.'

– Lord Militant Jahkel to the joint chiefs,
Lysander Theatre, 795.M41

'The cold start or "dead drop" practice of machine launch is not recommended or approved for use under any circumstances.'

– Munitorum Advisory 435F, item 1161521,
issued 520.M41

'Given that the bastards are putting some effort into killing us, why are we trying so hard to kill ourselves?'

– Pilot Officer Bree Jagdea, at Vesperus

DEAD DROP

VESPERUS HIVE

IMPERIAL YEAR 795.M41, DAY 81

The ADF-C module weighs three-quarters of an ounce and is approximately the size of a human fingernail.

It is one of 38,047 micro components in the fuselage systems of the Voss-pattern (Primaris) Lightning, situated below and slightly aft of the compressor assembly, between wiring loom 14-kappa (primary) and wiring loom 126-ki (aux). It may also be found in flight systems of other Aeronautica craft, including earlier Cypra-M-pattern Lightnings, Thunderbolts and, in a slightly revised form, Avengers (which have two ADF modules, fore and aft, synchronised in combinatory flow). The ADF-C (Standard Template Construct number 4562-77-1) is a hydraulic pressure sensor, data-linked to the Systems Monitor Package (FFG-24) and thence to the Cockpit Advisory Display. Its purpose is to monitor hydraulic capacity and integrity. It may be inspected and, if necessary, replaced, via inspection plate 16 (belly) or during a top-down overfit of the turboram engine assembly. It is item 672 on the pre-flight mechanical check.

The ADF-C module in Voss-pattern Lightning tail number 451091 was in perfect order, and had passed inspection at 04:23 that morning, when the enginseers and fitter crew checked it both manually and via a logis diagnostic. At 05:55, with the pre-flight complete, Tail 091 was rolled out, anointed, and secured for launch on its landing claws, nose-down, tail raised at an angle of seventy degrees to the platform lip. Fuelling then commenced, and the bombardier did a walk-around to remove the tagged pins in the underslung air-to-air munitions.

The ADF-C module was not damaged, but the hydraulic flex it was attached to had suffered an accidental perforation point four inches from the module. The puncture was less than two millimetres wide, and had been caused when the probe-limb of a servitor had accidentally snagged against it during inspection of the 126-ki loom at 04:31. This contact had not been observed or noticed, not even by the high-grade servitor responsible. The ADF-C did not detect the puncture because, with the aircraft sitting level, hydraulic pressure remained stable.

When Tail 091 was raised into launch, or 'dead drop', position, the tiny puncture began to bleed hydraulic fluid due to gravity. In the first ten minutes, less than a quart of hydraulic fluid was lost, and this was not spotted, because the aircraft was nose-down over the drop and no one could see the small but steady drip as it was obscured by the platform lip. The ADF-C module did not detect the fluid loss, because it was attached to a loop of the flex below the perforation, which acted as a reservoir for hydraulic fluid below the leak point.

After thirty minutes, the aircraft had lost almost five quarts of hydraulic fluid. The puncture had not increased in size, because the flex was an armoured composite weave designed not to split or rupture in the event of damage, but the angle of the aircraft optimised vascular flow rate.

At 07:03, a remote observation post at Maladine Circus (ROP 54) reported engine noise in its vicinity. No visual observation was made, but doppler mapping showed the sound-source to be moving east, and the acoustic signature was an eighty-nine per cent match for a hostile power plant. ROP 54 relayed this track immediately to Squadron 66 (Intercept). Campanile Control verified the track, and an intercept was instructed. At 07:10, Squadron Leader Hyram Lungrim quit the morning huddle early, leaving his executive officer, Garrant, to finish the blessing, and went directly to his aircraft. Lungrim was alert-ready and already wearing his flightsuit. By 07:16 he was strapped in, and running a slam-check of Tail 091's control displays. The fitter crew closed the canopy, disconnected the fuelling lines, and withdrew the bulk-lifter truck that had been sitting behind the raised aircraft. As the truck's forks withdrew, Tail 091 settled fully onto its landing claws. There was a creak of metal as the weight shifted, and Tail 091's tilt angle increased to seventy-three degrees to the platform lip.

Lungrim was a veteran combat pilot, with five thousand hours logged and a tally of forty-six. He was an undisputed bat-killer. His slam-check was a fluid and efficient combination of experience and familiarity. He had been flying the formidable Voss-pattern for most of his career. He threw the voltaic master switch, and watched the instruments light up. All gauges, including hydraulic pressure, showed prime. He cleared the stick, and checked the display for rudder response, and then for all flight surfaces including flaps and speed brakes. All showed green. He then, as per recommended practice, worked left to right around the cockpit, prepping the vector thrust secondaries, and presetting the nozzles for both attitude and aperture. He activated auspex and modar systems, allowing their pre-start diagnostics to run, primed the starter, engaged the fuel pump, adjusted ad-mix, and then manually checked target acquisition settings. He toggled the guns on, off, and on again (an old, superstitious habit), armed the countermeasure package, and verified the hardpoint connections. By then, the starter compressor was beginning to whine as it spun up, and the auspex was painting the prediction track as relayed from ROP 54. Lungrim tightened his harness, connected his air-line, comms-line and visor-display cable, ran a vox check, and armed the seat. All flight instrumentation showed prime and green.

Just six minutes after the shout had reached the war deck, he was go-ready. He signalled his status to Control, and Control cleared him for immediate release. Auspex prediction gave a time-on-target estimate of two hundred and forty-five seconds, but Lungrim was confident he could shave fifteen seconds off that.

He released the landing claws. Tail 091, with a ramp weight of ten and three-quarter tons, dropped nose-down off the lip.

The landing claws were a non-standard variant used for urban zones. Each 'foot', avian in pattern, had four digits of dendritic design. Hydraulic pressure governed their ability to close and grip, but a simple mechanical system actuated their release. They were used, against Munitorum advice, for dead drop launches, which conserved fuel load and optimised fast-launch in crowded or obstructed airspace environments, greatly improving time-on-target intercept response times.

Engine primed but unstarted, Tail 091 fell nose-first down the side of the Campanile. The hive floor level, in this case Orundo Street, was three thousand feet below. A second after he threw the release lever and the bird began to plunge, Lungrim fired the starter. The forced-plasma exciter, also used in flight for afterburner boost, was designed to ignite the fuel aspirating into the already spinning turbine. The principle was to flash-start the turboram once the aircraft was already in free-fall, obviating both the fuel-cost and time-lag of a traditional launch. The engine would light on the way down, and as the pilot pulled the plane up, it would already be approaching engagement speed.

Lungrim's indicators were all still green and prime.

However, the aircraft's hydraulics had almost entirely drained by that point. Only two fluid ounces remained, trapped below the puncture in the reservoir of the flex loop. These two fluid ounces caused the ADF-C module to report a false green. To the sensor, the hydraulics were still fluid-rich, with only a slight, non-optimal but non-critical loss of pressure.

In reality, the plane had bled out.

When Lungrim fired the starter, there was a thump of negative response. Despite the fact that he was dropping, powerless, towards the street at terminal velocity, he remained unfazed. He was a veteran combat pilot. He had known plenty of misfire starts. Calmly, he tried the starter again. Negative response. This time, his board went red, as all systems, including engine, vector thrust secondary, and flight surfaces tried to draw on a hydraulic system that was unavailable. With hydraulics dry, the plasma starter would not fire. The engine would not light. The fuel pumps seized and locked. The rudder went soft.

Lungrim didn't speak, or attempt to alert Control to his situation. There were only seconds left. He did not even bother trying the starter again. Five thousand hours' experience told him when a bird was stone dead. He wrenched on the over-seat handle, knowing the chances of surviving an ejection at this height and angle were slim, though comparatively greater than the alternative. He knew he was likely to hit one of the neighbouring buildings before his chute deployed. He knew that even if his chute opened clean, windshear would probably throw him into an architectural obstruction. He knew he was looking at a high probability of severe injury, and the end of his flying career.

All of this, in one or two seconds. One or two seconds that lasted forever. All of this, and the thought of the woman he would never see or hold again, the fraternity of the Intercept 66 blessing huddle, the dark and caustic humour of the nights in the refectory, the rapturous liberty of flight.

The ejection system, a chemical/mechanical process, fired. Seat-release was synched to the canopy jettison system, which was designed to blow the armoured canopy off and away from the cockpit as the seat fired, but the canopy-jettison system relied on hydraulic pressure.

Lungrim ejected directly into the locked frame of his armoured canopy. The rocket-assisted impact pulped and killed him instantly. Two seconds later, Tail 091 hit the deck nose-first and fireballed.

Though Lungrim was not alive to see it, at the last instant before impact, his Cockpit Advisory Display showed red everywhere except the lone, green indicator of hydraulics.

GLORY STORIES

ORISON HIVE-PLEX

IMPERIAL YEAR 795.M41, DAY 86 – DAY 89

DAY 86

Oceanic Approach (Safe Lane 345), 16:56

They had been flying through rain for nine hours, following Transoceanic 27, the convoy spread out in a long, straggled line, like migrating geese.

Bree Jagdea was lead stick on the convoy principal, a ponderous Kazin-pattern Firmament. It had been dark for more than an hour; they had flown towards the encroaching terminator and into nightfall. With the darkness, and the rain, visibility was now zero-zero. But the convoy was so spaced out, none of the other birds would have been in sight even in clear conditions. Eased back in the pilot seat, she watched the progress of the tiny amber cross-runes on the scope, a chain of aircraft almost forty miles long. The runes blinked, repositioned, blinked, repositioned…

Rain pissed against the cockpit's side windows, but the main screen was kept clear by air ducts below the seal. There was nothing to see; just a vacuum of darkness. Somewhere far below, the heaving sea. Somewhere far ahead, the invisible destination.

'A ping soon, surely?' murmured Menomar, her co-pilot. He was in the pit space directly behind her, hunched on a pull-down seat, playing tarotti with the payload specialist and two cargomen. The ping came almost at once, a tone bleat from the transponder console.

Jagdea smiled. Klay Menomar was like that. He had an instinctive knack for time and distance logging that ticked over in his head as accurately as any logis-engine. They'd been flying together for eight months. Menomar never set a wake-up alarm.

She yawned, and took her feet down off the instrument panel. Behind her, Menomar picked up his cards, riffled them into a block, and offered his commiserations to the payload boys. They left the pit, grumbling. Menomar latched the bay door behind them, inviting them to try again next run, strapped the pull-downs upright, and damped the cockpit lights. In the blue gloom, he took his place beside her, their faces lit by the coloured constellation of the flight board.

The ping came again. The automated request pulse from Orison Traffic. Jagdea dragged her headset off her neck.

'OT Control, OT Control, this is Glacier Heavy Five-Nine. Verification request acknowledged, over.'

She threw a switch on the transponder. Her bird was now transmitting its identification signal. She checked the modar screen, watching the chain of runes, and tutted as she switched vox-channels.

'Glacier Heavy Five-Nine to all elements. Wake the hell up and verify, over.'

On the screen, one by one, green tags blinked into life alongside each amber cross-rune as transponders came on. Twenty-six freightbirds in the line. A couple were slow. She waited until they were all showing. Sometimes bats snuggled into a convoy line, passing as just another link in the chain. There were stories of intercept wings splashing whole convoys because some shithead forgot to activate verification. Orison Hive wasn't playing games these days. The last thing she needed was the thought of a Thunderbolt pack out there in the zero-zero dark, stalking her with weapons hot.

The vox crackled in her phones.

'Glacier Heavy Five-Nine, this is OTC. Verifying twenty-six – two, six – elements inbound at this time. Confirm, over.'

She switched channels back to Traffic.

'Confirm twenty-six – two, six, OTC. Approaching the marker. Request permission to depart Transoceanic Twenty-Seven and join Safe Lane Three-Four-Five, over.'

'Permission granted, Five-Nine. Make your height four thousand, and join Three-Four-Five. Advise cross-winds, over.'

'It's a dirty night, OTC.'

'It's always a dirty night here, Five-Nine, over.'

'Confirming instruction, OTC. Glacier Heavy Five-Nine turning north-north-east to join Safe Lane Three-Four-Five and descending to four thousand, over.'

Jagdea looked at Menomar.

'Remind them,' she told him.

He nodded, adjusted the sit of his headset, and began repeating the routing instruction to the other convoy elements. Jagdea took a breath, settled at the controls, and took the multiengine off autoguide.

At once, she sensed its cumbersome weight through the stick, a huge mass sliding, ungainly, in the wet air. Firmaments were among the largest Aeronautica transporters, eight-engine transatmospheric mammoths that dwarfed even the hulking Oneros. They were almost entirely logis-driven. Someone once joked they could fly and land themselves, but Jagdea knew it wasn't a joke. She'd seen basic-function servitors run them up and down the cargo lanes on Gereon after liberation. She and Menomar were present in what seemed a purely ceremonial role.

A pilot didn't ride a Firmament the way she would ride a

single-seat fightbird. There was no connection, no synergy, no ongoing contest with the stick. A Bolt was a racing animal, a steed, full of spittle and fury. You clung on and coaxed until it knew you. You tamed it and you broke it, or it broke you. You were in it together, fused as one, every second of the way. The heavies, like the Firmament, had personality too, but it was distant and aloof, the stubborn resentment of a pack animal as sensed through slack reins by a driver on the laden cart behind. It went where it was going, stoic and unspeaking, and you nudged it now and then to keep it true.

Jagdea had been on heavies for ten years and six worlds. Oneros, usually, sometimes Destriers. Occasionally something smaller, on a delivery run, a day out that would remind her of other times, and leave her with both heartache and zero regrets. She missed the spittle and fury, but she remembered the shred that had gone with it, the constant acid hiss of adrenaline, the searing stress, the physical and mental punishment. Combat pilots either died young, or lived long enough to wish they had. Veterans like her, long past their consume-by date, were patched and limping and broken. Fightbirds were a young smoke's game. You had to be young to be fit enough, to be sharp enough. To be dumb enough.

The chop was getting heavy. The stick twitched in her palm, like a door rattled by the wind. She felt the gale and the driving rain kneeling on the aircraft, pushing it off true with little jerks and bumps, like someone trying to move a sofa that was too big to lift outright. The Firmament scraped the air, shifting and fidgeting.

'You got it, Jags?' Menomar asked, glancing at her.

'Oh, piss off.'

'Only asking,' he replied with a grin.

'It's Four-A,' she replied, something she hadn't said in a long time. And it was. She edged the stick, leaned the big bastard into the wind. Logis-programs adjusted trim for her. It was almost like flying.

Five-Nine had run non-stop from Port Halgart on the Black Glaciers. The southern polar region was Lysander's main landfall point for orbital supplies: munitions, fuel, consumables, fighting vehicles, spares and sometimes even troops. The glacial region had been the primary war zone back in '74, when Innokenti's wounded host had hit the world during the retreat from Herodor. Rand-Huppert had them driven out by '75, and now the black ice plains had become crusted with city-sized Munitorum depots supporting the second phase of Lysander's conflicts, known as the Orison Wars or the Mainland Wars, depending on who you asked. They'd begun in '86, when the Archonate had attempted a take-back in the Cabal Systems, and they had been burning ever since.

Jagdea didn't really keep up with the minutiae. She was no longer required to appreciate combat objectives. She flew logistics. Her targets were times and destinations and cargoes-by-weight. The crusade was the theatre show, and she and Menomar were, as he liked to put it, stage hands, lugging the scenery so that the show could go on.

That summer, she'd made nineteen runs between Orison and Port Halgart, pretty much all of them freight turnarounds; standard bulk-lifts to the hive, then a run back empty, or with a hold full of blank-eyed Militarum rotating out, many of them carrying wounds.

Nineteen runs, but Orison still impressed. In daylight, it was an urban mountain range, a tiered cliff of a city that ran the length of the gulf coast for some two thousand miles. Ramparts of stone and ocean walls, and behind them, the hazy summits of the main spires further inland. This was the first time she'd seen it at night.

And she *could* see it, despite the darkness and the rain. Passing the marker forty miles out, she began to see the glow, the smudged fuzz of yellow and white, a smudge that slowly resolved into countless unfocused lights as the Firmament rumbled closer. A billion windows, tower lights, mast lights, search cones, the wash of radiance against curtain walls, the sodium cast of lamps along thoroughfares, the yellow glare of decks, the beady wink of red navigation markers on spire tops. It was like a mass of stars, a generous serving of the local spiral arm, scooped out and served on the black plate of the world. And behind them, the gauzy shimmer of the main spires, upright cities, illuminated staircases leading up to the heavens, and perhaps to some kind of god.

Jagdea wasn't sure whose.

'Glacier Heavy Five-Nine, this is Orison Traffic. Reading you now inbound. Slow your approach to one-twenty and descend to one thousand.'

'Copy that, OTC.'

'Routing you to Hymnal Four-One for put down. Make your turn zero-two-zero onto guidepath two-one and begin final. Switch to auto-track option, over.'

'Received, OTC. Turning zero-two-zero on descent, over.'

Jagdea eased the stick, watching the azimuth dial. On the display, the cross-runes had begun to bunch up as the convoy closed its spacing. They were crossing the coastline, coming in over the glow of the sea ramparts. They were close enough to buildings, either side and below, that the proximity warnings went off briefly. The cross-shear grew worse. The night gale was planing off the armoured walls and creating an eddying river of turbulence and backwash. Something loose in a cubby behind her seat started to rattle.

The transponder pinged. She ignored it, calmly cupping the stick as if she was raising a pot from wet clay on a wheel.

It pinged again.

'Autotrack?' Menomar asked.

She shook her head. Hymnal 41 Field was transmitting an autotrack datastream that would guide the bird in on full automatic via logis-engines. The complete, hands-free, autoglide experience, what Klay Menomar liked to call the 'full hat to sack service', micro-adjusting in real-time to smooth the buffet and shear.

'Autotrack, Jags?' Menomar asked again.

'Autotrack *option*,' she replied, eyes on the dials. 'Means it's optional. I like to earn my pay once in a while.'

'You do?'

'Keeps me honest,' she said.

Menomar chuckled. He leaned over and threw a switch on the transponder. A panel lit up: A/TRACK REJECTED.

She could see the strip lights ahead. The tower's voice was in her ear. The shear was really strong, and irregular. The enormous mass of the multiengine amplified the effect. It was pushing at the tail, causing both pitch and yaw. Jagdea corrected, each touch on the stick imperceptible, a little pressure, a little ease, smooth yet firm, not allowing an ounce of over-response.

Almost like actually flying.

The heavy was ducted, but only an idiot tried to set down a capacity-laden Firmament at night, in a storm, on vector only. Textbook recommended a short conventional down, with vector assist, and Jagdea was nothing but textbook.

Except for those few pages that, now and then, got stuck together.

She had the leviathan balanced at the happy edge of stall. Chin up, the phosphor glow of the Militarum field, and the glittering city beyond, flashing by at what seemed like a suicidal rate. The world was ripping past, breakneck, but she felt like she was floating, like a mote of dust.

'Cart down,' she said.

'Lowering cart,' Menomar replied. He slunked over the oiled steel levers. There was a thump, and they both heard the slow, straining groan of the gear extending. Lights flicked on over the levers, all green and prime.

'Cart clean, cart down,' Menomar said.

'Copy,' she replied. The stripway was rushing up at her, marker lights flitting past on either side, like tracers from a surface battery. She could see the veil of rain, the shimmer of standing water on the rockcrete. A little more chin, a squeeze less power. Vector ducts around to two-seventy, down forward, front. She did that manually, overriding logis-control, not even looking as she turned the rotary dial with her left hand.

The ground proximity alert started sounding. Menomar muted it.

'Ducts at five per cent, build to ten,' she instructed.

'Copy,' said Menomar. He smoothly switched in the vector thrust secondary system, diverting five per cent of thrust from the eight massive turbofans to the ducts aimed down and forward. A little judder as the ducts took up the slack and robbed out more speed. Menomar increased output to ten, and the Firmament felt like it was stuck to the air, way below stall speed.

'Little more,' said Jagdea. He obliged. They barely felt the touch as the wheels kissed the ground. Jagdea powered back and applied reverse thrust to arrest the roll. The Firmament hissed forward on its massive wheels, and gently came to a stop in less than sixty yards.

Menomar began the power down. Jagdea cross-checked, and damped the ducts. A cargo-4 ran out onto the bright stripway, swung in ahead of their nose, and lit up a bright, flashing 'follow me' indication display. She eased off the brakes, and taxied the heavy after it, steering off the strip onto the wide hardpan of a parking stand.

Behind them, the rest of the convoy began to thunder in, one at a time, two more Firmaments, a Destrier, three Oneros; gear down, nav-lights blinking, ducts wailing, home to roost.

Hymnal 41 Field, Orison, 19:03

They were idly looking at the routing board in the sickly glare of the wire-domed lamps when the assistant deck officer approached them. His name was Dillady, and he wore his dark blue battlefleet uniform with a fastidious attention to detail. The pins on his sleeve and collar, well-polished, indicated Imperial Navy, the Aeronautica Warfare Arm, and Logistics. He was career Aeronautica, which meant he had spent most of his time on the ground. He had data-plug ports over his left ear, and a moustache that looked like a crow that had failed to notice a cliff. He also had a data-slate, and Jagdea was always wary of career men with data-slates.

'Glacier Heavy Five-Nine?' he asked.

They turned, her and Menomar. They had just walked in off the field, ready-bags over their shoulders, and water was dripping off their coats. Outside, under the floods, servitors were unloading cargo from the whale jaws of their Firmament. The off-load would take another four hours, and one of them was supposed to stay on site until it was done, but those were pages in Jagdea's textbook that had stuck, and they'd left supervision to the payload officer because it seemed far more like his job. First down, first out, first look at the routing board. The other crews were starting to wander in. If there was anything remotely decent, Jagdea and Menomar wanted to stake it.

But, as ever, there wasn't.

'Yes,' Jagdea answered, with slight reluctance. She didn't know Dillady. She usually flew into Hymnal 32 or Spire Field 19. But she had a feeling she knew his type.

'Non-standard,' said Dillady. He glanced at his slate as though to confirm the diagnosis. 'Non-standard,' he repeated.

Jagdea and Menomar exchanged glances. It wasn't clear what Dillady was referring to. They were wet, tired and cold. Almost everything about their flight gear was non-regulation. Both wore heavy flight boots, black leather coats, and quilted flight bottoms with high waists and braces over thick, white knitted sweaters. Was it possible that they were too wet for indoor use? Or was it the sweaters? It was the sweaters, Jagdea decided.

'Your approach and landing,' said Dillady.

'I seem to remember landing intact,' Menomar said. He looked at Jagdea, widening his eyes. 'Shit, Jags, did we crash? Are we dead? Is this… paradise?'

Jagdea hid her smirk.

'What's the problem?' she asked.

Dillady looked at her, yearning for a 'sir' that would never come.

'Non-standard approach and landing,' he said. He checked his slate again. 'Which one of you is Jagdea?'

Jagdea pointed to herself. Menomar pointed at her too.

'Pilot Officer Jagdea,' Dillady said. 'You had craft command. You were also element lead. You were at the stick.'

'I was.'

'You did not engage autotrack.'

'Must've forgot,' she said.

'OTC instructed you. Logis would have prompted you. You did not engage.'

'Slipped my mind,' she said.

Dillady consulted his slate.

'It didn't slip your mind, pilot officer. System data shows that you manually rejected it.' He held up the slate to show her, and pointed at a line of metadata.

'Oh, that was me,' said Menomar. 'I turned it off. I'll be honest, it was bothering her. Very persistent. Borderline harassment, if you ask me. It kept making these advances, making suggestions, all kinds of stuff. So I said, no, that's got to stop. I'm not having it–'

'What?' said Dillady.

'I just shut it down,' said Menomar. 'It was the gentlemanly thing to do, really–'

'Is this a bit?' Dillady asked, frowning. 'Is this a bit you do?'

'It could be,' said Menomar.

'I decided on a manual landing,' said Jagdea. 'I didn't see the harm.'

'It was non-standard,' said Dillady. 'It was contrary to field protocol, and contrary to Orison Traffic regulations.'

'Still,' said Jagdea. She shrugged. 'Landed it.'

'In these conditions?' Dillady said. 'Night flight. Storm advisory. Precipitation. Over an urban zone. Eighteen hundred tons of aircraft. Use of autotrack is a safety countermeasure, which is why it is mandated. Guidance and guidepath regulations are fully enforced by Wing Command, and circulated on a more than regular basis to all multiengine drivers, including pool reservists like you. Besides which, you were element lead. You're supposed to set an example to the other pilots in your convoy. What do you have to say?'

'I felt like flying,' said Jagdea. She knew her reply was off-hand, but she just wanted to be left alone.

'If you'd misjudged,' said Dillady, 'and piled that bird in, we'd have had to close the stripway. Probably the field. We'd have lost a valuable air asset, and a vast tonnage of materiel. And we'd be frantically trying to reroute twenty-five *other* freight elements, all low on fuel after a transoceanic run, to other fields with capacity before they fell out of the sky.'

'And eight personnel,' said Menomar.

'What?'

'A valuable air asset, a vast tonnage of materiel, *and eight personnel*,' said Menomar.

Dillady stared back at him.

'I am not letting this kind of laxity slip through,' Dillady said. 'Inexperienced pilots making poor judgements when–'

'Inexperienced?' said Menomar. 'Do you know who this is?'

'Don't,' said Jagdea quietly. She felt a spike of anxiety. Menomar leaping to her defence was the last thing she wanted to handle.

'Pilot Officer Jagdea,' said Dillady, using his slate to make sure he got it right, 'Aeronautica Logistics Reserve.'

'Wing Commander Bree Jagdea, Phantine Twentieth Fighter Squadron,' said Menomar, taking a small but aggressive step forward.

'Don't, Klay,' said Jagdea.

'Flew Bolts, flew Lights, flew every last damn thing,' Menomar went on heedlessly. 'Flew the Cirenholm Air War, flew U-Minor, flew Lotun, flew Khan IV. Flew Srady Bay *and* Zinc Hill under Hydun. Flew Enothis in '73. The frigging Battle of the frigging Zophonian Sea. That one *must* ring a bell, for f–'

'Stop it,' said Jagdea.

Dillady looked at her. 'You were combat?'

Jagdea nodded.

Dillady glanced down at his slate.

'I don't pull up biographical data,' he said, the crow on his upper lip expressing mild curiosity. 'You were a wing commander? A squadron lead?'

'Yes.'

'But you don't use the rank or the pins?'

'I drive cargo,' she said. 'A squadron leader only exists when there's a squadron to lead.'

Dillady paused, then nodded. 'New routings will be posted at oh-six-thirty tomorrow,' he said. 'There are bunks and washrooms on level four. Carry on.'

Jagdea picked up her ready-bag, and pulled the still-glaring Menomar away by the arm. As they turned, Dillady called out to her.

'Jagdea? Report to the deck officer at twenty-two hundred. His office is East Block, level five. Be prompt.'

'The deck officer?' Jagdea said.

'You heard me.'

'Over this?' she asked. 'About *this*?'

'Follow instruction when issued, please,' said Dillady, and walked away. His 'please' irked her. People always treated her differently when they discovered her past. The courtesy rankled, but not as much as being sent up in front of the deck officer.

East Block, Hymnal 41 Field, 21:58

Deck officer. Such a mild, insipid title. But 'deck', more properly 'war deck', was a basic unit of measurement in the mighty Imperial Navy, referring literally to the carrier deck or decks of a battlefleet warship, and by extension to any field, ground base, port or platform out of which the Aeronautica ran squadrons. Hymnal 41 Field was a deck. On a big ship of the line, the 'deck' might mean thirty full wings or more. It was the deck officer's purview, his domain, his command. On a war deck, the deck officer was god, or at least a proxy, local god. He was base command, operations oversight, and wing commander, all rolled into one. On a war deck, even admirals and wing leaders saluted the deck officer.

She waited in the corridor outside the suite of offices. Most had shut down for night operation. Lights were only on in a few. She could smell food, decent food, from somewhere close by. Her stomach growled.

Klay had insisted on coming with her, to take his share of the heat, but she had out-insisted. Rank had its privileges. She'd sent him to catch some sleep. One of them had to be fresh in the morning to snag a half-decent routing.

The corridor was gloomy. Large ports on the opposite side to the offices overlooked the stripway. The windows were flushed with rain, like someone had turned a pressure hose on them. If she pressed close and squinted, she could see multiengines lined up on the rockcrete, crews working to unload them in the downpour. More distant lit pinpricks suggested the swell of the towering hive. She saw the wink of a wing light as a bird came in on an outside strip. Something big, maybe an Onero. Too far away to tell. Too much rain.

She turned her gaze back to the hive again, the glow of it. Orison wasn't really a hive. It was a hive-plex, and not even the biggest on Lysander. As far as she could remember, there were nine major conurbations. Orison was one of the key densities. It was a family of hives, hives that had prospered and grown to the point where they had started to blend into one. They covered the western seaboard and large territories inland, like thick lichen encasing a rocky outcrop. Like all families, some members had done well for themselves, and grown old and fat, while others were still young and breeding. And, like all families, there had been deaths.

Lysander had been free of the Archenemy for just over ten years when the enemy take-back began in '86. Jagdea had been on Gereon then, working with the occupation forces after the liberation nine years earlier, but she'd heard word of the big hit that Lysander had taken. An orbital attack, a year of land war, and then Great Haven, the easternmost hive of the Orison hive-plex, had fallen to the Archonate. Its neighbour, Vesperus, had followed a year later. Crusade forces, pushing out of the main Orison zone, had driven the onslaught back. Vesperus, already partly evacuated, had been smoked and killed outright. A whole hive, nearly as big as the one she was staring at, dead and empty, a city grave. Great Haven had survived. Since then, Great Haven and Orison had been slugging it out, a massive surface war mainly, but a major air fight too. Significant Aeronautica assets had been committed, some said as much as on Lyubov. There was glory out there in the rainswept darkness, glory to be chased and snatched by the brave and the reckless, the bat-killers and the gunfighters, the veterans who should know better, and the over-confident smokes who didn't, and who probably wouldn't live long enough to learn.

There was nowhere to sit. She waited. She leaned against the wall, easing the pins in her left hip. So many holes, so many patches, each one the souvenir of some shitfest or other. Jagdea believed she could make a popular mess game out of it: match the scar to the theatre. The burn tissue on her bicep? Tracer shot over Cirenholm, well done, sir! The blue, fibreweave grafts on her left arm, lower throat and shoulder? Cannon fire from a hell-bat over the Enothian littoral that had brought her down and opened her to the bone. Congratulations, everything still to play for. The scar on her thin cheek? Bursting canopy plex, Srady Bay, well spotted. The stipples on her belly? Aluminoid fragments, Urdesh Minor, correct. The hip, the ribs, the herniated spinal discs? Well, *that* crash on Lyubov, of course. Spectacular. The kind where they had to cut you out of the burning wreck of your career. The fibreweave patches on her throat, wrists, left forearm, groin, right calf and ankles? All elective reinforcements done at various times to armour circulation points against high-G compression, or repair thromboses or deep-vein collapses *caused* by high-G compression. Take your pick, but full marks to you, thank you for playing. Let's move to round two...

Dillady's words haunted her.

No, not his words at all. Klay's. Frigging Klay Menomar's. His angry defence of her. His roll call of her life. None of it fresher than a decade or more, all of it ancient history. Glory stories. She wasn't ashamed of them, of any of it. But actually hearing it, hearing it spill into the air out of somebody else's mouth, that had knocked the stick out of her hands. It had made all the faces come back.

They came back from time to time, but only when she let them, when she was ready for them. If she let herself remember, or was telling a story, like the ones she'd told to Klay, then she'd call them up and let them come to her.

Standing in front of Dillady, she hadn't been ready at all, not even slightly braced. And they had all come at once. Van Tull and Zemmic. Milan Blansher, of course. Espere. Clovin and Waldon. Darrow, always eager, and Viltry with his sad eyes. Scalter. August Kaminsky. Aggie Del Ruth. Larice, with her shit-eating grin. Marquall and Ranfre and Cordiale, laughing about something. Padmus, Rodine, Alia Tan, and all Jagdea's other peers from the Cirenholm days and the Urdesh Minor tour, from Halo Flight, and Orbis, and Talon, and always, always Umbra Flight, in each and every incarnation, like old flight-room picts, dwindling in the brutal years after Enothis. Zeto and Lal Mullane and the Dancers from Khan IV, the laughing boys and girls of the Bat Pack on Lyubov, gunfighters with their hair on fire and their claws out, forever fewer and fewer.

It had almost overwhelmed her. She had felt as though tears were about to explode her eyes. All the faces. All those years. All those fleeting friendships that were less than actual friendships, but far, far more all the same. Born out of the shred. Born out of the fire, and the stress, and the necessity. Bright and hot and gone, like las-bolts. Her combat years, and she'd had more than most and been blessed with far too many, had been a constant, extreme state, relentlessly high on adrenaline. For almost ten years, she had never come down, never, not once. She had stayed high in the shred until she couldn't stay up any more.

Did that make her lucky, or the unluckiest one of all?

She'd had friends since, co-pilots, wingmen. Menomar was one of the best. But the friends you make in the fire melt into you and fuse, and leave their marks on you like scars.

A door opened along the hall. A bar of light spilled across the corridor floor and up the wall.

'Pilot Officer Jagdea?'

She straightened up. She rubbed her eyes, and shook out the sleeves of her coat. She had thought about changing for this, putting on a uniform, but there was nothing in her ready-bag except two pairs of clean shorts, two fairly clean pairs of wool socks, a definitely-not-clean vest, and a rolled compression bodyglove. So she'd settled for a strip-wash in the billet sink. Menomar had offered her a comb, which was a typical Klay Menomar joke, because Jagdea's hair was about as short as hair could get and still deserve the name.

She walked down to the door, went in, and closed it behind her. She saluted, then stood, head up, hands behind her back. The room was a large command office, with hooded lamps over the desk, charts on the wall, and giant observation ports running with rain. The smell of food was stronger. She ignored her stomach.

The Hymnal 41 deck officer wore a clean, battlefleet regulation uniform that someone had probably pressed for him. He was standing with his back to her, pouring an amasec from a drink cart. She noticed his augmetic hand gripping the decanter.

'How are you?' he asked.

'*Well*, sir. Thank you,' she replied.

He put the decanter down and turned to look at her.

'You probably don't remember me,' he said.

Her eyes widened. It was hard to process what was happening. She felt like she was back in the hall with Dillady, the faces swarming back against her will.

'Shit,' she said.

'Oh, charming,' he said. 'It's hardly a face you forget, I confess, but still.'

'Kaminsky?' she whispered.

'Hello, Bree,' said August Kaminsky. 'How's the Emperor been protecting you?'

'I was trying to work it out,' said Kaminsky, handing her a second amasec. 'What is it? Nineteen years? Twenty?'

'Twenty, I think,' she said. She had taken an armchair by the desk before he'd even offered it. 'Twenty. '75. Khan IV.'

'The Dancers,' he said, raising his glass. His smile made an odd crease in the burn tissue of his face. 'My last go-around.'

'I was sorry to lose you.'

'Don't be,' he replied. 'I was done, and no good to you, or Umbra Flight. It was time. Thanks to you, I got, what, two extra years combat rotation I never thought I'd see? Three tours, and I wouldn't give them back. But the shred gets you. The smart ones know when it's time to step back. Yet you went on.'

'Which makes me not one of the smart ones?' she asked wryly.

Kaminsky laughed. 'No, you weren't ready. You had tour-time left in you.'

'Umbra didn't,' she said. 'It lasted about four months after you went. Not enough of us left. Wing Command retired us as a unit, but offered places to pilot officers, because they were desperate for decent sticks. So I signed off and folded into the Aeronautica. Two more tours with Fifty-Eight Aquila, then on to Twelfth Squadron Stratoraptors, and Lyubov.'

'Some show,' he said. 'And I question the adjective "decent" in that account. The Aeronautica was lucky to have you. Any of you.'

'What about you?' Jagdea asked.

Kaminsky shrugged.

'Same story but from the other side of the desk,' he said. 'Put in for transfer to Aeronautica after I stepped down from active combat, got accepted, served in munitions on the *Clarion*, then made junior deck. Then assistant deck on the *Grace And Majesty Of Khulan*. Eight years doing that, then four on the *Imperator Resurgam*. Then here.'

'So what rank are you?'

'Senior deck officer, Hymnal Forty-One Field, please and thank you and where's my salute?'

'You run the frigging place. I get it. But what rank does that make you?'

'Well, technically,' he mused, 'that makes me a wing commander, wing commander.'

'Good for you,' she said, and tipped her glass to him.

'I just can't quit the smell of aviation fuel,' he said, 'but this is as close as I'm prepared to get any more.'

'So,' she said, 'a question, senior deck officer… Dillady?'

'Good question.'

'Answer?'

'Oh, arsehole.'

'Good answer.'

'But I didn't appoint him,' said Kaminsky. 'Turns out you don't get to choose these things. We are obliged to get along. One does not join the Aeronautica to make friends.'

'Or keep them,' she said.

'Brutally true,' he replied. 'Look, Bree, I saw your name on the day log when I was reviewing the inbounds this morning. I had to call you in, just to say hello.'

'I would have been offended if you hadn't.'

'Glacier Heavy Five-Nine, was it?' he asked. 'What the hell are you doing driving multis and running airlifts?'

'I have one skill,' she said. 'I fly things. And I'm too broken for combat. So I wound up in the Logistics reserve pool, doing whatever jobs needed to be done.'

'Well, I think that's a crime. You know what, recon's crying out for decent sticks. A little mono fightbird, high alt, picters in place of guns, no shooting guaranteed? That's more you.'

She shook her head.

'Oh, come on. Bree Jagdea flying freightbirds?'

'They don't fly themselves,' she said.

'Well, I hate to break it to you...' he began, and they both laughed.

He got up.

'Hungry?' he asked.

'Hell, yes. I've been smelling food since I got up here. Good food, too. Is the canteen still open?'

He walked over to a sideboard and took the steel domes off two warming plates.

'Oh, Throne,' she said. '*That's* what I could smell.'

'I took the liberty of ordering supper from the officers' refectory,' said Kaminsky. 'I mean, if a senior deck officer can't treat an old friend to a good meal, where's the frigging justice in life?'

Kaminsky had been Enothian Commonwealth Aviation Corps when she'd first met him, invalided to service duties. In the crunch, before the Battle of the Zophonian Sea, she'd dragged him back into combat duty, got him a brevet assignment to the Phantine Air Corps, and handed him a place in Umbra Flight. Kaminsky had stayed there, through the rest of Enothis, then through Lotun, and most of Khan IV.

'I was junked,' he said as they ate. 'But you brought me back from the dead, and gave me a lease of life I never expected.'

'That's an overly generous description of what happened,' she replied. 'I pulled strings and bent more than a few rules to give you a chance to kill yourself. Because I needed a stick. That's not what friends do.'

'One does not join the Aeronautica to make friends,' he said.

'Who said we were friends?' Jagdea grinned, raising a forkful of steak.

'I was just thinking,' Kaminsky said, 'maybe I can return the favour this time around? Bring *you* back from the dead. I have connections.'

'I'm happy being dead,' she said.

'How long since you flew combat?'

'Not long enough, August.'

'But when? Lyubov?'

She nodded.

'Long time,' Kaminsky mused, refilling their wine glasses from the carafe. 'But still...'

'Drop it, Kaminsky. It's a young bastard's game. A smoke's game. I am well past my prime.'

'You were the hottest stick I ever saw.'

'Yeah, well, thanks, but that was then. I wore out. And I'm old. Reactions don't get faster.'

'But you miss it?'

'No,' she said firmly.

'You do.'

'It was what I did. Combat pilots burn bright and fast. What, five, six years, if they're lucky? Much less, usually. The attrition is brutal. If you survive, by some miracle, the mental cost is too much. Remember Viltry?'

'I do.'

'Well, then.' Jagdea sipped her wine. 'Those are the career arcs. Physical burn-out, mental shred, or just plain, old-fashioned fiery death.'

'The same could be said of the Astra Militarum,' he said. 'More so, in the meat-grinder. But there are Guard veterans pushing sixty, seventy… more, even, with augmetics and enhancement juvenat.'

'Yeah, but a seventy-year-old colonel in the Guard doesn't get out of bed each morning, strap himself to a ramjet, and fire himself at the enemy, does he?'

'I believe there are a lot of people who would like to see that happen.'

'I'm sure,' she said, smiling. 'My point is that the only gunslingers who last more than a decade, by means of luck or damnation, are freaks. Crazy, psychopathic freak-monsters. And they are, thankfully, a rare breed. No, the only outs are switching to non-combat stick work, or desk duties, or promotion to Navy Command.'

'Or death.'

'Or that.'

Kaminsky paused, glass in hand, and studied her across the table.

'No, you miss it,' he decided. 'I know this because I chose to fly a desk, Bree, but you're still flying actual birds.'

'Multis,' she corrected.

'And you reject autotrack during a class-three gale. I saw the report. Why would you do that, unless you still wanted to be tested?'

'It was a cheap thrill,' she said. 'Change the subject.'

He shrugged. 'Do you ever wonder what happened to them?' he asked.

'Who?'

'The ones that aren't here. Those friends we didn't make?'

'Now and then,' she said.

DAY 87

East Block, Hymnal 41 Field, 01:45

The rain had stopped just before midnight. They took their amasecs out onto the observation gallery and watched the field while a servitor silently cleared away their plates in the office behind them. The night air stank of promethium and petrichor. Two Destriers were rolling out into the floodlit glow of a launch slip. A late-flight Arvus was coming in on the boundary pad.

'Zemmic went down on Lyubov,' she said. 'We lost so many there, actually. It was a shitshow. Prycel, Mullane, Banerjee… but you probably don't remember them.'

'Lal Mullane, I do. He joined on Khan IV.'

'Right, right.'

'Van Tull?' Kaminsky asked.

Jagdea pursed her lips.

'No idea. He was with us all the way to Lyubov, and made it through that. Transferred to Thirty-Three Angelic, I think, or Forty-Three Angelic, and was posted to the Erinyes front. I don't know after that. I like to think he's out there somewhere. Aggie Del Ruth retired to Phantine after Enothis. Ended up as senior instructor at Hessenville.'

'Still there?'

'I think so. We haven't kept in touch.'

'What about...' Kaminsky tapped his brow as he tried to recall. 'What was her name? Asche? Larice Asche?'

Jagdea had often wondered that herself.

'I never knew what became of her,' she said. 'Always was bound for glory, one way or the other. The Apostles stopped posting pilot lists after '75. Probably because they didn't want to admit they were mortal. Their attrition rate was the worst of all, because they took the biggest chances. Had that reputation to preserve. I doubt very much that she's still alive. If she is, she'd have burned out of the Apostles years ago.'

'Maybe she's Queen Apostle?' said Kaminsky.

'Maybe. But the Apostles are exactly what I was talking about before, August. You get to that level, multi-ace, the best of the best, and there's nowhere left to go. You kill until you're killed, and you *will* be killed. They're the freaks, the ones with the skill and luck to outrun Fate's wheel longer than anyone else. The Apostles seemed so brave and glorious to us, but they were dead inside. Dead from shred. Terrified, because every day was another day overdue, another hour stolen, another I.O.U. to death. I never, ever wanted to end up like that. And, Throne knows, I was headed that way.'

Kaminsky nodded and sighed.

'I hear you. That's why I got out. That moment you realise you're not so quick on the stick any more, not so tight in the turns. Breaks your heart, but you walk away if you've got any sense.'

'That's right, August. And that day, for me, was about seventeen years ago.'

They stood in silence for a while. Down below, trolley starters banged and coughed as the ground crews got the compressors running on the brace of Destriers.

'I think that's about all of them,' Jagdea said. 'Oh, Darrow, of course. Transferred to Aeronautica after Lotun. I don't know what happened to him after that.'

She looked at Kaminsky, noticed the crooked smile.

'What?' she asked.

'I do,' he said. 'I know. Darrow's upstairs.'

She frowned at him. Kaminsky pointed one prosthetic finger at the sky above them.

'Darrow is deck officer on the *Naiad Redemptor*,' he said.

'You're joking?'

'I am not joking.'

Jagdea shook her head in wonder, took a slug of her amasec, and started laughing. The *Naiad Redemptor* was one of the great battleships of the crusade fleet, sister ship to the mighty *Antitor* and *Cerulis*, an Incarnate-class voidshaker, if she remembered correctly. It was also the capital ship of the Lysander campaign, and Lord Militant Jahkel's flag vessel. To be deck officer of that was to command fifty wings, minimum.

'You're joking,' she said again.

'Still not,' he chuckled.

'You speak to him?'

'Couple of times. Six weeks ago, we chatted. Just holopresent. He tends to stay orbital. But it was good to see him. The boy's done well for himself.'

'Not a boy any more, I would imagine,' she said.

'Not at all. Filled out. Bit of a paunch.'

'Throne, *no*!'

'Yes, unlike us, who have remained in peak condition, obviously.'

She snorted, and punched his arm.

'Frig, we got *old*!' Jagdea said, still laughing.

'Oh, I started old, I assure you,' Kaminsky replied.

She looked at him, and cocked her head.

'So when you said you had connections…' she began.

'I meant it,' said Kaminsky. 'I mean, I can easily place you here. Throne knows, I need hot sticks, but Darrow, well… he'd kick his best bat-killers out of an airgate to get you as a flight leader.'

Her smile faded.

'He'd do that because he's ridiculously loyal,' she said. 'He'd do that for old times' sake, and that would make him an idiot, because those are not good reasons. I wouldn't even pass the physical.'

'You're still rated, aren't you, Bree?'

'Technically. Certified for monos and multis, but hardly–'

'Darrow would do it for morale reasons. To have the legendary hero of the Zoph and multi-ace in his officer cadre? That's prestige.'

'*Darrow's* a Zoph hero and multi-ace. And I'd be dead in a week, so the morale effect would be counter-productive.'

'Admit it, you were tempted there, for a moment, weren't you?' Kaminsky said.

'Less than a moment,' she replied. She locked eyes with him. 'What is this really, August? Some romantic notion of a last bat-fight reunion? Reliving the good old days, showing the smokes how it's done? You and me, and Darrow, flying Umbra's last hurrah? Like something out of a glory story?'

He shrugged. 'I happen to like glory stories,' he said.

'You do not!'

'I do.'

'You read them?' she asked, astonished. 'You do understand they're propaganda for the masses, right? Made-up shit full of valour and daring that bears no resemblance to actual combat life?'

'I like them,' he said. 'You'll find they're very popular in the fleet and the Militarum. Everybody reads them. Every time a carton arrives at the commissary, it sells out.'

It was true, and she knew it. Cheap and lurid chapbooks like *Victory In Battle!* And *Imperial Action Tales* were a common sight in all mess halls and billets. They were filled with almost unreadable bullshit about courageous lasmen triumphing against the odds, or valiant pilots surviving the impossible. In tale after tale, these invented and impossible warriors always won the day, and never got trench rot, or lice, or gut worms, or got blinded by gas attacks, or seared by surging voltaics, or had their bowels opened by shrapnel. In glory stories, the Imperium never suffered defeat, lines never broke, and people didn't die stupid and unnecessary deaths. Campaigns that had been lost in real life were spectacularly won in the pages of *Indomitable Guardsman Stories Quarterly*, and worlds that had burned to ash were alive and well in *Majestic Battlefleet Illustrated*. Jagdea understood why such tawdry publications were beloved by the civilian populations, but she had never, for a moment, understood why they appealed to people who were living war for real.

'They provide an escape,' Kaminsky offered.

'They're borderline pornographic,' she replied.

'They offer hope and an ideal,' he said. 'Something to aspire to.'

'You can't aspire to something that isn't real,' she snapped. 'So, this glory story you're writing in your frigging head… it's Umbra reuniting to save the day? The heroes of the Zoph? You and me, knife-fighting bats? What do we do, Kaminsky? Do we take down Great Haven's finest aces in a six-on-one tumble-scrap? Or is ten-on-one better? Frig it, make it twenty-on-one! Wait, I know… do we single-handedly win the air war on Lysander? Save Orison?'

'Bree–'

'No, no, seriously. There's got to be a big, sentimental finish, right? A real tug to the heartstrings. How does your glory story end, August? Are we swarmed by enemy bats? Mobbed out? Does Aggie Del Ruth blaze out of the sun to save us, with the doughty Hessenville cadets in formation behind her? Does Darrow climb into a Bolt, one last time, and burn through everything to reach us? What about the frigging Apostles? Let's not leave them out. Last-minute saviours, flying in, claws out, to relieve us just as our ammo count reaches zero?'

'Just a hunch,' said Kaminsky, 'but I have a feeling you're mocking me.'

'Not at all. That's how those stories end, don't they? Nice big finish, all heroically neat and upliftingly tidy?'

'That... *is* the usual structure, yes,' said Kaminsky. 'They're rather formulaic.'

'No shit,' she said. She looked down, and her energy dropped. 'Sorry,' she said. 'Is that why you called me up? Is that what you thought might happen here? One last, glorious go-around? The long-awaited sequel to Enothis?'

'No,' said Kaminsky quietly. 'Not any of that. I called you up here to say hello. To greet a friend I hadn't seen in a long time. And I thought, maybe, I could do her a good turn, return the kindness she once did me. Give her another chance at life.'

'My life is over, August,' she said. '*That* life is over.'

'All right, then. Even though I can see there's still fire in your belly?'

'Wrecks keep burning long after they've augered into the strip-way,' she said.

He nodded. 'Fair enough, Bree,' he said. 'End of conversation.'

She felt bad about it suddenly. She'd been too fierce. He'd only been trying to help, maybe offer some lively break from the monotony of multi-engine hauls, and she'd taken the piss. She wanted to say something to lighten the mood, to show she appreciated his intentions, no matter how misguided they'd been.

But before she could think of anything, a siren started to wail. Others quickly joined the chorus. Kaminsky marched back inside his office, put down his glass, and checked his desk displays.

'What is it?' Jagdea asked from the observation gallery doorway.

'Night raid,' he replied, studying the data.

'Expected?' she asked.

'In as much as Great Haven throws something at us pretty much every night. Bomber formations, approaching the eastern 'plex.'

He straightened up, and glanced at her.

'I have to get down to Control,' he told her. 'We'll be ordered to ready, and we may have to run up intercept formations if the eastern fields are overstretched.'

'Of course,' she said.

He walked to the door.

'Stay here, by all means,' he said. 'Make yourself at home. There's amasec, and this week's copy of *Victory In Battle!* somewhere.'

'Thank you. And thank you for dinner.'

Halfway out of the door, he looked back at her.

'Or you can come and watch, if you like,' he said.

Control, Hymnal 41 Field, 02:05

The chamber, a nocturnal cave lit by bright screens and holo-lithic projections, was in uproar.

It was a silent uproar, just the murmur of voices and the clatter of keys, but Jagdea could feel it the moment she walked in. A constricting snake of tension, every one of the seventy-plus personnel present intensely alert. She could smell recaff, and stimulant-rich sweat. Voices were clipped tight and lashed down. Anyone moving, walking data-slates or papers between consoles, moved with a brisk urgency, as though they would break into a sprint at the slightest excuse. She knew this sensation. It reminded her of the old days. This was the shred, bottled-up and waiting to blow. It was menacing. It would have been less alarming if they'd all been screaming and yelling and running around.

'Is she cleared?' Dillady asked, looking up from his station.

'Wing Commander Jagdea is my guest, Dillady,' said Kaminsky. He was staring at the main displays.

'Very good, sir,' said Dillady.

'Might be a better use of your breath to get me to speed,' Kaminsky said.

'Mass swarms extending in Areas Three and Four,' said Dillady. 'Secondary swarms approaching Area Six, and the Selberg Boxes. Four hundred miles out. Altitude fifteen and a half.'

'Escort cover?'

'Detected. Principally Blades and Razors, holding at seventeen thousand. All eastern and northern decks have scrambled intercepts. Tracking the first engagements now.'

'Saturation hits reported at Selberg and east Area Three, sir,' a controller nearby called out.

Kaminsky nodded. 'Command directive?' he asked.

'Western fields are directed to stand ready, sir,' said another controller. She was a tall young woman, her hair clipped back so she could wear her headset unobstructed.

'Well,' said Kaminsky, 'we can stand ready on the stripway as well as anywhere. Roll out Rush Flight, Gyre Flight and Sunray Flight, and get them go-ready. Have Sabre and Rapier flights prepped for pre-roll. If we have to overlap, I want it done fast.'

Jagdea hung back to keep out of the way. The chamber was a tiered amphitheatre encircling the central strategium station. To her left, the modar operators, then the vox-stations, then primary auspex, then supplementary auspex, the warfare control stations, condition mapping, standby auspex, threat mapping, the AD/G stations, principal plotting, additional plotting, CRX/K, resources, traffic coordination, resources oversight, relay operations, grading and evaluation, binharic vox, tactical assessment, strategic assessment, data-link management, and high watch.

She kept her eyes on the big display projecting above the font of the main strategium, a multi-coloured sheet of light. It twitched and shifted every few seconds. She tried to ignore the tension burn rising in her gut and the swim of too much amasec. She could see cross-rune threat markers crawling west across the continental mainland from the contoured mass that represented Great Haven. Bright blobs on the left of the updating image indicated the eastern formations of Orison Hive-Plex. There were a few blue markers edging right, showing intercept groups already in the air. The rest was a dull blur that looked like a dense and circulating weather system.

'Is that climate patterning?' she asked.

Dillady shot her a dirty look. Kaminsky glanced her way and gave her a thin, patient smile.

'No, Bree,' he said. 'That's the hostile formations.'

She said something. She wasn't sure what. It drew ugly looks from several controllers.

'I have a plateful right now, Bree,' Kaminsky said softly. He took her by the arm and steered her towards the warfare control stations.

'Of course,' she whispered. 'Sorry.'

'Supervision Officer Brodie?' Kaminsky said to the woman with the clipped-back hair. 'This is Wing Commander Jagdea. Would you let her ride in back, and answer any questions she might have?'

'Of course, sir,' the woman said. She glanced at Jagdea, unsure what to make of her.

Kaminsky squeezed Jagdea's shoulder and then went back to join Dillady.

'Sorry,' said Jagdea quietly. 'I'm getting in your way.'

The supervision officer shook her head.

'Nothing to get in the way of, mam,' she replied. 'Not yet. Warfare's just watching the map until we get anything aloft. Just watch and wait, this side of the room. You must remember that?'

Jagdea winced. *Yes, of course I do. I remember that despite the absolute frigging aeons that have passed since I did this for a living.* The woman, Brodie, sensed her stiffen, and frowned.

'Did I say something, mam?' she asked.

No, you didn't, and even if you did, you didn't mean anything.

'No,' said Jagdea, and forced a friendly smile. 'I just...' She hesitated, then gestured to the swirling repeater screen on Brodie's station. The blue glow of it underlit their faces. 'That's really the enemy mass? Bomber swarms?'

'Yes,' said Brodie. 'Fairly major tonight, but I've seen bigger. Fifteen, maybe twenty thousand. Hard to scale it on this. I can find out for you.'

'No, your estimate is fine.'

'They've been throwing mass raids like this at us since last year,' Brodie said. 'Daylight raids at first, but we attained airspace superiority by winter. Then they switched to night raids, which poses more problems for us.'

'Why?' asked Jagdea.

'The Archenemy uses the night well,' Brodie replied ominously. 'They bring the darkness with them, screw with our auspex. But we're holding them.'

Some of Klay Menomar's rambling monologues began to make sense. Menomar was ex-Marauder, bomber wing, and he'd maintained a keen interest in the unfolding war. Jagdea realised she had not. She'd almost deliberately ignored it. She'd kept her mind occupied with payload dockets and fuel loads, almost wilfully disinterested in any form of strategic overview. But Menomar had banged on about the bombing campaign during long flights. Mass raids – savage, but shut down in short order by Aeronautica efforts. Then night raids, which had required new strategies. Seeing the screen, Jagdea realised why the Navy had deployed such serious Aeronautica strengths to Lysander.

'How far west do they get?' Jagdea asked.

'We're quite safe here, mam,' said Brodie.

'I wasn't worried about personal safety,' replied Jagdea.

'Well, we usually stop them at the front door. Area Three, Area Four. Sometimes they get lucky. It's a numbers game, really. They come in wave after wave, every night, and we knock them down in their hundreds. Sooner or later, they will simply run out of things to throw at us.'

'Not from the look of that,' said Jagdea.

'Yes, it's terrifying,' Brodie agreed. 'But it's containable. We've got their measure and we can last them out. No, the emergent threat these past few months is Vesperus.'

'The hive-grave?' Jagdea asked.

Brodie looked at her, puzzled. 'Pardon me, mam,' she said, 'but are you really a wing commander?'

Jagdea laughed. Brodie was twenty years her junior, and well over a head taller. She was young and powerful and professionally disciplined. Jagdea never struck anyone as short, because she was lean and compact. People thought of her as tall, due to her athletic build and commanding presence, but she wasn't. That was why she'd flown combat, and why Brodie was a supervision officer working a ground job. Jagdea doubted Brodie could even tuck her frame into a Thunderbolt cockpit, and if she did, Throne help her if she ever had to eject, because she'd probably amputate those long legs of hers.

Nevertheless, the question was fair. Jagdea was old and lean, and dressed like a scrap-hunter, and there was alcohol on her breath, and she was patently ignorant of even the basics concerning the Lysander war.

'I am,' Jagdea replied. 'So they tell me.'

Brodie nodded, still uncertain. 'So... you're cleared, mam?'

'To group level,' Jagdea replied, which wasn't a lie because no one had ever bothered to rescind her command clearance.

'Well,' said Brodie, with a little reluctance, 'Vesperus is dead, yes. It's a burn-out. But we've been denying Great Haven's mass raids with such persistent success, they've started to use Vesperus as a back door. For flank attack.'

'Vesperus airspace?'

'Not really. Between auspex, modar, regular intercept and the Nightstalkers, we can spot, match and take down just about anything that comes across at us. Mass raids especially. They're hard to hide, even with the Archonate manipulating darkness to their own advantage. So we can splash anything coming at us over Vesperus.'

'And?'

'They've started to come *through* the hive,' said Brodie.

'Through it?'

'Yes, low level. Through the actual infrastructure and the ruins. Insane stuff.' Brodie paused, and reclipped her hair. 'They can't throw any significant numbers through, no formations, and it's absolutely suicidal. There's no room to move inside those structures and streets.'

'I can imagine.'

'So they send singletons, sometimes pairs, occasionally small groups. Razors, Talons, and so on. All rigged with high-yield ordnance. And they're running so low, they're cheating our auspex. We just don't pick them up when they're masked by the hive. So these loners are hitting the south-east 'plex, Vanberg, Solace, Yllsbruck, that sort of area, and they're hitting it hard. They come out of nowhere. Precision bombing. Significant tactical targets. We've got our hands full with the mass raids. The Vesperus assaults are minuscule by comparison, but if they keep it up...'

'What?' Jagdea asked.

Brodie frowned and shrugged. She dropped her voice to a proper whisper. 'I've seen reports. Assessments. Projections. We could lose the south. That would be bad.'

'I can see that.'

'If we lose the south hem to airstrikes, especially the main shield lines, it would pivot the land war, and open our belly to the ground armour.'

'Can you close the door?' Jagdea asked.

'That's the idea,' said Brodie. 'Wing Command has stationed several forward intercept groups in Vesperus. The lord militant demanded it. It's their job to keep the run closed and denied.'

'In the hive? Stationed inside the hive?'

'Inside the hive, yes, mam.'

Jagdea raised her eyebrows. 'That's the shittiest job I've ever heard of,' she said.

'Oh, it will get you killed, no doubt,' replied Brodie, almost cheerfully. 'Get you killed faster than standing outdoors under that.' She pointed at the shadow of the bomber swarm on her screen.

'Flights up and go-ready!' a controller called out across the chamber. Jagdea saw Kaminsky acknowledge the report.

'Let's take a look,' said Brodie, adjusting her control and switching data-links. 'We probably won't lift anything tonight. We're way west. But who knows?'

Her screen flickered, and shifted to a stripway pict-view of the field. Jagdea saw eight Thunderbolts on their elevated launch ramps. Ground crew were still withdrawing, dragging back the flopping loops of fuel lines. The Bolts were bright blue, with red-and-white checkers on their tails. The flight lead had a glossy yellow nose.

'Rush Flight,' said Brodie. She toggled the picter-select, and flashed up angles on two other Bolt packs on adjacent pads, one tan and black, one sea green. The sight of them, even over poor-resolution imaging, made Jagdea feel a hollow longing. 'Gyre, and that's Sunray,' said Brodie.

Jagdea's hands trembled, so she made fists. Years later, and the addiction remained. The speed and power. The intensity. The focus. Nothing else like it. So pure. She knew she'd been right, absolutely right, to give it up and walk away after the ground came up to meet her on Lyubov. That had been gravity telling her it was time to admit she had a problem, that it was time to stop, that combat flying was something she was no longer capable of doing. If you ignored a friendly reminder like that, if you gave in to your addiction and kept on, then it burned you away. Viltry had known that, and Kaminsky, and Aggie, and Darrow in his way. Mullane had not, nor had Zemmic, and probably not Larice Asche, wherever she had fallen.

Bree Jagdea knew, more certainly than ever, that she'd made the right choice.

But Throne of Terra, the sight of those Thunderbolts reminded her she would never, ever *not* miss it.

An hour passed. The go-order did not come from Command. Reports chattered in of bulk intercepts along Area Four. The displays became swirls of cross-rune markers. From the scrolling tally, it seemed to Jagdea that the swarms were losing dozens of elements every minute.

Kaminsky kept Hymnal 41 on stand-ready. The knotted snake of tension in the chamber cinched tighter, and got harder to bear. The shred was always ugly at the start, but the longer it lasted, the worse it got. Everything grew tight. Breath got sour, eyes dry, throats choked up. It was like the harsh buzz of too much caff. The first cup got you sharp, but you kept going for refills to maintain lift, and after a few hours, your gut was sore, and there was a hard-edged noise in the top of your skull like someone had hooked it up to a trolley starter.

'We'll probably be standing down in another hour, mam,' said Brodie. She'd brought Jagdea a cup of recaff. Jagdea was still watching the display.

'That says one-six-four kills,' said Jagdea.

'So far,' said Brodie. 'Decent bag. One swarm's already turning back.'

'Was that Bolts?' Jagdea asked. 'The eastern intercept groups?'

'Some of it,' said Brodie. 'The Nightstalkers did the heavy lifting.'

'One sixty-four in a single night,' said Jagdea, impressed.

'I know,' said Brodie. 'That's almost Zophonian Sea numbers. Can you imagine?'

'I can,' said Jagdea.

Brodie laughed. 'Doesn't compare, really,' she said. 'The Zoph was proper air war. This is more a game shoot. Target-rich. It's easy to become a multi-ace fast if you're flying out of an eastern deck on Lysander. There's a pilot out at Hymnal One-Oh-Six who has four hundred and eighty-six, confirmed. And I know for a fact that he's a shit pilot. He just goes up every night, high alt, pushes the nose over, and dives into the swarm, guns live. It would be difficult to miss. That's not combat flying, that's harvesting. He wouldn't have lasted five minutes in the Zoph.'

'You know Deck Officer Kaminsky flew the Zoph, don't you?' Jagdea asked her.

Brodie's mouth spread into a broad grin.

'Why do you think we worship him so much, mam?' she asked. She paused, and then frowned at Jagdea. 'Why do you know that?' she asked.

'He mentioned it over dinner,' replied Jagdea, and quickly changed the subject. 'What are Nightstalkers? The name keeps coming up.'

'Do you have clearance?' asked Dillady, appearing behind them.

'I believe she does, sir,' said Brodie.

'The words "I believe" suggest you have not verified, supervision officer,' said Dillady. 'Carry on, and I'll attend to the wing commander.'

Brodie nodded smartly, and turned to her console. Dillady eyed Jagdea.

'I think you've seen all there is to see,' he said. 'No big show for us tonight, but we should thank the grace of the God-Emperor for that. Is there anything else?'

'No, I was about to leave anyway,' said Jagdea. 'I appreciate the opportunity to observe.'

Dillady nodded. 'Nightstalkers,' he said. 'Marauder Vigilant variant, not yet formally adopted. We've worked some up here in the 'plex out of necessity. They are dedicated night-fighters. Stripped right back of all excess weight and plating, including standard weapons systems and most of the crew. Light armour and virtually zero modar profile.'

He walked her over to a side console, entered his authority code, and pulled up an image. The aircraft was a sleek beast, entirely matt-black, with no markings, and a nose that bristled with masts and whisker antennae.

'Marauder Nightstalker,' Dillady said. 'It carries more high-gain auspex than anything we've ever put in the air. One pilot, one auspex operator slash gunner. It flies high, ceiling at forty, forty-two, unpressurised, so full flight armour. Silence protocols, sterile cockpit. When the swarms first started to come over, they quickly got used to breaking as soon as they spotted standard intercepts, and if that happens, you've got a sky full of madness that you can't predict or corral. The Nightstalkers stay high, then drop in behind the swarms, picking up targets in zero-zero conditions. High-gain augury at close range. Pinpoint. They come up behind the Archenemy bulk bombers, Harbingers, Tormentors, the big Apocalyptors, that sort of thing, very close, without detection. The bastards don't even know they're there. Hard target lock, then the 'stalkers bring them down, single shot. Under optimum conditions, they can splash three or four, maybe even half a dozen, before the swarm realises it's under fire and breaks. It gives us a significant percentile improvement in kill-rates.'

'How do you bring down a Harbinger with a single shot?' Jagdea asked. 'That's not possible.'

Dillady tapped the screen, pointing at the long, fat chimney sticking horizontally from the plane's nose under the aerial clusters.

'It is if the one gun you're mounting is a modified volcano cannon,' he said.

'You mounted a volcano cannon on a Marauder?' said Jagdea.

'Yes,' replied Dillady, as though this was perfectly sane behaviour. 'It's good for about six shots before the cells are drained. That's when you peel off and run for altitude, because when the fighter bats come after you, you haven't got turrets to fend them off.'

'Well, thank you for explaining, Assistant Deck Officer Dillady. Very illuminating.'

'A pleasure,' he said.

'What's the loss rate for Nightstalker crews?' she asked.

'High,' he said. 'Why, wing commander? Does it appeal?

Commander Kaminsky said you were quite the hot stick. The Nightstalker squadrons are crying out for expert pilots.'

'I'll bet they are,' she said.

She paused beside Kaminsky before she left the chamber. He looked weary. He was studying a printout of raid data.

'I'm going, August,' she said. 'Thank you for the look-around.'

'Any time,' he said.

'I hear it was a good night, all things being equal.'

'Yes, overall,' he said. He glanced at the printout again.

'Something the matter?' she asked.

'No.' He sighed. 'I just saw we lost Ingram over the Selberg Boxes. No chute.'

'I'm sorry. Good stick?'

'Exceptional,' said Kaminsky. 'And he was due here this morning to complete a transfer.' He paused and looked at her. 'Have you got a routing for tomorrow yet?' he asked.

'It's tomorrow already, August, so no. I'll find something.'

'Could you handle a delivery run? You do those, don't you?'

'Sometimes. Aircraft delivery. It happens.'

'What do you think? It would help me out, and get you in a mono again for a few hours.'

'A Bolt?' she asked.

He shook his head. 'No. Lightning Strike. Intercept Six-Six is in desperate need of replacement aircraft.'

'Voss-pattern?'

'That's right.'

Jagdea frowned. She'd got her wings on the Cypra M Twin Lights. They were such bliss to fly; moving to Bolts had been a slog. But the Voss, which she'd flown a few times, was an unforgiving bastard, over-teched, over-engined, and prone to hideous instability.

'Can I think about it?' she asked.

'If you think quickly,' he replied. 'It's got to go up tomorrow. I mean, today. Sorry, tired. Ingram was slated to do it. It'd be a straight run, escorting supply carriers. Overnight at most. Get there, sign the bird over to the deck officer, then ride the carriers back here.'

'All right,' said Jagdea. 'But only because it's you asking.'

'Thank you,' said Kaminsky. 'I'll get the papers processed. Ten hundred hours, sharp. You'll enjoy it.'

'That's what I'm afraid of,' she said.

She walked up the stairs into the communal levels, trying to remember the way back to the billet block.

A voice behind her called, 'Mam? Mam?'

It was Supervision Officer Brodie. She raced up the stairs behind Jagdea, two at a time. Her faced was flushed. One of her hair clips had shaken loose.

'What's the matter?' Jagdea asked.

'I checked your clearance,' Brodie said, out of breath. 'Assistant Deck Dillady made me doubt myself. So I ran you. You're Wing Commander Jagdea.'

'I think you knew that already, Brodie,' said Jagdea. 'We were introduced.'

'Yes, mam. But I didn't realise you were *that* Jagdea! Wing Commander Bree Jagdea of the Phantine XX! I'm so sorry, mam, I was burbling on about the Zoph, and you were actually *there*! I... I should have realised that's how you knew the chief! You must think I'm an idiot!'

'I don't think that at all, Brodie.'

'Well, I'm sorry anyway! I just wanted to say it was an honour meeting you. I've read all the monographs, and studied your tactics, mam.'

'Yet you still didn't recognise me?'

Brodie faltered and her cheeks went pinker.

'You… you are shorter than I expected, mam,' she mumbled.

Jagdea chuckled. 'We all come up shorter than we expect, Brodie.'

'Mam?'

'Skip it. It was nice to meet you, Brodie.'

'It was an honour, mam,' Brodie spluttered. 'To meet *the* Bree Jagdea!'

'Well, you didn't, Brodie.'

'I'm sorry?'

'I don't think she exists any more,' Jagdea whispered, and walked on up the stairs.

Ready station, Hymnal 41 Field, 08:55

She'd got three hours of deep, heavy sleep before her chronograph's alarm roused her at 06:45.

That was her party trick. Klay Menomar could measure time, awake or asleep, in his head, but she could steal sleep at the drop of a hat. Anywhere, at any point, even if she was shred-wired or buzzed up on caff. She'd put her head down, and slept. It was a habit she'd picked up in the early years: you got your sleep when you could, and accumulated it through the day, because you needed to bank as much rest as possible. Jagdea couldn't actually remember the last time she'd slept a whole night unbroken.

She left the service billet, got a shower, and pulled on her compression bodyglove. By 07:15, she was at Allocation to collect her papers. The duty chief signed her in, and handed her the tearsheets.

'Strip K,' he said, with little interest. 'Tail Four-Four.'

'I need some kit,' she said.

'Stores,' he replied, a flat response. She stared at him. 'There's a requisition code top left,' he added, pointing at the sheets in her hand.

She nodded, and turned to go, reading the flight orders as she walked away. She stopped, and swung back.

'This is correct?' she asked.

'Of course,' said the duty chief, who had returned to his caff.

'The destination...' she said. 'That's not a mistake?'

'Intercept Six-Six, yes, mam,' the chief replied.

Jagdea used a word the chief hadn't heard in a while, and she noticed him flinch.

'He never said anything about...' Jagdea growled. She looked at the officer. 'I need to see the deck officer as soon as possible.'

'I'm sorry, mam. He's off-field. Group tactical review all day.'

Jagdea stood there for a moment, clutching the tearsheets. Then she sniffed and went to find Klay.

Menomar was in the ready station with a cup of caff and a plate of suspect breakfast. The place was bustling with crews coming in to collect food from the hatch, or to sit and talk. The air hung with lho-smoke.

Menomar was at an end table. He was intently reading a dog-eared glory story. On the cover, a technically inaccurate representation of a generic Imperial tank was dramatically crowning an unfeasible redoubt. The sky was on fire, a garish mono-print red, and a ragged banner read DRAMATIC DEEDS WITHIN! Klay's enthusiasm for the crap-rags was one of the things that had sharpened Jagdea's dislike of them. When she pulled out a chair, he said, 'Sorry, that's taken. Waiting for someone,' without looking up.

'Yeah, me,' she said.

Now he looked up. He stared at her, quizzical.

'What are you wearing?' he asked.

'I got it from stores,' she replied, and sat down, dumping her helmet and her over-stuffed ready-bag at her feet.

'All right, *why* are you wearing it?' Menomar asked.

'Did you get a routing?' she asked, helping herself to his caff.

'No, there was nothing,' he said. 'I waited for you, but you were spark out. Late night?'

'Yeah. Look–'

'Is this the part where you explain why you're dressed up like a frigging gunfighter?' he asked.

'I got a job,' she said, in no mood for his bullshit. 'A favour for a friend.'

'Is it fancy dress?' he asked.

'Delivery run, monojet,' she said. 'So I need an actual flight-suit.'

Stores had issued her with a green, quilted one-piece. It was a good fit. Unlike the notorious practices of the Militarum, where any old scrap would do, the Aeronautica took kit seriously. A compression flightsuit had to fit well, or it wouldn't tighten properly. It wasn't about personal safety, it was about asset safeguarding: a dead pilot equalled a dead bird. They'd given her heavy boots, leather gloves, an over-harness, a flight-cap, glare goggles, and a gloss-white, Maxin-pattern helmet with a slide-down integrated visor. She'd put them all on over her own socks and bodyglove, all except the helmet and the gloves.

'Fightbird?' Menomar asked.

'Yes.'

'Bolt?'

'Light,' she replied. 'Voss.'

'You hate those,' he said.

'I do,' she agreed. 'It's a favour to a friend.'

'Some friend. Some favour.'

'Look, I'm sorry,' she said, sipping some more of his caff. 'I know we had a plan. This came up last minute. A simple run and drop. I'll be back later tonight, tomorrow morning latest.'

'All right,' said Menomar.

'I scrounged this up for you,' she said, and slid a docket strip across the table. 'Forty-eight hour pass, off-base access. Knock yourself out and have some fun. I'll be back tomorrow, latest.'

'So you said,' he replied.

'Then we can pick up a return haul or something,' she said. 'Transoceanic, whatever.'

'I can grab something myself,' he replied. He seemed relaxed and blandly cheerful. 'There will be other rotations. They said they would post more routings this afternoon.'

'No, use the pass,' she said. 'Then we'll stake something tomorrow.'

Menomar picked up the docket strip and studied it.

'You want me to stay around, then?' he asked. 'Wait for you?'

'Yes.'

'Like we're… a team?'

'Shut up, Menomar,' she said.

'You can say it. Go on.'

'Shut up.'

'Say we're a team.'

'Actually, smart-ass, I need you to watch my kit,' she said. She kicked the ready-bag under the table. In it were her own boots, her leather coat, her flight bottoms, sweater and other minor effects. 'There's not room on a fightbird for a carry bag. Just stay here and watch it, have a drink or six. I'll be back tomorrow.'

Menomar shrugged. 'All right,' he said.

'All right?' she asked.

'I said so, didn't I?' He smiled. 'I know the bag's just an excuse. You think we're a team. You don't want to break up the team. Because you'd miss me. You just won't say it.'

Jagdea sighed. 'Just look after my frigging belongings, Menomar.'

He sat back, smirking. 'See?' he said. 'That wasn't so hard.'

'Please will you look after my bag as a favour to me?' she asked quietly, her expression fierce. 'I'll be back tomorrow.'

'Sure,' he said casually.

'Good. I've got to go.'

She rose to her feet, grabbed her helmet, and put her bag on the table in front of him, planted directly across the open spread of the glory story.

'Voss?' he asked again.

'Yes.'

'You hate those,' he said.

'It's just a job,' she replied.

'But that's not what's pissing you off, is it?' Menomar said.

'No,' she admitted.

'What, then? Jags?'

'The destination,' she replied. 'It's the destination.'

'Where have you got to go?' he asked.

'Frigging Vesperus,' she replied, and walked away.

'Jags!' he called after her. Everyone in the ready station turned to look.

She stopped, and glanced back at him. 'What?'

'Good flying,' he said.

Strip K, Hymnal 41 Field, 09:14

The Lightning was waiting for her on the hardstand.

Jagdea walked out towards it, helmet swinging from her hand. Light rain spattered across the field at an angle. Low cloud veiled the vast, drab hive-rise beyond the wire.

There were three Lightnings on the pad, the ground crews still milling around them, pumping fuel and running the check lists.

The birds sat with their canopies open. Two of them had magazine panels raised, like miniature speed brakes, while the fitters locked in new powercell blocks.

The Voss-pattern (Primaris) was a handsome creature, with aggressive lines, wide, forward-raked wings, and a snarling intake under the snout. It looked like it was yawning wide, about to pounce and chew you up. Given its performance dynamics, that wasn't far from the truth. The Voss was a fine bird, but you had to know what you were doing, or it would bite your arse and eat you.

Jagdea had enjoyed a lifelong love affair with the Cypra-M-pattern, the smaller, lighter, twin-engine machine from which the Voss had been derived. She had flown them, especially the III-IX, in the early years at Cirenholm and many times since. The Cypra possessed a near perfect mass-to-power ratio. Its twin F100-XB thrust tunnels gave it neck-cracking speed, and its generous wing surface made it a superb manoeuvring fighter. It could race faster and turn tighter than almost anything in the sky. On top of that, it always forgave you. It was constantly lenient with a pilot's excesses, and supple enough to cushion mistakes. You could bend it through insane multi-Gs without it folding up, it seldom flamed out, and you had to actively *try* to stall it. When a smoke came to a Cypra Light, the Cypra was the veteran, absolving all novice errors and youthful indiscretions, teaching the pilot how to please it, making the pilot a better fight-driver. The functional, fit-for-purpose simplicity of a Cypra extended outwards from the cockpit layout. The instrumentation was stripped back, just the essentials. You didn't need to rote-learn a fist-thick book to understand the board. Jagdea's friend, the long-departed Milan Blansher, had once said that you flew a Lightning for the joy of flying.

He'd also said, in the same breath, that you flew a Thunderbolt for the joy of killing. After Cirenholm, in the Urdesh Minor scrap, Jagdea and her flight had switched to Bolts. She'd found them cumbersome at first – bigger, slower, heavier, and plated like ground armour. They were harder to drive well, and much less forgiving, but she'd quickly come to adore them. They were robust and long-limbed, and they shook off the kind of beating that would total a Cypra. What they lacked in speed and agility, they more than made up for in muscle power and heft. By the end of the Urdesh Minor tour, the Thunderbolt had become her weapon of choice. It was an unparalleled multi-role, the quintessential bat-killer, the fightbird of a true gunfighter. Once you learned its ways and its foibles, you could even throw it around like a Cypra. They weren't quite as nimble, but Jagdea had trusted them, and gained the confidence to bend them way past the book-recommended dynamic envelope. Bolts had been her mainstays ever since. She'd flown them in the Zoph, on Lotun, on Khan IV, and ultimately right smack into the ground on Lyubov.

In the forges of Voss, the Mechanicus adepts had taken the Lightning basic and, using rediscovered STC patterns, bred their surly variant. Like its Cypra cousin, it was agile and fast, capable of outdancing a Bolt, but it packed armour plate like the multi-role, plating so heavy it would make a Cypra whimper and wonder why it was being punished. The Voss-pattern used the same basic air frame, but that's where the similarities ended. Gone were the twin turbofans, replaced by a single, centre-line Gladius-XV-pattern afterburning turboram. The ram developed almost as much power as the twin fans combined, but the weight differential of one engine rather than two meant that its effective max was higher. It was dangerously fast, with no subtle register. The throttle went from nothing to a sledgehammer-in-the-face unless you were ready and excessively light of touch. The lithe, and perfectly generous, wings of the Cypra had been supplanted by massive forward-rakes, downswept and belligerent. The turning ability of those wings was undeniable, but between them and the mid-mount engine, the centre of balance was too far forward. The Voss was alarmingly nose-heavy. The most common, and almost always terminal, pilot-forced accidents were the results of over-gunning and going arse-up.

That, or the frustratingly high stall speed. Or the ram's habit of flaming out without warning and for no apparent frigging reason. Or the excruciating lag between the stall limit and vector uptake, an agonising hiccup of thrust-and-lift loss that those in the know referred to as 'the stumble'. Or the turboram's low-speed cough, the shuddering *bang!-bang!-bang!* of an airbreathing engine gasping for breath and aspirating its own fuel. That was known as 'the choke'. Or the basic dynamic instability of the front-ended platform. Or the fact that Voss Forge had laden the monster with a full suite of logis-systems, which gave it the most over-specced and overwhelming cockpit in the Aeronautica. There was a logis-system or automation for just about everything, which denied the driver a vast range of nuanced manual control, but you couldn't switch those systems off, because they were essential cogitator management processes, and without them, the pilot could never perform every simultaneous thing necessary to keep the bird stable or, indeed, in the air. It was impossible to fly a Voss manual only. The logis-engines moderated trim and thrust ratios in real time faster than a pilot could do it, and without their constant oversight backing the pilot up, the bird would go into an uncontrollable spin, or a terminal stall, or a choking fit, or drop arse-up, or flame out dead, or any number of other non-ballistic outcomes that didn't end well for anybody involved.

Voss drivers called the instrument display 'the headache' or 'the seizure' because of its bewildering complexity and array of indicator lights. Jagdea couldn't think of another machine that had acquired so many slang terms for so many things that could turn to shit.

Plus, there was a book, and it was two fists thick, and it was essential reading, unless you wanted to forget coming home.

The Voss was a brute. It was a pig to fly, a bastard to handle, a nightmare to learn, and it had a personality, simultaneously snooty and feral, to match. You could take your Bolt home to meet your mother. The frigging Voss would never, ever be your friend.

Still, it looked mean. Jagdea liked that. The Voss had lost the Cypra's peppy wide-eyed 'face'. It had an intimidating stance, a threat posture that felt like it was trying to out-menace a Thunderbolt in a display ritual. The Voss wanted to be pack leader, it wanted to be alpha beast, and Old Man Bolt was in its way.

The ground crew bull, a big man in dungarees with arms like hams, walked over to her, wiping the lubricant off his hands on a rag so he could fish out his data-slate.

'Gumm?' he asked her.

'What?'

'Are you Gumm? Sagittarius Gumm?'

'No,' she replied. 'Jagdea.'

'Ah,' he said. He took her paperwork, read it over, and noted the hand-off on his data-slate.

'Zero Four-Four,' he said.

Tail number 044 was her assignment. She walked over to it, smelled the oily stink of it, and looked it in the eyes. Tail number 054, sitting beside her bird, was drab-washed in pale grey undercoat from head to toe, new out of the fitting shop. There clearly hadn't been time to dress it in the colours of Intercept 66. She presumed that would have to happen on site. Tail

044 and Tail 035, however, were a matched pair, their undersides egg-shell blue, their topsides a deep forest green. Basic intercept two-tone, dark from above, light from below. Both had scarlet stripes across the wingtips. They mounted heavy lascannons either side of the snout, twin-linked Urdesh-pattern K68s, serious firepower that matched a Bolt's punch and could splash even big prey. But that was all. No hard guns, and nothing on the hardpoint rails, not even drop tanks. The Voss was a heavy drinker, and Intercept 66 was nigh on five thousand miles away, allowing for the indirect routing, which would push the edge of the Lightning's operational range. Unless there was a stopover, they would be flying in on fumes.

She checked her paperwork. No stopover.

So, no joy-riding, no showboating, no tricks and gimmicks, and definitely nothing in reserve for a tangle. Fair enough. She was just the valet. Done and done.

The lack of hard guns always disappointed her. Bolts had twin lascannons *and* quad autoguns, all stacked in the nose, and the Cypra M had wingtip las mounts, which afforded a glorious arc of fire, and a hefty ventral autocannon that could ruin anyone's day. The Voss, with its six hardpoints, was intended as a missile platform, with its heavy twins as backup in case there were any follow-up questions. Jagdea wondered how many canisters of Skystrikes were reaching somewhere as remote as Intercept 66, and how often. Surely not enough to keep these animals in the manner to which they had become accustomed, especially if they were out hunting on a daily basis? A scramble-intercept flight with a regular stream of game would burn through missile stocks. And a scramble-intercept flight had to be light on its feet anyway, with rapid turnarounds. You could replace a powercell or a shell drum pretty fast. Missiles took far longer to hook up.

Somebody, somewhere, hadn't thought things through. Wrong

tool, wrong job. More likely the case, Jagdea decided, was that somebody, somewhere, probably high in the chain, had ordered that something got done, and somebody, somewhere else and lower down, had thrown together whatever was available, without thought to (or, perhaps, actual knowledge of) appropriate warfare application. And someone else, somewhere else, in this case right down the bottom of the chain at Intercept 66, would have to make do, and try to fulfil the top-level demands with whatever they had been given. Inter-urban, fast-response intercept out of a remote and undoubtedly under-resourced deck? Here, have some over-teched missile platforms that are pigs to fly, way too hasty for ultra-tight conditions, and require the highest levels of thorough and specialised technical know-how to maintain. Perfect.

'I'm frigging glad it's not my fight,' she told the bird.

'Did you speak?' asked a voice behind her.

Jagdea turned. There was an aviator standing nearby. He was compact, almost stocky, and clad in a grey flightsuit and white pressure vest. The Ryza-pattern helmet under his arm was gloss-black. His face, framed by the leather inner helmet, was odd: bland and flawlessly white, like porcelain. Not a hint of stubble, or scar, or blemish. His expression was entirely neutral, like a doll. Only his eyes, small and blue, had any life. Jagdea was taken aback. His frame and eyes seemed to belong to a middle-aged adult, but his face was that of a child.

'I...' she said. 'I was just talking to myself.'

'You know what they say about that,' he replied. His voice was as soft as fur.

'The first sign, I know.' She smiled, trying to make it look authentic.

'Better that than talking to your machine,' he added.

'Throne, yes.' She laughed. Her cheeks burned. When was the last time she'd felt remotely embarrassed?

'You Jagdea?' he asked.

'Yes,' she said.

'Pilot Officer S. Gumm,' he said.

'S for Sagittarius,' she responded.

He frowned. In fact, his face didn't move at all. Zero expression, except for a slight narrowing of his eyes.

'How did you know that?'

'The crew-chief mentioned it.'

'I tend to avoid using the name,' he replied. 'A moment of parental madness. Gumm is fine. Preferred, actually.'

She shrugged. 'I've got Four-Four,' she said.

'Five-Four,' he replied. 'Mine's the naked one.'

'Delivery?'

'Yes,' he said.

'Me too,' she said. 'We'll be coming back together.'

'You flown a Voss before?' he asked.

'A few times,' she said.

'Brutes,' he said, 'unless you know what you're doing.'

'Let's assume I do,' she replied.

Gumm crouched down and stared under the wing at the undercart of her bird. 'You notice that?' he asked her.

She crouched next to him. There were brand new gear nacelles attached either side of the landing struts. She hadn't spotted them.

'I've only just started my walk-around,' she said.

'Landing claws,' he remarked. 'A requested fit-out by Intercept Six-Six. You ever use them?'

'Ice landings,' she said. 'Lotun.'

He nodded. 'These are the dendritic variant,' he said. 'They must be out of their minds up there.'

Jagdea looked at him. She realised what he meant.

'Dead drops?' she asked, frowning.

'That would be my guess.'

'Shit,' she said.

'Very much, and very deep,' he agreed.

'Well, not our problem, Gumm,' said Jagdea.

He shrugged. 'No, but *that* might be,' he said.

The third pilot had just jumped off a cargo-4 and was ambling towards them. He was tall, and he was young, striding the cocky walk of the too-confident-to-know-better in his black suit and flame-yellow helmet. The helmet had a black stripe, front to back.

'Smoke?' Jagdea murmured to Gumm.

'Worse,' he whispered back. 'Ace *and* a smoke.'

'Is that a thing these days?'

'It happens here,' said Gumm. 'Miracles, born in a bat-rich sky.'

The pilot strode up to them.

'Hello!' he said. 'Good to know you. Tilo Wilzar, pilot officer. Three-Oh-Three Skyknifers... Well, I was, until yesterday. Transferring to Six-Six. Probably my record, they need hot sticks. I've been out at Hymnal Eight-One-Eight all summer. Out east, you know? Area Four, right in the brunt. Seen some shit, I can tell you. The swarms. Eight kills, though, so can't complain.'

He stuck out his hand.

'Jagdea,' said Jagdea.

'Gumm,' said Gumm.

Wilzar shook with them both. Firm and brisk, and just a hint of assertive power grip.

'Jagdea, eh? And Gumm, was it? Good to know you.'

His voice was plummy and refined, and he was much taller than either of them. He was also very handsome, with high cheekbones and a strong brow. He reminded Jagdea of someone. As Wilzar began, without invitation, to describe a 'particularly balls-out tangle' he'd been in to the deadpan Gumm, she racked her brains to remember who he put her in mind of.

When it came to her, she had to turn away and cover her

mouth to disguise her laughter. Wilzar looked like a character on the cover of one of Menomar's wretched glory stories. *Heroic Dogfight Escapades*, some shit like that.

'You all right there, Jagdea?' Wilzar called.

'Something in my eye,' she replied.

'Well, we'd better get on,' said Wilzar. 'Which one's mine?'

'Tail Three-Five,' said Gumm.

'The one on the end,' said Jagdea.

'Bloody beautiful,' Wilzar replied, and rubbed his hands.

'Eight kills, then?' said Jagdea, her composure recovered.

'That's right,' Wilzar replied proudly.

'But surely... your first tour?' she asked. 'You seem very young.'

'It's been a busy summer,' he said. 'Baptism of fire. The Emperor has blessed me. First tour, garlanded with glory.'

'How many hours?' Gumm inquired quietly.

'All told, Gumm? Three hundred and some.'

'On the Voss?' asked Jagdea.

'No, Jagdea. In the Knifers, we flew Bolts.'

He kept using their names. It seemed like familiarity, but she knew it was a power thing.

'But you've put in time on the Voss?' she pressed.

'Oh, yes,' said Wilzar. 'Twenty hours. I got myself fully rated.'

'Twenty hours... *upstairs*?' she asked.

'No, simulator, Jagdea. But I made them set it to high dynamics, the full shake. Didn't want to get caught napping.'

'No one wants that to happen,' said Gumm, without any inflection at all.

'Well, shall we get lifted?' Wilzar asked. 'Our slot's coming up.'

'Oh, let's,' said Jagdea.

'Yes, let's,' agreed Gumm.

Wilzar shot them a smile and snatch-away salute, and marched off towards his bird.

Jagdea looked at Gumm. He shrugged, turned, and strolled away to his.

Strip K, Hymnal 41 Field, 09:56

Jagdea checked the tearsheets to make sure she had got the routing details correct, and marked them down on her thigh-slate. Then she folded the sheets and put them in her flightsuit pocket. It seemed she had been assigned as element leader. They would be escorting two Destrier tankers, and two replenishment Valks, both laden with munitions, spares and consumables. Due to the lower cruising max of the transports, they would lift first, and the fightbirds would follow on and catch up. That suited her. It was nearly 10:00 already, and transport elements were prepping for lift on an adjacent stripway. In the time it would take them to clear away, she could finish her slam-check properly.

She walked around her bird as the crews cleared their equipment and unlatched the fuel hoses. Alongside her, she could see Gumm doing the same. Down the end, Wilzar was already strapped in. Gumm was an odd little man. She didn't know what to make of him. He didn't seem like a smoke, or act like one, but that face. He looked prepubescent. Like an infant standing on the shoulders of another infant, wearing a grown-up's big coat. Just another pool driver like her, she decided.

Wilzar… Well, she knew what to make of him. She was hoping he would fail to match her expectations. If he didn't, she'd be garlanding him with *something*, all right.

'Any quirks?' she asked the ground crew bull.

He shrugged. 'Checks Four-A,' he replied. 'Prime up and down. The throttle has a little give, so watch for the choke. Oh, and the hydraulics indicator keeps coming on red.'

'Faulty ADF?'

'No,' he said. 'Faulty bulb. I haven't got time to lift out the whole SM Pack and the CAD to replace it, so if it indicates red, give it a flick, or ignore it.'

'Reassuring,' she said.

She ran her slam. First, on herself. She checked, and where required, tightened, the straps on her boots and suit, zipped up and buttoned, and then settled her harness. She didn't have a sidearm. There had been no time to draw one from the stores. She put on her cap, then her helmet, and rechecked the dangling leads – air, vox and data; re-plugged each one into the suit's belly-box. Then she put on her gloves, and strapped down her suit cuffs over them so they wouldn't ride up. At altitude, the interior metal in a fightbird cockpit could reach 120, or drop below freezing. Either way, brush a surface like that with a bare wrist or forearm, and you would be looking at serious burns.

She was set. One last circuit of the plane, checking the panel seals. The air reeked of prom. She got up on the wing-board, and side-stepped elegantly to the cockpit along the WALK ONLY strip. Then she swung in, feet-first.

It was as tight as she remembered it. A squeeze compared to a Bolt, and she hadn't even been in one of those for a long time. She was used to the pit space of a multi, where there was room to put your feet up while people played cards behind you. The cockpit smelled of metal and oil. She pulled on the straps, and locked up the quick-release chest buckle with a satisfying metal clack.

The crew bull loomed above her, preparing to close the canopy.

'Stand by,' she said, raising a finger. He waited.

She flipped the voltaic master switch. Power on, the bird woke, and the instruments lit up. And *there* was the headache. She sighed. Why had anyone seen fit to pack this much instrumentation into a bird? The Cockpit Advisory Display alone looked like a floral arrangement. She made a quick pass, left to right. All gauges showed prime, except hydraulic pressure, which had stayed dark. She gave it a flick. It came on, red. She flicked it again. It stayed red.

'Told you,' said the crew bull.

'You did,' she agreed.

'Canopy, then?' he asked.

'I want you to sight-check surfaces first,' she said.

'It does that for you. Look, it's green right along.'

Jagdea didn't trust logis-systems unless she had to. If there was an opportunity to manually or visually confirm at pre-flight, she always took it. And from inside the cockpit, she couldn't visualise the brakes or tailerons.

'I want you to sight-check surfaces, please,' she repeated.

The crew bull looked baffled, and shrugged.

She cleared the stick and ran it: rudder response, flaps, tail, leading edge, speed brakes. Each operation in turn got a solemn nod from the waiting crew bull.

'You can lid me up.'

The crew bull closed the canopy and set the latches. Then he jumped down.

Green everywhere, except for the frigging hydraulics. She flicked it again. No change. That was going to piss her off. She pressed on with her slam-check, nice and slow. Left to right. That practice had arisen from twin-engine birds. You worked your checks from cockpit left, then started the right engine and then worked back to start the left. Veterans called that walking the parish, and it was an efficient way of double checking everything. Even in single engines, it was still a good habit.

From the left, she checked and prepped the vector thrust secondaries, and preset the nozzles for lift. Then she activated the auspex and modar systems, and watched their warm-up diagnostic cycles flick on. She primed the starter system, engaged the fuel pump, and gently adjusted the ad-mix until it felt right to her. She followed that with both a manual and auto verification of the target acquisition system, and tweaked the settings to her preferences. She toggled the guns on, checked the indicators – full load, power available – and then off again. They were there if she needed them, which she wouldn't. The starter compressor was now spinning up. She could hear the whining chug of it. She armed the countermeasure package. Hardpoint connection check was unnecessary, as she wasn't loading anything, but she checked the connector indicators anyway. The auspex lit up, an amber glow, and the route-track, auto-loaded via data-link, drew out a little jagged line marked with rune tags. She checked that against the version written on her thigh-slate. Out in front of her, the stand marshal was cross-arming his luminous paddles. *Yeah, yeah, keep your frigging hair on,* she thought. *I'll go when I'm set, and no one's leaving without me.* She tightened her harness, and connected her lines. Air, comms and visor-display data, plugging each one in neatly.

'Vox check, Tail Four-Four,' she said. 'Vox check.'

The link crackled.

'Vox check, Tail Four-Four, Tail Five-Four receiving.'

'Copy that, Five-Four,' she replied.

Another crackle, then she heard Wilzar.

'Vox check, Tail Four-Four, Tail Three-Five receiving. Repeat, this is Tail Three-Five.'

'Copy you, Three-Five.'

She armed her seat.

'Four-One Control, this is Tail Four-Four. Flight elements are ready to lift, Strip K. Waiting on clearance, over.'

'Tail Four-Four, this is Four-One Control. We read you ready, Strip K.

Your transport elements are already away, heading for the turn. You are cleared for lift and ascent approach to Safe Lane Seven Six, repeat seven, six. Proceed when ready, over.'

'Confirm seven, six instructed, Four-One Control. We are going to lift.'

All flight instrumentation showed prime and green, except hydraulics, which she was now ignoring. She raised her right hand, and hand-signed to the stand marshal through the canopy. He acknowledged, opened paddles wide in an almost theatrical flourish, and got the hell out of her way. Down the stand, the other paddle-boys were clearing away from her wingmen.

'Tail Four-Four to elements,' she said into the vox. 'Gun-up when ready and follow me into a slow-roll lift. Three-Five, Five-Four trail. We are cleared by Control. Safe Lane Seven Six – seven, six – instructed. Request confirm, over.'

'Five-Four, confirm, over.'

'Three-Five confirming, over.'

She wasn't sure why she'd ordered Gumm to the back. For all she knew, he could be as much of a smoke as Wilzar, or just a pool driver with no actual fightbird time. But she wanted Wilzar between them, where they could both watch him. Tilo Wilzar was not going to wing them out into hostile air.

Jagdea pressed her starter. There was a sudden, startling roar as the forced-plasma exciter lit the prom mix aspirating into her spinning turbine. The turboram howled into life. The Voss shook, as though straining at the leash, eager to break and sprint. She cooled it slightly, disconnecting the plasma to lift starting torque, checked she was still all-green, and then just enjoyed the roar. Throne, but it wanted to run. She made some fine adjustments, easing regulation, nudging back the red lines logis was showing on output. The ram was a bit too frigging eager. She was sitting on a lot of engine.

Above the howl of her own bird, she heard Gumm's Voss light up beside her. A swirl of flame spat from its jet exhausts, but it was quickly tamed into a tighter, steadier, regulated tongue. Yeah, Gumm knew what he was doing. He'd sweet-talked his Voss as swiftly as she'd soothed hers.

Then she heard a series of loud bangs, like a heavy bolter being fired on rapid. For a second, she actually thought they were under fire. In that second, the shred, which had been bubbling low-key since the moment she walked out onto the stand, began to boil up in her chest and throat, and tighten her arms.

Black, sooty smoke whipped past her screen.

'Four-Four, instruct!' Jagdea shouted.

'This is Five-Four,' Gumm's voice said, flowing over the vox like silk. *'Power down, Four-Four. Repeat, power down. Start-fail reported, over.'*

'Copy that,' she replied.

No. It wasn't possible. Had he choked? Had he actually choked out on the frigging *ground*? The bangs hadn't been a bolter. They had been the hacking death-cough of an over-aspirated ram. For frig's *sake*.

Jagdea powered down, quickly but methodically. Her engine roar died away and the Voss stopped trembling. Red CANCEL indicators came on to keep hydraulics company. As the bird's systems died back into dormancy, muttering, complaining, whining, sighing, she hit her quick-release, yanked out her plugs, and popped the canopy.

Gumm was climbing out onto his WALK ONLY too.

Wilzar's bird was dead, canopy closed, black fumes boiling out of both the pipes and the front intake.

Jagdea jumped down off her wing.

'Smoke by name...' Gumm called out to her as she marched past him.

'Frigging looks like it,' she replied.

Ground crew were running up. Wilzar had opened his cockpit, yelling something to the crew bull and two hooded enginseers. He looked like he was registering a complaint, or trying to explain something. He didn't have to explain anything to her, except perhaps why he dared to wear an Aeronautica patch. Wilzar had underestimated the power of the ram and over-throttled, choking the engine out.

No, it was worse. He also hadn't shut off the fuel when the engine first cut, and fuel flooding had occurred. A wet start. Wilzar should have shut down everything except the compressor, and windmilled the engine to empty excess fuel back into the tanks or evaporate it. But no, he'd just kept going, and torching had occurred. She could tell just from the quality of the smoke.

A wet start itself was no big deal. It happened. You retarded the throttle, made damn sure the exciter was off, and applied air to clear the flood. *Then* you repeated the start sequence. Wilzar hadn't waited or cleared, and as a result, he had ignited the excess fuel in the combustion chamber. He should have been able to read from his instruments that he was in a wet start condition. As the compressor showed a positive rise, there should have been a commensurate rise in engine efflux temp. Not only that, logis sensors would have told him he was emitting fuel vapour from the pipe. It wasn't as if the Voss wasn't comprehensively instrumented. There was probably a gauge for flatulence pressure, and a meter to measure testicle circumference.

But, no, he'd torched it, igniting the fuel soak residue.

'Wet start,' the crew bull said to her as she came up.

'Coughed out, wet start, *and* torching,' she snapped.

'The trifecta,' he agreed.

Wilzar had got out of his cockpit and was staring down at

them. He looked like he was angry with them. With *them*. He seemed about to say something. *That* wasn't going to happen.

'Get back in!' she yelled at him.

He gazed at her, with a look on his face like she'd slapped him. Again, he started to say something, as though it was still a good idea.

'Get. Back. In,' Jagdea shouted. 'Shut everything down and prep to start over! And don't do it until the chief's cleared you and I say so, you frigging arsehole!'

Wilzar glared at her. His jaw tightened. Was he gonna? Was he going to go for it? *Go on,* she thought.

No. No bite back. Wilzar nodded, and climbed back inside.

'Probably just a lot of noise and burn,' said the crew bull.

'You mean the driver?' she asked.

'No… I meant…'

'I know what you meant,' said Jagdea. 'Let's hope. But can you run a diagnostic? Hot box damage?'

Given the ferocity of the Voss' output, Wilzar's over-gun might have spooled the ram up far too fast and shredded the stator blades.

The crew bull nodded.

'Won't happen again,' Jagdea told him.

'Wanna bet?' the bull asked. 'Things I've seen out here–'

'It won't,' she declared, 'because I'm going to switch guns hot and splash the little shit the moment we're clear of the field.'

The bull liked that. It made him laugh.

She turned on her heels and marched back to her bird. Gumm was still standing on his WALK ONLY.

'Looks like rain,' he remarked as she strode past.

'Shut up,' she snapped, without looking up.

Jagdea got back into her bird and re-plugged. She switched the electrics back on, and watched the voltaic needle bounce up.

The headache relit in all its elaborate glory. Hydraulics remained red. A fitter began to re-close her canopy.

She buckled her mask back on and pressed vox.

'Four-One Control, this is Tail Four-Four. Reporting start failure, Strip K. Resetting for lift. Request standby, over.'

'Copy that, Four-Four. We show you at standby, Strip K. Do you require additional tech assist, over?'

I need a different frigging– 'Negative, Four-One Control. It's in hand. Appreciate your patience, over.'

'Not a problem, Tail Four-Four. Everyone here enjoyed the performance, over.'

'Frig you very much, Four-One Control, hope you all die in a fire, over,' she replied, but only after she'd switched vox off.

She sat back and closed her eyes. She made her breathing deep and slow, and began to quell her temper and the queasy, bubbling slosh of the shred. She'd had half a cup of caff that morning, but she felt like she'd drunk five. No wonder a lot of aviators took to stimulant fixes and performance enhancers.

She took another deep breath, and let it ooze out of her slowly.

Then she began to repeat her slam-check from the start. Every last item, from the top.

Safe Lane 76, Orison Hive-Plex airspace, 10:58

They'd been in the air for thirty minutes, having finally made the lift on the second attempt.

They'd come off the field into overcast, a dense layer of low cloud that was virtually zero-zero. Flying instruments only, and following autotrack, they had headed west to the turn, then begun the gradual ascent towards the low flight bands of Safe Lane 76. Visibility outside was just a dull, luminous fog, like trying to peer through a dirty sheet. The swaddling cloud seemed to muffle everything, even the growl of the bird's ram. There was just an annoyed throb, as though the Voss was sulking and displeased. Jagdea kept one eye on the track, and the other on the auspex, watching the little yellow cross-runes that indicated 054 and 035. Wilzar and Gumm were in long-line formation behind her. Their spacing was decent. Wilzar kept closing the gap on her a little, but she'd edge out slightly to drop him a hint. Gumm, at the back of the line, maintained precise distance on Wilzar's six.

A little higher. The cloud was noxiously thick and yellow, top-lit by hazy sunlight. Jagdea took the time to refamiliarise herself with the Voss-pattern, running practice drills around the systems, as though she was in an active simulator. With the bird in actual motion, the instruments performed differently, meshing together better, complementing each other, making more synergistic sense. You could spend hours sitting in a sim cockpit, or studying the book, but Jagdea believed that nothing taught you more about a bird than the actual experience of flying it.

Except, perhaps, for the actual experience of trying to kill something with it.

After thirty minutes, they climbed again, rising to the approved cruising level as Safe Lane 76 angled from a southward bearing and started to run south-east. That brought them up out of the top of the overcast.

And that was a moment. She enjoyed it. They broke the top of the cloud deck like surfacing submersibles, and rose into hard sunlight. Clear air, immediate long-range visibility. They could suddenly see for hundreds of miles in all directions.

It was almost serene. The light was golden, as if her canopy glass was running with honey. Below them was an endless plateau of cloud-top, like a soft carpet of filthy yellow wool. It was silent, and seemed almost motionless. It reminded Jagdea of the Lotun snowfields, the endless wastes, stained by chemical ash after the fall of Litzon. The three birds ran the top of the cloud like they were riding a long, straight nap-of-the-earth sprint over the snow cover, hugging in at a hundred feet. The actual ground was six thousand feet below them, below the overcast, but it felt like they were bombing along over snow on a belly-scrape approach vector.

High above them, a dome of dark cloud, a second, high altitude layer, the roof of a world-cave, purple fading to black. This had become their kindom: an endless plain of dirty snow, an eternal ceiling of thick smoke-darkness. Between the two, a sandwiched realm of golden light, three thousand deep, and endless in its lateral dimensions.

And there were islands. The huge, silent atolls and outcrops of Orison's main hive-rise towers, standing waist-deep in the snow, hazed and soft, tinged pink, orange and yellow. Specks of light twinkled on them, revealing their scale. Some were so vast they continued up into the blackness, their summits obscured by the darkness.

Jagdea dropped the glare visor of her helmet. Emerging from the cloud cover, the sudden dazzle had been almost blinding. Now she could see, she practised her visibility regimes and her situational awareness: the stray wisps and tufts of white cloud passing her by; the distant black masts of lower hive spires poking up out of the cloud like half-buried fence posts in a snowy acre, each one slowly flashing a red marker light; the pencil-thin line of white vapour running back off her nose and past her canopy left; the winking lights of four aircraft fifty miles east, crossing at a higher level in the opposite direction, following High Lane 80, leaving stripes of white trail behind them that slowly vanished in the glare.

An hour in, and burning south-east, they began to overhaul the other elements. The transports had departed well ahead of them, and were gunning at the top of their cruising limits, but they didn't have the long stride of the Lightnings. The three fightbirds began to catch them up at last: the two big Destriers, Hydraphur-pattern tankers, fat and heavy, blinking their running lights, following the two transport Valkyries, specks a fraction of their size. The auspex and modar picked them up first, then Jagdea eyeballed them. She lined up on their contrails, and followed them as though she was following footprints in winter.

At six and a quarter thousand feet, the transports were at the upper range of their operational ceiling. They were running in formation, as per the routing track instructions, above the cloud deck, just rattling along at a steady rate. Jagdea opened the vox and made contact, informing the transports that her escort wing was bearing in at their six, though she knew they already knew that. A brief exchange, pleasant, matter-of-fact. No recrimination or complaint, no, 'Where were you?' Just professionals making the necessary routine acknowledgements.

Because that's all any of them were. Just drivers, delivering freight and machines. Just drivers, not pilots.

Cruising speed for the formation was determined by the comfortable max of the slowest elements, in this case, the Valks. So, in these conditions and at this altitude, they would be moving at a touch under nine hundred miles an hour. That felt like a slogging crawl to the lusty fightbirds. The Voss-patterns had to drop speed once they'd caught up, and Jagdea knew her bird didn't think much of that. It had been free and clear briefly, up where it belonged, running without a care. It wanted to horse around the sky. Now it was forced to match step with sluggish creatures that couldn't do any better. It resented it. As she gently eased back to match pace, 044 seemed to fidget. It didn't cough or buck, but she distinctly felt like it wanted to clear its throat. It wanted to run. It didn't understand why it was being forced to wait for anyone or anything.

She brought them in alongside the thundering transports, dipped her wingtip slightly as a courtesy nod to the lead Destrier driver, and then pulled ahead. She dropped into the lead spot, out ahead of the Valks. At her instruction, Gumm and Wilzar sank back, adopting trailing positions to the left and right of the rear transport, flying as wide escort cover.

Jagdea signalled to OTC that the formation had joined up, that all elements were Four-A, that they were en route and on schedule. She checked the track instruction again to be sure. Hymnal 41 to Intercept 66 could not be safely achieved in a straight line because direct would take them out over Area Five and into war space. They were obliged to go the long way round, well out of their way, south along the gulf coast over the 'plex, then south-east, then east, and then north-east for the final stretch. They would stay over the hive-plex for most of the way, sticking to approved safe lanes, entirely skirting disputed airspace or any actual war sky. The roundabout route would add a full third again to flight time and distance. But that was fine. That was how it had been instructed.

She compared the data on the autotrack to the details on her thigh-slate. One last waypoint in two hours' time over Gahlborn, then they would turn north-east, and run the Vesperus Corridor, Combat Lane 90, all the way to the hive-grave.

Done and done.

The sky was clear, a golden heaven. As Klay Menomar had wished for her, it was good flying, straight and true. Jagdea was glad she had said yes to Kaminsky. It was good to be back in a bird, just for old times' sake. It soothed the lingering pangs of withdrawal. Her addiction was sated, for another year or two.

She edged ahead, and watched her pace and spacing. The Voss still wanted to let go and run.

To be fair, so did she.

Combat Lane 90, disputed airspace, 15:20

The landscape had changed. The day had grown darker and colder. They had long since left behind the sprawling, sunlit coral reefs and stacks of the vast hive-plex, and even the vast outer 'bergs and sub-cities that fringed the 'plex territories. They were cruising above endless tracts of industrial territory, the heartland of the continent, an almost flat patchwork of treatment plants, silos, vapour mills and refineries. Dirty smokestacks and venting pipes exhaled stained vapour that trailed in toxic palls. Vast manufactory complexes, like cancerous, rusted circuit boards, passed slowly below them. Jagdea saw the pale arterial threads of highways and the coils of polluted rivers, the etching of canals, and the undulating vistas of waste ground and spoil heaps. Occasionally, they would track slowly over a titanic open-cast mine, a vivid wound in the ground thirty miles across, garishly red or pink like an open sore or an infected boil. Lakes of chemical waste striped the countryside with bright greens and purples, colours that did not exist in nature.

They were heading north-east along the Vesperus Corridor, on the edge of war sky. Compass-south of them lay the coastal agri-plains, chequered tiles of hydroponic farms, livestock farms, cities of poly-plastek grow-tents and artificial irrigation grids. Auto-harvester units, big enough to land a Destrier on, were tiny red or yellow dots in the geometric pattern. Stands of giant wind turbines ran along the horizon, slowly turning as though they were trying to screw the white sky to a backboard. Beyond them, a blue smudge, was the defensive seawall that framed the wide Bay of Cadmus.

Compass-north was the warzone itself, a grey nothing blurred by distant rain storms and banks of low smoke. It seemed endless and empty, but Jagdea knew that down there in the distant murk, armies were grinding and churning and digging in.

They flew in silence, transponders on. Now the fightbirds were formed up with the transport elements, they had become one entity, designated Carry 74. Jagdea made sure she made her regular vox checks with Control, and watched their route. Deviation from the Combat Lane, even with transponders transmitting, would make them viable targets. They ran scopes up, auspex and modar set on wide-gain, watching for any other movement in the air. One missed identifier, and they could find themselves targets for an overzealous combat patrol group.

And it wasn't beyond the bounds of belief that the Archenemy could have opportunist poachers in the area.

She watched the auspex carefully. It sang a few times: some low-level transport craft; a recon bird moving high and fast; a lumbering flight of Marauders returning from a bombing mission, crossing their track eight miles behind them. Once, a pair of Bolts, racing north-west under them at very high speed. Someone, somewhere, was about to have a problem.

Then Carry 74 had a problem of its own.

Her vox crackled.

'Four-Four Lead, this is Three-Five, over.'

'Read you, Three-Five, over,' she responded.

'Three-Five, reporting fuel load warning, over.'

'Say again, Three-Five, over.'

'Three-Five, fuel load warning, over,' Wilzar said.

Jagdea clenched her jaw. It was cold in the cockpit and her hands were numb, but she felt a sudden spark of heat inside her.

'Three-Five, what range are you showing, over?'

There was a long pause.

'Four-Four Lead, I am indicating three hundred on gauge estimate, over.'

Wilzar's tanks were almost dry. He must have been running on reserve for a good half an hour without speaking up. Out of shame, probably. Jagdea knew what it was as well as Wilzar did. There was very little chance he had holed his tanks or fuel line and drained them in flight. No, his wet start had burned far more fuel than anybody had realised. He must've flamed two-thirds of his fuel allocation when he torched on the strip. Why the frig hadn't he said anything sooner? Vesperus was still several hours and several thousand miles away. He had nothing like enough to get there.

There was no point tearing him yet another new arsehole over the vox. She half-considered ordering him to drop out and find a friendly deck, and then catch them up, but she was element lead, and Wilzar was as much her responsibility as the transports.

'Three-Five, stand by,' she said. She checked her auspex and her mapping. There was very little out this way at all, just a handful of combat fields all well off the assigned route. The closest was Psalter 96.

She had no choice. She opened the vox.

'Control, Control, this is Carry Seven-Four, over.'

'Go ahead, Carry Seven-Four, over.'

'We have a fuel deficiency issue with one flight element, Control. Request permission to deviate from assigned route soonest. Request permission to set down at Psalter Nine-Six for refuel, over.'

There was a long pause, in which the static spat and clicked like insects at dusk.

'Copy that, Carry Seven-Four Lead. Are you requesting your whole group divert, over?'

'Confirm whole group, seven elements, Control, over.'

'Stand by, Seven-Four Lead, over.'

The wait made her fidgety. She could imagine the control centre thrown into urgent activity as it tried to accommodate the routing change request. They would have to run a confirm by Psalter as well. What if Psalter 96 was flight blocked by hostile action? What if it didn't have the prom surplus to handle them? The next deck was Hymnal 131, and Jagdea was pretty sure Wilzar didn't have the juice to get there. He'd clearly been over-optimistic about everything so far, perhaps idiotically hoping for the best, and had only spoken up when it became apparent he was in shit. If he'd been estimating generously, what did he really have? One-fifty left? Less?

It was his frigging mess but, as element lead, it would go on her transcript.

'Carry Seven-Four Lead, this is Control. Permission given. Immediate reroute authorised. Descend to one-two-five-oh and redirect. Psalter Nine-Six is advised, over.'

'Instruct confirmed, Control,' she replied. 'Seven-Four descending to one-two-five-oh and onto approach, over.'

Quickly, she informed the other flight elements, and then led the turning descent north.

They came in, low and slow, over tracts of grey wasteland and the scabby remains of derelict agri-factories. Jagdea had wanted to let the transports go in first, but ten miles out it was clear that Wilzar was flying on frig all. His Voss had dropped back, as though it was out of breath, and lost height. It was pluming a thin cord of grey vapour from his tail pipes, the dirty burn of a ram gagging on residual. Jagdea advised Psalter deck control to keep Gumm and her transports in a steady holding pattern and allow 035 first approach. She went in with him on his wing, circling out in a wide burn-and-bank to settle in beside him.

His Voss was unsteady, and showing signs of choke. Throttling back and trying to match his step, she got in close. She could see Wilzar in the cockpit, mask on, goggles down, anonymous. But still she seemed to sense breathless terror in him. She knew she was probably projecting.

Still, what was he afraid of? Crashing? Dying? Being forced to eject from a starved bird that would no longer fly? Trying to land a brick like the Voss on glide?

Facing her afterwards?

They saw the deck ahead, a dirty cluster of modulars, modar masts, armoured barns, bunkers and perimeter emplacements. It had three stripways, rough rockcrete decks that the pioneers had expected to be temporary when they laid them down five years earlier.

She was forced to fly so slow to match Wilzar that her own bird was growling, closing on its high stall limit, threatening to choke. She prepped her vector secondaries, ready for the inevitable stumble. A little burst of throttle and she could bring herself in easily and safely, but she wasn't going to leave him alone.

'Three-Five, keep it level,' she voxed. 'Switch three per cent thrust via your forward vectors, over.'

'Can't spare the fuel. I need all the lift I can get, Lead,' he replied. There was a twitch of agitation in his voice, the tell-tale fingerprints of the shred.

'Three-Five, do as I say,' she replied. 'Wilzar, you have to keep the nose up. Switch three per cent vector front to maintain flight stability before you drop like a stone.'

She glanced sideways, saw him in his cockpit. He didn't appear to be moving. He was terrified of burning fuel on anything except forward thrust. *Dammit, Wilzar.*

Then she saw the front ducts of his Voss reset. He was taking her advice. Tail 035 lost a little speed immediately, but its uneasy wobble corrected and it ran a little truer.

'Three-Five, keep it there,' she voxed. 'Nice and steady. You've got all the time you need, over.'

He said something in response, but it was indecipherable.

The assigned stripway came up fast, a small and forlorn target after so much open sky. Wilzar's bird was limping dangerously low, almost low enough to clip the top of fence lines. He was choking hard, his bird vibrating with each bang, leaving donuts of greasy black smoke in his wake like pops of flak.

But he brought it in. A fair landing, a little awkward, a little heavy, but down. As soon as she saw he was deck-side and properly grounded, she opened her throttle, burned hard, and ran out what was left of the stripway at zero height. She nosed up, climbed hard, turned out east, and circled into her own approach, bringing her Voss in for a book-perfect vector landing about sixty yards from Wilzar's bird.

Ground crew teams rushed out to clear them both off the strip. Jagdea popped her canopy and watched the rest of her flight, low and heavy, begin their approach.

Psalter 96, 16:52

'Are you going to talk to him?' asked Gumm.

He'd been in a huddle with the crews from the transport flights outside the deck's ready station. He turned when Jagdea walked up.

They both looked over at Wilzar. He was some distance away, sitting on a munition trolley, his helmet at his feet, gazing at the perimeter fence. It was getting dark early, an indigo gloom, and rain had started to come down. Sheet lightning, at ground level, wandered around the horizon rim below a heavy sky like strobing searchlights.

'No,' said Jagdea. 'I can't tell him anything he's not telling himself.'

Gumm nodded.

'Yes, let him be,' he agreed. 'A little self-evaluation never did anyone any harm.'

'I never learned much when people shouted at me,' said Jagdea. 'Knowing that they wanted to was enough. It made me dwell on why.'

'It's ironic,' said Gumm.

'What?'

'Intercept Six-Six is keenly awaiting three new birds and a new combat pilot,' Gumm replied, 'and when we get there...' He shrugged. 'The two combat pilots with any experience will be on immediate turn around and leaving again,' he said, 'and they'll be left with a smoke who's had the confidence kicked out of him. It won't seem like a great result for them.'

'Wilzar will learn,' Jagdea said. 'Pretty frigging fast at Six-Six, I should think. It's not our problem.'

'I guess we won't be making it back tonight now,' said Gumm.

Tail 035 was being refuelled and given a thorough check. Psalter Control had also agreed to fuel the rest of Carry 74's elements back to capacity for the last leg. It would be another two hours at least.

'We'll be late in,' said Jagdea. 'Early morning return run, I should think.'

Draden, the commander of the lead Destrier, wandered up beside them, clutching a steaming mug of recaff.

'Any word, Lead?' he asked.

'Couple of hours at least,' said Jagdea. She gestured at Draden's drink. 'Where did that come from and is there any left?'

Draden tipped his head in the direction of the ready station. 'Should be,' he said.

Jagdea went inside. She felt leaden and earthbound in her thick flightsuit. The station hall, a long and low shelter, was warm and well lit. It was also virtually empty apart from eight combat pilots in full gear who were sitting in silence, drinking recaff. Call-ready, no doubt, mentally preparing. Jagdea nodded to them courteously as she came in, but none of them responded.

She went to a sideboard and poured a cup from one of the brass urns. A battered servitor was refilling the other, whirring quietly. Jagdea saw the wall behind the sideboard was covered in names, scrawled on the flakboard or scratched in. The names of pilots and crews, people leaving their mark, an informal honour roll. Some were dated, and were two or three years old. Some had little comments like 'good flying' and 'always a hot stick'. Jagdea wondered how many of the names were still at the deck, or had long since moved to other postings. She wondered how many of them still even existed.

She took her cup to a table at the far end, away from the combat pilots. She'd half considered joining them, maybe making a little small talk, but they were clearly getting their mental game ready. Besides, she was nothing to them. A nobody pool driver, and not part of their breed at all. Approaching them would have been an unwelcome intrusion.

Gumm entered, got a refill, and sat with her.

'So you've flown combat?' she asked.

'Yes,' he replied, a casual response that suggested some surprise that there would be any doubt.

'Much?'

'Some.'

Jagdea smiled to herself. Like that curiously expressionless and, Jagdea was beginning to think, artificial child's face, S. Gumm didn't like to give much away. The face had to be a reconstruct. Now she could see it up close, it seemed to be moulded white ceramic with subtle augmetic articulation. That was an expensive repair. Pilots, even good ones, usually only got basics, and they were seldom pretty, merely functional. The patches of blue skin-weave on her throat and shoulder attested to that. But Gumm had a high-function mask with clearly intricate motor function. Only the eyes were real, or at least appeared to be. She wondered what had happened to him. What was the last thing his real face had seen? What trauma had taken it? Had it taken his combat rating too?

'So you're a pool driver?' she asked.

'Like you,' he said.

'Before that, where?'

'Here and there,' he said. 'A few years' service.'

Jagdea smiled. 'This is clearly a subject you wish to avoid, Gumm,' she said.

'It's not pertinent,' he replied, though it wasn't unfriendly. 'I'm a pool driver in the reserve. And I don't know you very well.'

'I could tell you things,' she said.

'And after tomorrow, we'll go our separate ways again, so the sharing of intimate stories seems like a waste of breath,' he replied.

'It passes the time,' she said.

He sat back and glanced at her. Not once had his voice been anything except soft.

'It smacks of competition,' he said. 'The comparing of reputations, the immortalisation of glories, real or imagined. The Aeronautica is obsessed with reputation. The legend of the hero pilot, and the influence and favour that bestows. It's exceptionalist bullshit, and I never had any time for it. I knew too many gunslingers who got so used to their own prestige they became sloppy. I joined the Aeronautica to fly and to serve, not to compare length of manhood.'

'That's not a contest that will go well,' said Jagdea wryly, 'for either of us.'

Gumm laughed, a gentle chuckle.

'I'm sorry, Jagdea,' he said. 'With genuine respect to whatever your reputation may or may not be, I've always found it the ugliest part of the job. The bragging. The notoriety. The elitism. I believe the obsession with reputation gets in the way of service to the Throne. I have no wish to mark a tally on my nose cone for all to see.'

'But you could if you wanted to, right?' she asked.

He would not be drawn. Instead, he leaned forward to her, and tipped his head towards the combat pilots at the far end of the hall. His voice became even softer.

'Did they speak to you when you came in here?' he asked.

'No.'

'Me neither.'

'They're probably getting their heads together, Gumm,' she said.

'Probably. I'm sure they are,' he said. 'But they are also combat aviators, basking in their own significance, conscious of their status. They didn't speak to you because you're just a pool driver on a stopover. An embarrassing stopover. They wanted *you* to speak to them. They wanted you to approach them, like a supplicant, and beg for a morsel of their time, so they could bless you with stories of their wonder and magnificence. They wanted you to beg for it, to beg for a little vicarious whiff of their glory, because it flatters their egos and helps convince them of their inherent superiority.'

'If that inherent superiority makes them fly well tonight, I don't have a problem with that,' said Jagdea.

Gumm sat back and shrugged. 'That's fair,' he conceded.

A buzzer sounded. A caged amber light on the wall began to flash.

The combat pilots got up immediately, gathered their kit, and left the hall through the field doors, leaving their tin mugs on the tables for the servitor to collect. None of them so much as glanced in the direction of Jagdea and Gumm.

'So you just joined the service to fly?' Jagdea asked once they had gone.

'Yes,' said Gumm.

'And that's enough?'

'Isn't it enough for you?' Gumm asked.

Jagdea nodded. 'It's all that matters.'

Gumm rotated his empty mug on the table thoughtfully.

'There's a quote,' he said, 'from long ago, long before the principles of artificial flight were established. It was said, allegedly, by an inventor. A genius. It runs… "Once you have tasted flight, you will forever walk the earth with your eyes turned skyward, for there you have been, and there you will always long to return." It resonates with me. Especially as the man who said it had never flown. He knew, even then.'

An inner door opened, and a cold draught fluttered down the hall. A woman in Navy uniform came in with it. She was handsome but severe, with a slightly haggard face, and short hair greying at the temples.

'Jagdea?' she called out. 'Tail Four-Four?'

Jagdea got up.

'Bryntow, assistant deck officer,' the woman said, looking Jagdea up and down.

'What's the situation, mam?' Jagdea asked, saluting.

'We've checked Tail Three-Five over,' Bryntow replied. 'It had blown some gaskets on the feeder manifold.'

'It torched on take-off,' said Jagdea.

Bryntow nodded. 'That would do it. The torching cost it fuel, but the rest bled out through the busted seals. We're refitting them now, but it'll be a few hours.'

'Will we get to lift tonight?' Jagdea asked.

Bryntow shook her head. 'Probably be past midnight before the work's finished, but that's not the issue,' she said. 'We've just had an amber advisory, raids due. So this is now active war sky and our priority is getting combat missions up. I can't allow a resupply in the air until we're threat-clear.'

'I understand, mam.'

'I've advised Control of the situation, and also informed Intercept Six-Six of the delay. I estimate an early morning lift. So, sit tight. Help yourself to the amenities. Crash billets on the far side of the yard. If a situation arises, follow instruction. Shelters are marked.'

'Understood. I'll inform the crews.'

Bryntow nodded. It felt like there should be something else to say, but there wasn't. Bryntow half-shrugged, and left the hall.

'You hear that?' Jagdea asked Gumm.

'I did,' he said.

Psalter 96, 21:20

Later, in a break between downpours, Jagdea walked along the inner hardpan beside the deck buildings to get some air. Everything smelled wet, or smelled of prom, and water gurgled in the decrepit gutters of the flight huts and service barns.

It had got dark very early, a thick blackness with heavy undercast. The silent sheet lightning still stalked fitfully around the rim of the world, making its thin flashes beyond the outer chain-link, as though it was signalling some secret and urgent message to her. The sky to the north, the whole horizon, was a fuzzy orange glow. Something in the outer areas had been punished hard. But the wind didn't carry any sound to her, not even the distant tremble of detonations.

She stood and watched as a four-bird flight of Avengers went for lift. Psalter 96 primarily ran ground-attack operations, flying missions across Area Five to hammer the enemy's fluid armour lines. The hook-winged Avengers, heavy, noisy, two-man thugs, were lifting in a diamond quartet. They were dressed in dusk camo, and their hefty cannons, either rotary or multi-las, were capable of ripping up tread units, even the most heavily plated. Most anti-armour missions were conducted in daylight, but these birds had heavy modar adaptation for night tracking. The fact that they were going aloft during an active raid alert suggested it wasn't merely bomber swarms on the move. The Archonate's land armies were making another push in the darkness.

The Avengers lifted in formation, engines screaming like wolves. She watched the pinprick glows of their burners until they vanished into the night and the pulsing blankets of soundless lightning.

Her flight's birds were all under cover in one of the deck's largest sheds, the fitter crews finishing work on them under the hard glare of lamps. In the next shed along, two birds were being prepped for lift by silent adepts and enginseers. Jagdea stepped through the weighted blackout curtains and stood watching the work through the half-open shutter.

Two Nightstalkers, sitting heavy on their gear. Blacked down and unmarked, they exuded menace. Their extravagant detector arrays and unfeasible weapon mounts looked even more preposterous in the flesh than they had on Dillady's screen. Aeronautica machines were generally stripped down to basic functionality, but these big multis took that ethos to an extreme. These were suicide birds, ultra-specialised, fundamentally single-purpose and devoid of frills. The crews that flew them did so because it was necessary. There was no joy or thrill, no comfort, no reward in driving a machine like that. It was a forced extremity demanded by the cruel escalation of endless war. How far could birds be pushed, she wondered, how far could pilots be pushed? War made its demands, like a screaming infant, from the moment it was born, but as it grew older and bigger, those demands became more and more outrageous.

She stepped out into the cold, wet night. Rain had started to spit again. The sheet lightning continued to flash its incomprehensible message.

She saw a figure standing nearby in the lee of one of the loading huts. She only noticed it because she spotted the coal of the lho-stick it was smoking, an orange dot like the receding engine flare of an Avenger.

It was Wilzar.

He looked at her as she wandered up to him. His collar was up, and she couldn't really see his face. He exhaled smoke, and ground the lho-stick out under his heel.

'I'm sorry,' he said.

'Don't be sorry,' she replied. 'Be better.'

DAY 88

Vesperus Corridor, Combat Lane 90, 08:32

It had been light for an hour by the time they entered the outskirts of Vesperus, but the hive had been visible long before that, a ragged black mass filling the horizon ahead.

Daylight, feeble and grey, seemed to curdle above the hive-grave. It was a dead realm, a kingdom of decay, but it endured, monumental, its primary spires and hive-rise structures reaching four or five miles high into the barren sky.

Carry 74 closed formation and flew into the hive territory in slow, single file. They had been instructed to low altitude, which put them below rooftop level of even the outer habs. An approach route had been transmitted in code, a pathway that threaded the principal streets and transit corridors. Auto-track guidance, Jagdea had been told, would be activated as they closed on Intercept 66.

Jagdea led the way, with the transport elements in line behind her, then Wilzar, and then Gumm. She would have preferred a wider spread, with the Lightnings as outriders, but the environment did not permit it. It was uncomfortably claustrophobic. They were flying along streets of majestic Imperial scale, vast canyon trenches of 'crete and steel, but from inside the Voss, they felt like murderously narrow ravines where no bird had any business being.

There was distance and clearance on both sides, a generous amount, and she knew it. Her instruments told her so. But it felt enclosed and unnatural. She, and her bird, and all the other pilots in the formation, were accustomed to open sky. Now habs and towers loomed around them, they were often in shadow, and there was no room whatsoever to manoeuvre.

As soon as they passed the outer markers of the hive proper, a mangled and long-dead belt of low-rise habitats and suburbs that had been destroyed by the war, their proximity sensors began to ping at regular intervals. Once they were inside the hive, and following the street plan, the pings came almost continuously, the aircrafts' modar systems stirred into a frenzy by the facades of buildings, skeletal masts, clusters of pipework and broken rafters menacing them. The pings intensified into shrill, continuous squeals every time they passed over, or under, an elevated roadway or the lip of a broken dome.

After a few minutes, Jagdea muted her proximity indicator, and then turned off her modar altogether. She instructed her crews to follow suit. The modar tone was merely rattling her nerves, and the display was telling her nothing useful anyway, just false echoes and bounces, the misleading artefacts of systems baffled by solid structures crowding the airspace.

She could feel the acid fizzle of the shred rising in her chest. This was no place to fly. It was simply insanity. Everything was too close, and distances so difficult to gauge, even at enforced low speed. It was hard enough to fly into and through the dead hive zone: she could not imagine the madness of trying to fight-fly, to turn, to bend or chase, to race at any kind of velocity. One push of the throttle, and she would shear off a wing against a wall or turn smack into the face of a tower.

It was also hard to judge what was coming next. The charts she could access were of little use because they had not been composed as flight-route maps. Street plans showed nothing in the way of aerial obstructions. Turning south at a place called Garrovin Circus, she found a conduit bridge instantly in front of her, and had to dip hard to avoid it, yelling as she did so to warn the elements turning in behind her. The auspex was scant help. Like the modar, it was jammed with clutter, returning ghosts and phantom traces, hobbled by the environment. Every street or avenue was a nasty new discovery, every slow, banking turn a horrible surprise. It was impossible to scan adjacent streets or parallel routes to watch for anything else in the air. Her probing signals were blocked or mystified by layers of rockcrete and ashlar.

Twice, she detected movement on a parallel route, her auspex briefly indicating an acoustic signature, perhaps that of a moving power plant, bounced and distorted by the architecture. But each track vanished again as quickly as it came, a fleeting illusion, a lie, a false alarm.

The sound was odd too. Despite the steady growl of her ram, everything seemed muffled. The swaddled echoes of Carry 74's engines reflected back to them from dead-eyed towers, and sometimes seemed to stalk and chase them, as though a second invisible convoy was following right behind.

They were travelling at a thousand feet, but it felt even lower and tighter than that because of the walls around them. Shadows were pitch black. Jagdea tried to maintain her situational awareness, but dared not take her eyes off the route ahead. Her eyes were the only things she felt she could truly count on.

Bridge spans, or the broken remains of them, loomed, and then whipped past, above and below. Buildings, even the most massive hive-rise structures, were blackened and scorched, their windows blind. Spools of cables and wiring trailed like decaying wreaths. The light, where it came, was orange, as though the hive-grave was exhaling rust. The facades of buildings were pock-marked, or had collapsed entirely, exposing empty floors, flaking rockcrete edges, and severed utility pipes. The cladding of some towers had been burned away, and they stood as though flayed, adorned with scraps of skin that had bubbled and blistered. Window glass had melted, and hung like frozen cataracts, or flowing icicles. Walls were scarred and punctured, or spalted like burned wood. Waste chemicals had poured down others, staining stone and metal. Ash billowed into the air as their jetwash disturbed dust that had collected like snow on ledges and arches.

They maintained single file, and Jagdea realised how much they must resemble some airborne cortege, a funeral procession of keening, hook-winged creatures, bearing the nameless dead to some final rest in the heart of ruin.

A thousand feet below, the hive floor was a well of darkness, a toxic underworld she had no wish to visit. Where the frail sunlight got in, she glimpsed the oily glimmer of liquid, black or dark green. The seawall that framed Vesperus' southern limits along Helot Bay had been breached by warfare, and the hive's sub-sections had flooded. Down in the lightless depths, the streets had become canals, swamps choked with debris, ruined war machines, and the unrecoverable bones of the fallen.

Above her, the sky was rapidly vanishing, as though a lid was being shut and nailed down. As they flew deeper into the hive's bulk, the structures grew more massive, until there was often far more architectural height above them than there was below. What sky remained visible became long, thin, angular rivers of white light between the cyclopean tops of habitats and towering manufactory blocks.

It was easy to become disorientated. With darkness below and long slits of light above, it felt as though she was flying inverted above a lit city. She focused, and tried to retain spatial awareness. She fought the shred, fought the tremble in her hands, and fought the occasional twitch and cough of her bird. The Voss was flying too slow for comfort, but it was also fenced in. It bucked and fidgeted, a bird in a cage, spooked by the oppressive confinement, yet unable to bolt.

They had to be close. Another dozen miles, perhaps. But there was no sign of the promised autotrack, and Intercept 66 Control refused to respond on the secure vox.

'Four-Four, this is Five-Four, over.'

Gumm, at the tail end.

'Go, Five-Four.'

'Track detected, Lead, over.'

She thought he meant the autotrack, but he didn't. Her auspex, clouded with doubt and confusion, was suddenly showing something too. A moving bounce, a signature behind them and high up. It had to be a mistake, a track error. It was moving too fast. Nothing could travel at those kinds of speeds in this environment.

'Stand by,' she said. She tried to adjust the return gain and the directional focus, but dared not take her eyes off the way ahead.

The track vanished as quickly as it had appeared. A ghost return after all.

No, there it was again, to their left. Impossibly, the auspex placed it inside the row of habitats off her port wing, travelling parallel, moving at nearly fifteen hundred miles an hour.

Jagdea looked left in panic, trying to spot it. Even her sense of panic distressed her. Her old self, her younger self, would never have panicked. She couldn't see anything. She fleetingly saw her own Voss reflected in the filth-streaked glass frontage of a municipal tower. She looked back front, and flinched as a pedestrian bridge appeared ahead of her. She barely lifted her nose in time to avoid it. The cross-hive walkway flitted underneath her, far too close.

She cursed. There was no time to warn the others, but they had seen the hasty jolt of her bird's trajectory, and corrected. The second Destrier had to skim low, beneath the cross-walk.

Jagdea steadied herself.

The track had gone, a phantom, a figment. She was breathing far too fast. She tried to cycle her breath rate, remembering her instructors long ago, back at Hessenville. First week, very first week, before they even let you near a bird, they taught you biopathic control to master nerves, adrenaline and hard-G resistance.

Frig this. Frig this to hell. She longed to be out of it, to be on the transport Valk home, to be leaving this treacherous crypt of a city behind. She tried to vox again, and still Intercept 66 did not respond.

The track reappeared suddenly, with a shrill of tone alarm. It was right behind them, high at their heels, moving fast and about to pass right over them.

'Seven-Four, maintain formation!' she yelled into the vox. It was the only choice. If they broke or evaded, it would end in disaster. She turned and looked back, craning to see out of the canopy. *Where was it? Where was it? It had to be over her already–*

She heard a boom, then startled exclamations from other elements on the vox, a cross-chop of voices.

And she saw it. Not above her, but below. Far below. A bird, moving four or five times their speed, had just shot under them at virtually zero level, burning away into the distance, leaving them behind.

'What the f–'

She saw the flare of its afterburners as it stretched away from her into the darkness. The configuration was unmistakable. It was a bat. It was an Archenemy fightbird. It was a Hell Blade.

Jagdea's whole body tightened. A long-dead fire relit in her heart, an ancient feeling that she thought had left her forever. It was the first time she'd seen an Archenemy bat in eight years, the first time in nearly twenty she'd been in gun range of one in an active war sky.

A hardwired instinct seized her, pure impulse. Her hand was already on the throttle, ready to burn off in pursuit.

But the bat was gone as soon as she had clocked it. A second later, another bird screamed past under them, moving just as fast, chasing the first. Jagdea saw the gout of flames as it kicked in its afterburners. It began to accelerate. A Voss. A Voss-pattern Lightning. She got the briefest impression that it was bright pink.

'Cut chatter now!' she yelled into the vox. Voices were yelling back and forth. 'Maintain formation and–'

Another boom. Another Voss. This one was pale, bone-white, but she only saw the belly because it passed *over* the convoy line rather than beneath it. It was gunning hard after the first two craft. It passed over her so suddenly it made her wince. The moment it was gone, two more squealed past, below her again.

Both were Hell Blades.

Five birds, in high-speed linear pursuit. They'd all shrieked past the convoy, high and low, as though it wasn't there, or didn't matter.

Throne, did the wingman know? Did the pilots of either Lightning, hell-bent on insane pursuit, even *realise* they had two hostiles pursuing them?

'Unidentified tails, unidentified tails, respond! This is Tail Four-Four Navy! You have two, repeat, two bats at your six! Respond, over!'

Nothing. All of the fightbirds had vanished from both view

and scope. Jagdea was sure they were all pancake thick by now, flattened against a tower facade. How could they manoeuvre at that speed? How could they–

'Carry Seven-Four to Intercept Six-Six Control, respond!' she yelled, switching channels. 'Respond now! Intercept pursuit observed, Mantium Avenue! Two Navy tails with hostiles at six. Standing ready to break and chase. Advise now, over!'

She couldn't hang them out to dry like that. The two pilots didn't know, they *couldn't* know they had bats on their backs. If she gunned the throttle, she could–

If she gunned in *this*? The idea, now conscious and no longer gut instinct, terrified her.

'Intercept Six-Six, respond now!' she barked into the vox anyway. 'Requesting authority to–'

'Authority denied, Carry Seven-Four. Maintain route.'

The sudden voice surprised her. It was dull, deadpan, muffled by vox-cast.

'Intercept Six-Six, this is Carry Seven-Four,' she snapped. 'Confirm ident, over.'

'Ident confirmed, Seven-Four.'

'Show transponder ident, over!'

'Negative at this time, Seven-Four.'

'Show your damn transponder, over!'

'Negative, Seven-Four. Circumstances dictate you trust us. The Emperor protects, over.'

Jagdea exhaled hard.

'Intercept Six-Six Control, confirm authority-to-chase denial, over.'

'Denial confirmed, over.'

'Intercept Six-Six Control, request autotrack, over.'

'Carry Seven-Four, unable to activate autotrack at this time. Maintain agreed routing. We'll activate when we have you visible, over.'

'Control, that's not good enough. Control? Control, respond, over?'

The link was lost. All she got back was dead air.

Intercept 66, Vesperus, 13:23

The silence lasted for nearly twenty minutes, which was about a century too long for Jagdea's liking. The shred coiled around her guts and sank its fangs deep into her throat. Sweat trickled cold on her skin, as though coolant was leaking inside her flight-suit, and it became hard for her to swallow. She kept Carry 74 in formation, following the agreed routing, coursing along the dark ravines of the hive-grave's canyons. They maintained low cruise rate. It still felt too fast.

But it wasn't the strangle of the streets, or the constant forced vigilance to avoid collision that quickened the shred. Those hazards seemed secondary now, though she wasn't used to them, and knew she never would be. Flying inside the hive structure was a fool's duty, and she wanted no part of it. However, the environmental dangers had been pushed into second place on her mental shit-list. This was active war sky, and there were enemy bats in the vicinity. At any moment, one could fall on them, from any direction, and prey on the tight, slow-moving convoy. There was no space to turn or evade, and certainly no room to break.

The shred came in different flavours, and none of them tasted good. The most savage was the hyper-focus terror of a tight-turning fight, the combat rush, which gave you no time to think, and left you shaking afterwards. The flavour that had her in its coils right now was a different kind; the slow, corrosive burn of tension, of waiting, of blind exposure. Though less intense, it was lingering and insidious, and by far her least favourite.

Seventeen years. She had forgotten what it felt like. She was glad she had forgotten.

They maintained route, driving their birds through the emerald shadow, under soaring arches, between towers, and over derelict walkway spans. The pitch darkness of the street-level floor was a dirty secret far below. Her skin started to itch, and she could smell the ugly stink of her own breath inside her mask. According to the routing, they were on the destination now, right on it. Without an instruct, they would soon have to start turning in some mindless, makeshift holding pattern.

The autotrack suddenly pinged and the CAD headache lit up as it received data.

'Carry Seven-Four, this is Intercept Six-Six. Instruct for landing, immediate. Hard in, hard arrest.'

Jagdea exhaled.

'Copy, Six-Six Control,' she responded. 'Confirm, we have autotrack. Fightbirds will maintain top cover while convoy elements–'

'Negative, Seven-Four. Read the damn track. All elements, down hard, down fast.'

The voice on the link didn't sound angry. It sounded tired and unimpressed, exactly the tone she would use when speaking to some know-better smoke. She reviewed the autotrack guidance data and saw that two landing sites were indicated in a massive structure ahead of them. One was lit green, indicating a guidepath for the cargo elements. The other, red, was for her and her wingmen, painting an approach route to a deck higher in the structure. All of her experience, along with basic Aeronautica operational protocols, told her that the fighter elements should hold back and stay mobile while the Valks and Destriers set down. If a bat was waiting to pounce, it would pounce during a landing run when the slow cargo birds were at their most vulnerable. The fightbirds should be covering them.

But the instruct was clear. All elements, hard in, hard arrest. And 'hard arrest' meant a short vector landing, suggesting that the deck was going to be small and tight. She cleared her throat. She literally could not wait to be on her way back to Orison.

'Copy, Six-Six Control. Beginning down-fast approach.'

She signalled her birds, switched the autotrack data to her visor display, and led the way. They began to climb, obeying the logis-plot. Her Voss seemed to wake up with a growl, as though roused from some sulk and expecting combat. She nursed the throttle to soothe its eagerness, and prepped the ducts.

The structure was dead ahead, an immense and soaring bell tower with a sharp, pyramidal spire. It formed the western end of a gigantic templum. The place must have been one of Vesperus Hive's main Ecclesiarchy buildings, a titanic and magnificent piece of architecture, a place of worship and solace. Most of it was ruined. As far as Jagdea could see, the templum had been heavily shelled or punished by airstrikes. Its outer towers were crumbling or decapitated, and the long span of its main roof was holed, exposing its rafters like a ribcage picked clean by crows.

The bell tower was largely intact. As she closed in, she saw the stippling of damage where ornamental features had been shot away, and the panelling of flakboard and rusting metal plates that blocked and armoured many of the window ranges. She saw anti-air gun batteries, half-concealed, nested in exterior alcoves and on the lips of the traceried parapets. And there, vox-masts sprouting from upper rooflines, and modar arrays clustering like fungal growths under the eaves.

Though she was nudging stall speed, it was coming up fast. The autotrack for the cargo elements was indicating a fairly large aperture in the face of the tower about two hundred feet below her, the mouth of a hangar or landing deck big enough to receive Destrier tankers and bulk landers. It looked as though an entire run of ornamental windows had been removed, and the excision reinforced with heavy steel props to form the cargo bay without collapsing the tower above.

On her visor, the autotrack display pulsed towards another aperture, much smaller than the cargo port, wide and shallow, like the mail slot of a quartermaster's office where you posted your requisition slips after hours. It had been some kind of ceremonial gallery, she presumed, a long balcony, once backed by windows, on which the High Ecclesiarchs would parade and sermonise on holy days. The windows were long gone, and the slot reinforced. The remains of the balcony's stone balustrade and rail were still visible at either end of the slot, like a last few teeth in the corners of a smile that has otherwise been smashed out.

It was tight. It was hellishly tight. Her pulse started to chase as the Voss began to cough and stumble, raging at the crawl speed it was being forced to keep. She pumped the rudder to maintain control. Jagdea had landed birds on carrier decks many times, and had never enjoyed the process of flying a fighting machine into a small compartment. The slightest misjudgement would clip the top or bottom of the slot and pile the bird in, and though the speed felt painfully low, it was still high enough to tumble the fightbird into a spin-and-shred. She eased the stick. The logis-engine was screaming data at her across her instrumentation and visor. Carrier decks were tight. This slot was about a quarter the size of the smallest deck she'd ever landed. It didn't seem remotely big enough to accommodate the wingspan, tail and angry mass of the Voss.

'Approaching bird, hard in and prep for hard arrest.'

'Copy,' she replied, one hand on the stick, the other on the throttle, gusting the vector thrust in an effort to mitigate the stumble. The vector control was almost at the hover stop, and the Voss was whining like a hurt animal, hanging in the air, vibrating hard. If she got this wrong, there would be nowhere to pull up, or abort. She couldn't shake off the approach and circle to try again. If she missed the slot, she would go straight into the face of the tower.

'Approaching bird, hard in. Hard in now.'

'Copy.'

'We don't have all day.'

Her speed was now so low, she was feeling the gyroscopic effect of the engine's rotation, pulling the nose to the side. She made authoritative use of the rudder to correct.

A heavy shadow was suddenly passing over her. She crossed the lip, and entered the slot. It felt like she was scraping paint off every surface. The moment she was over steel, she sensed the Voss threaten to lift as the downward vector thrust that had been holding her in the air kissed the landing deck. She'd been waiting for that bite. She killed forward thrust and let the Voss stumble, using its design idiosyncrasy to drop her and prevent a sudden reactive lift into the ceiling. All engine power was flowing into the ducts, and all the ducts were hard-angled down, except for the front assembly, which was tilted up at forty degrees to achieve a hard arrest. The bird was still lurching and screaming.

The deck space was incredibly small. It was dark too, with only a few strip lights laid to outline the landing space. Her airspeed, which had seemed like a painful crawl outside in the open, now seemed like a headlong charge. There was no room. The back wall of the landing deck was just yards away, and she was going to slam into it nose-first.

Hard arrest. Hard arrest, by the book. Unlike a Navy carrier deck, there were no decel fields or magnetic traps here to catch her and set her down. Not even a cable to catch a tail hook. The Voss had to stop itself. *She* had to stop herself. She pushed the vector control past the hover stop to the braking stop, and threw power to the front ducts until they shrieked. The walls stopped moving. She stopped moving. The back wall stopped rushing at her. She cut right back on her thrust, and the Voss settled with a hard, solid jolt on its struts.

Jagdea swore to herself loudly, and idled the turboram right back. She had landed.

'Tail Four-Four down,' she reported, beginning her landing checks.

'Copy, Four-Four. Kill power to systems, hands up, and remain canopy closed.'

She hesitated. You didn't just land and execute a full shutdown–

'Four-Four, repeat, kill systems, hands on your head, and remain canopy closed. Now.'

Bewildered, she executed shutdown, disengaging the fuel line, cutting voltaics, and making weapons safe. The Voss shuddered, as though it was suffering a choking fit, which rapidly led to unconsciousness. The plane passed out around her, inert on the deck, hazed in a wash of its own fumes.

She placed her hands on her helmet, the Aeronautica's accepted signal of compliance for ground crew safety. If a pilot visibly had her hands on her head, there was no chance of them being out of sight below the canopy frame, fiddling with something that might accidentally kill attending fitters.

Jagdea sat tight. What now? Where were the ground crews? Why were no fitters running forward? She sensed movement to starboard, and glanced around in time to see a cargo-8 truck driving straight at her. To her horror, it was about to broadside her.

There was a hard thump and a sidelong impact, then a grating squeal of metal. Suddenly, she was in the air again. She threw out her hands instinctively to brace against the sides of the cockpit.

'Control, what the f–'

'Hands up, Four-Four.'

The cargo-8 was an open-topped tractor, just a heavy wheelbase mounting an open driving position and a hydraulic array. Jagdea could see the driver, a huge ogryn, hulking and impassive. She gestured at him. He ignored her. He had run his vehicle forward and picked her fightbird up with the fork cradle of his hydraulic lift, just picked up the whole damn plane. She put her hands back on her head and glared at him. He hitched the Voss a little higher, then turned his head away, looking over his shoulder as he reversed the cargo-8 and its helpless cargo off the deck.

It was absolutely non-standard operational procedure. It was contrary to all safety regs. And it was undignified. Jagdea was trapped in her cockpit, still strapped in, as the cargo-8 swept her backwards off the deck. Immediately, she tilted again as the cargo-8 reversed onto the pitch of a rockcrete ramp. It hauled her down it at a speed that felt both reckless and precisely practised.

At the base of the long ramp was a large hangar space, a windowless cavern strung with sodium lamps and glow-globes. Through the cockpit glass, Jagdea saw two lines of parked fightbirds. She glimpsed a pair of Cypra M Lights, one electric blue, one dirty sand, a Bolt dressed in funeral black, and at least two more Voss-patterns. The ogryn spun his steering wheel furiously with one thickly muscled arm, winding them around in a tight turn, then spurred forward and set Tail 044 down unceremoniously on an empty stand. Hydraulics hissed as the forked cradle withdrew. The ogryn circled his wheel and, without a second look at her, swung his tractor around and sped back towards the ramp.

She sat there for a moment, shaking. Nothing happened.

'Control, this is Tail Four-Four.'

No response.

'Intercept Six-Six Control, copy. This is Tail Four-Four.'

Nothing. The link was dead. Furious, she took her hands off her head, wrenched off her mask, and started to unstrap and unplug. What the hell was this frigging shitshow?

She popped the canopy and started to climb out. She could hear the echoing squeal of vector thrust from the deck above the ramp, another bird straining as it came in on hard arrest, just like her.

She jumped down, and took off her helmet. The hangar reeked of jet fuel, oil and fumes. She could hear extractor fans humming in the ceiling. The shred was still in her, seething and alive, refusing to die. She couldn't execute a full shutdown on herself the way she had on her bird.

Ground crew appeared from somewhere, hurrying towards her Voss, one of them dragging a trolley.

'What the hell–' she began.

They ignored her and began an immediate post-flight close-down on her Voss, opening covers and releasing valves while an enginseer intoned the litany of the machine spirit and anointed the bird with chrism.

'Who's in charge here?' Jagdea demanded.

One of the fitters, a broad and very muscular woman in a sleeveless black vest, glanced at her.

'Just stand to,' the woman said.

'Who is in charge?' Jagdea snapped.

The woman straightened up from her work. She had a Mechanicus electoo on her left cheek. Her hands, heavy augmetics, clutched a dirty wrench.

'This is a down-fast situation, driver,' she said with a cold glare. 'Stand to and wait. Somebody will get to you.'

Jagdea opened her mouth, then closed it again. She didn't like the pugnacious look on the woman's face, or the wrench, and the woman had turned aside anyway. Another fitter was taking a torque gun to the retaining bolts of the Voss' belly housing, and the shrill rasp was a further barrier to communication.

The cargo-8 reappeared, reversing down the ramp at a high rate with Gumm's Voss in its jaws, like a cat carrying a wounded bird away to toy with and devour. It rattled past her, swung around hard, and lurched forward to deposit Gumm on another empty stand. Jagdea glimpsed Gumm in the cockpit as he shot past. He had his hands on the top of his helmet. His face didn't show shock or surprise, because it couldn't, but she caught a look in his eyes that told her he was no happier than she was.

The ogryn slid the forks clear, turned his truck around, and raced away towards the ramp. Jagdea paused, looking both ways for sudden hazards like an ogryn driving a tractor too fast, and then crossed to the side of Gumm's plane. He clambered down.

'All right?' she asked him.

Gumm took off his helmet, and nodded.

'Not a landing execute I'd be happy to repeat in a hurry,' he replied.

'Agreed,' she said. She was trying not to think how Wilzar might be coping. 'I don't know who's running this place,' she added. 'Every safety protocol in the book seems optional. Who the hell forks birds off the deck without–'

Gumm shrugged. 'It's a war deck, Jagdea,' he said. 'I imagine the situation demands certain short-cuts. That landing box is small. Too small, I'd say. But anyway, in a down-fast, they need it cleared almost instantly for the next bird.'

'I suppose,' she said. Her pulse was beginning to settle. The bell tower was exactly that: a bell tower. It wasn't a carrier deck with hoists and elevator pads that could lift and slide warbirds clear of the strip to affect constant arrivals or departures, nor did it have the space for multiple, simultaneous set-downs. Now she was calmer, the shred tamed a little, she could appreciate the crude and practical logic a little better.

But she didn't like it. It smacked of desperation, of the sort of reckless haste and improvisation that led to too many accidents and avoidable deaths. She'd seen it, from time to time, back in the day, decks pushed to the limit and cutting corners, developing bad practices due to combat pressure, bad practices that ultimately did more damage than the enemy.

'I'm going to speak to someone,' she said.

'Jagdea...' Gumm sighed.

'And file a report when I get back.'

'You're not going to make any friends,' he said.

'I'm not here to make friends,' she replied. 'In fact, I'm not here period, and neither are you. I'll file a damn report. If this operation is so critical, it needs to be run better. Or, at least, delivery drivers like us need to be better briefed. What to expect, the type of approach, the set-down conditions, the lack of comms and autotrack–'

'You're angry,' he said.

'Yes,' she agreed.

'That's active war sky,' Gumm said, with a nod of his head towards whatever lay outside the hangar's thick walls. 'You saw the bats. So did I. They keep comms to a minimum here, and activate the autotrack at the last minute to avoid detection. They don't want the enemy pinpointing this deck and turning it into a target.'

'I suppose,' she admitted. The necessities and obligations of warfare, long dormant and laid to rest, were beginning to wake up in her memory. The hard choices, the requirements of secrecy and surprise for an interceptor station. In order to hunt bats in Vesperus, Intercept 66 had to keep its location secret, or it would get knocked out.

'We should check in, at least,' she said to Gumm. She felt kind of stupid. She hadn't been thinking like a warrior. She hadn't been applying warfare logic. She hadn't had to in a long time. 'We should find the deck officer, sign off and get ready for the haul back.'

'Yes,' said Gumm. 'I don't want to stay here any longer than I have to.'

'I'll buy you a recaff in Orison,' she said.

'Accepted.' He nodded. 'And we can laugh about this.'

They walked up the hangar, past the line of parked birds. Behind them, teams of fitters and enginseers were tending both of their cooling Strikes. The air was fuzzy with exhaust smoke, and from above, they could hear the scream of overstressed vectors.

The planes in the hangar space were misfits. Despite the fresh paint of their often garish colour schemes, Jagdea could see the hull patches and armour welds, the scabs and scars, and the often mismatched or non-standard modules they had been fitted with to replace lost or damaged components. The bright blue Cypra M Twin sported autocannons that looked like they had been salvaged from a Bolt. An orange Thunderbolt had a Voss-pattern's auspex module crudely mounted under its chin like a goitre. One of the Voss Strikes was missing its lascannons, but carried twin Urdeshi hard-guns on its wing rails, and two more strip-fitted into the snout, recessed at the back of long gun troughs. It seemed to lack a targeting unit, which meant those guns were boresight only. Gumm appeared to notice these scratchwork fixes too, but passed no comment.

They reached the ramp. A flight of rockcrete steps led up the edge of it. As they started to ascend, the cargo-8 reappeared, thundering backwards down the ramp into the hangar with Tail 035 in its forks. They watched it go by. Jagdea could see

Wilzar, hands on head, in the sealed cockpit; his flame-bright helmet, his fear-pale face.

'He's had quite the adventure,' Gumm noted.

'His is only just beginning,' Jagdea replied.

They reached the top of the steps and the floor of the landing box. The box was empty, but Jagdea could see a group of pilots and ground crew standing in conversation on the far side.

Now she was de-planed and on foot, the landing box seemed huge. It was a massive chamber, with a high, reinforced ceiling, and walls lined with pipework and extractor vents. The slot was a wide and immense aperture full of daylight. She could see the dirty skyline of the dead city outside, the smog and low cloud. She felt like an idiot. You could land three birds in formation in this space. How had it seemed so treacherous and impossibly small from behind the stick?

'Let's find the deck officer,' she said.

An alarm started to bleat, making an ugly, tinny noise in the landing box. Gumm put out his hand and stopped her from striding forward. There was another bird coming in.

The pair of them stuck to the side of the box, well out of the landing path. They craned to peer out through the slot to see what was on approach. Nothing seemed visible. Then Gumm pointed and she saw it. A hard light, bobbing and blazing against the urban skyline. A forward running light. It seemed to shake, unsteady, but Jagdea knew that was just air current vibration. A blob began to take shape around the burning light, a shape, an outline. A Voss Strike.

As it closed in, Jagdea could see it was bone-white. Jagdea was pretty sure it was the gunfighter that had streaked over the convoy, claws out, during their approach.

She could also see that it was trailing grey smoke, and that it seemed too low, and coming in too hot.

'Give it some lift,' she murmured to herself, gazing in horrified fascination. 'Duct it, duct it, for frig's sake...'

Gumm glanced at her.

'We should get off the deck,' she said.

'That bad?' he asked.

'What does it look like to you?' she asked.

Gumm stared at the incoming bird. It was lifting a little, but it seemed to be accelerating too. The alarms continued to bleat.

'Yeah,' said Gumm. 'We should get off the deck.'

Tucked in against the dirty wall, they started to edge back towards the steps. She could hear the turboram now, flailing and coughing. She glanced back.

The Lightning seemed to fill the slot suddenly, blocking out the daylight. It entered the box in a blitz of raised dust, with an engine roar that, now confined, hurt her ears and shook her diaphragm. It was going to plough down the length of the box and auger into the end wall.

But it didn't.

Its vectors howled then died as the pilot killed the turboram in the air, and dropped it dead on its struts with an impact that seemed to shake the tower.

Jagdea stared. Had that hard-down been deliberate or an act of necessity? Just kill the engine early and drop strut-down on the steel? The pilot had either done this too many times to care about delicacy, or had been left with no other choice. Either way, Jagdea was weirdly impressed. Rather than the catastrophic overshoot she had been expecting, the Voss had actually set down less than a quarter of the way into the box, with ample room to spare.

But smoke was bleeding messily from its intakes, and she could see a stitched line of blast holes in its flank. It had made its way home wounded after a scrap. The entire engine compartment needed to be flooded with retardant immediately, before it started to burn. The ground crews on the far side of the box were moving forward, some carrying suppression portables.

Gumm started to run towards the bird. He was shouting, and waving his arms. Jagdea wondered what the hell he was doing. Then she saw what he had seen.

'Weapon hung!' Gumm was yelling. 'Weapon hung! Starboard wing!'

The Voss had been carrying missile stores on its hardpoints, and had clearly launched them all during its sortie. All except one. A missile, long and white, a heat-seeker of a pattern she couldn't immediately identify, was dangling off the starboard wing's second hardpoint rail, its tail fins almost trailing on the deck. The rear lock had released from the rail, but the forward lock was still attached, bent out of shape by the weight of the munition that it, alone, now held in place.

Jagdea started to run too. She caught up with Gumm as he ducked under the wing to grab the back end of the missile and support it. The arming pins would have been removed at launch. The weapon was live, and if it fell, or its motor belatedly ignited...

Gumm didn't hesitate. He grabbed it, steadied it, and got his shoulder under it to ease the strain on the remaining clamp. Jagdea got in beside him, and added her grip and shoulder to the front end. Up close, she could see the twist in the forward lock, the ugly crease of metal fatigue.

'Can you detach it?' Gumm yelled, straining.

She groped around. She couldn't reach. If she shifted more, the weight might tear it free. And she wasn't sure she wanted to, either. When the hardpoint locks released, they not only dropped the missile away from the wing but also triggered motor start. The forward lock might be the only thing stopping the missile from firing and launching.

Inside the landing box.

While they were holding it.

'Jagdea?' Gumm growled.

'Wait!' she grunted. 'Wait!'

From her position, hunched under the wing, she could see straight up at the bird's cockpit. She could see the face of the pilot staring right back at her. He looked sickly and pale, thin yet puffy in the face. His hands were resting on his helmet, which was glossy red, and had the word BLOODSPOT scrawled in white across the visor plate.

'Weapon hung!' she shouted up at him. She saw his eyes widen in alarm.

'Get out!' she yelled at him. 'Get out and get clear!'

The pilot just sat there, gazing at her.

'Get out!' she yelled, trying to brace the weight better.

The pilot lowered his hands, popped his canopy, but remained in his seat.

'Voltaics off!' he called down. Well, that was something.

'Get out!' Gumm snapped at him. Still, the pilot did not exit the cockpit.

Suddenly, they were no longer alone. The ground crew had reached them, along with fitters from the hangar below. Hands reached in to help steady and take the weight.

'Pin!' somebody was shouting. 'Pin!'

A woman in black with severely short grey hair moved past, followed by a member of the ground crew. They began squirting retardant foam into the engine ducts, damping the threatening burn.

'All right?' the woman called up to the pilot.

He nodded.

'Sit tight,' she told him. He nodded again.

'Why the hell won't he get out?' Jagdea yelled at the woman, fighting to keep the missile stable.

The woman looked at her.

'He can't,' she said simply.

'Let me see it,' a voice said over Jagdea's shoulder. Jagdea leant back a little, making space for a man behind her. There were now six people trying to keep the hung munition in place.

The man squeezed in beside her. He was handsome, grizzled, unshaven, his short hair salt-and-pepper. He was wearing a black compression suit. One of the pilots. Squashed up against him, she could smell his sweat. She could see the gold icon of the Ecclesiarchy on his collar.

'Get me a pin!' he called out. 'Chief Tarr! A detent pin, right now!'

'A pin isn't good enough,' Jagdea snapped. 'If he's committed to fire, a pin won't unprime this frigging thing! If we release the lock, it'll just trigger launch.'

The man looked at her sharply. There was a look in his eyes that said he knew she was right, and that he'd known it anyway, but he had run out of ideas, and he didn't appreciate being spoken to like that by a no-mark pool driver.

'She's not wrong, Lead,' said a voice beside them. It was the heavy-set female fitter from the hangar. She was holding out a tagged pin in her augmetic hand, but seemed reluctant to let him take it from her. 'If he's committed, the heater will be ready to flame the moment the lock parts, pin or no pin.'

The man looked at her, then at Jagdea.

'Dampier!' he yelled over his shoulder. 'Did Bloodspot commit all?'

The woman with grey hair looked up at the pilot. 'Did you commit all stores?' she asked, tight and precise.

'Confirmed, commit all, mam,' the pilot answered.

'Commit all confirmed,' the woman, Dampier, relayed back.

'Then I'm open to suggestions,' the man beside Jagdea said. 'Tarr, you're the bombardier. What now?'

The fitter frowned, and wiped her mouth with the back of her forearm. She peered at the hardpoint. 'That lock's twisted bad,' she said. 'If we get a sling under it–'

'A sling?' Jagdea exclaimed.

'To hold it steady,' the bombardier sneered back. 'Just shut your hole, driver, and let me think.'

You're not the one holding this frigging warhead, Jagdea thought. Not that it mattered. If it detonated, the whole landing box, and everything in it, would be vaporised.

Two fitters were pushing in close under the wing, carrying a roll of heavy tarp between them like a makeshift stretcher. Behind them, Jagdea saw the huge ogryn who had driven the fork lifter.

'Let Boa take it!' somebody called out. 'Better than a frigging sling!'

'Can we disconnect the whole lock?' Gumm asked. His voice was squeezed with effort. 'The whole lock assembly?'

'Yes!' said Jagdea. 'Gumm's got it! If we can disconnect the lock on the hardpoint side so it doesn't actually release, the sequence shouldn't complete–'

'Shouldn't?' the man in black asked.

'Shouldn't seems better than *definitely will,*' Jagdea replied. 'Tarr?'

'The driver might have something,' the female fitter said. 'Keep the lock whole. Take it right off the rail. Let me see it.'

She elbowed in, and called for a pneumatic wrench. Someone handed one through. She took it, and tried to stretch up.

'Can't reach, Lead,' she grunted. 'I need more space.'

'Give it to me,' Jagdea said.

The fitter glanced at the man in black.

'Do it, Tarr,' he said. 'We can't let go to make room.'

Tarr looked at Jagdea and held out the torque gun. Jagdea

eased her shoulder further under the missile to free her right hand, and took it.

'Keep it steady!' someone yelled.

'Done this before?' Tarr asked Jagdea.

'Never,' Jagdea replied.

She reached up around the missile, and pressed the power-driver head against the first of the suspension lugs that held the lock assembly to the rail. It suddenly went very quiet. There were now more than a dozen people crowded in under the wing of the plane, at least half of them supporting the missile. The first buzzing rasp of the pneumatic tool made them all inhale sharply.

'Everyone back off!' the man in black ordered. 'Everyone who is not actually holding this thing, get off the deck and behind the blast baffles. Now! That includes you, Dampier.'

People started to withdraw one by one, some of them running back across the deck to the cover of the blast shields. Dampier stood and watched for a moment, then followed them.

'You too, chief,' the man said.

'I'm staying, Lead,' Tarr replied.

Another squealing buzz, and the first lug fell out. The bodies pressed in around Jagdea seemed to wince as it bounced off the deck at their feet.

'Easy does it,' Tarr whispered.

Jagdea got the tool on the second lug, and freed it with two, quick bursts of power.

'One more,' she said.

'When it goes, it'll feel ten times as heavy,' the man in black said.

'Or get very, very much hotter,' Jagdea replied, shooting him a grin.

He didn't smile back. But some kind of bleak amusement seemed to drift in his eyes.

'Boa, get in here!' he called. The ogryn hunched down and crawled in under the Strike's wing beside them.

'You're going to take it when it goes, nice and steady, all right?'

'Lead,' said Boa.

The man in black looked at Jagdea.

'Do it,' he said.

Jagdea reached up. It was a bad angle. The air-tool's bit slid off the lug as she pressed, and banged against the wing's underside.

'Frig's sake, driver!' Tarr growled.

Jagdea ignored her. She reached up again, secured the bit, and drilled the lug free.

The missile came away from the hardpoint with the entire lock assembly intact. They all took the strain, even Tarr, reaching in beside Jagdea. Then the ogryn slid under it, and took the whole thing in the curl of his massive arms, as though he was lifting a log.

One by one, they let go and stepped back. The ogryn held it perfectly steady, without a hint of effort. Then he started to edge out, shuffling on his knees. Tarr placed her hand gently on the top of his head to keep him down until he'd cleared the plane's wing. If he rose too soon, and brained himself...

'You're clear,' said Tarr.

Slowly, almost majestically, Boa rose to his feet, first one leg, then the other.

'Where?' he said.

'Blast box?' Lead asked Tarr.

'Blast box,' she agreed. 'If I can safe the heater, I'll put it back in the bomb farm. If not...'

The man in black nodded. 'We'll need a new blast box,' he said.

Two fitters came over with a munitions cart, and the ogryn gently laid the missile on the rack. Then they wheeled it away towards the ramp, with Tarr following them. The cart rattled, and it had at least one squeaky wheel. Jagdea grimaced every time it shook and clattered over a divot in the deck.

Gumm leaned back against the plane's fuselage and exhaled. Jagdea breathed out, and then, quite suddenly, had to stop herself from vomiting. The shred was deep, deep inside her, a fury in her gut and chest. She'd been oblivious to it in the moment, just blocking it so she could concentrate. But as soon as the tension lapsed, she became hyper-aware of it, and it almost swept her away.

'Clear the deck!' the man in black yelled. 'Right now! Get the lifter up here for Bloodspot! Gangster's still circling, and we need the box empty to bring her in!'

The group began to disperse. The man in black didn't give Jagdea a second look as he strode away. Gumm took her by the arm, and walked her over to the wall near the ramp.

'Ease back,' he whispered. 'Ease right back to idle. We'll be gone in the morning.'

She was about to reply when they heard and felt the blast. The huge blast of a major detonation. For a moment, Jagdea thought the hung missile had finally cooked off.

But it wasn't that.

It wasn't that at all.

Intercept 66, Vesperus, 15:01

'What's happening?' Wilzar asked as he approached them. 'Was that an explosion?'

He arrived in the landing box just as a tractor was carrying the bone-white Voss away down the ramp. He looked pasty and damp from fear, concentration and fatigue.

'Definitely,' said Jagdea. Sirens were sounding. Not the tinny bleat of the landing advisory alarms, but a deep, plaintive howl that echoed out of the bell tower below them.

'Are we... are we under attack?' Wilzar asked.

Jagdea shrugged. Gumm turned without comment, and strode towards the open slot.

'Look! Jagdea!' he called out, and they joined him. Outside, dense clouds of black smoke were boiling up the face of the bell tower from somewhere far below. Jagdea knew the smell of that burn. Jet fuel. Lots of it.

'Prom burning,' said Gumm. He was standing right on the crumpling lip of the slot, the sheer drop to the street yawning below him. Jagdea inched closer, cautious of the edge. She tried to peer down. It was a terrifying plunge, at least fifteen hundred feet to a street level below that was rendered invisible by shadow.

She swallowed, and tensed.

Gumm glanced at her, carelessly indifferent to the precipice. 'Are you afraid of heights?' he asked.

She nodded.

'I'll remind you what you do for a living...' he said, amused.

'I'm not afraid of heights when I'm inside a bird,' she said. She peered down again, clutching his arm to steady herself while she leaned out. He didn't seem to mind.

There was fire below the immense black smoke plume. She could see licks of it, fierce and wild, leaping out of a lower part of the bell tower. The rippling blooms were orange. It was a huge blaze, molten hot. As she watched, there was another blast rumble and a fireball expanded, fed by fresh combustion.

'Shit,' she said, pulling herself back. 'That's bad.'

'We're under attack,' said Wilzar. Jagdea looked at him, and realised it was a statement this time. Wilzar was staring out across the hive. He pointed.

The smoke had sharp eyes.

Jagdea heard the power plant first, a confusing echo bounced by the deep streets. Then she saw the bat. A Hell Talon was coming straight at the tower along the ravine of a cross-street avenue, almost level with them. A full-burn approach. Dead on.

Then it banked away, sharply and steeply. Jagdea had no idea why. Another second on that angle, it could have laced the facade of the bell tower with cannon fire.

'Throne's sake!' Gumm exclaimed. 'Look at that!'

It was happening fast, almost too fast to follow, but they had front row seats. The bat was rolling out of its line of assault in a high-G evasion. A fightbird came across it, out of nowhere, shockingly low and insanely fast. The fightbird was a Voss Strike. It was bright pink. It barrel-rolled over and under the escaping bat, which then started to tumble with it, locked in a tight and fatal dance.

'Too low! Too low!' Jagdea cried.

Somehow, both aircraft managed to miss a roofline, and soar between a pair of ruined towers. They vanished from sight behind the hulk of an immense hab, then appeared again on the far side, looping a spire and bending back towards the bell tower. They were locked. The bat was trying to shake the Voss, but the Voss was stuck fast like a leech.

It had three choices, Jagdea thought. Turn out hard... and undoubtedly collide with the buildings around it. Light its burners, and try to out-race the Voss. Or hard brake in an attempt to force the Voss into overshoot so it could drop in behind and make a kill from the six.

And, of course, the fightbird pilot had precisely the same options.

The bat chose option three, just as she had anticipated. She saw its nose pitch up as it throttled back hard, lurching its airframe. The pink bird shot past it, now square in its sights.

Then the Voss did the very last thing she was expecting. Instead of braking in an effort to slide back out of the bat's cone of fire, it lit its afterburner. It accelerated. It accelerated with the bat on its six. It accelerated past any sane limit of speed for a constricted urban environment.

Jagdea flinched as it ran out of space and ran out of street. But the fightbird rode its kick of a burn upwards, and missed the roofline of a hab by no more than six feet.

The bat did not. Racing to catch the extending Voss, and stay on its six, the bat was too intent on its prey. It misjudged. She saw the flash as it impacted the roofline, the spinning fireball that travelled on, bouncing across the rooftops, the brief spray of disintegrating airframe, the shower of debris from the ruptured roof. The pink Voss climbed, banked away, and vanished from sight.

It was the closest near-miss she'd ever seen. The closest, closest call. That was a matter of pure luck, not skill. They were both meant to die. One didn't.

She looked at Gumm. He looked back at her with an astonished shake of his head.

'Now that was some damn flying…' Wilzar murmured, still gazing out.

'No, it wasn't,' Jagdea told him. 'No, it frigging wasn't, Wilzar. That was nothing like flying at all.'

Intercept 66 had been hit hard. Jagdea and Gumm left the landing box with Wilzar trailing them. The station's old hallways, poorly lit, were glazed with smoke rising from below, and ground crew ran past carrying fire suppression equipment. Sirens were still sounding.

They found a stairwell, and Jagdea led the way down. The smoke grew thicker.

'What are we doing?' Wilzar called out, coughing.

'We have to help,' Jagdea replied. 'They're going to lose the entire station if the fire takes hold.'

She glanced at Gumm.

'So we'll never get out of here,' she added.

But it wasn't that, not really. Logistics Reserve or not, the old instincts came back. In a crisis, everyone got stuck in. If you didn't, you weren't really Aeronautica, and never had been. It wasn't about rank or role, it was about survival.

Ancient plumbing ran down the walls of the stone stairwell. The pipes were shuddering and rattling. In places, at bad seams or old joints, they were blurting water and leaking. Jagdea reached up and felt one of the juddering pipes. She could feel the pressure.

'Water suppression,' she said. 'They must have tanks on the roof.'

'Rainwater,' Gumm nodded. 'Just open the taps and flood.'

'Please Throne it's enough,' she said.

They continued down, and moved aside to let a stretcher team come up past them. The body on the stretcher, a fitter, was writhing and gasping, his skin and clothing blackened. Behind them came several more station personnel, choking and coughing, damp cloths pressed to their mouths. One of them, an older man in a brown leather coat, saw them and took his makeshift mask away. He was wearing red leather gloves, and he waved his damp cloth at Jagdea with a brisk and theatrical flourish.

'Back up!' he wheezed. 'Up, up! The smoke's too dense. Go back!'

Jagdea hesitated.

'Listen to me,' he said. 'You'll be dead in minutes if you go down.'

'Lopard?' a voice called out from above them.

Jagdea looked back. It was Dampier, the austere woman with

the cropped grey hair. She was on the stairs behind them, prepping a breather mask.

'What's the situation?' she asked the man in the brown coat, ignoring Jagdea completely.

The man in brown coughed hard, trying to clear his lungs. His eyes were reddened with smoke.

'Appalling,' he replied. 'Major fire right beside primary fuel storage. The freight box is a complete loss. But we managed to get the valves open, so we're flushing it. With luck, that will contain it. And Asa is getting the vents on, to pump the smoke out. Right now, it's too thick.'

'Asa's down there?' Dampier asked.

'Last I saw.'

'I'm going down.'

'Dampier–'

'I'm going, Lopard. Get highside. Get some air.'

She began to descend, and then seemed to notice Jagdea and her companions.

'What are you doing here?' she asked.

'Trying to help,' said Jagdea.

'You're getting in the way,' Dampier replied curtly. 'You heard Lopard. You can't go down without a mask.' She looked at the man in brown. 'Lopard, take them up to the rec room.'

'I don't even know who they are,' he replied.

'Logistics drivers,' Dampier said. 'They just brought the new birds in.'

'Actually,' said Wilzar, 'I'm Pilot Officer W–'

'Not now,' Jagdea growled at him. Close up, she was keenly aware of the woman's aura of authority, and saw that her severe uniform wasn't black at all. It was dark, battlefleet blue. She could also see the small rank pins fixed either side of the coat's high collar. To the left, Deck Command. The right, Prefectus.

'Get them stowed, Lopard,' Dampier said. 'I need a headcount, and I want to know where everyone is.'

She pushed past them, and continued her way down.

Rec room, Intercept 66, Vesperus, 15:51

'You picked a bad day to join us here at the Campanile,' Lopard remarked as he led them into the rec room high above. He was still coughing, trying to clear his airways. He tossed the damp cloth he had been using as a mask on the floor with disgust.

'We're not,' said Jagdea. 'Joining you,' she added.

'Ah,' said Lopard. 'Of course. Just pool drivers.'

'I'm joining,' said Wilzar proudly. 'Tilo Wilzar.'

Lopard looked him up and down, then nodded. Some judgement had been made.

'Are you?' he said. 'Well, then.'

He produced a clean, spotted kerchief, shook it out, and began to wipe the soot from his face. Jagdea thought he was what some might describe as very handsome, with a lingering smirk as the default set of his features. She judged him to be about her age. Lopard sauntered towards the drinks cabinet.

That gait. Jagdea could tell he was a veteran aviator just from the way he moved. Years of G-strain took its toll on a body. It caused the skin of the face to sag slightly, to age prematurely. It loosened the joints, and left thread capillaries and g-rash spots on the throat and chest. She knew that from her own experience. Most of those things weren't immediately obvious, thanks to Lopard's darker skin and striking features, but there was no disguising the louche roll of a backbone and limbs stress-slackened by years of hard-G punishment. Lopard was a career pilot.

He poured a glass of some dark spirit from a bottle, and

knocked it back in one. He coughed, and dabbed his lips with the back of a thumb.

He looked over at them.

'Where are my manners?' he said, with a sly smile. 'A drink?'

Gumm shook his head.

'Thanks,' said Jagdea. Wilzar nodded.

Lopard refilled his glass, and poured two more. He handed them to Wilzar and Jagdea. She saw the red gloves. Finely made. Hand-made to fit.

'May you return to deck before the bats know you're up,' Lopard said, raising his glass casually.

The rec room was a small and shabby chamber. Mouldering furniture, some armchairs and three sofas, had been reclaimed and dragged in from somewhere. A large scale chart of Vesperus decorated the wall. The room smelled of dead smoke and desperation. The rusted pipes running along the top of the wall were still juddering with pressure and, in one place, leaking a dribble of brown water down a framed portrait of Lord Militant Jahkel that hung askew over the fireplace.

'So, what happened?' asked Jagdea.

'Where to start?' Lopard sighed. He set his drink down, and produced a silver smoking case. 'First of all, I was born, then many horrible, regrettable things occurred–'

'I mean this,' said Jagdea, unamused. 'The attack.'

'A bat found us,' said Lopard. 'It happens. As I was told it, Gangster and Bloodspot scrambled a few hours ago when a track was flagged, and they tangled. Splashed one, drove the others off.'

'I think we saw part of that,' said Jagdea.

Lopard nodded. He opened the case, and offered it. 'Smoke?' he asked. He smirked at Wilzar. 'No pun intended.'

'I say–' said Wilzar.

'No, thanks,' said Jagdea.

Lopard shrugged, took out a lho-stick for himself, and tamped it on the lid with a gloved hand.

'Bloodspot took a knock, so they headed back,' he continued. 'I think that was while you were arriving. Hard-down, and the autotrack wasn't supposed to be on for long because of hostile activity. But there was some delay.'

'A hung weapon,' said Gumm.

'That'd do it,' said Lopard. 'So the box was full. Gangster was circling. And one of the bats came back. Sniffed out the autotrack, which someone had lamentably left running in all the fuss. Took a run at us, unloaded into the freight box. Nearly hit the damn fuel reserves. We were lucky, I suppose. But it's still a mess. Casualties.'

'How many?' asked Jagdea.

'No way to know yet,' Lopard replied. He lit his stick.

'Your pilot... "Gangster", was it?' said Wilzar. 'He splashed the bat.'

'He did not,' said Jagdea. 'The bat splashed itself. He was merely present and insane at the same time.'

'Ah, the Six-Six motto,' Lopard chuckled.

'It was a fine piece of flying,' Wilzar insisted. 'Absolutely Four-A, the best I've ever seen. I'd like to shake him by the hand.'

'Her,' said Lopard. 'Pilot Officer Disa Yesof, call sign Gangster. And I would not recommend it. If you do, count your fingers afterwards.'

Above them, the pipes suddenly stopped knocking. Lopard glanced up.

'Well, either the fire's out, or we've drained a tank.'

He raised a finger, listening, waiting. With a clang, the plumbing started to rattle again.

'There,' he said. 'They've switched to tank two. We've got three, bulk reservoirs. Let's hope it's enough to get that blaze doused. And leave enough left for basics like washing, cooking and, you know, drinking. Rainwater's our only source. We have a purification plant. Might have to start rationing again.'

'Can't you pump a supply from the hive floor?' asked Gumm.

'It's a purification plant,' said Lopard, 'not a miracle. Word of advice. Do not drink from the hive's water table. Ever. And if you go down, don't ditch in the water. The streets are flooded. Try and find a friendly rooftop.'

'We won't be here long enough to face that situation,' said Jagdea. She sipped her drink. It was poor quality joiliq, the local alcohol of choice. It burned like dirty ad-mix, but it was warming her belly.

'You are very insistent on the brevity of your stay,' Lopard said.

'We're just here on delivery. Overnight turnaround,' said Jagdea. 'Pilot Officer Gumm, Pilot Officer Jagdea. Aeronautica Logistics Reserve.'

'Harlot,' Lopard replied.

'I'm sorry?' said Jagdea.

'My call sign,' said Lopard, grinning mischievously. 'We all have call signs here, and mine is Harlot.'

'And how did you come by that?' asked Gumm.

'One does not choose one's own call sign, Pilot Officer Gumm,' said Lopard, exhaling lho-smoke in a languid plume. 'It is bestowed upon one by one's fellow pilots, usually in a derogatory fashion. I can't imagine why they chose Harlot for me.'

'Reputation is a terrible thing,' remarked Gumm.

Lopard laughed. 'My dear sir,' he said, 'it's like you know me.'

'I know you were bomber wing,' said Gumm. 'Marauders?'

Lopard cocked an eyebrow. 'And what makes you say that?'

'That toast you gave. That's a bomber's toast.'

Lopard nodded, impressed. 'Old habits,' he replied. 'I was

bomber wing in the early days. I switched to monos. I've been fightbirds for, well, more years than I'd care to count.'

He leant back against the sideboard on one elbow, face turned to his raised lho-stick in a feigned aristocratic pose.

'So many, many years,' he murmured, then sighed. 'I suppose I should sign you in. I imagine no one's been in any position to do any paperwork. Though I might leave it to Dampier.'

'What's her call sign?' asked Wilzar, trying to be genial.

'Dampier is our Fleet Prefectus discipline officer,' said Lopard, suddenly cold, 'and also our senior deck. The Six-Six circus is her show, son. She does not have a call sign, and I wouldn't go inventing one.'

He straightened up.

'I suppose I should at least find you billets,' he said.

'We can crash on the floor,' said Jagdea. 'We're only here overnight.'

'Oh dear,' said Lopard, looking at her. 'You don't seem to have grasped it. That bat shot up the cargo box. Those freight-birds you escorted in today were sitting on the deck. They're gone. The crews too.'

'All of them?' asked Jagdea.

'All of them,' said Lopard. 'That burn is the fuel they were carrying. Fuel we dearly needed. They'd only just begun unloading and pumping. They were hooked up, sitting targets. Went up like a bomb. You won't be going home in the morning, because the birds that were due to take you are cooked. So let's find you a billet.'

DAY 89

Crash room, Intercept 66, Vesperus, 01:02

Her ability to sleep on demand had abandoned her. She lay in the darkness of the dirty crash room on a cot that smelled of other bodies. Gumm was asleep on the far side of the room. She could barely hear him breathing. Wilzar had been sent to the aviator billets.

Sometime before midnight, the pipes had stopped knocking. Either the tanks had emptied, or the fire was out. She hoped it was the latter. The stink of smoke permeating the station had decreased.

She lay in the dark thinking of Orison, of Menomar. Of Port Halgart far away on the Black Glaciers. Of August Kaminsky, whom she felt like cursing for landing her in this shit.

But it wasn't his fault. It was what Oskar Viltry had once called Fate's wheel. She wondered how long they'd have to wait for another routing to be sent out this way. A while, she suspected. How often did a remote deck get a resupply? Infrequently, except that Six-Six had just lost a replenishment carry-flight, and all the fuel, food and munitions it was bearing. There would be an urgent request. A *priority* request. Six-Six would be pleading with Air Command so it could maintain its operational function. So maybe a relief flight would be put together fast, which meant that she and Gumm could be on their way back out in a day or two.

Provided there were supplies to be drawn. The Aeronautica was overstretched on Lysander. What if it took a week, two weeks, before someone, somewhere managed to requisition a fuel load that wasn't earmarked for the Eastern Areas and the front line?

She thought of Draden and the crews of the Carry 74 Valks and Destriers. She tried not to imagine the sudden wail of the bat running in, the cannons firing. She tried not to imagine the blinding flash of fire and light that had been the last split second of their lives.

She hoped it had been quick. There were two ways to die in a fuel ignition event.

Once midnight had passed, her edginess had increased. She wanted to get up and pace, but she didn't want to disturb Gumm. She considered her options, and resolved, selfishly, to request a link to the hive-plex first thing. As soon as it was light. If she could speak to Kaminsky at Hymnal directly, she could get him to pull strings. Send a Valk. Get her and Gumm out. Maybe she could get Kaminsky to chase the replacement resupply? That would help Six-Six out, so it wouldn't be so selfish.

Maybe... maybe Six-Six had a Valkyrie or a carrier bird that could take them back. If there were casualties that the Campanile couldn't handle, they'd need extraction to a home field surgical unit. She found herself wishing for casualties that needed a fast exfil, so she stopped thinking about that.

Just after 01:00, the door opened without a knock, and light spilled in.

'Jagdea? Gumm?' a voice called. 'I'm looking for a Jagdea and a Gumm.'

It was Senior Deck Dampier.

* * *

Dampier led them up the bell tower's hushed central staircase, a grand affair of aethercite and marble, lit by hooded glow-globes. Even at the late hour, there was a bustle of activity, with ground crew, Munitorum, and pilots heading up and down. Their footsteps echoed off the high vault.

'Is the fire out, mam?' Jagdea asked.

'Yes,' Dampier replied.

'Casualties?'

'Too many,' said Dampier. She was clearly a stranger to smiles or long sentences.

'Is there any indication,' Jagdea asked tentatively as they hurried up the steps, 'when Gumm and I can expect a transit back to the hive-plex? We're just pool drivers, and we'll be required for freight routing. I appreciate that's not a high priority–'

'I'm glad you appreciate that,' said Dampier.

They crossed a broad marble landing, overlooked by a vast mosaic of the God-Emperor Ascendant. The feeble glow of the hooded lamps made the huge and defunct chandelier suspended over the main stair-drop seem even more neglected. Its crystal beads caught the half-light, twinkling like a forgotten constellation.

Large double doors led through to Six-Six Control. The chamber, large and high-vaulted, had evidently been one of the Campanile's principal belfries. Heavy bell yokes and bearings were still suspended from the thick timber headstocks overhead, and cracked, muted bells sat under dusty tarps along one wall, with loose clappers piled beside them like stacks of rocket munitions. The belfry's floor traps had been closed, and rubberised matting laid down. Four warfare officers and three servitors manned the control station in the blue gloom.

'You have your tearsheet?' Dampier asked.

Jagdea and Gumm produced their instruct papers from the pockets of their flightsuits and handed them over.

'Wait here,' said Dampier. She walked away, and vanished through a door on the far side of the control room.

Campanile Control resembled every forward operation centre Jagdea had ever seen, a command-and-control set up in whatever space was available. It was an abbreviated version of Kaminsky's more permanent control at Hymnal Field. Around the room, modar and vox-stations, primary auspex, warfare control, condition and threat mapping combined, the AD/G station, principal plotting, CRX/K, binharic vox, tactical assessment, strategic assessment, and high watch. The belfry windows, high lancets, had been sealed shut with welded steel plates. The duty officer stood by the strategium table in the centre of the room, watching the moving glow of the display. The squadron's exec, Jagdea presumed.

He looked over.

'Have you brought the caff?' he asked them.

'Sir?'

'The caff,' he repeated. 'The recaff.'

'No, sir,' said Jagdea.

The man frowned. He wore a dark green flightsuit and a flight coat. If he was the exec, Jagdea thought, he was young. He looked like a smoke, thin-faced, thin blond hair.

'Who are you, then?' he asked. Jagdea recognised the exec's voice as the weary controller who had directed her approach the day before.

'Just pool drivers, sir,' said Gumm.

The exec sighed, and turned back to his display.

Dampier returned. 'Just a moment,' she told them. She stood with them and they waited, watching the quiet but intense activity, listening to the low-level chatter of transmissions.

'Do you lift at night, mam?' Gumm asked.

'When we have to,' Dampier replied.

Jagdea shivered at the thought of night-flying the lethal labyrinth of Vesperus. It was bad enough in daylight.

The awkward silence continued. Jagdea felt obliged to fill it.

'Why couldn't that pilot de-plane today?' she asked. 'Call sign Bloodspot? Standard operating procedure in a weapons-hung scenario is for the pilot to dismount and get clear while the crews safe the ordnance.'

Dampier looked at her, deadpan.

'Pilot Officer Sorrentine,' she replied, 'call sign Bloodspot, is one of three pilots here rigged for bio-impulse bonding. You know what that is?'

Jagdea did. It was a rare thing in the crusade, but she'd seen it a few times, usually in high-alt or orbital carrier ops. The pilot, surgically augmented, was brain-plugged to his logis-engine and wet-linked to his bird, his blood decanted and replaced with a synthetic neuroreactive plasma, fed from tanks behind the seat. He effectively shared an artificial blood supply, circulation and nervous system with his plane, and had direct neural awareness of his bird's control surfaces and instruments. The bio-impulse gestalt was supposed to greatly improve alertness, acuity, G-strain resistance limits, and reaction time. A symbiosis; pilot and machine fused as one, partly-living unit, flying by nerve impulse and thought-command more than stick. Jagdea had always thought of it as an abomination, and it was only ever done in extreme circumstances. She wondered what theatres this Sorrentine had been flying before coming to Six-Six that could have warranted such conversion.

'So there was no time to detach him and transfuse him with blood product?' Jagdea asked.

'He could have dismounted,' Dampier replied, 'and walked as clear as the feed tubes allowed. About four or five yards. It wasn't an option. Besides, we don't have the blood product for repeat transfusion.'

'Are you saying the pilots stay linked all the time?' asked Jagdea.

'Yes. By necessity.'

'But you have to flush their systems,' said Jagdea. 'It's required. The toxin build-up and bio-waste debt–'

'It is what it is,' said Dampier. 'We don't have the resources out here. We can unplug and flush them once a month, max, but they all refuse. They're used to it.'

'Prolonged neuropathic linkage results in brain damage, organ failure, tissue collapse, and death,' said Jagdea.

'Yes, long term,' said Dampier. 'Long term is not a parameter that concerns us here at Intercept Six-Six. Our attrition rate sees to that.'

The door on the far side of the control room swung open, and someone called her name.

'Follow me,' Dampier said.

As they reached the door, Jagdea saw it had the word LEAD stencilled on it in yellow. They entered. The office was small. It was an old rope loft. Bundles of bell ropes, with their wound ribbons and coloured woollen sallies, still hung from wooden racks, gathering dust. The man in the black leather flying coat was standing beside the desk, studying their tearsheets.

'Pilot Officer B. Jagdea,' Dampier said. 'Pilot Officer S. Gumm. Both Aeronautica Logistic Reserve.'

'Thank you, Deck,' said the man in black.

Dampier glanced at them.

'Squadron Leader Asa Garrant,' she said. 'I presume that even drivers from the Reserve know how to salute?'

Jagdea and Gumm snapped to attention, and made the sign of the aquila.

Garrant looked over and raised a hand.

'At ease,' he said. 'Your transfer back to Orison has been postponed, as I'm sure you've realised by now.'

'Yes, sir,' said Jagdea.

'We'll await the next transport run, sir,' said Gumm.

'Unless you have an evac going back,' said Jagdea.

'We have four medicae recovery Valks,' said Dampier. 'None to spare.'

'And that's beside the point,' said Garrant. 'I don't have your full books at my disposal, but I see from this that you're both certified.'

'We're pool drivers, sir,' said Jagdea. 'We've maintained rating for multis and monos, but we're Reserve.'

'But you've both flown combat, and you're rated for it still,' said Garrant.

Jagdea didn't like where this was going.

'We are pool drivers, sir,' she said flatly. 'I can't speak for Gumm, but I haven't flown a war sky in seventeen years.'

'You'll be flying combat from tomorrow,' said Garrant. 'I'm retaining you both for Six-Six.'

There was a short silence.

'I... don't think that's a good idea, sir,' said Jagdea.

'Well, it's my idea, Jagdea,' said Garrant, 'so it's not a decision you get to make. Deck, can you see to the transfer papers?'

Dampier nodded.

'Sir, we are not combat fliers,' said Gumm.

'But you were,' said Garrant. 'You both were. I can see that just by looking at you. You both know what you're doing. That was obvious in the landing box today.'

'I know what I'm doing,' said Jagdea, 'and I'm not doing this.'

'Moderate your tone, pilot officer,' said Dampier. 'That is not a valid response.'

'Permission to object,' said Jagdea.

'Granted,' said Garrant. 'I'd like to see what that looks like.'

'I am no use to you, sir,' said Jagdea. 'I burned out a long time ago. I drive transports. That's the top and bottom of it.

Put me at the stick of one of your fightbirds, and you'll lose a fightbird. To a building. I may be rated on paper, but I am not combat fit. Sir, I formally request a link to Hymnal Field Control. I want to speak directly to Deck Officer August Kaminsky.'

'Who?' asked Garrant.

'Comms are restricted to priority operations only,' said Dampier. 'This station stays as sterile as we can keep it. Request denied.'

'Please–' Jagdea said. She realised she was on the verge of begging.

'Jagdea's right, sir,' said Gumm. 'We're no use to you.'

'You weren't when you came in yesterday,' Garrant replied. 'Things have changed. I shouldn't have to explain the mutability of a deck in an active war sky to a pair of veterans.'

'Yesterday, we had too many pilots and not enough planes,' said Dampier. 'Now the reverse is true. When that bat hit the freighting box, we lost sixteen people along with the carry-flight crews. Twelve ground crew and four pilots.'

'Longbow, Bard, Slingshot and Whisker,' said Garrant. 'Two of them were veterans with decent hours on the dial. With the birds you delivered yesterday, I have empty sticks. I also have a mandate direct from Lord Militant Jahkel to maintain a functional intercept station in Vesperus. I need pilots. You are both pilots. You're also both Aeronautica, so this is an instruct not a debate. You're assigned. End of discussion.'

'Will we be rotated out when new pilots arrive, sir?' asked Gumm.

Garrant shrugged. 'I would imagine so,' he said. 'Consider it a temporary posting, if that makes it easier to swallow.'

'I'd like my objection to be formally recorded, sir,' said Jagdea. 'I'd like–'

'I'll tell you what I'd like, Jagdea,' said Garrant. 'I'd like not to be here. I'd like to be flying a war sky environment that wasn't so murderously difficult. I'd like better replenishment and provision. I'd like to be supplied with birds that were fit for purpose, not the over-engined Voss monsters they keep sending our way. I'd like a decent fuel supply. I'd like a payload of Skystrikes or Hellfuries so we didn't have to rely on old stocks of Urdeshi ground-to-air rockets that don't mate cleanly with the hardpoint rails. I'd like to stop burning through smokes at the currently atrocious rate. I'd like experienced sticks who won't fly into a wall the first time they drop, because these children, Jagdea, these children they keep sending us, are young and overzealous, and they think they're immortal, because all they've ever known is thirty or forty hours in the wide open skies of the Eastern Front.'

Garrant had sat down at his desk, and he slapped the desktop hard to emphasise the words 'experienced' and 'sticks'.

'God-Emperor bless and protect us all,' he said quietly, gazing at the floor, 'they are so damn young, and they are so damn eager, and they are so damn useless. And they keep dying.'

He looked up at her, and involuntarily touched the golden Ecclesiarchy icon on his collar. 'I'd like not to have been in this job for just eight days,' he said.

Jagdea held his gaze and said nothing.

'Captain Garrant was squadron exec until eight days ago,' said Dampier. 'We lost Squadron Leader Lungrim in a cold-start incident.'

'I am the fourth person to sit at the desk since the squadron arrived at Campanile,' said Garrant. 'I am making the best of what I have, and what I have today is you. Deck will assign you billets. I want you both alert-ready at oh-eight-hundred. There is no time or, more crucially, fuel, for drills or familiarity sorties. Look at a map. Get some sleep. Dismissed.'

* * *

Billet, Intercept 66, Vesperus, 05:09

She managed an hour of poor quality sleep. Her billet, assigned by Dampier, was a small room on a lower floor of the tower's occupied portion. It was cold, and all the lower levels stank of smoke. There was a cot, a bedroll and a chair. Kit lockers were in the hall outside, numbered. Dampier had assigned her one of those too. Jagdea had been allowed to visit stores, because neither she nor Gumm had so much as a ready-bag with them. 'Stores' turned out to be a generous term. There was little on offer. She got a bar of soap, used, and a bottle of dextrose tablets, which she chewed on her way back upstairs. The only things that stores had in any plentiful supply were cartons of lho-sticks and piles of dog-eared glory story chapbooks, both of which she declined. There was no ready-issue clothing at all. The Munitorum store manager pointed her to some plastek bins filled with rags and second-hand garments, all personal effects emptied from lockers that were no longer needed.

'Help yourself,' had been his advice.

She'd found a couple of vests that almost fitted, a pair of baggy black work trousers of the kind favoured by fitters, a woollen sweater with moth holes, and a tan leather flight jacket, Navy issue, from which all patches and insignia had been unpicked. She slept in them because the billet was unheated, and she needed to get out of the compression suit's crush for a few hours.

She slept in them, or lay awake, the stale scent of dead fliers in her clothes, feeling her circulation settle and blood pinprick its way back into her extremities.

Just after five, she got up in the zero-zero dark, found her boots and put them on, unlaced. She knew a shower was out of the question. She could hear movement in the hallway outside; a Munitorum junior knocking doors and rousing pilots for early readies. She wondered if there was food, but she wasn't hungry. Her breath tasted nasty from the joiliq Lopard had given her.

The shred was coiled, waiting for her, in the corner of the darkened room.

She ventured out into the hall, shuffling in her unlaced boots. There were a few other fliers around, starting prep, all glazed from sleep or the lack thereof. No one spoke to her. They were all in their own worlds.

She went to her locker to fetch her flightsuit, harness, gloves and helmet. She saw Wilzar. He was the only person on the corridor who seemed fresh and active. *So damn young and so damn eager…*

'Jagdea,' he said brightly. 'I hear you're joining us.'

Us. Like he hadn't just got here too.

'Seems that way,' she replied.

'Splendid,' said Wilzar. 'Four-A. Well, good flying.'

She nodded.

He went to his locker, just a few down from hers.

'What the hell is this?' she heard him exclaim when he opened the door.

He took out his striped, flame-yellow helmet.

'Is this a bloody joke?' he spluttered.

Aircrew staff juniors would have checked their kit overnight. Someone had written the word SMOKE across the visor guard of his helmet in white paint.

Jagdea almost smiled. *One does not choose one's own call sign. It is bestowed upon one by one's fellow pilots.*

She opened her own locker. In black paint, across the brow of her white Maxin-pattern helmet, was the word DRIVER.

'DRIVER'

VESPERUS

IMPERIAL YEAR 795.M41, DAY 89 – DAY 94

DAY 89

First drop, Intercept 66, Vesperus, 08:41

Garrant had stated there would be no time for familiarity sorties, and he hadn't been lying. When Jagdea walked out onto the launch deck, fully suited, Tail 044 was waiting for her. It had been carried up via the Campanile's internal ramp system, rolled out, and secured for launch on its landing claws. It was nose-down, tail raised at an angle of seventy degrees to the platform lip.

The day was gloomy, and heavy with smog. Visibility was poor. A cold wind harried the platform. They were almost at the top of the bell tower structure, just below the base of the spire. It felt horribly exposed. The view across Vesperus would have been spectacular, but the smog had turned the towering skyline into a menacing phantom of cliffs and peaks.

Jagdea thought about walking to the edge and looking over. She decided not to. Orundo Street was about three thousand feet below. She'd see it soon enough, one way or another.

The ground crew was still finishing checks on her bird, and on the other two secured nearby. To the right of Tail 044 was Garrant's bird, the blue Cypra M Twin. Further down, to her left, near the corner of the high parapet, perched a Thunderbolt, black with a black-and-white chequerboard pattern on the wings and tail.

Garrant stood nearby with the other pilot. He was wearing his black flightsuit and holding his helmet. His head was tilted down, solemn, as though in prayer.

The other pilot was a very tall, very thin young woman, incongruously wearing the black and white robes of an Ecclesiarchy nun. She was murmuring quietly, her head also bowed. Jagdea decided not to intrude, but Garrant saw her, and called her over.

'No time for a squad huddle this morning,' he said. 'Pilot Sister Meredith is providing a quick blessing.'

It didn't appear to be optional. Jagdea had her own faith, and it was her business. She had learned to keep the ferocity of the hardline Imperial Truth at arm's length. But she stood with them, head down, hands clasping her helmet-strap. The Sister continued a short blessing in a voice so small that, thanks to the wind, Jagdea could barely hear.

Pilot Sister Meredith was tall, taller than Garrant. She was one of the Aeronautica's preachers-militant charged with maintaining devotional rigour. Jagdea had never seen a squadron preacher who was also a rated pilot before. Meredith had a shock of frost-white hair under her wimple. Her face was painfully pale and utterly deadpan. Her lips, eyes and brow had been ritually darkened, and marked with black powder.

'...that we may find the sinners and castigate them, in the name of the God-Emperor...' was all Jagdea could make out.

It was over, apparently. Garrant and Meredith made the sign of the aquila. Jagdea did too, fumbling clumsily with her helmet to free her hands.

'Let's get to it,' Garrant told them. 'Slam-checks. Make yourself go-ready. Pilot Officer Jagdea, do you have any words to share?'

'No, Lead,' she replied. 'Only to formally repeat my objections for the record. To both my transfer and the application of cold-start launches.'

The Pilot Sister glanced at her, aloof and stony, her black-shadowed eyes narrowed.

'Not what I meant,' said Garrant, 'but so noted. Jagdea, once we're up, follow my instruct. There is no space for formation in Vesperus.'

That was it.

'The Emperor protects,' Garrant said, and walked away to his bird. Sister Meredith turned away without a word, and strode towards hers. Jagdea could see the words MERRY DEATH stencilled below the black Bolt's cockpit.

Jagdea went to her own bird. The fitters, led by Tarr, were clearing their equipment and unlatching the fuel hoses. Jagdea saw that Four-Four's rails had been fitted with four white missiles of the same Urdeshi pattern that she'd wrestled with the previous afternoon.

'Get in,' said Tarr. Despite the cold up on the platform, her heavily muscled arms remained bare. She'd been working hard.

'I always do my own walk-around,' said Jagdea.

'Not today,' said Tarr. 'No time.'

Reluctantly, Jagdea strapped on her helmet, and climbed in. It was much harder with the plane nose-down, and as she swung into the cockpit at an awkward angle, she was afforded an unwilling view down over the nose into the hideous drop below.

Chief Tarr crawled up on the walk-strip beside her.

'Checks Four-A,' Tarr said. 'All prime. The throttle has a little give, but you'll know that. Be advised, the hydraulics indicator shows red.'

Jagdea glanced at her.

'Faulty bulb,' said Tarr. 'I lifted out the SM Pack and the CAD to make sure. No hydraulic issue, just a faulty bulb.'

'But it's still showing red?' asked Jagdea.

Tarr nodded.

'You lifted out the whole SM assembly, but you didn't replace the bulb?'

'No spares,' said Tarr. 'Just ignore it. Lidding you up.'

'I want you to sight-check surfaces first,' said Jagdea.

'There's no time for that sort of business,' said Tarr. She looked at Jagdea. 'Done this before?' she asked.

'Never,' said Jagdea.

'Good flying,' said Tarr, and latched the canopy.

Fuming, Jagdea sat for a moment, tilted forward against her tight straps, and then flipped the voltaic master. The instruments lit. She began her slam-check, walking the parish. From the left, she checked the vector thrust secondaries, and preset. She activated the auspex and modar, then primed the starter, engaged the pump, and adjusted the ad-mix. She began a manual and auto verification of the target acquisition system, and toggled the guns on. The starter compressor chugged as it began to spool up. She armed the countermeasure package, keen to verify the hardpoint connection for those clearly unreliable missiles, missiles she had no experience of at all. This had started out as the stupidest thing she'd ever done in her life, and gone rapidly downhill from there. Then she tried not to think about the phrase 'going rapidly downhill'.

'Vox check,' Garrant crackled over the comms.

'Vox check, Lead, Tail Four-Four receiving.'

'No tail numbers,' he replied, *'use call sign only.'*

Jagdea took a breath.

'Vox check, Lead. Driver receiving.'

'Copy, Driver.'

Another crackle, then she heard the Sister.

'Vox check, Lead, Merry Death receiving.'

'Copy you, Merry Death.'

Jagdea armed her seat, and continued her meticulous but now disordered slam-check.

'This is Lead, deconflict auspex.'

'Copy,' she replied, annoyed. She wasn't done with the weapon systems yet. She moved to auspex, and made adjustments. Her strict walk of the parish had turned into a hapless meander. She tried to remember where she'd got to, and what was still left to be completed.

'Control to wings. Receiving shout from ROP Three-Two. Hostile track reported Zado Avenue. Go for start. Go for start.'

'Copy, Control,' she heard Garrant reply. *'Track received. Going for start, immediate release.'*

Frig, no– Jagdea thought. *I'm not even–*

'Lead to wings. Dead drop now.'

Jagdea felt her bird rock as Garrant's Cypra dropped off the lip. Then again, as the Pilot Sister's Bolt followed it.

'Shit,' she said, and released her landing claws.

Engine primed but unstarted, she fell nose-first down the side of the Campanile.

Free-fall. The face of the bell tower rushing past her belly. The hive floor, so far away, approaching so fast. *Madness, madness, utter frigging madness–*

She fired the starter. The forced-plasma exciter ignited the fuel aspirating into the spinning turbine.

There was a thump of negative response.

Misfire. She was already at terminal velocity. Everything on the headache was still green, except the frigging hydraulics. There was nothing calm or composed about her, despite her years of experience. This was panic, a desperate effort to remain alive. She fired the starter again.

Flash-start. The turboram lit.

She barely heard the roar as the forced-plasma exciter lit the prom mix aspirating into her spinning turbine. The engine was running, but there was no time to regulate the red lines that logis was displaying. Getting the ram fired was only half of her problem. She had fired late, and dropped too low. She had to impose control and bring it up.

Somehow.

She was already carrying a heavy g-load. She'd gone into grip position, tensing her stomach, thigh and buttock muscles to compensate. She felt her flightsuit constricting to reinforce blood flow. With the ram lit, her downward velocity had rapidly increased. There was already no room left. Could she even force the bird up out of a dive like this? It was like riding a bullet that had been fired at the ground.

And there was the ground, an unlit blur of rubble and wreckage, a glint of stagnant water. Jagdea wrenched the stick full-back and decreased the throttle hard. She needed power to come up out of a hard dive, but too much would load the airframe with extreme G, way past structural capacity. That could shear off the wings or the tail. The Voss was shaking. Everything on the panel looked like it was flashing red, and every advisory alarm was blaring.

Pull up… Pull up… Pull up…

The bird's entire suite of complex logis-arrays was emphatically telling her she was wildly exceeding safe tolerances, and bleakly insisting that recovery was impossible.

She took her left hand off the throttle and clamped it over her right to lock the stick back and hold it. The nose would not rise. She wanted to scream out a curse, but the bladders of her flightsuit had inflated so hard they were almost winding her, and she dared not exhale what breath she had left.

The nose lifted slightly. She pulled harder, and it came up a little more. It would have been easier to arm-wrestle Boa.

She came out of the dive at zero level. She was so low, the altimeter refused to read it and merely pulsed red. She was travelling along the length of Orundo Street with no height, far too fast, waking out a vast fan of filthy water from the flooded road behind her. She was running out of street. Now she needed to climb. She realised she was below the tops of ornamental light-poles that ran down either side of Orundo. Somehow she'd missed a collision with either row at the bottom of her dive, but now she risked clipping a wing on one side or the other. The posts were massive and wrought iron, with huge overhanging lamp-heads that seemed to curl in over her like ribs. They were whizzing past on both sides. She needed to lift, but was absolutely certain there was not enough clearance. The lamp-heads were more closely spaced than the span of her bird. She saw that three of the posts on the right had been felled, a tiny gap that was barely a microsecond away. She pulled back hard, and by luck more than skill, slipped her bird up out of the trench.

Hard climb now, almost harder than the dive. The end of the street was literally a wall dead ahead. Grip position. The G-load was even more fierce, and the strain intense. She was going to be striped with bruises from her compression suit. Blood was pooling in her legs, starving her brain. Her vision was starting to tunnel. She began to lift clear, advancing power hard to counteract the shudder of a stall. At the top of the climb she managed to bank and roll out into level flight, a thousand feet up, now racing back down the street the way she had come.

Her vision misted back. Her compression suit eased. The shred, sharing the cockpit with her, did not. Her heart was punching at her ribs. Ten years of combat flying, and she'd never executed a manoeuvre so needlessly reckless.

But the ride was only just starting. Even though she was level and flying, the city was coming to kill her. She was barely at a fraction of advised combat/pursuit speed, and she was being forced to wrench and flick the stick to avoid obstructions: walls, buttresses, rooflines, masts, hanging debris. Each flick adjustment snapped g-load right or left. It made her perilous flight into Vesperus the day before seem like a measured advance. She was certain she didn't have the hand-eye reaction to handle the endless stream of near-misses, nor the fortitude to endure the G-strain, and nothing like enough of either to maintain the rate. Each frantic bank or dip just threw her at another obstacle, and into another forced evasion.

There was no sign of Lead or Merry Death. They hadn't waited to see her fate. Jagdea dared not glance down at her instruments for even a split second to watch the track, but she didn't have to as logis was painting it across her visor. Lead and Merry Death were far ahead of her, closing on the plotted intercept. She was miles behind them. They must have lit burners. How? How had they dared? She was crawling by comparison, yet it was already faster than she wanted to go.

She knew she'd got old. She knew she'd grown slow. She'd told Garrant that straight up. She doubted that she could have coped with this even at her best, twenty years earlier. This was simply proving everything she had known. She was no longer the hot stick, the multi-ace. She was exactly what it said on her visor plate. She was not fit to fly combat, and she'd never, ever been fit to fly this special brand of madness. If she made it back to the Campanile alive, maybe the whole sorry episode would demonstrate to Garrant his mistake, and force him to send her home.

She did her best to catch up and keep up. The intercept had already moved past Zado Avenue, and was running east. The plot wasn't clear, and kept bouncing. She couldn't distinguish Lead or Merry Death. Sometimes it looked like one track, sometimes five or even six. Even though the data was displaying on her visor, she couldn't take her eyes off the way ahead long enough to unpack it. There was nothing on vox: either her ears were bunged by G-strain blood pressure, or the dead drop trauma had stripped the vox-aerials off her fuselage.

She banked hard into another wide avenue, and immediately had to pitch viciously to avoid an overhead gantry. She tried to correct, and barely missed a walkway bridge. The Voss' systems were shrieking at her, insulting her and shaming her ineptitude, and the bird itself was bucking and fighting, sick of the constant corrections to velocity and attitude.

She ignored her screaming instruments and the jumbled flashing of the headache. The bird couldn't tell her anything she needed to know, nor could it tell it to her fast enough. She blanked it all, trusting only in hands, feet and eyes. Let the logis-systems do their job and correct for her excesses automatically. The only way to stay alive was to rely on herself.

A strange detachment came over her, a distancing, as though she was watching herself and not sitting in the bird at all. The headlong, twisting flight path did not ease, nor did the pummelling assault of G-strain, but her mind sharpened. She started to coach herself, like she was a Hessenville cadet. Not aloud, because the suit bladders made it impossible to breathe, let alone speak, but in her head, where only she could hear it. Ignore instruments, she told herself. Just look at what's coming and evade. Make those evasions soft and fluid. Minimise the extremity of corrections, because that only led to equally extreme re-corrects. Don't let one error propagate into others. Let the bird flow from one hazard to the next, and ride that flow. Forget each hazard as you pass it. Think of the next and the one after that. Slow your mind, not your speed.

Now get the shred out of your head. Regulate breathing.

Embrace basic biopathic principles. Tense into G-strain instinctively. The shred wants you hasty and scared. Speed is required, not haste. Put the tension into your locking muscles where it belongs, not into your mind where it has no place. Feather the stick and the throttle, despite the mindless thrust. Crush the urge to react too hard. Missing an obstruction by a yard is just as good as missing it by six. Pick the shortest line, the racing line. Anything else is extravagance, and an invitation to over-stick and die.

Jagdea became acutely aware of her own instrumentation, the processes that had seen her through ten years of combat. They'd been dormant for a long time. The total concentration. The absolute fixation. Her obstacles weren't gantries and bridges and pylons, not really. Her obstacles were shame, and fear of failure, and self-doubt. Those were the collisions to avoid. Her power plants were pride and dignity. They drove her forward. She might be long past matching the prowess of the Six-Six veterans, but she would make a good enough account of herself so she could damn well look them in the eye back at the bell tower.

She soared into Zado Avenue and turned east, trying to pick up the intercept track. She was so far behind now, badly lagging and out of position, that–

Two birds shot past ahead of her. She glimpsed them for a second as they crossed Zado at high speed. A bird, electric blue. A bat, in hard pursuit. The fight had tumbled back in her direction while she'd been busy not killing herself. Jagdea gunned and banked, turning east into the cross street in time to visualise the two aircraft briefly as they raced ahead. She saw the hot flare of their burners boosting as they vanished behind a manufactory. She coaxed out a little more power, and threw the Voss around the rotting hulk of the manufactory, then under the decayed bridge of a loading spar. The birds were turning up ahead. The bat, a Hell Blade, was at Garrant's six, firing. She saw the stream of tracers. They were banking hard around a wide civic plaza. Garrant's blue Cypra M rolled out of the enemy's firing envelope, but it was stuck to him.

She turned into the plaza airspace as hard as she dared. The tightness of the turn made her drop speed, and the Voss threatened to stumble. She eased up the power, g-loaded. Garrant was already extending away from her down a long, deep street canyon that led off the plaza. The bat was following, unshakable. Jagdea tried to get it in her sights, but it was too far out for a clean missile lock. She burned after them both. The street was deep, and so heavily shadowed they were moving through a sickly green gloom. The exhausts of the birds ahead were spots of hot orange, leaving her behind, mocking her. She pushed harder, trying to catch them up.

She was so intent on them, she only realised at the very last second that the street had no end. There was no turn. The sides of the street ran like cliffs into the facade of a massive structure. She had to pull up. They had to pull up.

They didn't. Jagdea stared in horror as Garrant flew into the building. The bat did the same a moment later. She expected to see the double flash of fireballs. Nothing. They hadn't collided with the building. They'd literally flown inside it.

Jagdea had no choice. She'd left it too late, and any attempt to climb out would spread her and the Voss across the face of the structure. She followed them in. If Garrant had flown inside the structure, then it had to be flyable, and he had to have known it.

Or else he was as mad as the rest of them.

She flew into the building through one of the huge holes torn in its side. She ignored the fractured rockcrete and twisted rebar that seemed to snatch at her as she entered. There was no floor. The levels below had collapsed into the deep, dark pit of the building's shell. But there was a ceiling, the ragged floor above, and she was suddenly running below it so close she thought she would scrape off her tail assembly. There were obstacles too: the huge upright support pillars of the building, spaced at regular intervals, and spills of broken pipes and rockcrete hanging down from the ceiling above. She jinked and turned frantically to evade, dodging in and out, eyes fixed on the bright coals of the engines ahead of her in the darkness.

She started to laugh. The space she was in was far, far tighter than the landing box, yet she was ploughing through it at many times the speed at which she had made her cautious hard-down the day before. Had she lost her mind too? Flying the hive-grave was about precision and zero hesitation. It didn't matter how tight the space was, and it didn't matter how close things came, as long as you missed them. If the bird fit, you could fly through it. The only thing stopping you was common sense. And if the bird didn't fit, you'd never know anything about it.

She forced herself to stop laughing. It was destroying her breath control.

Ahead, the snaking bat fired again. Its shots missed Garrant's bird as far as she could see, but they unstitched a section of the sagging ceiling, which peeled away and began to collapse as she reached it.

Desperate, she tried to evade, but there was a rockcrete support pillar to her left. She pitched hard to avoid both, and shot through the descending swirl of dust. She heard debris ping and bang off her hull. She tried to level. She'd lost both speed and height, and was convinced that the debris strike had clogged her intakes or broken her control surfaces.

Higher than her, the two birds exited the structure through the gaping hole of a huge observation port. She was too low. She stood the Voss on its left wing and followed them out through the tall, narrow slot of a lancet window lower down.

Outside, the chasing birds turned up and right, climbing. Jagdea barely saw them. She was still too low, and exiting into a very narrow cross-street. There was another structure straight ahead, and Jagdea understood at once that its ranges of glassless windows were far too small to enter.

She threw power from thrust to vectors, and turned as hard as she dared. Grip position. G-force crushed her into her seat. The Voss stumbled and stalled into a sickening flutter of intake momentum drag, its tail swinging right out as though it was skidding on the air.

Then... then she was steady again, the bird righting. She advanced thrust hard to compensate for the bilious tumble of the stall, and shot off after the receding planes.

She had no idea how she'd survived that turn.

Garrant and his pursuer had already vanished. She dropped speed, and turned her head from side to side, frantically hunting the airspace around for a visual contact.

Her threat indicator pinged furiously. There was something behind her, and it had a lock.

She couldn't see it, but her gut told her it was overhauling her fast. There was no possibility of an evasive turn. She dropped her speed even harder, and an accelerating Hell Talon shot past, low off her starboard wing. She glimpsed its red, barbed lines as it rushed by, extending. She kicked after it, and almost immediately obtained a hard lock. Before she could toggle to missiles, it braked and reversed the manoeuvre, spitting her out in front. Jagdea cursed, and banked, climbing hard across the face of a towering Administratum building. Las-fire chased her, stitching up the building's facade, shredding casements and stonework, and showering glass into the air. She rolled to evade, almost clipping the face of the building with one wingtip. Then she inverted, diving towards the street and turning out as wide as she dared.

The bat was still behind her. Hard threat lock. This was her first actual knife-fight in twenty years and she was in the worst possible position. Ninety-nine per cent of the evasive plays she'd learned in her years of combat flying were unavailable to her, incompatible with the breadth of the street. They were plays meant for open sky and a turning fight, not this.

She threw the speed brakes again, killing her thrust. It was her only option, and it had worked once. But the bat pilot was not fooled a second time. He dropped his rate too, sat on her six, and lined up. Hard lock tone. Then the urgent chime of missile launch.

A hard climb was her only choice. She yanked the stick and punched the burners, ascending almost vertically into a vice of hard g. The suit bladder winded her like a fist, and her vision coned. The missile was still on her, pulling up on her superheated efflux. The G-crush was so intense, she could barely lift her hand. Her finger, all ten tons of it, found the countermeasures button and mashed it. The Voss vibrated hard as it popped a long, blooming plume of flares into her wake. There was a flash. The heater had swallowed her bait and detonated. She tried to regain control and twist off the climb. The bat was still on her, chasing vertically. Hard lock.

She cut power and fell past it, dropping towards the street, forcing the Voss into viff control to level it. It choked hard, yawing wildly. The engine was so far into the red line she expected it to depart the airframe and melt.

Stability, barely. High above, the bat inverted and began to dive back onto her. Tracers tore past her port wing. She accelerated–

There was a bird coming right at her. Head-to-head. An instant away from collision. Its guns blazing.

Jagdea flinched as Merry Death's black-and-white Bolt crossed her with less than a yard to spare. It was the perfect aerobatics pass, but if they'd planned it for some parade display it would have been cut on sanity grounds, unless they'd promised to affect a much greater separation. Jagdea jerked her head around as the Bolt went by, trying to follow it. Merry Death had been moving at six times her rate. The Hell Talon suddenly went past her on the right. It was pouring flames from its rear, and its back vanes were disintegrating. It arced ahead of her, snaking and uncontrolled, and fell. Then it hit the hive floor below and filled the street with an astonishing cloud of fire.

The shockwave rocked her in the air. What the hell had it been carrying? Special ordnance intended for Yllsbruck, Vanberg and the south-east 'plex. Enough to level a hab or blitz a stripway.

Merry Death had disappeared. Jagdea resumed visual scanning, trying to control her heart rate, and almost at once saw Garrant again. His blue Cypra was on the tail of a bat, chasing it through the eaves. Both birds jinked hard, dodging ducts and slumping gutters. They vanished from sight, then reappeared, turning, diving towards the street. The Cypra's belly cannon strobed out a stream of shells. The Hell Blade tried to lift. The Cypra lifted after it. The G-forces they were pulling were so fierce, the stream of tracers from the cannon seemed to lash like water from a hose.

They found the bat. It juddered and then tore apart, its bright dagger-form becoming a swarm of component parts that continued to fly and tumble in formation for a second before a central detonation – once again viciously powerful – scattered them towards the ground.

Garrant rolled in beside her, matching her speed.

'Return to deck,' he voxed. Just that. Nothing else. Then he pulled away and began to extend.

Pulling a hard arrest into the landing box seemed easy after what she'd been through. There was so much room. She killed systems without being told, and sat in silence with her hands up as Boa ran the tractor in, and carried her down into the hangar. Then she sat in silence while the ground crew safed her unused stores and took them off.

Tarr unlatched the canopy and tapped Jagdea on the top of her helmet. Jagdea stirred, slid up her visor, and pulled off her mask. She climbed out without assistance, trying not to let the fitters see how unsteady her legs were. Her gut, thighs and chest felt like they had been kicked repeatedly, as though she had been beaten up in some alley and left for dead. The shred slithered out of the cockpit, and followed her.

'Well?' said Tarr with a grin, wiping grease off her augmetics with a rag. 'A successful intercept, so I hear. And you were there when it happened.'

Jagdea ignored her. She walked away, taking off her helmet, trying to remember how to walk. She left the hangar, and found the washrooms in the adjoining service block. In a filthy toilet stall, she vomited violently. There was nothing to bring up except bile and what looked like bloody water, but her punished body didn't care. It kept her retching and heaving and shaking for a long time, until the pain of her bruised gut muscles forced her to sit back.

She was sitting on a metal chair in the hall outside the washrooms when Garrant found her. Her flightsuit was unzipped, and she was clutching her gut. Her helmet was on the floor at her feet, and she was staring straight ahead. There was nothing to look at, and nothing inside her looking out. She had never felt so empty or so lost.

'Get some food,' he told her. 'Rehydrate.'

She looked up at him, her eyes glassy.

'I was useless,' she croaked. 'Worse than useless.'

'You went out,' said Garrant. 'You came back. That's a start.'

'I didn't even get off a shot...' she began.

'Food, water, now,' he said and walked away.

Refectory, Intercept 66, Vesperus, 13:17

She found the refectory by following the smell of cooking. The smell turned her stomach, but she knew Garrant was right. She needed calories and she needed hydration. The G-forces she had pulled would have wrung litres of sweat out of her.

The refectory was a large, high-ceilinged, wood-panelled chamber on the tower's mid-level, and possibly the only chamber in the Campanile that retained its original function. Once it had served as a dining room for the choristers, bell ringers and templum population.

Now it was a mess for flight crews and ground staff. Militarum field kitchen units had been set up along one side, broiling and stewing food in their modular steel caskets. Jagdea took a metal tray and was served a bowl of oatmeal, a tin mug of soup, and some fried strips of canned slab. She took a chipped glass from a stack. There were pitchers of drinking water on every table.

There were quite a few people present, eating, laughing and, it appeared, drinking. She didn't know any of them. The dining space held five rows of long tables, each flanked with benches. She sat alone.

She filled her glass from the jug on the table, drank it down, and refilled it. It tasted metallic and bitter, overprocessed. She drank the second glass. Then she picked at her food.

Her hands were still shaking, and her mind was still wound tight. She couldn't let go. The sortie replayed in her mind, every crushing movement of it, not because she wanted to run some kind of evaluation, but because it wouldn't *not*. Every aspect came with a bump of shock, as though she was reliving it: the drop, the dive, the climb… every impossible switch and turn, then flashes of the combat. Getting locked. The frantic evasion. The near-miss. Flying through a ruined structure.

Flying through a ruined structure.

The thought almost made her gag. Tangling with bats again, she thought that would be the trigger, but it wasn't. The enemy was still the enemy, out to kill her, and she knew she was in harm's way when she shared the sky with bats. It was the structure-pass that truly shocked her. Flying through that ruin. That hadn't been the enemy trying to kill her. That had been *her* trying to kill her.

'Hey,' said a voice. She looked up. Three pilots were sitting nearby, two men and a woman. One offered her a bottle of joiliq.

'You don't want to go drinking that neat,' he said, nodding to her water glass.

Jagdea shook her head.

The pilot shrugged. 'You'll feel better,' he said.

She doubted it. She couldn't speak. The pilot turned back to his comrades.

A lot of the personnel around her seemed to be openly drinking. Some were smoking lho-sticks, and she could smell harder narcotics and the unmistakable stink of sweat laced with combat stimms. Many of these people, aviators and ground crew, were alert-ready or at least call-ready. But they were drinking and buzzing themselves. What would they do if a shout came in? Would any of them be remotely competent? Or was this a permanent state, to blot out the feral existence of Six-Six?

She took a forkful of oatmeal. It tasted bad, and her stomach hurt as though she'd been knifed.

The wood panelling above and around the refectory's huge fireplace was covered with lists of names, written up in chalk.

A roll call, an honour board. Many names had at least one tally mark beside them, some multiple. Far too many of the names had lines through them. Down at the right-hand end, she saw the most recent additions: DRIVER, SMOKE and DOLLFACE. The latter had to be Gumm. These people were unsparing.

Most squadrons put names on the ready room wall when a pilot had been lost, as a mark of respect. At Six-Six, evidently, your name – or whatever insult they had decided was your name – went up when you arrived, and then got bluntly crossed out when you died. It seemed brutal, and devoid of empathy. There were more names on the wall struck through than not.

Jagdea looked up as applause began. Pilot Sister Meredith had walked in, solemn. The preacher dragged a chair to the fireplace, stood on it, and took a stick of chalk off the high mantel. Stretching up, she marked a tally line beside the name LEAD and another beside MERRY DEATH. The personnel present began to cheer and bang the tables. The Sister turned to face them, still standing on the chair. She made the sign of the aquila and bowed, accepting their approval. Then she stepped down, and knelt before the fireplace.

Jagdea saw that the dead cave of the fireplace itself had been turned into some kind of shrine. A large golden aquila was surrounded by dozens of smaller icons and figurines, along with candles and offerings in pots and jars. Medals, icon pins and strips of parchment had been fixed to the wood of the fireplace surround. To Jagdea, the shrine seemed tribal, a far cry from the trappings of an Ecclesiarchy chapel.

The Sister lit a candle and some incense, then bowed her head and recited something. A hush fell. Jagdea couldn't hear what Meredith was saying, but a good number of those around her joined in, intoning with the Sister, heads down. Those that did so appeared to be the more sober present; the ones dressed in black and darker hues, the ones not drinking. The others, the drinkers and the rogues, fell silent out of respect, or raised their glasses to toast.

Meredith rose, and business resumed. As the Sister walked past, Jagdea scraped to her feet.

'Thank you,' Jagdea said.

The Sister looked at her, expressionless. She had marked her eyes and lips again with black ash from the grate, and remade the shape of the aquila on her brow with a fingertip.

'You saved me,' said Jagdea, in case it wasn't clear.

'I did not save you,' Meredith replied. 'I was killing sinners as the God-Emperor has asked me to do.'

She walked away.

Jagdea sat back down, and picked at her food.

Lopard dropped his tray on the table beside her, and took a seat. Like her, he was still in his flightsuit, and his face was streaked with sweat. His tray was piled with food. He lit a lho-stick, but tucked in anyway.

'I hear you dropped,' he said, chewing.

Jagdea nodded.

'Exhilarating, isn't it?' he smiled. He tucked the stick in his teeth, and produced a bottle of amasec from his coat pocket. He filled his glass, and went to fill hers.

'Don't,' she said.

He did anyway.

'I've been here longer than you, Driver,' he said. 'These are the rules.'

'I may still be called to go-ready,' said Jagdea.

'Me too,' said Lopard.

'And you don't care if your head's not clear–'

'I don't care. Try not to care yourself. Life won't get any better. I know the remedy for a shit day, and we're both having one.'

'You dropped?'

'Yes,' he said. He drank his shot, and refilled. 'Splashed one. And lost one,' he added, and knocked back the second glass.

'You lost one?'

'Some poor smoke who arrived a month ago. I didn't even see it. He'd never really got the hang of this.'

'Does anyone?' asked Jagdea.

'No,' Lopard said with a chuckle.

He stood up, abruptly, drink in hand. Senior Deck Dampier had walked into the refectory, her face like stone. A stillness fell. Everyone stood. Dampier crossed to the fireplace, stood on the chair, and marked a tally beside the name HARLOT. There were some noises of approval, but they were muted. Jagdea realised that Dampier only came in to mark the wall for one reason. Dampier drew a chalk line through the name VOXBACK. The name had no tally beside it.

She got down.

'Call sign Voxback,' she said to the room. 'Lost oh-nine-fifty this morning. The Emperor protects, the Aeronautica remembers.'

Everyone present raised their glass, of water or otherwise, and chorused, 'Voxback.'

Jagdea barely sipped hers. The stink of amasec made her gag.

'Carry on,' said Dampier, and left the refectory.

Jagdea sat down. Lopard was already digging back into his meal.

'That wasn't even his name,' said Jagdea.

'Who?'

'Voxback,' she said. 'What was his name?'

'Hell if I know,' said Lopard.

'You were with him?'

'Didn't see it,' said Lopard. 'Longlas and I were gunning through a vent between the manufactories at Haleside Point. Hard chase. Two Talons. Both of us realised Voxback was no longer with us.

Longlas peeled back. Nothing but debris. Side of a tower on the approach.'

'Bat-kill or mis-judge?' asked Jagdea.

'Same thing, here,' said Lopard. He sat back, frowning. 'You know, if I could, I'd spare them all. All of them,' he mused. 'Spare them the pain and the shred. Four weeks he'd been here, that boy. Four weeks, screaming inside every second of it. Not even a kill. Not even close. He had no hope. If I was a good man, Jagdea, a properly good man, I'd have gone into his billet the night he arrived and put a pillow over his face. Just let him go before he had to suffer any of that.'

He fell silent, his mind somewhere very far away and very dark. She stared at him.

He smiled suddenly. 'No wonder I drink,' he announced, raising his glass in a red-gloved hand.

'To dull it?'

'To stop me saying things like that out loud,' said Lopard. He looked her up and down.

Jagdea turned away. She picked up her glass, and managed to knock back a little of the amasec. It was actually decent stuff.

'Smoke?' he asked, offering her his silver case.

'No.'

'Something stronger?' he asked. 'I know who to ask. Yellodes. 'Roma. Obscura. Stimm.'

'No,' she said. 'I need to sleep.'

'You won't sleep now,' he said, 'I can see how wired you are.'

The room was full of voices again suddenly. Three more aviators had entered. One was a small, athletic woman with her flightsuit zipped down and peeled from her waist. Her hair was black, and her tanned skin was covered in tattoos. Behind her came an older pilot with an augmetic eye embedded in scar tissue. Behind them, Gumm.

Gumm stood back. The older pilot offered the woman his hand, and she stepped up onto the chair. People were beating the tables. The woman grabbed the chalk and marked a tally stroke beside the name BLINDSIDE, then turned, teetering on the chair, to wildly clap the older pilot, who took a mock bow. Then she turned back, and marked a tally beside the name GANGSTER. The table-pounding got louder. She looked back at the room, a coquettish glance, a finger to her lips, like an exotic dancer teasing the crowd before removing her last garment. Then she added a second tally mark beside GANGSTER.

'Splash two! Splash two!' the audience chanted. Gangster stood on the chair and began a little snake-armed, sway-hipped dance.

'The infamous Gangster,' said Jagdea.

Lopard nodded. 'Disa Yesof. The infamous Gangster.'

Billet, Intercept 66, Vesperus, 15:20

'I didn't have time to grasp any of it,' said Gumm. He was sitting on her chair while she sat on the cot.

'Me neither,' said Jagdea.

'I mean, nothing,' said Gumm. 'Just so fast, every second on the stick. I pushed past everything I knew, and it still wasn't enough. I was just hanging on for dear life. Vesperus is no war sky. Not like any I've ever known.'

'I hear you,' said Jagdea.

'I got off a few shots when a bat went over me. It turned out. I got a missile lock, but these damn things they fit us with… It ran wide like it had no guidance. Took out a silo nowhere near the bat, which was, by then, exiting my weapons envelope at full burn.'

'Better than me,' Jagdea replied. 'I didn't even fire in anger. Came back racks full.'

'But you came back.'

'And so did you.'

'I'm trying to replay it all in my head,' said Gumm. 'You know, dissect it? See if there's anything I can learn from it. Anything.'

'Me too, I suppose. I made one turn that I have no idea how I recovered.'

He nodded. 'I mean, there have got to be tricks, right?' he said. 'New tricks. The veterans here have survived, because they've learned how to cope.'

'I think they've learned how not to frigging care,' said Jagdea.

'That,' agreed Gumm. 'I could barely track Gangster or Blindside. It seemed to me their approach was "fly as hard as you can and don't die". I wouldn't say either of them are very good, as fliers. They just monster in at full burn like nothing matters.'

'Fearless.'

'Fearless. But there's got to be more to it.'

'Has there?' asked Jagdea. 'Really?'

'Got to be,' said Gumm. 'This is a new kind of theatre with very specific challenges. There have got to be techniques we can learn and employ. They may well be techniques that bend an aircraft further than we've ever pushed, but even so. Turning, for instance. Anticipation. Reaction.'

'Or we're just old and slow, Gumm,' she said.

'No one's fast enough for this,' he replied. 'The longer we live, Jagdea, the more we'll learn.'

'Well, there's another happy motto to add to the list of stupid things that get said around here,' she replied.

She looked at him.

'Sorry,' she said. 'I'm tired. I need to sleep.'

'We're both supposed to be alert-ready.'

'Then someone can wake me.'

* * *

She didn't sleep. After Gumm had gone, she peeled off her compression suit. As expected, her flesh was so banded with bruising it looked like she had been camo-striped. Everything hurt, and everything ached. She stank, but water rationing was in force and there was no hope of a shower.

Naked, she sat on her cot and fished out the bottle of good amasec that Lopard had insisted she keep. There was about a third left. She took a swig. She thought that Gumm was probably right, but she couldn't break down her recall well enough to analyse it. The sortie just kept playing back, full-bore, too fast to deconstruct.

She lay back, feeling the bruises on her spine and shoulders. The marks of her harness, pulling her through the flightsuit at every g-turn, still had not faded. There had to be something, some small detail she could tease out, and unpack, and use. She thought about that turn. That turn, how had she recovered from it? Stumbled into a hard stall, stick slack, yet…

Her mind drifted. She thought about the deck at Psalter 96, waiting in the cold darkness. It was only the night before last, but it seemed like years back. She remembered what she'd said to Wilzar. *Be better*.

That was all she had.

DAY 90

Second drop, Intercept 66, Vesperus, 06:53

Jagdea limped onto the launch deck. Her bruises had become more painful overnight. Her legs were weak. Tail 044 was secured for launch on its landing claws, nose-down.

The day was a mauve haze, underlit by the distant rusty glow of municipal reactors that had been left to cook, untended, for years. Same deck as the day before, though the Campanile had several.

Different pilots, though. The young, thin executive officer was checking his jet-black Voss. She had learned the Exec was called Ricou Badler, but all it said on his visor plate was EXEC. He glanced at her with the same look of disappointment that had been on his face when she'd told him she hadn't brought the caff.

The other pilot was call sign Joiliq. Jagdea didn't want to know how he'd come by that. He was wearing a crimson compression suit. His bird was another Voss, dark green. Jagdea had assumed that her Lightning, and Wilzar's, had been pre-painted in the squadron colours for delivery, but perhaps they had just still been wearing their old squadron colour schemes. Or maybe people chose their colours? Or maybe, after patching and repair, a bird just ended up whatever colour ground crew had left in the stocks?

Exec approached. A huddle, she presumed. A blessing. Joiliq wandered over too, but seemed disinterested.

'Any words?' Exec asked her. His face was so young, so slender. His eyes were so old.

She shook her head. Joiliq didn't bother replying.

Exec nodded. He bent his head, mumbled a few lines of blessing, touched the Ecclesiarchy pin at his throat, and stepped back.

'Saint preserve you,' he said.

'Saint?' asked Jagdea.

'Saint Sabbat, who has returned to save our souls and our arses,' sneered Joiliq.

'Shut your hole,' Exec told him. 'Deck says we have moderate vis, but there's a smog-storm closing in the next hour.'

'Let's get up before that shit blows in,' said Joiliq.

'We'll get up when there's a shout,' said Exec.

Joiliq muttered a curse. Jagdea glanced at him, eyebrow raised.

'They'll use the storm,' he explained. 'Bet your arse. The bats. They'll use the storm.'

'Go-ready, please,' said Exec. 'Mount up.'

She got in her bird. The ground crew was still finishing their checks. The fitters, led that morning by a man called Voris, were bull-whipping the fuel hoses clear, and starting to coil them. An enginseer chanted, hands raised. Boa was reversing the lifter truck back. Jagdea saw that, once again, Four-Four's rails had been hooked up with the unreliable Urdeshi missiles.

'No walk-round?' asked Voris.

'Why bother?' said Jagdea.

Voris grinned. He had lost teeth to serious obscura use. 'I heard you like a walk-around, Driver,' he said. 'We got time.'

Jagdea cinched in her straps, and felt them bite the sores on her collarbones.

'Run me,' she said.

'Checks Four-A,' Voris replied. 'Nice and prime. The throttle has a little give. Hydraulics will show you red, but it ain't nothing.'

Jagdea glanced at him.

'Find me a spare bulb and I'll buy you a drink,' she said.

'If I find a spare bulb every bastard in the squadron will buy me a drink,' Voris replied.

'Lid me up,' said Jagdea.

'Don't you want me to sight-check your surfaces?' he asked. 'Maybe fetch you a glass of tea on a silver tray?'

'Piss off and lid me up,' said Jagdea.

He sniggered. 'Done this before?' he asked.

'Once,' said Jagdea.

'You'll be an expert, then,' said Voris, and latched the canopy.

Jagdea flipped the voltaic master. The instruments lit. She walked the parish, quickly, efficiently. There was time, but she did it fast. Her slam-check was complete before the vox woke up.

'Vox check,' Exec said over the comms.

'Vox check, Exec, Driver receiving.'

'Vox check, Joiliq, copy.'

The comms fell silent, apart from a brief instruct to deconflict auspex. Jagdea armed her seat, and sat very still. Her own slam-check now, biopathic: pulse, heartrate, breathing, mind.

Do better.

'Control to wings. ROP Nine-Zero reporting hostile track Machinko Circuit. Go for start. Go for start.'

The bats weren't waiting for the storm after all.

'Copy, Control,' she heard Exec reply. *'Track received. Going for start, immediate release.'*

Her hand was already on the release lever.

'Exec to wings. Dead drop now.'

Jagdea thanked someone, maybe Saint Sabbat herself, that they weren't going to have to wait in harness for hours. The last thing she needed was time to dwell on her thoughts.

Engine primed but unstarted, she fell nose-first down the side of the Campanile. Free-fall. She fired the starter. The forced-plasma exciter ignited the fuel aspirating into the spinning turbine. The ram lit.

The dead drop was more terrifying than it had been the last time. Now she knew what to expect.

Logis was red-lining. She tensed into the G-load and felt her suit bladders puff. Orundo Street rushed up. She dragged the stick full-back and decreased throttle. The Voss shook as its nose came up. The headache blinked its blizzard of red lights. She held the stick back and gradually levelled out. No street dive this time, no slalom around light-poles, no savage climb out.

She banked east, onto Exec's tail. Joiliq was lagging behind, still rising. Exec accelerated to full military power and began to pull away. An intercept required to-the-second response. Joiliq ripped past her at full throttle.

She cursed them both. This was the game now. The hive-grave game.

She advanced her throttle too.

They came out into Machinko through the shell of a burned-out hab. Exec was in clear lead. Jagdea was in tail spot. One hundred and ninety-six seconds to intercept target. Not bad.

They peeled hard left into the wide bowl of the Circuit, a massive habitation zone that still retained some of its original hard-shell geodesic dome. The light caught below it was arsenic green.

'Don't see 'em,' Joiliq voxed.

'Negative tracking,' Exec confirmed.

Jagdea leant her bird over to improve visibility.

'Three position, west-west, floor level,' she voxed. 'Two contacts.'

'Copy that,' Exec replied. *'Target acquired. Follow me in.'*

She banked after him. They chopped down ultra-low, ripping along a hab-street at sub-roof level. Joiliq broke away to port. He seemed to have a different understanding of the instruct, 'Follow me in.'

Two contacts, moving south-west at zero alt. Now they were low, and street-clipping, she no longer had visibility. She tried for auspex lock, but the clutter was too bad. She tried modar, but turned it off again right away when it started to squeal.

Hard right. Hard right. Hard left. Under a bridgeway. She stuck to Exec's tail. Hard right. Over a raised processional. Hard left. Along a thousand yards of echoing drainage duct, like flying down a plug hole. Daylight, turn out hard. Drop. Street level. Hive floor.

Bat.

It streaked past at twice their speed. Exec rolled and took off after it. She stressed her airframe to turn and follow.

But there had been two bats. Two contacts, at least. Where was the other? Were they on the lead or the chasing wingman?

Hard left. Hard left. The hive was doing its best to kill her again. Hard right. Hard pitch. She could still see Exec on the bat's tail. It was jinking to evade his lock.

Las-fire sprayed past her starboard wing and she felt a knock as something hit. Damage buzzers sounded and, after a second, a belated weapon lock warning. The second bat was behind her. She went into evasion, zagging hard, but it wasn't going to be enough and, as ever, there was no space to break. She attempted a hard-brake overshoot, but the bat was wary. It stuck to her.

Jagdea swore as another stream of fire raked past her. Another hit warning. She hoped to the Throne she was taking it on her Voss' heavy plating. It seemed so, because no systems were going dead. She tried to visualise the bat, but she couldn't detect an engine echo over the shrill chorus of her protesting logis-systems, and she kept mistaking the reflection of the headache's constantly flashing panel lights for shots passing her canopy. She'd lost sight of Exec, and there was no turn out. None she could see.

She flipped the modar back on, ignoring its howling confusion. She switched over to terrain only. She got a modarlock on a tight left ahead, a cross-street impossible to visualise from her speed and position.

Shots streamed past. Hit warning. She turned at the very last second.

Hard turn. Hard, *hard* turn. She threw power from thrust to vectors, braced into grip, and veered as sharply as possible, G-force crushing her into the seat. Frame-load warnings went off. The bat shot past behind her, unable to match her turn.

The Voss stumbled, and stalled into an uncontrolled flutter, overstrained. It was exactly like the impossible turn she'd recovered the day before.

But worse. Deeper. Harder. Serious intake momentum drag threatened a brutal departure from controlled flight. The bird's tail swung out in the stick-slack air-skid.

And then settled true. A sickening lag, but it settled. She had control.

For a second, she began to understand something.

There was no time to contemplate or review the thought. She gunned into a hard climb, inverted over the ridgeline of the hab's high roofs, and dropped back onto the street she'd been running before.

There was the bat. A Hell Razor. It was in front of her now.

Tone lock. Missile lock. She toggled and fired. One of her

underwing stores streaked away. She felt the knock of its motor wash. Jagdea began to grin.

The grin faded. The missile seemed to have decided on its own journey. It raked right and destroyed the facade of a hab.

Was the bat jamming guidance? There was no trace of logis countermeasures showing.

The bat started to jink, aware of her threat. It hard-braked, trying to throw her past. She dropped speed, obtained missile lock and fired again.

Nothing. A thump. A rune lit on her panel.

MISFIRE.

She had a hung weapon.

She throttled back, and selected FIRE again. Nothing. The bat was extending. Her mind raced. She'd heard of pilots hard-spinning or hard-rolling to tear hung stores off a rail by means of centrifugal force, but there was no room for that.

Nothing she could do. She kicked in the burner briefly, and poured up speed to get back on the bat's six. It decelerated hard and managed to spit her out. She snarled and did the same, rocking the bat back onto her nose the moment it thought it had the upper hand. Hard right. Hard right. A ductwork bridge. The bat split under it, and she went over. The jolt made something bang. A strip of smoke streaked away from her.

The hung weapon had finally fired, all by itself. It must have come off her rail skewed, maybe losing a fin to her wing, because it immediately tumbled into a non-ballistic spin, end over end, motor sputtering and seething.

It was… tumbling back towards her.

Without thinking, she stood the Voss on its wingtip and let the heater swirl past her belly. It detonated behind her, levelling another hab.

She tried to stabilise. The vicious bank had robbed her of

speed and lift. She pulled into a climb to reload power. Ahead and below, the bat climbed too, inverting and coming at her. It had so much more vertical pull than her.

They were under the lid of the Circuit's ruined dome, climbing into green shadow and smoke-clotted air. Shots striped past her. Jagdea banked out and almost collided with a vox-mast. She jerked to avoid it, then fumbled as the fightbird slipped away from her. The Voss started to roll, and threatened to depart flight again for a second. She applied opposite stick to counter.

Overburning, the bat went past her and began to turn. She turned after it and they both started to climb hard. Vertical rolling scissors. She squeezed off a burst of guns, but the bat forced a split. Above her, the fractured roof of the dome was coming down at them fast.

The bat rolled flat and began to skim the dome's underside, dodging stanchions and dangling girders. She levelled her wings as she turned out at the top, and then chased after it down the belly of the roof. It started to burn again to widen the space differential. She stuck to it, waiting for the tone, her thumb on the gun switch.

Tone lock. A clean modarlock. *Murderlock*.

Before she could fire, something got in her way. A dark green Voss. Joiliq.

She braked off to avoid clipping him. He followed the bat down the curve, gunning hard.

So that was it. Joiliq was a poacher. She'd met his kind before. He hung back high and let his wing-mates do all the hard work scaring bats up, then dropped in to steal a kill.

She cursed him. No warning, no courtesy. He'd almost steered her into the dome with his surprise arrival.

And now that he had her kill, he was botching it. He was firing wildly, without waiting to get his nose on. His las-fire was chewing down the dome's underside, spalling debris in a huge, lethal cloud.

Jagdea pulled clear, debris thumping off her. She bent the stick to dodge a large chunk of dome plating that Joiliq's shots had torn loose.

He could have her kill. She had no wish to wing that kind of crazy. She curled into a dive towards the hab roofs below. A flash. Light on canopy glass. There was Exec. The other bat, a Talon, was on him, chasing him relentlessly. He couldn't shake it.

Jagdea stamped the rudder into a tight corkscrew. She went down after the chasers, loading enough g to clench her jaw shut and reduce her vision to thirty per cent. On the vox, dulled by the blood in her ears, she could hear Joiliq whooping and crowing. He'd finally scored his kill. Clean or messy, it was still a kill.

The Talon spotted her, and broke off its chase to engage. It wanted Exec, but it was smart enough not to leave its back exposed to his wingman. It came at her, climbing fast, head-on. Far below, she saw Exec, freed from its threat, turn up hard to reverse the chase positions and get back on it.

Jagdea and the Talon passed each other, nose-to-nose, at a combined speed of almost twelve hundred. Both were gunning, but Jagdea couldn't get off more than a quick squirt. She was about to turn, knowing the bat would too, but held her trajectory at the last moment as Exec came burning up past her. They also passed nose-to-nose.

Now she turned. Max g. Exec was chasing the Talon back up towards the broken lip of the dome. She saw him fire. One burst. Two. Both missed. The Talon was rating hard and forcing him to the outside. It was starting to get lateral separation. Out of the corner of her eye, she saw Joiliq's bird muscling up on a hard burn to close the box. And, she was certain, steal a second kill.

Then. *Then*. It was too fast, really. She was too far back to do anything but watch. As the Talon tried to separate, Exec switched from guns to missiles, and launched a brace. They had just started running on their dirty plumes when Joiliq ripped between them, guns hammering, trying to blow the Talon's tail off from a passing side attack. She saw a puff of debris as his shots hit the Talon. A second later, one of Exec's missiles took it square in the engines and the Talon went up like a small sun. But the other heater was still running, curving. It heat-locked Joiliq as he shot between them.

She heard Exec screaming, 'Pop flares! Pop flares!'

Joiliq must have known. He must have heard the sudden wail of missile lock. Jagdea saw him turn, a good, strong turn. She saw countermeasure decoys, phosphor-bright, sown like spring flowers in his wake. The missile streaked into the cloud of tiny flashes, half a second off Joiliq's exhaust.

And detonated. Joiliq had evaded a friendly kill by the skin of his teeth. But the blastwave rocked him hard. He tried to level off. His un-centred Voss flew straight into the overhanging lip of the dome.

The last thing Jagdea heard on vox was Joiliq laughing at the near-miss.

Hangar level, Intercept 66, Vesperus, 08:52

Jagdea popped her canopy and climbed out the moment Boa's tractor set her down on the stand. Tarr and the crew crowded in.

'Joiliq?' Tarr asked.

'Gone,' said Jagdea.

Tarr swore.

'Because he was stupid,' said Jagdea.

Tarr shot her an ugly look. Jagdea didn't care. She was angry.

She peered under her wings. There was blast scorching on the armour, but no real damage. Her two remaining missiles were secure. No hang.

'Don't rack me with missiles any more,' she told Tarr.

Tarr shrugged, sullen. 'Standard order-out,' she replied. 'We have plenty of them.'

'Because we keep bringing them back,' said Jagdea. 'I don't want them on my rails again.'

The cargo-8 was reversed back down the hangar, Exec's black Voss in its hoisted forks. They watched him go past. Exec was still masked and visored.

'The Voss is a missile platform,' said Tarr reluctantly.

'I don't care,' said Jagdea. 'Tell me that when you have decent ordnance that will synch guidance with logis.'

'So what then?' Tarr asked. 'What do you want?'

'Cannons,' said Jagdea. 'Hard slug cannons.'

'That's non-standard...'

'Me all over. Find me some.'

'I might be able to...' Tarr hesitated. 'There might be something in the Tomb. I think I can scare up a belly cannon from a Twin. Maybe. But not two.'

'One is fine.'

Tarr shook her head. 'Nah, the load displacement. A cannon and its munition pod on one wing? That'll frig up your load symmetry real bad...'

'Then you'd better find me two,' said Jagdea.

She walked away. Fitters were approaching Exec's fightbird, but he was still sitting, canopy closed.

'Back up a sec,' she told the crew. They stood back, waiting. She hauled herself up onto the WALK ONLY. Exec was at the stick, harness on, visor down, mask up. Jagdea unlatched the canopy. He still didn't move. She glanced down, and checked the cockpit side for puncture marks. She thought for a moment he was dead, shot through in his seat.

'Exec?' she said. 'Badler?'

She reached in, pulled off his mask and slid up his visor. His old eyes were filled with tears that were streaming down his young, thin face.

'You gotta get down,' she said.

'Can't let them,' he whispered.

She leaned in. 'Can't let them what? Exec?'

'Can't… can't let them see me like this. The crews. I'm the frigging exec.'

'No, you can't,' she said quietly. 'I don't know how long you've been exec. Not long, I imagine. But no, you can't let them see you like this.'

'Ten days,' he sniffed.

She nodded. Badler had moved up to fill the exec slot when Garrant made lead. The Six-Six turnover. No one stayed anywhere long, not even alive. Had he been over-promoted? Probably. He was so young. But he was a good stick. She'd seen that much. More natural talent, or experience, or both, than the average multi-ace smoke from the Eastern Front. In another theatre, he'd have prospered. But like all the young pilots – no, scratch that, all the pilots period – he was coping with the non-stop shred of flying Vesperus, and now command responsibilities on top of that. She could see from his face that he was broken, living on his nerves.

'Joiliq…' he murmured. He refused to look at her. 'He just…'

'Wasn't you,' she said. 'You didn't kill him, Badler. He killed himself.'

He glanced at her, flushed.

'Don't say that,' he said. 'He was one of our best! And I–'

'He flew into your track,' said Jagdea quietly. 'He was a poacher. You know he was poacher. He flew into your track. He must've known you'd go for missiles at that separation. Badler, he was an idiot.'

'Don't say that!' he snarled. He pulled off his helmet and glared up at her. 'Shut your hole, Driver! He's frigging dead! Why would you say that about him?'

'Because now you're angry, you're not crying and you can get out,' said Jagdea.

He breathed hard, staring at her.

'Let's go, Exec,' she said. 'Stay mad at me, and walk out like an executive officer.' She dropped her voice to a whisper. 'Get to the washrooms. Cry there. Splash some water on your face.'

'There is no water.'

'Then slap yourself a few times and pretend.'

He stared at her, then rubbed his eyes, and unclamped his harness. Jagdea jumped down. He followed, and strode out of the hangar without a word to anyone.

Refectory, Intercept 66, Vesperus, 12:26

Senior Deck Dampier chalked a tally mark beside the name EXEC, then another beside the name JOILIQ. Then she put a line through Joiliq's name. Jagdea stood watching. Exec hadn't cared to attend.

'Call sign Joiliq,' Dampier said to the room. 'Lost oh-eight-twenty this morning. The Emperor protects, the Aeronautica remembers.'

Everyone raised their glasses and called out, 'Joiliq.'

Jagdea got a tray of food. She saw Gumm at a table already, dining alone. He was eating a forkful, then taking a sip of water. Gumm took his refuelling and rehydrating routines seriously. As she came close, she passed Voris on his way out with some member of his fitter crew.

'Hey,' Jagdea said. 'Is there a copy of the Voss-pattern book in the workshop?'

Voris looked at her with an amused leer. 'Just realising you know shit-all?' he asked.

'Is there, or isn't there?'

'Maybe,' he said. 'I'll take a look. I think we burned all the books last month in the cold snap. We don't need them, see? We know 'em by heart.' He tapped a grubby finger to his temple knowingly, as though that's where he thought his heart might be.

'Tell me if you find one,' she said, and moved on.

Gumm glanced up as she sat down.

'Why d'you need the book?' he asked.

'I'm having trouble sleeping,' she said.

'No, really, why?'

She tucked into her fried slab. She had a pile of it. 'I want to check something. Loading thresholds. Logis parameters. The book limits.'

'On a Voss? Why?'

'Just something. Nothing, maybe. A turn I made. Twice now. A bad turn, if I'm honest. But–'

'But what?'

'I want to find out how far I can push it,' she said.

'Why?'

'Stop saying "why". Just an idea I had. Maybe a trick. A technique. We want those, right? You said as much.'

'New tricks? Sure.'

She drank some water. 'So, how was your day, dear?' she asked.

Gumm sat back, and pointed to the wall. Jagdea looked. She didn't see it at first. Then she noticed the fresh tally mark beside the name DOLLFACE.

'You got one?'

'Yes.'

'You got one, Gumm?'

'Lucky, but yes.'

'Good for you,' she said. She clinked her glass against his.

'It's unlucky to toast with water,' he remarked.

'It's unlucky to *drink* this water, Gumm,' she replied. 'And I don't have anything stronger.'

'Unlike... almost everybody else in this room,' said Gumm.

He took another bite. He had to cut his food into small, neat pieces because his porcelain mouth didn't move much.

'So tell me all about it,' she said.

'Just lucky, as I said,' he replied. 'I was up with Gangster. Again. And Rockcrete. Went out south, towards the big reactor burn, chasing a track. Track was bogus, but then we fell over three Talons that were short-cutting in from Intercept Five-Two's area. Had a high angle of attack, so we just went for it. Well, Gangster went for it. I rolled in. This Talon just flew into my lock. There was no skill involved.'

'I'm sure there was a little skill involved...'

'Maybe some.'

'Well, good for you,' said Jagdea. 'Finally putting to use all those years as a multi-ace in... where was it again?'

He looked at her. She grinned.

'Oh, right. You never said,' she continued.

'I never did.'

'Because we don't brag, and we don't make friends.'

'The former,' he replied. 'Maybe not the latter.'

Two pilots suddenly joined them without invitation, dumping their trays down and taking seats opposite. One was a hard-faced young man that Jagdea didn't know. His flightsuit was purple, and he had a thin crease of pink scar running right up his face. The other was Gangster. She had a bottle of joiliq, which she uncorked and swigged from before filling all of the glasses.

'So, come on, Dollface,' the man said. 'That was some kill.'

'Real nice,' agreed Gangster.

'Real smooth,' said the man.

'Real smooth and nice,' said Gangster.

'Some chops,' said the man. 'You got serious hours, Dollface? Which shows? Where'd you get those hours?'

'Tell us your glory stories,' said Gangster.

'Pilot Officer Gumm prefers not to share his record,' said Jagdea.

'What are you?' Gangster sneered. 'His personal frigging secretary?'

'Should call you "Killer",' the man told Jagdea. 'Or "Unlucky Charm".'

'Won't fit on a visor,' Gangster advised him.

'Just "Bad Luck", then,' the man said. 'Should call you Bad Luck. You go up, Joiliq doesn't come back.'

'Should call you...' Jagdea replied. She paused, and shrugged. 'Can't think of a good insult. Don't even know who you are.'

'That's my boy Rockcrete,' said Gangster. She looked at Gumm, and started to wriggle off the top of her compression suit to free her arms for eating.

'Come on, Dollface,' she purred. 'Just one good one.'

'I was Aeronautica Logistic Reserve,' said Gumm gently. 'That's the top and bottom of it.'

'Yeah, but before that?' Gangster asked. She was fighting with a sleeve that was too tight because the cuff bladder hadn't deflated. It seemed every aviator lived in his or her compression suit at Six-Six. To hold in the stink, Jagdea thought. She would kill for a bath or even a scrub wash.

Gangster wore a tight black support vest under her suit. Jagdea had a clear view of the ink on her arms and hard belly. Half of them were actually compression bruises, Jagdea realised. Gangster sported a navel piercing, and several strings of beads and charms on chains around her neck that draped, along with her tags, into her uplifted cleavage.

'There was no before that,' said Gumm. 'I was Reserve. Just like Jagdea.'

Gangster looked at Jagdea oddly for a moment. Something crossed her face, some expression. What was that?

'You're Vervunhive?' Jagdea asked her.

Gangster grinned. 'Verghast strong!' she barked, and slapped palms with Rockcrete.

Then she frowned.

'How'd you know that, Driver?' she asked.

'The accent,' Jagdea said. Then she gestured. 'Also the shoulder tatt. Vervunhive gang mark. I served with some.'

'Where was that?'

'Years ago, before I was Reserve.'

'But where?' asked Gangster.

'Pilot Officer Jagdea prefers not to share her record,' said Gumm.

That made Gangster laugh. Her necklaces jingled. Some of them were holy icons or Imperial symbols. Some were tiny pieces of junk, or what looked like human teeth because they were human teeth.

'I brought joiliq,' said Gangster. 'Joiliq for Joiliq. He was a poacher. A gak-head poacher, but he could fly, until he couldn't.'

'Until he went up with Driver,' said Rockcrete.

'Shut up, 'crete,' said Gangster. She raised her glass. 'Joiliq!'

They echoed her, and drank. Jagdea noticed that Gumm didn't really sip.

'Everything here seems in short supply,' said Jagdea, trying not to grimace at the burn as she swallowed, 'except liquor.'

'Plenty of that,' said Rockcrete. 'We cook our own. Voris and some of the crewers built a still down in assembly. Right next to the bomb farm.'

'Shhhhh!' Gangster snorted, pouring another.

'That's an excellent place to keep a still,' said Jagdea.

'Keeps people away,' said Rockcrete. 'Stuff Tarr keeps there, she should've dumped most of it. Says it's safed, but safed my arse. It's about as safe as...'

He paused, trying to complete his thought effectively.

'Something not safe?' Jagdea suggested.

'Vesperus?' offered Gumm.

'Yeah, those things,' Rockcrete agreed.

'There seems to be good stuff around too, though,' said Jagdea. 'Not this wet start flush. Amasec.'

'There's plenty here,' said Gangster. 'Plenty. If you know where to look.'

'And where is that?' asked Jagdea.

'Ask Harlot,' Gangster replied.

Jagdea saw Wilzar across the refectory. He had fetched a tray, but had sat alone. He wasn't eating. He was clearly not Four-A.

'I'll be right back,' she said to Gumm. 'Don't tell any good stories while I'm gone.'

Wilzar looked up at her as she sat down opposite. His eyes were glassy.

'All right?' she asked.

'They said food and water,' he replied. His voice was reedy, and his hands had a tremble. 'I can't face it.'

'You need it,' she said. 'Starch, calories, fluids. I've barely seen you since we got here. How many times have you lifted?'

'Twice,' he said. 'This isn't flying.'

'It certainly isn't Area Four,' she agreed.

'It isn't flying, Jagdea,' he insisted. 'These people are psychotic. Bloody insane...' He looked at her. 'I can't do it,' he said.

'You can. You have.'

He shook his head. 'First drop, I barely pulled out,' he said quietly. 'I was so bloody scared. The bird wouldn't lift. Thought I was going to die. The rest of that sortie, I don't even remember it. A blur. I was useless, and I don't know how I got back intact.'

'It's not you, Wilzar. It's everyone.'

'Every turn, there was something to dodge–'

'Vesperus is a nightmare war sky,' she said. 'Unforgiving and brutal. It's not like anything I've–'

'I can't do it,' he repeated. 'I just haven't got the skill. The reaction. The... nerve. Smoke by name, right?'

'I've got some hours,' said Jagdea. 'I am still shit-scared every time I'm up. It doesn't get better. So you have to.'

Wilzar exhaled, exasperated.

'Be better? Like you told me before? I'm trying.'

'I have no doubt.'

'Now I'm grounded for two days.'

'What did you do?' she asked.

'Second drop. This morning,' he said. He wiped his mouth. 'Winging Garrant, no less. Made a mess of everything. Garrant and Bloodspot took off after the track. I tried to keep up. I wanted to hit the burners, like they had, but everything was too close. I didn't dare. They were already in the knife-fight, and I was still miles out. Two drops, two fights I haven't even seen.'

'And?'

'One bat broke. Garrant voxed it was coming my way, ordered me to break west and chop it. Ordered me to burners.'

'*And*, Wilzar?'

'I hit afterburn,' he said. 'Barely missed a bloody tower, then tore my wingtip off on the gantry of a passenger dock.'

'Not good.'

'Barely got out of the spin. Bat was long gone. No idea whatsoever how I made it back or executed hard arrest. I'm stood down for two days while they repair the torn wing. No bird, no fly.'

He met her eyes.

'Which is fine by me because I can't do it anyway,' he said.

'You can,' she said. 'You will.'

'Do better?' he asked, hollow and cynical. 'You telling me that again?'

'We all have to do better,' she replied. 'We all have to learn how to fly this space. The drop rate is so punishing, no one's got time to teach anything. No one's got time to learn. No one's even got time to pass on tips. I think it's been like that since Six-Six set up here. No time for anything. A squadron's supposed to support itself. Share best practice. Veterans bringing the less-experienced pilots up to spec. We never really leave flight school, Wilzar. Every lift is a lesson. But there's no culture of that here.'

'What do you know about squadrons?' he asked.

'I was combat once,' she said. 'It doesn't matter. Look, Gumm and I, we're trying to put some ideas together. Maybe devise some tricks to help.'

'Gumm was combat too?' Wilzar asked.

She nodded.

'What sort of tricks?'

'Techniques,' she replied. 'We don't know yet. Anything that could give us an edge. Anything that might work. When we have some, I will share them with you. I promise.'

He sort of nodded.

'Now, follow the instruct,' she said. 'Eat. Hydrate. That's technique one right there. Doesn't matter if you don't feel like it. Get calories and fluids in you. You can't fly on empty tanks. You'll fatigue too fast. And g-load will knock you out faster.'

'All right,' he said. He picked up his fork.

She got up, and walked away, then turned and looked back at him.

'Wilzar?'

'Yeah?'

'You said passenger dock? You clipped a passenger dock?'

'Yes,' he said.

'What do you mean by passenger dock?' Jagdea asked.

Intercept 66, Vesperus, 21:40

The storm that had been threatening all day finally rolled in late in the afternoon. Jagdea had returned to her billet to think and sleep, and by the time she woke up, the storm was moaning and lashing outside.

The darkness seemed solid, as though the smog-storm was seeping into the bell tower around the flak-boarding and shutters. Lighting had dropped to half-power, and the lamps in her room, and the hall outside, throbbed and wavered. She had an ugly sense that something was sucking power out of the deck station, or simply drinking the light.

She wasn't properly awake, and her whole body felt more wretched than ever before. Her joints seemed loose and floppy, as though they'd all been overstretched, and her fingers felt weak. There was an ache in the base of her skull that dripped all the way down her spine.

When she peered out into the twilight of the billet hallway, she saw two pilots walking past. One was Blindside, the veteran who'd winged Gumm and Gangster the day before, and chalked a kill.

'What's going on?' she asked.

The pilots glanced at her dourly.

'No fly,' said Blindside.

'Storm?' she asked.

'Storm,' he replied.

She could hear the howling gale outside, and the thump and bang of poorly secured shutters. She wondered if it was the murderous windshear or the zero-zero visibility that was keeping the squadron grounded.

Blindside and his companion were already walking on. Jagdea saw a bottle of liquor swinging from the hand of Blindside's friend.

'Hey,' she called after them. 'Where did you get that?'

'Usual place,' he replied.

She went back into her room, and sat on the cot. The light from the glow-globe winced and trembled. She thought about banking some more sleep, but the eerie wail of the storm outside wasn't going to let her settle. She considered going back down to the refectory and piling up another plate.

She looked at the wall of her room. She hadn't been able to scrounge a data-slate, or any paper, or even a stylus from anywhere, but she'd borrowed a stick of chalk from the refectory fireplace and turned the scabby wall of her room into a memorandum. She'd scratched out a list of priorities in block letters, then two sub-lists of reminders and half-formed notions. She'd even drawn in a few arrows linking items on one list to another. It had made sense before she'd gone to sleep. Half-awake, it read back as the rambling last testament of a convict in solitary.

A sudden squall of wind shrieked outside and shook the casement. The lights dimmed sharply for a moment. She'd drawn a ring around the word DOCK. She wondered why, then remembered. The things she'd written down in the rush of her combat-high earlier in the day now seemed futile and worthless, fool's gold notions that were not worth the effort of chasing. She sat back, easing a cramp in her thigh. The storm squalled again, so hard this time, the entire tower seemed to shiver, and every billet door in the hallway rattled in its frame.

Her door kept rattling for a few moments after the gust died down. Jagdea leapt up, and threw the door open.

Voris, the fitter, was crouching on her doorstep. He looked up at her in surprise, like a discovered thief.

'Didn't want to wake you,' he said.

He'd been about to leave something outside her door. He rose, and handed it to her instead. It was heavy, and she needed both hands to take it. A battered copy of the Voss-pattern spec-book.

'Like you asked,' he explained, and turned away.

'Thanks,' she called.

He shrugged indifferently, without looking back.

'I owe you a drink,' she said. Now he paused and glanced back. A bad-toothed grin.

'Kind of you,' he replied.

'Where would I lay my hands on some, Voris?' she asked.

'Harlot,' he replied.

She hefted the book back into her room, and sat on her cot, flicking through its pages. She tried to locate and read certain sections, but the combination of tiny typeface and the wobbling, fretful gloom began to give her eye strain.

She got up and laced on her boots.

Lopard was alone in the number two hangar. She found him by accident. He was standing by his bird, a snow-white Bolt with a crimson muzzle that faded back from a dark gradient at the nose.

The storm was still moaning around the tower, and through-draughts were raising little whirling dust-devils of soot off the wide deck. Smog particles were clotting the air too, smudging the light. Jagdea could feel the grit in her throat.

Lopard saw her approach. He took a lho-stick out of his silver case and perched it on his lip to light it, oblivious to the prom-stains on the decking and the reek of fuel in the air.

'Not a good idea,' she said as she joined him.

Lopard took the stick off his lip, and considered it.

'I suppose not,' he said. 'Though comparatively low down on the list of things that are not good ideas.'

He put the lho-stick back in the case and snapped it shut.

'Not sleeping?' he asked.

She shook her head, and looked at his plane, appreciating the muscular reassuring lines of the mighty Thunderbolt. It was very much like its pilot: handsome, dangerous and confident, but older than it looked, and more worn-out than it cared to admit. Harlot, with what seemed to her characteristic vanity, had allowed a kill tally to be marked on the fuselage below the canopy. Jagdea counted thirty-six black bars.

'Did you fly Bolts?' he asked her.

'When?'

'In your other life,' said Lopard. 'The one before this?'

'This is a life?' she asked. He smirked. She could see how he was observing her, reading her. Could he instinctively sense her affinity with the Thunderbolt, or was he studying her for other reasons?

'Yes, I flew Bolts,' she said. 'Weapon of choice.'

'And how did that go for you, Jagdea?' he asked. His eyes seemed to be appreciating her form exactly the way she was appreciating the Thunderbolt's.

'It was Four-A,' she said. 'Four-A for a long, long time, until I missed the sky and hit the ground instead.'

'Unfortunate,' he murmured.

'Inevitable,' she replied.

'And now you fly Strikes?' he said.

'Now I drive cargo,' she said. 'Sticking a Voss is just the culmination of a recent and unfortunate sequence of events.'

'Like flying a Bolt into the inevitable ground?'

'Exactly like that,' Jagdea shrugged. 'Anyway, it's just temporary.'

Lopard grinned. In the curious half-light, his dark good looks seemed amplified, and his wear and tear all but invisible.

'You really are determined to live up to your call sign, aren't you, Driver?' he remarked.

'No,' she said. 'It's temporary because I'll be dead soon.'

Lopard sniffed.

'Anyway, where are your manners?' she asked.

'I'm sorry?'

'On our previous encounters,' said Jagdea, 'you've all but forced liquor on me. But now...'

Lopard smiled again, and straightened his jacket.

'What do you need?' he asked.

'Amasec,' she said. 'The good stuff. I was told Harlot knows where that is.'

'Well, he does,' said Lopard. 'Why didn't you say so?'

'Take one of these,' Lopard said, fishing a pair of tactical flashlights out of a derelict locker. He had led her from the hangar, through the fitting shops, past the Tomb, and then down through a labyrinth of gloomy halls and stairwells into the depths of the ruined templum. They were almost outside the official bounds of the Intercept 66 Deck, and straying into the structures that adjoined it.

The storm continued to moan and howl outside, and clouds of black dust billowed down the decaying passageways, driven by the intruding wind. On these levels of the vast building, windows, doorways and damage-punctures had not been braced and shuttered as efficiently as they were inside the base itself, merely boarded and blocked. The storm leaked in, playing in abandoned chambers, swinging broken doors on rusty hinges, driving gusts along vacated hallways, and producing odd whistles and wails as it blew in through tight cracks and loose frames. It also stank of burn-ash and hive-grave waste.

'Is this area out of bounds?' Jagdea asked, slapping the flashlight and testing it.

'Of course.'

'I thought you had rules?' she said.

'I do,' he replied. 'This is one of them. I know this area is out of bounds.'

She followed him down a hallway. The overhead lights were at the lowest power they could be without actually being out. Lopard dragged some crates out of the way, and revealed a rusted hatch. Jagdea could see the last traces of Ecclesiarchy engraving under the corrosion. Lopard freed the bolts. Unlike the door, the bolts were cleaned and oiled.

He pushed the hatch open and led her through. It was dark beyond, with no voltaic supply at all. From somewhere came the sound of panicked screaming. It was just the wind.

'You are now leaving Intercept Six-Six,' Lopard said, switching on his flashlight. 'Officially. This is the precinct of the templum of Saint Kiodrus and Saint Sabbat Martyr, which the Campanile once served. And also, a dead zone, just so you know.'

'You've been here before?'

'That's a very silly question,' said Lopard. 'Obviously, I have. All of us have. Well, maybe except Dampier. She is very much a rule-keeper. Someone has to be, I suppose. But the rest of us... we all need to stretch our legs once in a while. Get out, you know?'

The floor was a fine ashlar tile. Jagdea thought the tiles were probably coloured, but in the gloom they seemed black and white. Even with her flashlight, she could read little of the chamber they were in, except that it was very large and grand. Tilted upwards, her torch-beam seemed to find the remains of a high, gilded ceiling, and the faces of faded cherubs and sad saints.

'So we all come down here,' Lopard said. 'Once in a while. To escape. To be alone. And there are events too.'

'Events?'

'Informal,' he replied. 'Six-Six is fairly lax, but you can only blow off so much steam in the rec room or the refectory. There are occasional parties down here. Recreations that can take place without running the risk of getting written up for conduct unbecoming.'

Jagdea's flashlight beam had already discovered empty and smashed bottles on the floor. Lopard opened another door.

'You'll find yourself coming down here eventually,' he promised her. 'Wanting to come down here.'

'Will I? It's not a charming environment.'

'Indeed it is not,' he agreed. 'But it's the only *other place* there is.'

The adjoining room was also large. There was power here. Lopard threw a switch and broken glow-globes came on, casting a feeble light. He turned his torch off to save the cells. The room had been some kind of chantry. It had a high arched ceiling strung with dead electroflambeaux, and the sectile marble floor was crusted with broken glass, from smashed bottles, and from the coloured glassaic that had once filled the tall windows. They were now boarded up.

The wind groaned. Window boards slapped and rattled. The dead, black remains of what had been a vast bonfire spilled out of the huge hearth, surrounded by regiments of empty bottles, and glasses filled with cold wax and dead candles. There was a litter of lho-stick butts, spent combat-stimm vials, and crushed injectors. Intoxicated hands had covered the walls with scrawlings, curses and bold statements that could not be written up on the boards of the refectory. Near the dead bonfire, a small shrine had been raised against the wall. It looked even more feral and primitive than the one in the refectory fireplace, except for the small brass aquila perched on top. It was draped in offerings: beakers of spirits, broken goggles, squadron badges, crude votive figurines, spent shell cases, and strings of dog-tag necklaces.

'This is where you mourn the dead?' she asked.

Lopard shook his head.

'This is where we mourn the living, Driver,' he replied.

The chantry walls were covered with ancient frescoes of very high quality. The images of angels and champions were almost invisible behind the dirt and the graffiti. Jagdea could make out the figure of a woman dominating the main fresco, a saint, clad in gold and selpic blue, haloed in light. Her face stared out of the filth, its expression impossible to read. Was she offended by the riotous desecration of her shrine, or silently approving that some raw brand of faith in the human spirit still found expression?

Lopard took out his silver case, and offered it to her. It was almost empty. She glimpsed a series of scratch marks, like little crosses, that had been gouged into the liner. She was more interested in his hand. The finely-made red glove.

'No, thanks,' she said. Lopard shrugged, took out a lho-stick for himself, and closed the case.

'You're Glavian,' she said.

'Is it the accent?' he asked, lighting the stick.

'The gloves,' she said.

He nodded, exhaling smoke. 'Seen them before, then?'

'Heard of them. Heard of the Glavian prowess at the stick. Bred in the bone.'

'So they say,' Lopard replied. 'But bred in the culture, too.'

He clamped the lho-stick between his teeth so he could peel back the cuff of his right glove and show the glint of the intricate dermal microcircuitry.

'Hardwired for flight,' he said.

'Is that much of an edge?' she asked. 'As much as they say it is?'

He took a slow drag on his smoke.

'I'm still alive,' he suggested.

'And a long way from home,' she said.

'Glavians travel,' he replied. 'You don't get to be born into a pilot culture and then stay put. It kind of defeats the object. Anyway, you're a long way from home too.'

'Not quite so far,' she said.

'How far is "far"?'

'Phantine,' she replied.

Lopard nodded, and pulled a face that suggested he was almost impressed.

'We should sleep together,' he said.

'What the f–'

'The offspring of a Glavian and a Phantine?' he said, chuckling. 'Two worlds famed for the calibre of their pilots? What a hot stick *that* child would be.'

Jagdea backed down, and found a half-laugh.

'I'm not having sex with you,' she said. 'I'm definitely not bearing your child.'

'I am aware,' he said.

'I'm too old. Too old for babies. Too old for combat flying.'

'And yet here you are,' said Lopard. He flicked the lho-stick onto the floor, and ground it beneath his heel. 'Right,' he said. 'This way.'

He led her to the door on the far side of the chamber. There was a crate on the floor beside the door. He opened it, and took out two battered rebreather masks. He tossed one to her.

'You'll need this,' he said. 'And the flashlight.'

The inside of the mask stank, and Jagdea could barely see through the tinted lenses. Lopard reached out, took her hand, and made her grip the back of his jacket.

Then he opened the door.

Darkness blew out at them. Jagdea staggered as the wind hit them. She protested, but all that came out was just an unintelligible grunt with the mask on. He guided her through the door into the darkness beyond, and closed the door behind them. She kept a fierce grip on his coat.

It was hard to see anything but blackness, and hard to stay upright in the assault of wind and soot. The next part of the templum complex had been entirely blown open during the fall of Vesperus, and there was nothing to keep the night and the storm out. The wind howled in her ears, and shoved at her, trying to knock her down. Lopard steadied her.

She followed him, head down, through the assaulting gale. She became aware of tiny red lights all around them in the darkness, the only things she could see. She realised they were the display runes of radiation counters that had been fixed to the remains of the chamber's floor and walls. The pioneers who had set up Intercept 66 had marked out the sections of the structure that were open and exposed to the toxins, dusts and other insidious by-products of the hive's catastrophic death. She fumbled with her torch, and tried to read the warning levels on the counters, but it was too bewildering. The lenses of her rebreather mask, fogged by dust, kept catching and reflecting the moving beams of their flashlights and the trembling glow of the runes. They were just lights, moving and dancing in the whirling darkness, as impossible to differentiate as the glint of passing las-fire and the reflection of CAD displays on her canopy glass during her last sortie.

Disorientated, she closed her eyes, and let him lead her, clutching his jacket. She heard a hatch scrape open above the roar of the gale, and then the wind dropped.

She opened her eyes. They were in a sealed section of corridor, and Lopard was securing the hatch to block out the fury of the chamber they had just crossed. He pulled off his mask, and she did the same, gasping. The only light came from their torches.

'Thanks,' she said sarcastically. 'We're probably contaminated now.'

'You were contaminated the moment you arrived on deck,' he replied.

'That kind of exposure was still stupid,' she protested.

'I've done it before.'

'That doesn't make it less stupid.'

'No,' he agreed, 'but as I said, there's a list, and what we just did comes a long way down. Besides, you want amasec or not?'

Jagdea spat dust out of her mouth.

'I don't know what to make of you, Lopard,' she said.

'They all say that,' he said with a grin. He set off down the corridor, playing his beam ahead of him. She hurried to catch up.

'Who's they?'

'Well, everyone who isn't me,' he replied. 'What to make of me? Hmm. Well, you could make a friend of me, though I think you've already done that.'

'I'm not here to make friends,' she said.

'And yet…' He winked. 'Or, I suppose, you could make me an attentive and talented sexual partner?'

'Knock it off.'

'Well, then,' he added. 'You could make a useful associate of me. A man worth knowing. A provisioner of the finest victuals.'

'Clearly, there's no beginning to your talents,' she said.

He turned and looked at her.

'Understand, Driver,' he said. 'This, where I'm taking you, is my secret. I found it. The location is known to me and just a chosen few others in the squadron. I am taking you into my confidence, and trusting you with great knowledge.'

'Why?'

'Because many would kill to know it.'

'I mean, why are you trusting me?'

'Because you need a drink.'

'Lopard–'

He laughed.

'Because I like you,' he said. 'And I pity you, which is much the same thing. And I sense that we are kindred spirits, hence my liking and my pity. And because we can't fly tonight, and there's frig all else to do.'

The maze of decaying corridors led them, by a route Jagdea was sure she would not be able to retrace, even in daylight, to deep, vaulted cellars. The heavy stonework was dank and, now they were so deep in the foundations of the ruined templum, the scream and howl of the smog-storm outside had changed in pitch and intensity. Lopard made her hold her flashlight steady as he unlocked the padlock securing a heavy door. The door was old. The padlock, a heavy security model issued to the likes of the Magistratum, was new. Lopard knew the code.

Inside, the cellar vault was lined with dusty bottles and shipping crates.

'Say what you like about the Ecclesiarchy,' said Lopard, 'they like fine living and the choicest spirits. The clerics who lived here, before they were atomised, stocked their cellars and pantries well. When I first found this place, Jagdea, I could not believe the treasures I found. Now we know where all the coin from the donation plates goes, I suppose.'

'The image of the venal cleric is a stereotype,' she said.

'Stereotypes are stereotypes for a reason,' he replied. 'Look at this. Wines from San Velabo and Ultramar. Altar wine? I think not. Cask-aged glayva from Cadia. Here, joiliq from Khulan, and Thracian kummel. What's your poison? Amasec?'

He slid a bottle off a rack and blew the dust off it.

'Amasec Regalis Balhaut,' he said. 'The drink of warmasters.'

He handed it to her, put down his flashlight, and used his igniter to light the multiple candles of a silver candelabrum perched on a nearby crate. A soft, golden glow filled the cellar.

Lopard took the bottle back, peeled off the lead foil, and pulled the stopper.

'No glasses, I'm afraid,' he said.

'Never mind,' she replied.

Lopard pursed his lips, then fetched a second bottle and opened it too. He held one out to her.

'May you return to deck before the bats know you're up, Pilot Officer Jagdea,' Lopard said.

'To the friends we won't make,' she replied.

They clinked the bottles, and took a swig.

'Shit.' She coughed, her eyes clenched shut.

'It's really not,' he replied.

'It really isn't,' Jagdea agreed. She took another sip. Lopard set his bottle down, opened a crate, and took out a carton of lho-sticks. He began to refill his silver case. She could see more cartons, some Militarum issue, some contraband, in the crate and the others around it, along with bags of tablets and blister packs of stimm-shots.

'You stash stuff down here too?' she asked.

'Of course. It's secure.'

'You score this yourself? Ship it in?'

'There are always deals to be done with the resupply crews,' he said. 'And hard currency is meaningless in a place like this.

But people still have needs and appetites. So a man can grease the wheels and maintain his status by providing for those needs.'

'Stimms too? Obscura? Prohib crap?'

'Whatever's in demand. Come now, Driver, we're both grown-ups.'

She took another sip. The amasec was the best she'd ever tasted.

'So when you said you knew who to ask, that "who" was you?'

Lopard chuckled.

'Among others. But for the *finest* goods…'

'Tell me,' she said, leaning back against a crate, 'is this why you seem so popular with everybody? So admired?'

He looked stung. 'Jagdea, I am without doubt one of the best bat-killers in the Circus. That is why the squadron admires me.'

His smile suddenly returned, wolfish, and he nodded at his stash.

'This is why they *like* me.' He started to poke around in the crates. 'Having trouble sleeping?' he asked.

'No,' she said.

'Having trouble staying awake?'

'No.'

'Having trouble with your reaction time?'

'Lopard, there's nothing in those crates that can help me with that.'

'You'd be surprised,' he replied. 'So, no combat stimms? No? No boosters?'

'Never touch them.'

'You will.'

He retrieved his bottle, took another gulp, then told her the code for the padlock. 'In case you change your mind,' he said.

'You really want me to like you, don't you?' she said. 'Why is that? Why trust me?'

'Reasons.'

'Such as?'

'Boredom. And many others. You're aware of the obvious one.'

'Painfully, and it's not going to happen. What else?'

'I told you. Kindred spirits. We can rely on so little out here, Jagdea. Except each other. If you're winging me, or vice versa, that becomes a matter of life and death. So anything that can be done to broker trust on a basic level extends to the air, where it really matters.'

'I would cover your six in a knife-fight whether you showed me this place or not.'

'Which is why I like you so very much.'

'It's not a matter of liking, Lopard, or being friends. It's not even a matter of trust. That's a given. We are both Aeronautica. We're both flying the same war in the same war sky. I'd cover your six because that's how it works.'

'I wonder how long it will take before that idealism is knocked out of you?' he said.

'Missing the sky and flying into the ground didn't do it, so...' She shrugged.

'Come on,' he said. 'Bring your bottle. It's yours. Take it. There's something I want to show you.'

They took both bottles, and the lit candelabrum. Lopard locked the cellar behind them, and led her up through the darkness of the gutted templum. The storm was still raging outside.

The chamber he brought her to had been the High Ecclesiarch's private sanctum, or so he claimed. Though the windows were boarded, and there was some trace of decay, it seemed almost untouched. The floor was a gleaming mosaic, and the pillars and traceries gilded. They glowed in the light of the candles. Shadows flickered across the high arch of the painted ceiling and the cloth-of-gold tapestries draping the walls. The plumply upholstered furniture, covered in red silk and pink velvet, was dwarfed by the scale of the chamber. Their footsteps echoed. Jagdea could detect the trace residue of incense burned long ago.

'I don't bring people here,' he said. 'Though I'm sure other explorers have found it. I think of it as my place. A sanctuary. It reminds me of home.'

'Does it?'

'My family was very rich. Glavian shipwrights. A whole dynasty.'

'Why did you ever leave?'

'Five older siblings. I was never going to inherit. I was expected to spread my wings.'

'You certainly did that.'

'Not quite the way the family expected.'

Lopard put his bottle and the candelabrum down on the top of a gold harpsichord that dominated the centre of the room, and lit another lho-stick. Then he tinkled with the keys, and filled the air with a trill of haunting notes.

'Why show it to me?'

'I don't know,' he said.

'I suppose,' she ventured, 'you've told me your biggest secret...'

'The cellar?' he asked, with a snigger. 'Oh no, that's my *second* biggest secret.'

'What's the first?'

Lopard put a finger to his lips and winked.

Jagdea took another swig of her amasec, and slowly turned, taking in the grandeur of the shadowed room. Behind her, bright music began. A sonata by Belique or Charmoday.

She turned. Lopard was sitting at the harpsichord, playing with some finesse, the lho-stick dangling from his mouth.

'You play?'

'In a high-born family like mine,' he said, still playing, 'one is expected to be accomplished in all aspects of the arts and sciences. My brother played the cornet, which was hateful.'

'For him or you?'

'For everybody in earshot.'

He stopped playing abruptly, and swung his leg around so he was straddling the cushioned stool.

'I want your trust,' he said, raising his bottle to drink, 'because you can fly... Really fly.'

'Once, perhaps–'

'It's still in you. So, if you're winging me–'

'I've explained this, Lopard. I'd cover your six anyway.'

'You misunderstand,' he replied. 'You can fly. The vast majority of the pilots in Six-Six cannot. Oh, they'd want to protect my back, but they can't. They can't even protect themselves. These babies. These children, who die so very quickly and so very often. How I wish I could spare them this, this nightmare, before they suffer it for too long. But I can't. I can't protect them all.'

He rose to his feet, bottle in one hand, half-smoked lho-stick in the other.

'I don't want friends any more than you do,' he said. 'Friends cost you. But if I'm going to make allies, if I'm going to broker trust, then I want to make sure it's with someone who is capable of returning that effort. The children in this squadron can't, though they wish they could and might intend to. But you can. You, and few others. You can deliver, because you can fly.'

'So this is all just self-interest?' she asked.

'Oh, Driver! Please! If you think that anything anyone ever does is not born out of self-interest, you're living in the wrong century.'

'Was there ever a right century?'

'Not! According! To! The! History! Books!' he declared, accompanying his statement with a sprightly, bouncing flourish up the keyboard.

The echo of the music died away. The wind grumbled and chewed at the window boards.

'You know who I am, don't you?' said Jagdea.

'You're Driver.'

'Don't eff around. You know.'

'You're Bree Jagdea of Phantine. I suspected.'

'And I confirmed it.'

'One is expected to be accomplished in all aspects of the arts and sciences,' said Lopard, 'and well-versed in history books, especially ones of aeronautic actions. Wing Commander Bree Jagdea of the Phantine Air Corps, multi-ace, commander of Umbra Flight, hero of the Zophonian Sea.'

'That's who I used to be. I fear your investment is shaky.'

'We'll see.'

'Well, now you have me at a disadvantage. All I know about you is that your name is Lopard, call sign Harlot. You're Glavian, from a good family, well-educated, dealer in alcohol, contraband and sundry prohibited substances, a dissolute, cynical rake–'

'Don't forget "multi-ace",' he put in, unfazed.

'And that. Over-familiar, sexually predatory, drunk–'

'You're drunk too.'

'I am,' she said. 'Right now. Half a bottle down. But when I said "drunk" in reference to you, I meant pretty much all the time.'

'Oh, that's just being picky!'

'I know you want to get in my good books, and my bed, and my shorts–'

'I've been fairly clear–'

'I don't even know your name.'

'Pilot Officer Reno Hewgin Lopard Delevane. I tend to leave off the dynastic portion.' He executed a curt but perfect bow.

'Lopard?'

'Yes?'

'Please don't tell anybody,' she said. 'About who I am.'

'Well, that's what trust's all about, isn't it?' he replied.

'I don't want to carry that rep around. I'm amazed you worked it out.'

'You'd be amazed at the things I know,' he said.

She paused. She took a sip from her bottle.

'Well then, here's a test,' she said. 'What do you know about the Vesperus public transport system?'

By the light of the candelabrum in his hand, Lopard pulled aside the folding metal shutter. The wind that blew in out of the darkness fluttered all the candles out, so they switched back to flashlights.

'Are you going to explain?' he asked.

'Maybe,' she replied.

'I'm very curious.'

'I have noticed that about you.'

Beyond the shutter was a wide gantry deck, with bench seating. It was derelict. Beyond the deck, brass-railed steps led down into the enclosed portico of a passenger dock. The dock's hatches were sealed, but she could hear the wind and rain beating against the outside.

They had climbed back up through the templum's ruined levels, then out towards the outside wall, which Lopard claimed was above the atrium port of the south facade. The dock gantry projected out, about eighteen hundred feet above street level.

'Wilzar said he clipped a passenger dock,' she said.

'Wilzar?'

'The relief pilot who came in with me. Smoke.'

'Oh, that bumptious child.'

'You saw that right off.'

'It was hard to miss,' said Lopard. 'Didn't you, the moment you set eyes on him?'

Jagdea had to admit she had.

'Wilzar said he clipped what he called a passenger dock on his sortie today. Nearly lost a wing. He's grounded for repairs for a couple of days.'

'Well, that's him safe for a while,' said Lopard.

'It made me think,' said Jagdea. 'I mean, it's obvious, really... a hive of this scale would have a public transport infrastructure. A considerable one.'

'Just how drunk are you right now?'

'Shut up. Listen. A public transport infrastructure. Road carriers, and rail links, all operating at street level, but also higher up. Serving the upper reaches of hive blocks and spires.'

'Yes, air-ferries. Lift-transporters. Shuttles. Gravs. The airspace here used to be busy.'

'And all accessed by public docks like this?'

'Yes,' said Lopard. 'There are passenger docks all over the hive. Everywhere. Three, I think, in the templum precinct alone.'

'I hadn't noticed them.'

'Well, you've had your eyes on other things, like not dying. The docks are just another hazard to avoid. Something your Wilzar needs to add to his list of things to do.'

'Stop it. Do you think there are records, somewhere? Archived data?'

'Of what?' he asked.

'Of public transport network routes? You've explored this templum, and Throne knows where else. Have you found any Administratum offices? Control centres? Anywhere that records might have survived?'

'A few,' said Lopard. 'Again, records of what? Of transport network routes?'

'Yes,' she replied. 'The routes. And the data-maps of those routes.'

'Why the frig would you want those?'

'Because,' she said, 'those ferry routes, between and through the structures in this hive, were airborne.'

DAY 91

Third drop, Intercept 66, Vesperus, 10:47

They were perched among the tangled girders at the summit of a hive-spire near Korazon Square, clinging by their landing claws.

The storm had blown out in the small hours, but it left behind a deep and impenetrable sea of smog that blanketed the hive and kept the squadron grounded until long after sunrise. No reports were coming in from the ROPs or other Intercepts. Jagdea had been able to bank some more rest, and sleep off the worst of the amasec.

By mid-morning the smog had begun to clear at the higher levels. Below two thousand feet, the air was still zero-zero soup with no light penetration, but Dampier had ordered flights up to prowl above the sinking dust.

She was flying with Garrant and Bloodspot. They'd made a conventional lift on ducts from the roof of the Campanile due to the conditions. Dead drops were out of the question. On instruments only, they had cleared the smog-shrouded pad, and then ascended quickly into clear air and shockingly bright sunlight.

The flight had turned out between the hive blocks and run as far as Maladine, then circled for a while. The view was startling. Vesperus looked as though it had been half-drowned by the ocean, with thick green smog standing waist-deep around the taller structures and obscuring others entirely. Above the smog layer, it was bright and very still, the sun blazing out of a grey sky.

Fuel concerns remained high. With the loss of the resupply, Six-Six's reserves were draining fast. There was talk in the refectory that the squadron might have to be cut to limited response or even stood down entirely unless a fresh replenishment could be arranged with the 'plex, and there was still no word of that happening. After twenty minutes in the air, and zero sign of contacts, Garrant had ordered them to roost to conserve fuel.

He had chosen a tower near Korazon Square that projected high above the smog. All that remained of the tower's upper portion was a mangled nest of girders and spars that leaned out over the drop, rusting in the breeze. There, they had settled, ducting in low and slow to seize the girderwork with their landing claws until they were secure. Anchored, they cut power and waited.

The three planes basked in the sun, side by side. They were essentially upright, their noses tilted down slightly. The twisted girders they were gripping creaked under their weight. Jagdea sat in her cockpit with Bloodspot's bone-white Voss to her left, and Garrant's blue Cypra just off to her right. Visibility was good. She could see for many miles, and the hard sun glinted off the remains of glass in distant buildings. She yawned. The Voss' cockpit was too tight for much movement, and she was fighting a persistent cramp in her thigh. The whole experience was bizarre. Just sitting, shut down, perched like lazy vultures, waiting for a war to start.

Half an hour in, she noticed Sorrentine, call sign Bloodspot, pop his canopy so he could stretch his arms and stand up in his seat. He waved over at her. She waved back. Even a semi-dismount looked precarious, but she unlatched her canopy too. The air wasn't fresh, but it was refreshingly cool compared to the stale recyc in the cockpit, and the sunlight was warm on her face. Garrant remained silent, lid down.

Lead was pissed off with her. At the huddle before lift, he'd demanded to know why she wasn't carrying any munition stores on her rails. Tarr had been as good as her word, and not loaded Jagdea with missiles at the fit-out. But the chief hadn't yet scrounged up any hard guns as replacements, and Jagdea's rails were bare.

Jagdea had apologised to the squadron leader. She'd mentioned an 'issue with her hardpoints' but hadn't got into any details. Garrant had let it go, but he wasn't happy.

They sat waiting in the hazy glare. Everything was so still.

Her thigh knotted again. Jagdea shouldered around in her seat, trying to find the space to flex it out.

Her intervox crackled.

'You look uncomfortable in there.'

It was Sorrentine. He was looking across at her from his bird's open cockpit, mask down, grinning.

'Copy that, Bloodspot. Leg cramp.'

'Well, get out and stretch it.'

Jagdea pushed her canopy higher and peered out at him.

'I'm not getting out,' she said, holding her mask to her mouth.

'Afraid of heights, Driver?'

'Yes.'

She saw Bloodspot nod. Then she saw him undo his straps and stand up in his seat again.

'Just watching you makes me uneasy,' she voxed.

'Then don't watch,' Bloodspot voxed back.

He climbed out of his cockpit, and stood on the WALK ONLY of his wing. The wing was a slope, and the drop below terrifying. She heard the tangled girders groan as his weight shifted. Bloodspot stretched his arms extravagantly, then stood upright, head back, face towards the sun. She could see the trail of loops of the bio-impulse umbilicals that wet-linked him to the neuroreactive plasma tanks behind his bird's seat. Bloodspot had no ejection system. The tanks had been fitted in its place.

He stretched again, languorous, knowing she could see him.

'Lovely out today,' he remarked.

'Stop it,' she voxed. 'It's making me nervous.'

He looked over at her, smiled.

'It's safe,' he said. *'This is the closest thing to fresh air and daylight I ever get. You know I sleep on a cot under the wing of my bird?'*

'I've seen you,' she replied. For Bloodspot and the other wet-linked pilots, a folding cot under the wing was as far as their umbilical tubes would let them roam. A miserable, limited life. She had no idea how Bloodspot could stand it.

Her thigh muscle locked again. She swore and then, exasperated, unlocked her harness and got up in a crouch on her seat, massaging her leg.

'Not so bad, eh?' Bloodspot voxed as he saw her head rise above the canopy line.

'I'm not getting out.'

'Try it.'

'Shut up, Bloodspot.'

'It's liberating.'

He walked down his wing-strip and then gently lowered himself off the wing until he was standing on one of the rusting girders supporting his plane. His umbilicals were stretched taut. The girder he was balancing on was only a foot wide. He was bracing himself against the plane's fuselage with one hand, but then he took that away and stood hands free.

'Will you stop frigging around?' she voxed.

He grinned over at her, and started to do a little hip-sway movement, a parody of Gangster's victory dance.

She couldn't look. She rotated her ankle and flexed her calf to try to loosen her thigh. Finally, in defeat, she stood up in her seat.

The wind was cool on her face, the sun a vague burn. It was almost like actually flying. Flying without a plane. All she could see was the sky and the top of the city. She inhaled deeply.

'Flying makes it better,' Bloodspot said in her ear.

She looked over at him. He was still upright on the girder.

'This,' he said, gesturing to the umbilicals trailing behind him. *'It frigging sucks. Until I get up in the sky. Then I'm free, and it's worth it.'*

She stood tall, easing her leg, and inhaled again. She almost knew what he meant.

Lead's voice suddenly cut over the comms.

'Stop being arseholes and wake up. We've got a track.'

The vox had gone live suddenly. Jagdea listened to the crackling reports as she sat down and strapped back in. A Six-Six patrol, led by Blindside, had picked up a pair of hostiles moving west near the Pallisades. For reasons that weren't clear from the message, the bats had slipped past them and were gunning towards Vanitas. Blindside's flight was in pursuit, but Garrant's was ideally placed to catch them on the way through.

'Immediate release and form on me,' Garrant voxed. She could already hear the whine of his starter.

'Driver copies, Lead,' she replied, hitting the voltaic master.

'Bloodspot, copy.'

Jagdea glanced left as she secured her canopy. Bloodspot had already hoisted himself back into his cockpit, and was lidding up.

She cinched her straps. She'd walked the parish at lift, but she checked all her dials as power brought the preset headache back to life.

Slam-check. Vectors set. Auspex and modar live. Starter primed, pump engaged. Acquisition on, guns on. The compressor rattled as it spooled up. The damn hydraulics still and forever showed red.

'Lead to wings. Dead drop now.'

Jagdea felt her bird rock as Garrant's Cypra dropped off the girder perch. She released her landing claws and followed it.

Engine primed but unstarted, she dropped nose-first into free-fall. Bloodspot went a second after her. The nest of girders swayed like a gorse bush behind them as their combined weight let go. The face of the ruined spire rushed past her belly. The hive floor, so far away, was invisible below the smog bank, and that green sea was rushing up at her.

She fired the starter. The forced-plasma exciter ignited the fuel aspirating into the spinning turbine.

Flash-start. The turboram lit.

All three of them plunged into the smog bank, submerged for a second in thick and muffling darkness. Then they climbed back out of it, leaping clear from the upper layer like flying fish skipping out of a wave. Lead banked hard right and they followed him in line, Jagdea, then Bloodspot, a tight, trailing formation.

Garrant hit the burners. The blue Cypra M's exhausts lit up like furnace slits. Jagdea advanced power and burned off after him. She could feel Bloodspot right on her seven, sticking close.

She heard Garrant on comms, requesting intel from Six-Six Control, Blindside's flight, or any nearby ROP, but the standing smog seemed to be creating interference. She kept hearing 'two bats', and 'low level'.

They raced hard, surfing the top of the smog layer in the sunlight, their jet-wash leaving long wakes across the green fog that swirled slowly, broadened, overlapped, and became oddly complex. Hard left. Hard left. High blocks rose like islands from the green sea, and every turn or roll to avoid sent up a lazy wash of smog that licked and coiled against the passing structures. They ripped under the hard shadows of three sky-bridges, strobing the sunlight and the noise of their engines. Hard left. Four seconds out from Vanitas.

Two contacts lit up on her auspex. Jagdea heard Garrant cry out.

Two birds went past them like bullets in the other direction. Too close for comfort. But not bats. She'd seen a flash of pink.

They'd just crossed Blindside's flight. Blindside and Gangster. A second later, a third plane, an orange Voss Strike, went by.

Where the hell were the hostiles they were supposed to be trapping between them?

There was a flash. At first, Jagdea thought it was sun glare reflecting off her canopy. Bloodspot yelled out on the vox. Garrant, directly ahead of her, suddenly flat-planed his Cypra and vanished above and behind her in a hard loop.

There was a bat on them. Somewhere.

She glimpsed Bloodspot pull away sharply behind her. She took evasive in a hard, hard roll as las-fire streamed past her. The manoeuvre dropped her into the surface of the smoke, which whipped and coiled around her in a slow, travelling splash. Then she copied Garrant's move, and flat-planed, pulling the stick full aft to turn the whole underside of her Voss into a giant speed brake. Into grip. G-crush. Her speed dropped from 400 to 150 in less than a second. The bat went past her, curving out and climbing. Gangster's pink bird came out of nowhere and started to chase it hard, followed by the orange Strike – Tantrum – the third member of Blindside's flight.

Jagdea tried to climb. In an instant, her master threat alarm sounded. Weapons lock. She had a second bat on her.

She tried to turn. She did it with too much force, and nearly clipped the facade of a building and the arched powerducts running into it. Hard left. Another hard left. Throttle up. A split second look to her left showed her the shadow of her Voss flickering along the face of a building, and the dancing shadow of the bat right behind it. She was still in its weapon's envelope. Shots went past. One clipped her starboard wing and rocked her.

She was riding a long thoroughfare. The shadows slanting across the heavy smog seemed to indicate a break to her left, a gap her modar was too bemused to detect.

She took it. Hard. Too hard.

For the third time since her arrival at Six-Six, she bent the Voss into a ridiculous turn, her tail skidding the air, her power red-lining, her bird uncontrollable and threatening to spin out.

But this time, it was deliberate. It had happened by accident twice, forced on her. This time, she wrenched it right out of its performance scope.

It was an experiment she'd been thinking about, but she hadn't had time to read the spec-book to study up. And this was no experiment, because the bat had a murderlock and she was dead.

Tail 044 somehow stabilised as it came out of the whip-turn. It felt like it was tumbling for a second, and stalled hard, but it recovered. Banking hard, she bellied across the face of the side street's building.

Almost immediately, a bat went over her.

The other bat was still on her six, but the turn had robbed it of its firing lock. Jagdea ignored it and pulled high after the second bat, trying to slide it into her envelope. The bat behind her didn't fire, perhaps afraid of an overshot hitting his own wingman, on whose tail Jagdea was now clinging.

'Driver, break off,' she heard Garrant instruct.

Screw that. Jagdea rode tight, the Hell Talon ahead of her bobbing and weaving furiously. She was determined to get it to sit, her thumb ready on GUNS.

It pitched low. She went after it. The Razor on her shoulders, which she couldn't positively visualise, came after her. Hard right. Two cross-bridges and a powerduct loomed from the smog like piers at high tide. The Talon dipped under the first bridge, then angled up and over the second and the scaffolded duct. Jagdea braked hard, and then blew under all three, pulling her nose up and climbing sharply as she came clear. She got a brief modarlock, but the threat warning suddenly screamed. The Razor behind her had achieved lock and launched missiles.

She rolled hard left, banging a horsetail of flares in her wake. The twinkling pops of mag-phos sowed out behind her. Something detonated in an airburst.

Her roll had been clumsy. She rolled back right, hard as she could, to avoid collision with the pylons of a drum tower, knowing she was effectively moving back into the chasing Razor's envelope.

Tone ping. She unloaded. The Talon she was chasing seemed to know the gunfire was coming, and banked left.

It was as though it had banked directly into the path of the tracer fire that caught it.

Lead's Cypra whipped past, overtaking her to port. It was still gunning. Her burst of gunfire had driven the Talon directly into Garrant's sights. The bat jiggled, shedding debris, then began to pour smoke. It arced away ahead of them, increasing in speed, and plunged into the smog. A moment after it had vanished, an immense flash lit the smog from within, and puffed the fog up in a soft boil, like a depth charge detonating, submerged.

'Driver, break high,' Garrant ordered.

Jagdea pulled, and went high, climbing hard into G-strain. Garrant peeled out left. The Razor behind them shot past between them. Braced into the strain, vision squeezed, she tried to loop back onto it. But there were Gangster and Bloodspot, in recklessly tight formation, tight on its heels. The Razor was trying to turn out right, but they were sticking to it, and the buildings either side were too high.

Jagdea rolled down and added some burn, trying to cut the corner and meet the Razor as it hooked right. She lost visual on it, and on Bloodspot and Gangster, as they crossed behind the long, misty bulk of an Administratum building.

Almost at once, she saw Tantrum's orange Voss. Tantrum – she didn't know his real name – was a young smoke, and clearly out of his depth. He was hauling arse towards her with a red Razor at his six. Jagdea could see, even in a split-second look, that he was concentrating too hard on avoiding the street-canyon's obstructions rather than shaking the red bat.

How many bats *were* there? Jagdea made that four so far, including the Talon Garrant had bagged. She'd never heard of a hostile track of more than two or three in Vesperus.

She tried to drop hard and cover Tantrum's wing, but he had already shot past under her. The red Razor started to fire. Opening the throttle, Jagdea executed another of her insanely hard, skidding turns, managing to squeeze her Voss down and around against the face of the Administratum building without collision. The Voss growled and stumbled, but recovered. She'd lost a lot of power, but she managed to chop out a burst of fire that discouraged the red bat and forced him out of his lock on Tantrum.

Tantrum tried to lift. Jagdea rated in after the Razor climbing after him, leaning hard on her starboard wing. She saw a flash. A spray of bright metal. Tantrum had clipped the rail of an overhead processional in his effort to extend. Debris was flying off his wing and belly, but he managed to right himself. Wounded, and trailing white smoke, he began to bend left.

Was his bird still flyable? The red Razor was determined to make sure it wasn't. She opened her stride to get on its heels.

Their pursuit suddenly met Gangster and Bloodspot's pursuit coming the other way. The Razor they were chasing, the one that had given her such a run just moments before, had snaked the Six-Six pilots in and out of the tight street-grid in an effort to evade, and was now coming back at her. It went past Tantrum. Bloodspot and Gangster broke left and right to avoid the orange Voss. The bat went under Jagdea and disappeared.

She didn't care. The red bat had her entire focus. The near-miss had caused Tantrum to shed far too much speed. Gangster went by Jagdea to starboard, still intent on her quarry. Bloodspot went past her on the left, but he was already pulling a huge, fast loop to come in beside her on the red bat's tail.

It was one hell of an execute. Jagdea knew for sure the G-load of the loop would have blacked her out. Wet-linked, Bloodspot could weather far higher G-strain than she could.

The red bat jittered in her target reticule. It slipped right. Bloodspot came up beside her on the left, then rolled in on the bat in a flare of burners. He caught the red bat with a precise stream of las-fire. It disintegrated in mid-air, and the burning debris stippled the facade of the building beside them like a rain of meteors.

Bloodspot levelled out. They both rocked past the limping Tantrum.

'Nice kill,' she voxed, as best as her clenched breathing would allow.

Bloodspot made some reply, but it was drowned out by the crackling whoop and holler of Gangster, who, eight or nine blocks away, had finally caught and gutted the other Razor.

'Form up,' she heard Garrant call.

Wing-to-wing, she and Bloodspot circled Vanitas Tower and

began to ride back along the street to find Tantrum. They were going to have to nurse the boy home.

She saw them at the last minute. She saw them far too late for the visual to be worth making.

A Blade and a Talon. They knifed up out of the smoke below. They had both clearly been running unseen beneath the fog level. She couldn't even begin to figure how that was possible. The Talon was iridescent purple. The Hell Blade was banded black and silver. They had both come out of cover to go for Tantrum.

'Break! Break! Tantrum!' Jagdea yelled. Bloodspot was already extending on her, cooking on burners far too fast for the street's profile.

She went after him. The Talon picked them up, and rolled out hard, climbing up and over the roofline to the right. The Blade forgot about Tantrum, who was turning in a desperate effort to get out of the street line, and braked back almost alongside Bloodspot, who was way out in front of her.

Locked, Voss and bat started to roll, each one attempting to squeeze the other out ahead, a bravura knife-fight move that had no place in an urban street-hunt. Just watching them, watching them scissor-cross around a pylon hub, an overwalk, and then between two tall municipal structures, made her sick and dizzy, and abruptly broke the adrenaline spell. Her flying had been decent that morning, more confident, but the sight of them came like a slap, reminding her how tight things were, and how full of potential collisions. She felt herself tighten, not in g-lock, but in fear, hyper-aware again of the span of her wings, the height of her tail, and how lethal every cubic metre of this war sky was. The shred, which had been silent since lift, was back in force, poking at her ribs and squeezing her organs.

She went after them, but she could feel an anchor of restraint and caution on her. Over the vox, she heard both Garrant and

Blindside closing. She lost sight of Bloodspot and his rival, then saw them again as they came out from behind a row of warehousing. The Blade suddenly broke away, pulling off hard. The Talon reappeared, out of nowhere, and went across fast, the blaze of his belly-guns forcing Bloodspot into a vicious evasion. Jagdea thought he was going to spin out, but he pulled it back, and banked to get on the Talon.

The silver-banded Blade dropped back in and raked Bloodspot with a sustained burst that ripped down the length of his fuselage.

Even from a trailing distance, Jagdea could see the puff of debris and the cloud of voiding fluids, hydraulics or oil. Bloodspot yawed, and his nose began to drop. The Blade peeled off and vanished into the smog. There was no sign of the Talon.

Bloodspot's white Voss was dropping slowly, almost as though it was gliding. A scarf of black smoke was streaking out behind it from inside its shot-up tail-frame.

'Bloodspot, respond.'

'Copy you, Driver.'

'Keep the nose up.'

'Engine fire.'

'Are you hit?'

A pause.

'Negative.'

She was closing on his tail, staying wide to avoid the smoke he was trailing.

'Bloodspot.'

Nothing.

'Bloodspot, copy me. Can you make it back to deck?'

'Negative, Driver.'

'Confirm that.'

'Confirm. Negative. Got to set down.'

She gunned up beside him. She could see the vibration in his decelerating airframe. The starboard side of his fightbird was stitched with ugly black holes and stained almost peach with venting, aerosolised oil.

'Hold it up,' she snarled.

Nothing.

'Bloodspot, do you copy?'

'Copy, Driver.'

'Hold it up.'

She was trying to match his declining route while she worked her modar.

'There's a Munitorum precinct three miles out. Reads as a flat roof.'

'Negative, Driver. Not going to make it that far.'

She saw his Voss turn slightly, clumsily. He was heading for the warehousing. The plated roofs of those long sheds weren't flat, but the pitch wasn't too severe. It would have to do.

'Driver to Lead. Bloodspot is making emergency hard-down on the roof of the warehousing at Vanitas South. Scramble Medivalks and recovery.'

'Copy, Driver. Control is aware. Twelve minutes out.'

She had to bank to avoid an aerial mast. It was hard to stay with Bloodspot. She tried to close up again. He was too low.

'Bloodspot, Bloodspot, you're not going to make the roof.'

'Copy you.'

'Get your nose up. Duct it.'

'Ducts out, Driver.'

'Then burn for some lift!'

He didn't reply. The bone-white Voss waved in the air. Then its ram coughed out more black smoke and she saw a flash of hot exhaust.

It lifted a little. A little more. The warehousing, an oblong black monolith rising from the green fog, was coming up fast, like a cliff. Another burn. A little more lift. Another.

'Bring it up, Sorrentine! Bring it up!'

He came in over the lip, just. Ducting to stay with him, high over his shoulder, Jagdea saw his ducts fire then gag out. She ignored her own choke, trying to keep her Voss level. Bloodspot's bird all but dropped onto the warehousing roof. The Voss bounced, then began to slide and drag, raking sparks and bright streaks of bare metal behind it. He was going to slide down the pitch and right off the–

His landing claws got a grip and dug in, tearing the roof panels. The Voss came to rest, and flopped wearily onto its nose.

Jagdea circled once, and set down higher up the roof, pincering her claws into the metal. She cut power, disengaged her straps, and threw the canopy up.

The wind was cold and unexpectedly strong as she climbed out. The sunlight glare was fierce. She was in such a rush to dismount, she forgot to detach her suit cables, and they yanked her back as she tried to step away. She unplugged with a curse, then jumped down onto the roof.

It felt precarious. The roof was vast and wide, but she felt very exposed. The wind was brisk, and the pitch of the roof steeper now she was standing on it. She had no harness, no securing cable. She scrambled down the slope towards Bloodspot's bird, following the ragged scraped and silvery metal gouges it had left as it slithered. As she got nearer to the plane, and the edge of the roof, self-preservation made her sink down and clamber belly-up like a crab on her hands and feet.

Bloodspot's listing Voss was exhaling smoke in a haze. He had opened his lid, but not emerged. As she got closer, she could see the huge puncture marks, black divots running down the length of the starboard side. She could hear the drip of leaking fuel.

'Sorrentine!'

She got up and braced herself against the tail. The metal was slick with sticky fluid that had vented out of the blast holes. It was watery and pink, like diluted fuel mix.

But it didn't smell like fuel. It was all over her gloves and her sleeves.

It smelled like rust. It smelled like loam, the wet, organic aroma of a peat-bog. It wasn't promethium. His tanks were intact. The bat's shots had blown out the plasma reservoirs of his bio-impulse system.

She got up beside the cockpit. Sorrentine's face was as white as his Strike's paint-job. His eyes were open. He was dead.

Neuroreactive tanks perforated, Bloodspot and his bird had bled to death in the air.

Refectory, Intercept 66, Vesperus, 15:10

'Call sign Bloodspot,' Dampier said to the room. 'Lost thirteen thirty this afternoon. The Emperor protects, the Aeronautica remembers.'

She put the stick of chalk down. Bloodspot wasn't the only name she had crossed out, nor the only name the room had raised a glass to. A smoke, call sign Tailend, had been lost on another sortie about an hour before Sorrentine. Gumm had been on that flight, and Jagdea wanted to ask him what happened, but there was no sign of him in the refectory.

The mood was low. Despite the tallies – kills for Garrant and Gangster, as well as Merry Death, Blindside and Harlot – the loss of Sorrentine stung. For a man who did not – *could* not – mix socially with the rest of the Intercept, he had made his mark. From what Jagdea had seen out at Vanitas, Sorrentine's gunfighter skill had spoken for itself. Gangster was sitting on her own at the end of the bench, and waved Rockcrete off when he went to sit with her. She was fidgeting with a bottle of joiliq.

'How did they get by you?' she asked Blindside. He glared at her across the table.

'They just did,' he replied.

'The track said two,' said Jagdea. 'Two bats.'

Her plate of food, untouched, sat in front of her. She helped herself to joiliq from Blindside's bottle, and he didn't stop her.

'Two at first,' he said. 'We got on them. Me and Gangster.'

'Where was Tantrum?' she asked.

Blindside glanced aside. The smoke, Tantrum, was sitting at the next table over, trying to eat. He was a stocky young man with thick, dark, curly hair tied back in a pigtail. Jagdea knew he could hear them.

'Lagging behind, as usual,' said Blindside.

'Or... left behind?' she suggested.

'If he can't keep up, he can't keep up,' scowled Blindside.

'Or wing you in a knife-fight?' said Jagdea.

Blindside sat back and stared at her.

'The bats were gunning hard,' he said. 'I don't have to make excuses.'

'Nobody ever does,' she said. 'There were more than two, though. Six, in fact. Maybe seven.'

'The rest came in after, using the smog. Low level. Didn't see them. Couldn't track them.'

'That's a lot,' said Jagdea. 'More than usual.'

Blindside nodded. 'We were on the first two,' he said.

'You and Gangster?'

'Yeah. Then the rest came out of the soup on our arses. Broke our pattern. By the time we'd pulled around, they were all past us.'

'So that's something new then?' she asked.

'Yeah.'

Jagdea took a sip of joiliq, then tucked into her food.

'How'd you pull that turn?' Blindside asked after a moment. He was watching her eat, his expression somewhere between a brooding frown and a sulk. 'That hard frigging turn. Non-ballistic. I saw it. How'd you turn like that?'

'Just lucky, I guess,' she replied.

'No such thing as luck,' said Blindside.

'We better frigging hope there is,' she said.

Blindside got up and left. Jagdea finished her food, then stood to clear her tray.

'How *did* you make that turn?' a voice asked her quietly.

She saw it was Tantrum. The boy had swung around in his seat, and was looking up at her nervously, almost cowering. His face was shred-pale.

'You saw it too?'

'Yes.'

'As soon as I know,' she said, 'I'll tell you.'

She turned to go, then hesitated.

'Did anyone tell the others about Bloodspot?'

'The others?' Tantrum asked.

'Mischief and Slipstream,' she said. Mischief and Slipstream were the squadron's other two wet-linked pilots. She didn't know either of them, but she knew their names. 'They don't come up here. They're stuck in the hangar. Did anyone tell them?'

'Probably,' said Tantrum. 'The fitters, probably.'

'Not their job,' said Jagdea.

The sky had gone grey, and torrential rain had set in. Jagdea hoped it might clear the smog. She made her way down to the hangars. Her thigh still ached, and her whole torso from the groin up was sore with g-lock bruising. She realised she was walking with a limp.

She was still alert-ready. She went to check on her bird. On her way through hangar three, she saw Slipstream and Mischief on the opposite side. Their machines, a dark green Bolt and a silver Cypra M, were parked on adjacent stands, and the pilots had drawn their cots together to play cards, each at the limits of their bio-link umbilicals. Mischief was a young woman with prematurely white hair, Slipstream an older man with a wispy beard and a blotchy, shaved scalp. Both looked tired and sickly, bleached out like Sorrentine.

Jagdea paused, and thought about crossing to speak to them. She hesitated. She didn't know them, and they didn't know her. Before she could make her mind up, an engine revved, and Boa trundled by carrying Bloodspot's bone-white Voss in his forked jaws. The plane had been brought back to the deck by the squadron's recovery Destrier. It seemed limp and sagging in the tractor's clamp, and it was dripping a wet trail along the deck behind it as rainwater flushed out its guts.

She saw Mischief and Slipstream get up when they saw it. They stood, side by side, their game forgotten, and watched it roll past. Their faces were paler than ever.

Jagdea's Voss was in hangar one. Tarr and her crew were working on it. The air was damp. Rain was leaking through the ceiling and splashing down into standing water on the steel.

'This do you?' Tarr asked as she saw Jagdea approach. She yanked the tarp cover off a munition trolley and revealed a pair of heavy ventral autocannons. They were the same basic pattern, but not matched. Tarr must've looted them from the carcasses of two different Cypra M Twins.

'Do they work?' asked Jagdea.

'Do they frig,' growled Tarr. 'Yes, they work. You owe me, finding them. A brace will balance your wingload.'

'Appreciate it. How long to hook them up?'

'Thirty minutes to lock them on the rails, then another hour to wire them in. I presume you want to be able to toggle?'

Jagdea nodded. 'Yeah, them or the twin-linked K-sixty-eights. And both?'

'Call it forty-five minutes, then. I can fix an ammo counter too. There's a spare slot in the F-thirty-one loom. I can run it via logis heads-up, but I can give you a mechanical counter as well. If you want.'

'How much is this gonna cost me?' Jagdea asked.

'All the favours,' Tarr replied. She scrubbed oil off one of her augmetic hands with a rag. 'Three-hour fit, all told,' she said. 'But you're alert-ready, so I can't start the job until you're stood down.'

Jagdea nodded. If a shout came, she'd be in hot water if her bird was mid-fit.

'We're just giving Four-Four a refuel, wash and brush up,' said Tarr. 'Got some plate scorching on the wing there.'

'Took a couple of knocks.'

'And reloading your countermeasures.'

Tarr nodded to a crate containing the little metal drums of the mag-phos decoy flares.

'You keep using those things up.'

'Yes, well,' said Jagdea, 'it was a busy day.'

'Not over yet,' said Tarr.

Billet, Intercept 66, Vesperus, 16:59

Back in her billet, Jagdea went over sections of the spec-book line by line. It was heavy going, the language both technical and archaic. She'd borrowed a stylus, a crumpled notepad, and a head-torch from the fitters. Without the head-torch, the manual's small print would have been impossible to read in the billet's gloom.

She made notes. Nothing she was reading was confirming her

idea, but nothing was denying it either. The spec-book was hardly going to state or recommend a non-standard manoeuvre, especially one that bordered on suicidal. But there was a sweet spot, a place in an invisible set diagram where 'book-recommended application' and 'book-outlawed practice' crossed over. Nowhere did the spec-book specifically state she couldn't perform that turn, or that the Strike couldn't take it. It had never occurred to the compilers of the spec-book that any pilot would be dumb enough to try it. What she had discovered, by accident, on her first sortie, was an unexploited aspect of the Lightning Strike's performance envelope.

And it was deeply counter-intuitive.

She glanced up at the list of priorities she had chalked on the wall. There was a knock, and Gumm came in. He flinched, and shielded his eyes with his hand as she looked up.

'Sorry,' she said. She turned off the head-torch and took it off.

'Busy?' he asked.

'Working something out,' she said. 'A trick. That turn I mentioned.'

He nodded. 'Go on.'

'Once I'm sure. It requires the pilot to bend the shit out of the plane. Outside specs. It would take a degree of confidence. And some praying.'

'Lot of that here,' said Gumm. 'Have you noticed the way this outfit is split? Lead Garrant and some others. Sister Meredith. A lot of hardline faith and Imperial Truth.'

'We're defending a templum,' said Jagdea.

Gumm shook his head. 'We're using the ruin of a templum,' he corrected. 'I've never been part of a unit that's so strict in observance. Zealous. And yet the other half, Gangster and the rest, they couldn't be much more profane in their attitude and behaviour.'

'Some are both,' said Jagdea. 'Sister Merry Death, for one. Doesn't seem to me to be a big difference between her and Gangster, apart from what they say they believe in.'

He nodded. 'Tribal,' he said. 'Feels to me like Six-Six collects two types of pilots. Crusading zealots breathing the fire of the Throne, or crazy heathens with a death wish. You fly here, you become one or the other.'

'Three types,' she said. 'There are the ones like us who didn't ask to be here.'

'True,' he agreed. He sat down on the end of her cot, and sighed. 'Still, we'll be going home soon. Word in the fitting shops is that fuel is really low. There's got to be a replenishment run soon, next few days, or Six-Six is out of business. So we'll get our ride back.'

'Shame,' she said. 'I was just starting to enjoy it.'

He looked at her, no expression on his porcelain face, but shock in his eyes.

'I was joking,' she said. 'The only thing I want more than a ticket out of this place is a shower.'

'This rain keeps up,' he said, 'the tanks should fill. Maybe they'll lift the washroom ban.'

He toyed with a loose button on his jacket.

'I may have devised a trick of my own,' he said.

'Share?'

'Target systems,' he replied. 'Shooting range in this environment is really short, in most instances. This is guns I'm talking about, not seeking munitions. Shooting ranges are short, shorter than any open war sky. We've got the weapons lock system, and modarlock. Both tied, usually.'

'Belt and braces.'

'Right. But they're both calibrated for prediction and lag. A lock tone isn't a solid lock. It's a lock on wherever logis is predicting the target will be by the time you've actually shot.'

'That's a reaction time lag way less than a second, Gumm,' she said.

'Agreed. We never notice it. But Vesperus is so tight, that tiny lag matters. I think our targeters have a pre-programmed lead that is too generous for local conditions.'

'A lead and draw designed for open sky? By how much?'

'Far less than a second,' he said, 'so less than a metre, would be my guess. It would take a tech-priest to calculate it. But our weapons locks are infinitesimally overcompensating, which means we're missing more than we should.'

'How did you figure this?'

'Today,' he said. 'I was winging Merry Death and Tailend out at Regulus Cross. We scared up two bats. I had a clean murder-lock at one point, but my burst went wide. Nothing wrong with my guns. It got me thinking.'

'I hear you lost Tailend.'

'We had these two bats,' Gumm said. 'Hard chase. Tailend was way back. That poor kid had no idea. Then four more hostiles came in from nowhere. It turned into a rolling scrap. Harlot's flight caught up with us. Harlot, Rockcrete and Slumbag. It got very messy. Harlot bagged one, and the Sister splashed another. Somewhere, in the middle of all that, Tailend went down. Didn't even see it, or the bat that nailed him.'

Jagdea exhaled slowly.

'Sounds like the knife-fight I went through. Six bats at least. Which is new.'

'New tactic, do you think?' Gumm asked.

'What do you think?'

'Felt like it,' he said. 'The enemy knows we're here, and it knows we're getting decent kills on the singletons and duos they've been using. So they're lifting larger groups. Two chasers out front, acting like bait to trigger an intercept, then the others to jump us when we commit.'

'Double formation?'

'No, one staggered formation,' he replied. 'Some of the Razors I met today were turning fast and tight. I don't think they were carrying payloads for ground targets. Too light on their feet. They were there, with unladen dynamics, to hunt interceptors.'

'That's a happy thought,' she said. 'What do we do about the target systems? Turn the damn things off and go boresight?'

'Maybe not,' said Gumm. 'I'm going to talk to the enginseers. There may be a zero-value default we can reset to, and wipe any logis compensations.'

'Our aim will be off, long range.'

'There *is* no long range, Jagdea,' he said.

An alarm sounded. Jagdea got up and grabbed her helmet.

'I'm alert-ready,' she said.

'Me too,' he replied.

By the time they were in the corridor, they could hear their names on the call-list crackling over the vox-speaker. They started to run.

Jagdea saw Wilzar up ahead. 'Hangar bay!' she yelled at him as she ran past. 'Tonight! New tricks!'

'New tricks?'

'Bring any smoke you know who wants to learn! Twenty-two hundred, Wilzar!'

Wilzar stood and watched them race away down the corridor.

'What if...' he said to no one. 'What if you don't come back?'

Fourth drop, Intercept 66, Vesperus, 17:51

Engine primed but unstarted, she dropped nose-first off the Campanile into free-fall. Into heavy rain. Into gathering darkness.

Gumm went a second after her. Merry Death led the way.

Flash-start. The turboram lit.

All three of them raked up on a hard burn and turned west into the rain.

There was less than an hour of daylight left, but the rain and undercast had reduced the light levels to a murky dusk. At least the rainstorm had cleared the worst of the smog.

'Merry Death to wings. De-conflict auspex.'

'Driver, copy,' Jagdea replied.

'Dollface, copy.'

'ROP Four-Two has a track,' the Sister voxed. *'Passing the refinery belt, moving south-west. Two hundred and forty-six seconds out. Accept track and form on me, over.'*

'Driver, accepting track,' Jagdea voxed, throwing a switch to let the plot load on her auspex display. The CAD display, in all its multi-coloured headache, seemed too bright. In the lousy light, she was getting reflections on her canopy, and without her visor lowered for optic boost, the brilliance of the display was going to mess with her night vision.

'Dollface, accepting track,' she heard Gumm report.

Could she dim the display? There had to be a dial for that, but the CAD was so damn complicated, she couldn't remember where. Maybe, though it was fitted with everything else, the Voss didn't have one. The headache was called the headache for a reason.

They climbed a little, whipping between the huge and blackened flanks of the mid-hive spires. Flying the hive in poor vis was a whole new kind of nasty. Everything was a hard jerk on the stick to maintain clearance and take hard turns. Shadows snatched at her. Some of the shadows were solid: gantries, derricks, pylons and spars. She kept her focus on the amber burn of Merry Death's bobbing, jerking exhaust.

Sister Meredith's voice came over the link.

'Offer now reverence and thanks to the Saint of the Sabbat and her

brother-in-light Kiodrus, hallowed be, that we may find the sinners and castigate them, in the name of the God-Emperor.'

A blessing huddle? In the air? The dead drop had been a slam, with no time for talk on the deck.

'May we find the foe, and the sinners who defy the light of all truth,' Merry Death continued. *'May we seek them out with all fury, and may we smite them with your wrath. Bless us this hour with your strength that we might not fail you. Grant that we may kill sinners as the God-Emperor has asked of us, copy.'*

She was waiting for a response.

'The Emperor protects,' she heard Gumm reply.

'The Aeronautica remembers,' Jagdea said.

They banked left at Westphor Union, and tore down the mile-long Union Transit tunnel in single file, their power plants echoing and howling off the vast rockcrete chute. Jagdea glimpsed torn roadway and burned-out ground transports below. The tunnel was big, a long tube, but it felt painfully tight. The shred was riding behind her again, and licking the back of her neck. She could smell the stink of her own breath and sweat.

'Stay low on exit,' Merry Death advised.

They were reaching the end of the road tunnel, rating hard. Jagdea saw Merry Death dip a little. She nudged down.

They shot out of the tunnel, directly onto the span of the Union Suspension Bridge beyond. The bridge was a massive superstructure, joining the mid-hive with the western conurbs. It crossed a four-mile-wide vent basin, but the basin had long since flooded, and was swamped with toxic black water almost up to span level.

There were heavy steel spars at regular intervals above the bridge road, fifty yards up. That was why Merry Death had told them to stay low. If they'd come out of the tunnel too high, they would have hit the spars. As it was, they were gunning across the bridge, boxed in; the buckled roadway below them, suspension cables and girder-work to either side, spars above. Though grand in scale, the bridge had not been built for aerial transit. They were in a cage. The spars strobed past overhead. High-tension bridge cables moaned and whined at the thunder of their engines. There was a ringing noise like a stick being held to spinning metal spokes.

'On exit, climb hard,' voxed Merry Death.

No shit. The end of the bridge was coming up fast. The roadway exit ramp sloped down into an unflyable street zone. The second they cleared the bridge spars, Jagdea pulled the stick hard back and hit burn to avoid spitting straight out into the buildings ahead. G-lock. Grip position. Her breath clamped. The shred chuckled. She followed Merry Death in a near-vertical ascent up the face of a soaring hab-block.

Ahead, Merry Death's black-and-white Bolt banked out across the roofline, and levelled. Jagdea matched her. Gumm followed her tail.

They turned in under the flying buttresses of a reactor complex, and opened out down a long canyon with walls made of dirty spires.

'Merry Death to Driver. Where are your stores?'

'I'm not loading stores, over.'

'Is there a fault?'

'A choice, over.'

'That is non-standard.'

'Driver, copy. That's me.'

'How will you kill sinners without missiles?'

'The God-Emperor will show me a way, over.'

'I will report you for this infraction when we return,' Merry Death stated.

For what? Jagdea wondered. The lack of standard order-out payload, or taking the Emperor's name in vain?

But it wasn't a lie. Her thumb was ready on GUNS. Tarr hadn't fitted the cannons yet, so all Jagdea had was the twin-linked K68s. But they were more than enough to kill something.

She thought about following Gumm's tip, and actually turning her targeters off, but that would take a display blank-down and a logis sub-system reset, which would require several seconds, several console controls, and sustained visual attention. She had none to spare. There was no time to look at the CAD because she had to keep her eyes on the way ahead at all times. Any distraction would pile her in.

Still, the multi-coloured lights of the CAD were glinting off the canopy. They reminded Jagdea of the lights on the radiation counters she'd glimpsed through the rebreather hood when Lopard had led her through the dead zone. Distractions. Visual noise.

They banked down a transit, under a series of powerducts, and swung out into the refinery belt, a vast industrial zone of processors, silos and reactor towers. The rain was heavy still, and the air was dirty from ash, micro-particulates and residual clouds of refinery waste.

Two hundred and twenty seconds. Merry Death's pace and hazardous route had chopped a whole twenty-six seconds off the intercept time.

'Contact, west-west,' Gumm called.

Auspex had just picked it up. Two contacts, moving fast and low. The three birds veered away, and came around the immense drum of a bulk reactor plant that dominated the landscape like a mile-high tree stump.

There was a red glow. Reactor fires were still burning inside it, over a year later.

They punched through a trailing plume of polluted smoke. Jagdea saw the tell-tale glint of exhaust flares at her low nine.

'Driver, contacts low nine position, south-east. Follow me,' she voxed, banking out hard in pursuit.

She heard Merry Death say something, probably an objection. She ignored her. Gumm was right on her wing. Guns live. Target system up. Hard steer around a venting scoop, fast dip under a derelict mining conveyer.

Two Talons, burning straight through a manufactory district. One suddenly banked out hard. They'd been detected.

'Stay on it,' Merry Death voxed. *'Pursuing the runner.'*

'Copy, Merry Death,' Jagdea replied.

She shunted the throttle and rode the kick. G-strain grabbed her as she pulled in past a factory siding to get on the Talon's tail. She gripped into it, into the squeeze of her pressure suit, feeling every bruise sing. Her thigh started to cramp. Her vision narrowed, then cleared as she pulled true and the load slid away. The Talon was trying to extend. She came in high, leaning on her port wing, hunting for a lock. Manufactory structures lashed past. The Talon executed a hard right onto an adjacent concourse without warning. It had shaken her.

But she pulled her suicide turn.

She heard Gumm yell her name as he shot past, unable to match.

She wrenched the Voss into the twist, feeling it stall out and stumble. She'd overcooked it this time, too confident in her ability to bend the performance beyond book limits. Logis red-lined and screamed. G-load greyed her out. The shred swallowed her, laughing at her stupidity.

Then the Voss levelled as logis compensated for her madness with ducts. The plane hated her. The logis-systems hated her. They did not wish to be treated with such disrespect. They would teach her how the plane wanted to be flown. Wild, fast, true.

That was fine with her.

The Talon ahead banked and faltered, startled to find that she was still, somehow, on its six.

Murderlock.

She let go with the guns.

The Talon wrenched to port, avoiding her chasing shots. But it was too frantic, and clipped a fuelling derrick, losing a significant portion of wing-edge.

She blew past it as it tumbled, trying to level. She banked hard right around a trio of waste tanks to come around and get her nose back on it. Hard G-strain, almost choking on bile and adrenaline. The shred wasn't laughing any more. It was gnawing her heart out through her ribs.

The wounded Talon was rising, climbing hard. It was slipping out of her reticule.

Gumm's Voss came across at ultra-high rate from the north, his cannons flashing. The Talon went up in an annihilating fireball, scattering burning debris.

Clean kill.

'Set them up,' Gumm voxed.

'Knock them down,' Jagdea responded, levelling out.

There was a bright flash, low in the darkening sky to the west.

'Kill!' they heard Merry Death shout on the link.

'Splash two,' chuckled Gumm as they turned out to find her.

Intercept 66, Vesperus, 19:41

'That's two for you,' Jagdea said to Gumm as they dismounted in the hangar.

'Technically,' he agreed, pulling off his helmet. 'That Talon was yours, to be fair. I only got it because you'd popped it up.'

'I don't think you get a tally mark for an assist,' she replied.

Jagdea peeled her gloves off. She could feel the sweat on her back. The liner of the pressure suit was either too old or too dirty to wick her perspiration away. Her shoulders ached from strap-drag, and her legs felt weak. She looked over at Tarr.

'I'm off the clock, chief,' she said. 'Can you fit the cannons?'

Tarr nodded. 'Be done for morning,' she said.

'I'll be back in an hour,' said Jagdea. 'Need some food, but there are some things I want to do.'

Tarr shrugged. She didn't care. 'Coming to the wake?' she asked.

'Wake?'

'For Bloodspot,' Tarr said. 'Midnight. Harlot says you know where to come.'

'Maybe,' said Jagdea.

They passed Merry Death on their way out of the hangar. She was climbing down from her Bolt.

'Good kill,' the Sister said to Gumm. 'I am reporting your lack of stores,' she said to Jagdea.

'May the God-Emperor forgive you,' Jagdea replied.

She limped up the corridor towards the refectory beside Gumm.

'That turn?' he said.

'You saw it?'

'I could hardly miss it,' he replied softly. 'That was the turn you were talking about? Your trick?'

'Not the best example, but yes. Want to learn how it's done?'

'I don't,' said Gumm, 'because I enjoy being alive.'

'You want to *really*.' She smiled.

'What I really want, Jagdea,' he replied, 'is to hear you trying to explain it to a bunch of smokes. You honestly intend to teach them that?'

'Well, they're dead anyway,' she said. 'Least this way, they'll go out with a bang.'

'That's a terrible philosophy,' he said.

'It is,' she admitted. 'I've been spending too much time with Harlot.'

'I don't want to know what you get up to with Harlot,' he said.

'Nothing to know,' she said. 'But we'll talk about something else. Let's talk about CAD displays.'

Hangar bay, Intercept 66, Vesperus, 20:47

Full of food and freed from her flightsuit, Jagdea wandered back into the hangar. It was quiet now, the exhaust stink dissipating. Rainwater was still dripping from the ceiling. Tarr, an enginseer, and two of her fitters were at work, under lamps, securing the cannons to Jagdea's rails.

Jagdea strolled over.

'We're nowhere near done,' Tarr growled at her before she could speak.

'Not here to chivvy you,' Jagdea said.

'Just want to watch the real experts at work?' Tarr asked with a sneer.

'Sure,' said Jagdea. 'When do they get here?'

Tarr glowered. 'What do you want, Driver?' she asked.

Jagdea thought for a moment. She pointed at a nearby tool trolley.

'That roll of lagging tape,' she said.

'Help yourself.'

Jagdea took the roll, a tight drum of grey adhesive taping, and climbed up onto Four-Four's WALK ONLY. The canopy was open. She peered in. The cockpit stank of her stale sweat. Or maybe that was just her. One of the wiring looms had been pulled clear of the CAD like a small drawer to expose the data-card slots, and a small mechanical roll-counter had been screwed to the left-hand slope of the CAD's cowling, its wires dangling. Power was off.

'Can I throw the master voltaic?' she called down.

'Wait,' Tarr's voice replied. A pause. 'All right.'

Jagdea flipped the voltaics, and the CAD lit up. Bright as ever. She peeled a short length of the adhesive roll, tore it off with her teeth and held it up to the lamp rigs. That wouldn't work.

'Chief? Have you got any hose tape?' she called down. 'The heavy-duty stuff?'

She heard Tarr swear somewhere below her, and a prone inspection cart trundle across the deck. Tarr rose into view.

'Hose tape?' she asked.

'The heavyweight kind?'

'Probably.' Tarr walked over to a tool trolley. 'This bitch wants everything,' Jagdea heard Tarr mutter to her crew, who were somewhere under the bird.

Tarr held up a roll of black tape.

'Like this?'

'Yes,' said Jagdea. Tarr tossed it up to her. Jagdea snatched it out of the air one-handed, and threw the lagging tape back with the other. Tarr caught it against her chest and dropped it back in the trolley.

'This bitch thanks you,' Jagdea said. She climbed into the cockpit. Inside, with some effort, she reached down, face pressed against the CAD, and slipped her utility knife out of its boot sheath. She tore off several short strips of the heavy black tape, and fixed them along the edge of her canopy frame. Then she took the strips one by one, and carefully began to stick them over various banks of the console, trimming each to fit with her blade. When the strips were used, she tore off more and continued. The tape was thick, thicker than the lagging tape. It was not light-permeable.

The work, painstaking, took several minutes.

'Frig are you doing, Driver?' Tarr asked, suddenly leaning in the cockpit at her shoulder.

'Masking to reduce light noise and reflection,' said Jagdea.

'You're masking controls,' Tarr began.

'None that I need,' Jagdea said. 'The Voss has way too much instrumentation. Half this stuff is completely redundant in a war sky like Vesperus. I don't need the distraction.'

'But–'

'Proximity sensors?' Jagdea said, pointing. 'Don't need them. I've got eyes. Secondary Auspex? Useless. Attitude?'

'You've got plenty of that,' said Tarr.

'So I don't need that either,' said Jagdea. 'Seriously, there's no open sky out there, Chief. You are constantly surrounded by verticals and horizontals to reference. Logis flow? No thanks. Logis activity? Not for me. Ad-mix monitor? I can listen for engine tone, and if it's gagging on a dead drop, I won't need six different red lights to tell me so. Hardpoint reporting? Surplus to requirement.'

'I suppose, with hard guns…' Tarr admitted.

'There's too much going on in here,' said Jagdea, 'when there's already far too much going on outside. In Vesperus, we shouldn't be looking at our CAD. We should barely be looking at our visor data. We should be looking at the city every second, or it will kill us. Plus, this frigging lightshow reflects off the canopy. Easy to mistake for passing fire, or distant exhaust burns, so that compounds awareness errors. I want everything I don't need masked.'

Tarr frowned, thinking. 'Done this before?' she asked.

'Never,' said Jagdea. 'Never flown a sky like this before.'

Tarr pondered for a moment more.

'You probably don't want Aux/Gfd or Range Graphing then,' she said, leaning in and pointing.

'You're damn right,' said Jagdea, tearing off more strips. 'And I'd kill the sound too if I could.'

'Sound?'

'The cautions. Again, so many. Proximity comes on auto-set, so I have to deselect. Analytics has a chime for everything. Countermeasure Dispense. Logis Instruct and Logis Compensate. G-load meter. Autotrack.'

'Some of those are important,' said Tarr doubtfully.

'Usually,' agreed Jagdea. 'But not if they all go off at once, and they keep all going off at once because of the conditions. In most cases, it's a false alert. If it's really something vital then, well, it's probably too late. I need comms. I need master threat and lock threat warning. And I need murderlock. That's all.'

Tarr rubbed the inside of her cheek with the tip of her tongue thoughtfully.

'I can get into the advisory hub and reset them all to a mute default,' she said. 'Except the ones you mentioned. If you like.'

'You can?'

'Sure,' said Tarr. 'If it works, it works. If it kills you, you can't come back and complain. Now are you done? I want to flip the power off again.'

'One more,' said Jagdea. She tore off a final, small patch of tape and stuck it down over the hydraulics indicator, hiding its red glow.

'That one was just pissing me off,' she said.

Hangar bay, Intercept 66, Vesperus, 22:05

'We're all scared,' said Jagdea. 'This is a hell of a sky, and there is no safe way to fly it. Me and Gumm, we've been trying to find new methods. New tricks. Ways of dealing with this particular environment.'

She paused.

'Scratch that,' she said. 'We've been trying to find ways to stay alive. Nothing I've got to say is recommended. Nor is it officially sanctioned. But if I say it out loud, and you happen to be in the same room in earshot…'

She shrugged. Gumm, seated to her left, said nothing. Her audience maintained an uneasy silence.

'I'm not telling you to do any of this,' she went on. 'Pick and choose. Take what you want. Ignore everything. It's up to you.'

'I just want to do better,' said Wilzar quietly.

'I just want to learn that turn,' said Tantrum.

Jagdea nodded. Four of them had turned up. Just four smokes. Wilzar, Tantrum and two others Jagdea didn't know. They had pulled up crates or folding stools to sit in front of her. None of them looked comfortable being there. Gumm was staying out of the way, off to her side, observing. Behind her, Tarr and her team were still working on Tail 044, the only other people in the hangar.

'You want to do better?' Jagdea asked Wilzar.

He nodded, weary. 'I thought I could frigging fly, Jagdea.'

'You can,' she said. She glanced at the others. 'All of you. Tell me, who are the best bat-killers in Six-Six?'

'Gangster,' said Tantrum. 'Gangster and Merry Death.'

'Lead Garrant,' said Wilzar. 'Blindside. Slumbag. Jongleur.'

'Harlot,' said one of the smokes, a young woman.

'Bloodspot,' said the other.

Jagdea nodded sadly.

'Yes, he was,' she agreed. 'So what have they all got that you haven't?'

'Kills,' said Tantrum emphatically. The smokes laughed.

'Yes, but not that,' said Jagdea. 'That's the goal. That, and being alive long enough to collect kills. I have no doubt that some or all of you have kills. You all got transferred to Six-Six from active units, recommended by your previous leads. Wilzar's a multi-ace. I know that for a fact.'

Wilzar looked at the deck, embarrassed.

'Something else,' said Jagdea.

'Hours,' said the girl.

'Right,' Jagdea nodded. 'Logged hours. They're all older. They're all veterans. Banking hours on the log doesn't necessarily make you a better pilot. But experience gives you confidence. You think less about what you're doing, and more about just doing it. Muscle memory. Familiarity. Maybe an adaptive attitude to regulations and the rules you learned in flight school. The names you mentioned are the best bat-killers, because they've accumulated the confidence to fly on instinct. You've seen them all in the refectory. Taking no shit. The swagger, in some cases. The way they act on the deck is the way they act in the sky. Proactive. Positive.'

'They're not afraid?' asked Tantrum.

'They're as shit-scared as you,' said Jagdea. 'But they use that fear, that shred, to be bold. Listen, you're all good pilots. I don't know you, but I don't have to review your records to know that. You are all Aeronautica. Just wearing that pin means you have trained to the highest level, shown potential and talent, made every cut, and reached the top percentile. You can all fly like bastards. It's in you. You can probably fly better than me or Gumm, because you're young. Sharper, quicker reflexes. I envy you. The bat-killers in Six-Six treat you like dirt, *because* you're young. They can taste your caution. And because you're young, you treat yourselves like dirt. Remember who the frig you are, and what you can do.'

'So this is about confidence?' asked Tantrum. 'An assertiveness seminar? Screw that.'

The others laughed, even Wilzar.

'What's your name?' Jagdea asked.

'Tantrum,' said Tantrum, stiffening slightly as she looked at him.

'No, your name.'

'Glick,' he said cautiously. 'Arvi Glick.'

'What you said right there, Glick,' she told him, 'that was exactly it. You took the piss. Just for a second, you remembered I was simply another arsehole like you, shooting my mouth off. You don't need me to tell you about confidence. But now I've put you on the spot, look at you. Tensed up, eyes averted. Look at me.'

Tantrum slowly raised his head, and made eye contact.

'I can't teach you confidence, Glick,' she said. 'But I can point out you've got some.'

Jagdea took a few steps, and looked around.

'What's your name?' she asked the girl.

'Kinny Inthimal,' she replied. She was slight, and good-looking, her blonde hair wrenched back in a bun. She was wearing round, pink-tinted sun shades. She regarded Jagdea with a curious intensity. 'Call sign Camo.'

'How'd you earn that?'

'I transferred in from the Fifty-Third Tropic,' the girl said. 'Day I arrived, I was wearing puzzle-pattern kit, because that was Fifty-Third issue. Someone called me Camo, and that was it. After three days, I burned the kit and went to the stores.'

She glanced down at the worn, hand-me-down crew gear she was wearing.

'They still called me Camo,' she said.

'Sucks,' said Jagdea. 'So wear it.'

'The... camo?'

'The name,' Jagdea replied. 'You're here tonight with Driver, Dollface, Tantrum and Smoke. I think you got off light. You know what's worse than a nickname? No nickname, which means they haven't even registered you.'

'Well...' Camo shrugged. 'It *does* rhyme with "Ammo".'

'Yes, it frigging does,' said Jagdea. 'What about you?'

The other smoke was a young, solemn man with very dark skin. He was wearing a red flightsuit and a black flying coat. He had sat furthest away, the most suspicious and dubious of the four.

'Maksim Steeley,' he said. 'Call sign Nosedive.'

'Let me guess... bad drop on your first day?'

'And every day afterwards,' said Steeley.

'Why did you come here tonight?'

'I wanted to hear about the turn,' he said. 'Tantrum... I mean, Glick... he told me about the turn.'

'Then let's talk about that,' said Jagdea. 'You all fly Strikes?'

Wilzar nodded. Camo, Tantrum and Nosedive all chorused, 'Yes, mam.'

'Oh, frig that,' said Jagdea. 'I don't work here. Call sign, or Jagdea. Again, you all fly the Voss?'

The group answered, 'Yes, Driver.'

'The Voss is a grox,' said Jagdea. She looked over at her own bird. Tarr and her adepts had finished work, but they were leaning on the airframe, watching, with amused looks on their faces. 'It's a grox to fly at the best of times, but it gives back plenty if you learn its quirks. However, it's the wrong plane for this war sky. It's way over-specced, and too fast. We can thank the Munitorum for supplying us with the wrong tool.'

'Is there a right plane?' asked Tantrum.

'No,' said Gumm, arms folded.

'Vesperus is a unique environment,' said Jagdea. 'It's determined to kill us. The Voss wants to run fast and high. The hive makes us fly low and tight. The Voss is battling you at every step. Choke. Stumble. Logis-correction. You're all flying it too slow.'

'I don't want to die,' said Nosedive.

'That's reasonable,' said Jagdea. 'But I bet every time you drop, you get left behind, no matter what the vets in your flight are sticking. Yes, we're back on confidence, Glick. I've said this to Wilzar, and I'll say it to you – a miss is as good as a mile. Everywhere you go in this hive, you'll be fitting through gaps, dodging obstruction, avoiding collision. Everywhere. So ignore clearance regs. Ignore proximity alarms. Mute them. Get your fitters to strip them out, even. If your bird's going to fit through a gap, it's going to fit, whether you have ten feet clearance all around, or you skin the damn paint. You know what your birds will fit through. You're hesitant because it seems unnatural, and it seems unnatural because it is. Flying cautiously, at a low rate, will get you killed, because there's no power in your wings for tight turning. Up that rate, you move quicker so you're more agile. And there's less time to think, and therefore overthink, and force an error. If you're going to fit, you're going to fit.'

'And if you don't?' asked Nosedive.

'Then it's over,' said Gumm, 'and you died trying, rather than failing.'

'The real killer is timidity,' said Jagdea. 'This turn Tantrum's so excited about–'

'It was frigging mad,' said Tantrum. 'Driver muscled her bird in, like, an "L"-shaped turn.' He gestured, using his hands to try to describe the motion and angle. 'No decel. Just hard over. Thought she was going to stall.'

'So did I,' said Jagdea. 'And I did. Hard. Trust me, I didn't mean to do it the first time it happened. I was scared out of my mind. A turn that tight is not in the spec-book, because the magi knew it would trigger the Voss' basic propensity to choke-up and stumble. A complete loss of pilot control.'

'So how did you come out of it?' asked Camo.

'I didn't,' said Jagdea.

'What–?'

'I didn't,' Jagdea repeated. 'The Voss did.'

'Wait…' said Tantrum, frowning.

'Every time I've done it, I've lost all dynamic control,' said Jagdea. 'If I'd done it in a Twin or a Bolt, there would have been more stability, and the stick would have stayed live for longer. But even a Twin or a Bolt would have stacked in. That L-shaped turn is unrecoverable.'

'But–' Tantrum began.

'For a pilot. Any pilot.' Jagdea paused. She sniffed. 'I'm not that good,' she said. 'But unlike a Twin or a Bolt, the Strike is logis-heavy. You all know that. It auto-corrects everything. Trim, lift, balance, power. The logis-engines are running constantly, compensating in ways that we don't even notice. And you cannot turn them off or shut them down, because the Voss would become an unflyable anvil, even fast and straight. So I didn't come out of that turn. The logis-engines compensated for a gross pilot error.'

'So… you crashed it, and it saved you?' asked Wilzar.

'Yeah, basically. I lost control, and bent the Voss into a stumble, its primary design flaw. Logis read that, read the critical loss of ballistic stability, and shunted power to the ducts faster than I ever could. Because the logis-engines are well aware of the Voss' primary design flaw too. They are templated to predict it and respond. Even in an extreme case.'

'I'd say *particularly* in an extreme case,' Gumm said, and stood up. His voice was, as ever, deceptively soft and silky. 'Jagdea accidentally learned that the Voss can do something its builders never realised. The Voss is oversensitive, but if you really bend it, way beyond the book, it bites back hard.'

'You're saying this turn,' Tantrum asked, in disbelief, 'you're saying we have to lose control?'

'You have to commit and turn into it hard, knowing that there will be a total control departure,' said Jagdea. 'Total. You have to submit. And that seems counter-intuitive. It seems insanely unnatural, like punching through a gap with zero clearance, because, once again, it absolutely is. You have to voluntarily give up the one thing we are trained to maintain. Pilot control.'

'Just give in?' asked Tantrum.

'There's more to it than that,' said Jagdea, 'as I will explain. You have to fight coming out of it. Fight to support the logis-driven efforts. But yes, in essence, you've got to give in. Relinquish control.'

'I imagine praying helps too,' said Nosedive.

'Doesn't hurt,' agreed Jagdea.

'So this L-shaped turn…' Wilzar began.

'J-turn,' said Camo with a smile. 'It's a hard jag. Should call it the J-turn. Because Bree Jagdea…'

Jagdea looked at her. Camo was grinning. What was that? Kissing instructor's backside? Or something else? What had the girl heard?

She ignored the lingering unease, and quickly ran through the basic combination of stick, rudder and thrust required to regain control from a logis-corrected turn.

'All right,' she said. 'That's enough. Go away and think about what I've said, especially the confidence part. Rest. If you haven't eaten, eat. If you haven't hydrated, hydrate. Sleep, food and water are the best tips I can give you. If you're still interested, come back tomorrow night and I'll tell you what I know about hose tape.'

'Hose tape?' Gumm asked, walking over to her as the smokes left.

'You'll love it.' She looked at him. 'I don't know if I've just done more harm than good.'

'We'll see,' he replied.

'I was disappointed there were only four of them.'

'There will be more tomorrow,' he said. 'I'd put money on it.'

'Are you going to Sorrentine's farewell?'

He shook his head. 'Not my kind of thing,' Gumm replied. 'See you tomorrow.'

He strolled out of the hangar. Jagdea turned and saw Tarr grinning at her.

'That was some crazy shit,' said the chief.

'You don't approve?'

'Not my place to say,' Tarr replied. 'But I'll tell you one thing. It's the first time I've seen any of those frigging smokes look more than plain terrified. You've just made them think. That's gotta count.'

'You finished with my bird?' asked Jagdea.

'Yeah,' said Tarr. 'I'm clocking off. You've got company, by the way.'

She pointed with a jerk of her chin. Down at the far end of the hangar, Exec Badler was standing beside a Twin.

'He's been here the last ten minutes,' said Tarr.

'Great,' said Jagdea.

Badler strolled towards her as Tarr stepped away to pack her tools.

'Interesting huddle,' Badler remarked.

'You have a problem with it?' Jagdea asked.

He made no comment.

'Garrant sent me down,' he said, instead. 'Sister Meredith filed a complaint. Said you went up without loading your rails today. Garrant said you'd done the same thing earlier.'

'This an official write-up?'

Badler shook his head. 'No, or he'd have sent Dampier, not me.'

'I had an issue with the stores,' said Jagdea. She gestured

towards her Voss. The heavy autocannons were hooked up under the raked wings, their muzzles extended proud of the nose guns. 'Chief Tarr found me some hard guns. I'll be lifting with rails loaded tomorrow.'

Badler frowned.

'The standard order-out is missiles,' he said.

'These will do,' said Jagdea.

'Was there an issue with munition connective, Chief?' Badler called out to Tarr. The chief was hooking spanners into a cart tray. She looked back, uncomfortable.

'Don't make her lie for me,' Jagdea said to Badler. 'The heaters we stock are shit, and you know it. I don't want them on my wings.'

'That's not your damn call, Driver,' he said.

'Well, I made it mine,' she replied. 'If Garrant has a problem with that, he can come and tell me so himself.'

'This isn't a circus, Driver,' said Badler.

'All evidence to the contrary,' Jagdea replied.

The exec glared at her for a moment, then turned and walked away.

'They've changed tactics,' she called out after him.

He stopped and looked back at her.

'The bats,' she said. 'Not just one or two bomb-carriers trying to run the hive. They've observed our hunting habits. Now it's bait and switch. Chasers out front to lead us in, then hunters in a pack behind to come at our six. Staggered trailing formation. Not all of the bats are bomb-heavy, so they are knife-fight ready.'

'We are aware,' said Badler. 'That seems to have been the case several times.'

'What are you going to do about it?' she asked.

'With the fuel we have left, and the birds and pilots available?' Badler replied. 'There's not a hell of a lot we *can* do.'

DAY 92

Dead zone chantry, Intercept 66, Vesperus, 00:25

Jagdea could hear and smell the wake before she reached it.

Past midnight, the rain still hammering. The dirty halls leading to the dead zone hatch Lopard had shown her smelled damp, and water trailed down the cracked walls.

She could hear music. The crates disguising the rusted hatch had been moved out of the way, and the hatch itself was ajar. A sallow, wiry man, a fitter Jagdea believed went by the name Fari, was slouching against the frame, smoking a lho-stick. A lookout. He watched her approach.

'Driver,' he muttered, then stood up straight to haul the hatch open for her.

There were still no voltaics in the large chamber beyond, but this time she could see more of it. Light – from lamps and flames – was shafting in through the door on the far side. With it came the noise of voices, laughter, and music. The golden half-light revealed that the chamber's floor of ashlar tile was inlaid with Ecclesiarchy emblems. It gleamed off the high, gilded ceiling, and warmed the faces of the cherubs and saints gazing from the walls. It also glinted off the broken bottles littering the floor. She could smell alcohol, woodsmoke and pungent narcotics.

She went through to the chantry. The glow-globes had been lit, and hundreds of candles burned in empty bottles and jars around the dirty floor. The bonfire in the massive grate had also been lit, and was burning savagely, creating an infernal atmosphere of flickering yellow and orange. The heat hit her like a wall as she came in. The bonfire had been banked too deep, and the chimney was not in good order. The air was sweaty, and thick with smoke.

The party was in full swing: men and women laughing, drinking, talking, clowning. A few were dancing, with careless and intoxicated abandon, to the loud music blaring from a portable audiocaster. The light of the bonfire threw the shadows of all present up the frescoed walls and across the ceiling.

Jagdea looked around. The smoke was getting in her throat, along with the scent of more prohibited substances. She imagined many of Lopard's customers were present, and partaking without discretion. She coughed the scratch of smoke away. She wasn't staying long. Just long enough to pay her respects.

A body stumbled into her. It was Rockcrete. He was sweating heavily, and his eyes somehow managed to be both bleary and dilated.

'Driver!' he bellowed, and handed her his bottle. Then he just stumbled away.

She sniffed the bottle. Cheap joiliq. She took a swig.

Most of the squadron's veterans were present, with the notable exception of Sister Meredith and any of the black-garbed, zealot persuasion. Jagdea saw Blindside and Jongleur, a trim, bearded man she hadn't spoken to yet. He had a decent reputation. There was Reaper, a compact woman with short, black hair and an apparently permanent sneer, and Longlas, a red-headed man with augmetic legs. With them, three others that Jagdea had not so far attached names or call signs to. Nearby, Slumbag, a heavy ape of a man who looked too big for a cockpit, was clapping wildly and whooping. Jagdea had heard he was another Verghastite, like Gangster.

Gangster was the cause of Slumbag's applause. She was standing on an upturned ammo box, dressed in combat pants and her tight vest, dancing a particularly rapturous version of her snake-hipped shimmy. Her skin was flushed and her eyes were closed. She had a bottle in one hand and a stimm-tube in the other.

The rest of the jostling crowd seemed to be ground crew, adepts and fitters, who had turned out in force. She saw Tarr, and Voris, and Boa, who was engaged in a contest of 'how many people can he pick up at once'. The answer, it seemed, was six. The ground crew seemed to be the real animals present. The number of broken bottles and used dispensers on the floor had increased significantly since her last visit. There were a few drivers from the service birds and Medivalks, and a few of the more experienced yet junior sticks. Jagdea couldn't see any smokes at all. They either hadn't been invited, or they were too timid to come.

Then she spotted Camo. The girl saw Jagdea through the crowd, and raised her bottle in a toast. A few things made sense. Camo was a smoke, but she was female and attractive. Someone would have invited her along. Someone who, perhaps in a private moment, had taken her into their confidence with regard to Jagdea's past.

Screw them. It didn't matter. Jagdea took another swig, and pushed through the crowd. Gangster jumped down from the crate, and lurched into Jagdea's path.

'Driver!' she announced.

'Gangster.'

Gangster thrust out her bottle, and Jagdea clinked it.

'You were with him,' said Gangster, slurring.

'Yeah?'

'With Bloodspot,' Gangster said, swimming her arms as if to improve coherence. 'At the end.'

'I was.'

'He was my friend!' Gangster barked, and drew a deep breath.

'I know that.'

'I hear... I hear you tried to get him down alive,' said Gangster, swaying, wiping her mouth with the back of her hand. 'All the way. All the way down. S'what Blindside said. You winged him all the way down.'

Jagdea nodded.

'Yeah,' said Gangster. 'All the way down. It was good you did that.'

She thrust out her bottle a second time, and they clinked again.

'Four-A,' said Gangster, and knocked back some joiliq. 'He was my friend.'

Slumbag and Rockcrete called Gangster's name, and she turned to stagger away, yelling.

'They joined the same day,' said Tarr, appearing at Jagdea's elbow. Tarr had a glass of amasec perched almost daintily in her augmetic hand. 'Winged each other whenever rotation allowed. Sorrentine was the only pilot here Gangster admired.'

Jagdea wondered if there was any more to the story, but Tarr had turned to look at the door.

'Well, here she is,' Tarr said.

Sister Meredith had just entered. The Sister, draped in black, came to a halt in the doorway, glaring at the hedonistic scene. Voices died away. Someone even turned the music down. Jagdea could feel the utter disdain with which the Sister was contemplating the spectacle of vice and sin she was beholding.

Tight-lipped, and very upright, taller than anyone in the room, Merry Death turned and looked at the fresco of the haloed saint. She made the sign of the aquila. Then she faced the crowd again. Her face expressed disgust and admonishment.

'Is there going to be trouble?' Jagdea whispered.

Tarr shook her head.

Blindside walked up to Merry Death. Merry Death reached out her hand. Blindside placed a shot-glass of joiliq in it.

Ignoring him, ignoring everyone, the Sister walked across the chantry floor, past the roaring fire, and knelt in front of the primitive shrine. She placed the brimming shot-glass on the foot of the shrine as an offering, and bowed her head.

Everyone stayed quiet while she said whatever prayer she had come to say. It was inaudible.

Merry Death rose again. She looked around at everyone reproachfully, as though she pitied and scorned them all, and then strode back across the room and left.

The sound of voices swelled again, and someone turned the audiocaster back up.

'She always comes,' said Tarr. 'She never stays long, and she never, you know, joins in with the recreation. But she always comes to show respect.'

Tarr looked at the glass in her hand.

'I need a refill,' she said. 'Get you anything?'

Jagdea shook her head. Tarr nodded, and pushed away through the throng. Jagdea looked for somewhere to put her bottle down. There was no point staying. She felt as out of place as Merry Death, and the night was only going to get rowdier.

'Not thinking of leaving?'

It was Harlot. He was glassy-eyed, buzzed on something. He grinned at her. She didn't smile back.

'I think you've got your hands full here, Lopard,' she said. 'And business to do, by the look of it.'

'What's wrong?' he asked.

'Nothing.'

'Stay,' he said. He nodded at her bottle. 'I can find you something better than that. Stay a while. You can tell me all about this turn.'

'Word gets around, I see,' said Jagdea.

'In a place like this? Of course. A little tuition, I hear? Smoke survival.'

'Got that from Kinny, I guess?' she said. She scanned the mass of moving bodies, and spotted Camo dancing on the far side of the chantry.

'Who?' asked Lopard.

'Camo,' said Jagdea.

'Shit,' said Lopard. 'Her name's Kinny? *Really*?'

'I can see you never asked,' said Jagdea. 'She's sweet. Little young for you, though.'

'We're all grown-ups, Driver,' said Lopard.

'Who talk too much,' said Jagdea.

Lopard looked offended. 'Yeah, she told me about your little huddle,' he said. 'It impressed her. Wasn't that the point of doing it? How has this pissed you off?'

'She talks to you. You talk to her. You tell her things. To impress her, I imagine.'

'Things?'

'Things I asked you not to tell anyone.'

Lopard reacted in surprise, and put his gloved hand on his heart.

'I never said anything, Jagdea. I swear.'

'Yeah?' said Jagdea, unconvinced.

'I swear,' said Lopard. 'If you must know, we don't do much talking. Look, there's trust between us, Jagdea. Between you and me. We established it. I wouldn't speak out of turn.'

He paused, and watched Camo cavorting in the firelight. She was putting her pink-lensed glasses on Rockcrete's face, and laughing.

'She knows?' said Lopard.

'She seems to,' said Jagdea. 'I got that distinct impression.'

'Well, she didn't get it from me.'

'Right.'

'Throne's sakes, Jagdea,' said Lopard. He looked genuinely annoyed. 'There is a trust between us.'

'Yeah, I thought there was.'

'Well, I wouldn't break it.'

'It doesn't matter,' said Jagdea. 'I don't care. Reputation, deserved or not, is just one more obstruction to fly around.'

She turned to go.

'Wait,' he said. 'Don't go like this. I've got something for you.'

'What?' she asked.

He was about to answer, but his face suddenly fell. He'd seen something over her shoulder.

'Oh, shit,' he murmured.

Jagdea turned.

Dampier had walked in. Her bearing was even more prim and stern than the Sister's had been minutes before. Merry Death had been detached and theatrical in her disapproval. Deck Dampier's look was one of plain, steel contempt. The chantry fell silent. Even the music cut off.

Dampier glowered, her hands clasped behind her back. Almost everyone present dropped their gaze, unwilling to meet her stare.

'Deck,' said Lopard, pushing forward to face her. 'This is just–'

'I know what it is, Pilot Officer Lopard,' she replied. 'Seriously? You think the senior deck officer doesn't know about this place, or the recreations that take place in it, or the delinquency involved?'

'Of course you would,' Lopard said quietly.

'Of course I would,' Dampier replied. 'This is a dead zone. Access is prohibited. I can count eight... no, *nine* banned substances just from where I'm standing. Look at yourselves. A disgrace to the service.'

Silence lasted. The fire crackled.

'If you're going to write anybody up, Deck,' said Lopard, 'it should be me–'

'Shut up,' Dampier said. She took a step forward, and removed the bottle of amasec from his hand.

'Sorrentine is dead,' she said. 'Unlucky for him, and all of us. Sorrentine was a first-class pilot. Lucky for you, all of you, the senior deck officer is not here. Not tonight. Julett Dampier is, to pay her respects to her friend Johan Sorrentine.'

She raised the bottle.

'Bloodspot!' she snarled, then took a swig. Cheering broke out. People stamped their feet.

'Shut up!' Dampier yelled, quietening the row. 'Shut it down! Enough of that. Six-Six! Straighten up, and present at attention. Leader on deck.'

Garrant stepped out of the doorway shadows behind her. He was grim. He took the bottle of amasec from Dampier with a nod, then raised a hand for quiet.

'Senior Deck Dampier isn't staying,' he said. 'Someone's got to maintain some discipline. But I am. I'm here to drink to the memory of my friend.'

He looked at Dampier.

'Senior Deck Dampier?'

Dampier scowled at the assembly.

'If anyone, and I mean anyone,' she said, 'is not fit to work or fly at oh-five-dark tomorrow morning, I will cut their legs off. Are we clear? Other than that, carry on.'

She threw a salute, and marched out. Garrant raised his bottle.

'Sorrentine,' he declared. 'The Emperor protects, and the Aeronautica remembers!'

* * *

After half an hour, Jagdea had had enough. It was too hot, and too debauched, and it was only going to get worse. She made her way to the door.

Lopard was waiting for her in the comparative quiet of the outer chamber. He lit a lho-stick.

'You're going?'

She nodded.

'I told you I had something for you,' he said, and reached into his coat pocket for his spotted kerchief.

'What is it?' she asked.

He unwrapped the carefully folded kerchief, and produced a small data wafer.

'What you asked for,' he replied. 'I found an Administratum hub down below, woke up the cogitators. It may not be complete, but that's a data-map of transport network routes in Vesperus.'

Jagdea's eyes widened in surprise. She reached to take it, but he pulled it back, and grinned.

'Now I know what it's for,' he said, 'I'm not sure I should give it to you.'

'Why not?'

He shrugged. 'This notion of yours, Bree Jagdea. Devising new tricks. Sharing best practice. Mentoring the poor little smokes, like Camo and Tantrum. Teaching them how to live just a *little* longer. That's just cruel.'

'How is it cruel?'

'They're all going to die, Driver,' he replied. He was no longer smiling. 'Every day, they live in shred and pain, waiting for it to happen. You're just prolonging that pain. Postponing the inevitable, giving the poor frigs more days of pain and terror. More days of suffering.'

'This from a man who wants to smother them in their sleep?'

'Oh, I talk a lot of shit,' he said, with a dismissive gesture. 'I don't mean any of it. Except the part about sparing them. No one deserves to suffer like this. Not that level of constant shred. And you want to give them *more* of it?'

'We're all suffering,' she replied. 'That's an active war sky out there, Lopard. Probably the worst I've ever seen. Someone's got to fight it. I want to give the smokes the best chance. *And* me. I want that chance too.'

'I think you're an idealist,' he said. 'Idealists are dangerous. In the end, they always kill more people. And those deaths, Bree, are the worst kind of dying.'

'Which is?'

'The hopeful kind,' he said. He looked down at the wafer he was holding between his red-gloved fingers. 'Take it,' he said. 'You'll have to live with the consequences.'

'If you're right,' she replied, 'probably not, because I'll be gone too.'

She took the wafer.

'Everything all right out here?' asked a voice. They looked around. Garrant was lurking in the doorway.

'Yes, Lead,' said Jagdea.

'We're good,' said Lopard.

'You both look a little tense,' said Garrant.

'Driver was just rebuffing my gentle advances, once again,' said Lopard with a smile.

'Driver sounds like a sensible woman,' said Garrant. He glanced down at his hands.

'I appear to be lacking a drink,' he remarked. 'Can you oblige me, Reno?'

'Happy to, Asa,' said Lopard.

'The good stuff, mind,' Garrant said as Lopard stepped past him into the chantry.

Lopard hesitated in the doorway and looked back at Jagdea. 'Kinny?' he said. 'Her name's Kinny? *Really*?'

He left the room. Garrant looked at her.

'You want a word,' said Jagdea.

'Was I that obvious?' Garrant asked, walking towards her. 'I don't drink much. Two shots of joiliq, and I'm giddy.'

'I was surprised to see you here,' she said.

'Well, Sorrentine was special,' said Garrant. 'A show of support was warranted. A mark of respect. Deck and I know about the parties. We've *always* known about the parties. We could shut them down. My predecessor tried. Lungrim was a man of strict faith. His predecessor too. It never works. In a high-shred deck like Six-Six, with no amenities, the crews need a valve. A release. So we turn a blind eye. Yes, it goes too far, too often. But the alternative is worse.'

He turned and looked thoughtfully back at the chantry doorway and the flickering flame-light. She studied him. Garrant was a big man, solidly made, his neck thick and shoulders broad. With his greying hair and noble profile, he was strikingly handsome, the model of an Imperial hero, not a glory story fantasy like poor Wilzar. He carried a weight on him, she could see that.

'I thought you were a man of faith too, Lead?' Jagdea asked.

Garrant patted the gold pin at his throat. 'I am,' he said, 'but not as hardline as Lungrim. The service thinks it sits better for the Campanile to be run by an observant. Holy ground.'

'Desecrated holy ground,' said Jagdea.

'This whole crusade has been about that, Jagdea,' Garrant said, 'and the aspect of faith has increased a great deal since the Beati reappeared. The Aeronautica is required to respect the Ecclesiarchy's interests in the prosecution of this campaign.'

'I've seen as much,' said Jagdea.

'Well, just as the crusade's militant seniors have to maintain a delicate balance between the sacred and the profane,' said Garrant, 'so too here. Tonight was about morale and solidarity.'

She nodded. There was an awkward silence.

'Is this about the missiles?' she asked.

He pursed his lips. 'It could be,' he said. 'Or it could be about the unauthorised mentoring…'

'One huddle, with four young pilots–' Jagdea began.

He raised a hand to quieten her.

'It could also be about the non-standard modification of your fightbird,' he said.

'I'm not the only one here doing that,' said Jagdea stiffly. 'I've seen your Twin, sir. I want to live longer.'

'No argument,' said Garrant.

He regarded her, as though appraising her. There was an odd look in his eyes. She had no idea where this conversation was going. He reached out. For a second, she thought he was about to embrace her. But he was taking the bottle from her hand.

'May I?' he asked.

She made a nod.

He took a sip.

'These… issues, sir,' she said. 'Badler told you about them?'

Garrant stepped away and leaned his bulk back against the worn, frescoed wall. They stood in the gloom, half-lit by the glow of the bonfire next door.

'Badler wants to be a good exec,' Garrant said. 'Badler's also young, and one of the more observant people here. Very strict in his faith. More than me. He worshipped Lungrim. So he is a little less tolerant of indiscretions and non-standard activities. I sent him down to pass on the instruct, so I could tell Sister Meredith I had passed on the instruct. He, however, takes things seriously.'

'I understand.'

'As far as I'm concerned, it's just protocol. Make the modifications you want. You know what you're doing.'

'Do I?' she asked. That was a mysterious remark.

'Yes,' said Garrant. 'As for these huddles, these classes…'

'I know they're out of line and insubordinate,' said Jagdea. 'But there is no culture of instruction here, with veterans supporting the young intake–'

'There's no time for it,' he replied.

'No time, Lead?'

'No,' he said. 'No time, no manpower, no budget. Of course I want a conditioning programme. Of course I want the older hands to bring the younger sticks up. But you've seen this place. There is no time for anything. I need people either flying, or resting. Those are the priorities.'

She walked over to him, and took back the bottle.

'I can stop,' she said. She took a sip. 'I meant no insubordination. I did it because I desperately need to improve, and it seems selfish to keep any insights to myself. I also took seriously what you said to me the night we met,' she added.

'I was in a bad mood that night,' he replied.

'Are you in a better one now?' Jagdea asked.

'Not really,' he said. He smiled. It was the smile of a man on first-name terms with tragedy. 'Look, Jagdea,' he said, 'I can't permit you to teach these kinds of things to the younger aviators. Your notions, just the ones I've heard about, cannot be sanctioned by regulations. The Navy would skin me if they knew I was allowing it.'

'I understand,' she said.

'No, you don't,' he replied. 'I can't be seen to permit it, but I can't control what goes on when I'm not looking.'

He glanced at the chantry doorway and the uproar coming out of it.

'Clearly,' she said, amused.

'So, informally,' he said, 'if you've got the time and the will, I'm saying do it. Please.'

'This is your *unofficial* instruct?'

'Entirely unofficial,' he said. 'I will deny knowledge if it comes out. The service doesn't understand the unique problems we face out here, nor will it appreciate your unique solutions. But Six-Six needs something. Maybe, in an illicit fashion, you can do something I can't.'

'Illicit?' she asked.

He took the bottle from her and drank.

'I actually think the smokes will listen better if they think it's subversive,' he said.

He handed the bottle back.

'Are you going back in to join the fun?' he asked.

'No,' she said. 'I was just leaving.'

'Me too,' he replied. 'Let me walk you back.'

Past the lookout Fari, who actually saluted as they went by, the hallways were gloomy and dank. The rain was still coming down.

'Don't worry about Badler or Dampier,' said Garrant, 'I'll keep them in check.'

'I don't know what to make of the exec,' she replied.

'If I'm honest,' said Garrant, 'Badler is a better leader than I am. I'm a good pilot. No, I'm a *great* pilot.' He grinned at her mischievously, acknowledging the arrogance. 'But I'm only a decent lead,' he continued. 'It was forced on me. With Badler, it's the other way around. He's a decent pilot. But he'll make a really fine lead or deck one day. So…'

They walked on.

'This was the matter you wanted to discuss?' she asked. 'My non-standard activities?'

'In part,' he replied. 'I've got news. Good news. Six-Six is nearly out of fuel.'

'That's good news?'

He laughed. 'No,' he said. 'In two days' time, we're going to get a resupply from Intercept Four-Three. As much as they can spare, which isn't much. But it's enough to tide us over for another twelve days when the replenishment from the hive-plex arrives. Full resupply, and some more pilots.'

She stopped walking. He turned to look at her.

'I can go back?' she asked.

'I'd honestly prefer you didn't. I don't want to lose you or Gumm. But we had an understanding with regard to your rotation, and I'll stand by it.'

'I can go?' she repeated, not believing it.

'Or you can stay,' he said. 'I'd like you to consider staying.'

'Why are you so keen on that?' she asked. 'I haven't even made a kill. I'm a waste of that Voss.'

'I was trying to arrange the transfer,' he replied. 'Trying to get it done right, through the proper channels. I had to pull biog transcripts from the hive.'

Now she understood.

'*My* biog data?'

'Yes, and Gumm's.'

'I see.'

'Yes, I think you do, Reserve Driver Jagdea,' he said. 'Or should I say Wing Commander Jagdea?'

'Shit,' she said.

'Kills or no kills, you're an asset I'd like to keep,' he said. 'You've been here five days, and you're already, of your own volition, working to improve squadron efficiency and decrease attrition. Only a veteran officer thinks like that. Only a veteran officer cares. You're not here for the kill tally. You appreciate the bigger picture. I want to keep you.'

'I think that's your prerogative as lead, sir,' she said. 'You could deny the transfer.'

'Yeah, of course. But I don't want to be remembered as the man who forced the conscription and service of the celebrated Zophonian Ace.'

'I'm not that any more,' she said.

'Whatever you are, think about it.'

'Have you told anyone?' she asked. 'About my record?'

'No,' he said. 'It's confidential. But I think people are beginning to figure it out.'

'Like who?'

'Gangster,' he said. 'It may surprise you to learn that Pilot Officer Disa Yesof, no matter her affect, is a keen scholar of Aeronautica history. She studies, Jagdea, and she knows the Zophonian Theatre back to front. You know it's taught at flight school now?'

'Shut up,' scowled Jagdea. 'Respectfully, sir. But shut up.'

'She recognised your name. Yesof is also a proud Verghastite, and when she found out you'd done a tour on Verghast, she put it together, because she knew her hero had flown there.'

'Her hero?'

'Whatever. Gangster worked it out. She's probably not the only one. And she's under no obligation to keep her mouth shut. In fact, it's not easy to shut her up, period. So the word is spreading. You're going to have to live with that.'

'I don't need the anchor of that reputation.'

'It might be an asset when it comes to getting huddles to listen.'

'Not if I'm only here for another fourteen days.'

He smiled sadly.

'I will offer you a deal, Jagdea,' he said solemnly. 'I will officially sanction your training efforts, and draw any flak they take, if you agree to stay on.'

She took a step back in shock.

'That's blackmail,' she said.

'Is it?' he asked.

'You're making my liberation from this shitty mess, a mess I never agreed to be part of, contingent on me abandoning the smokes to their fate. If I stay, I might... *might*... improve the odds for them. If I leave, they're on their own. If I want to leave, I have to sell them out.'

'When you put it like that,' he said. 'Throne's sake, Jagdea. This is war. You know all about that, better than many. We're the Aeronautica. Pitiless and ruthless precision is a fundamental part of our mindset. Target acquisition, then kill without hesitation.'

'I'm your target in this analogy?'

'I need you here, as a pilot and perhaps a survival asset,' he said. 'If I force your cooperation, it'll be half-hearted–'

'So you'd coerce it instead?'

'Jagdea–'

'I'll offer you a counter deal,' she said. 'You say we've got fourteen days? Let me see what I can do in that time. Hell, let me see if I'm still alive. If I can see positive results before that resupply arrives, I will consider staying. If I don't, I'm out.'

He sighed.

'Very well,' he said.

'Let me be clear,' she said. 'I am not promising to stay.'

'But you'll think about it?'

'Yes, Lead.'

They carried on walking in silence.

'Are you angry with me,' he asked. 'For my brutal efforts at coercion?'

'Yes,' she said. She paused. 'No, actually. It's exactly what I would have done if I was lead here. Leveraged an outcome rather than commanding one. You're a better lead than you think, sir.'

'You can call me Asa,' he said. 'When no one's looking.'

They walked a little further.

'Lead?' she asked.

'Yes?'

'You pulled our biog transcripts. The full sheet. Me and Gumm. What… what did you find out about Gumm's prior service?'

'Oh, come on, Jagdea,' Garrant said. 'You know that's classified. I kept your past a secret. I'll keep his.'

Fifth drop, Intercept 66, Vesperus, 13:11

Jagdea burned hard after Harlot, with Exec at her six. After the torrential overnight rain, the city was a misty graveyard, uncannily still.

ROP 12 had flagged a contact in the central hive zone. Jagdea had expected an early shout, fearing the Archenemy would somehow know that many of the Six-Six aviators would be the worse for wear, but the morning had been quiet. She felt tired. She'd been go-ready since five, as the roster had demanded, and spent the rest of the time waiting in-suit, fully prepped. Even a couple of at-will naps in a folding chair on the drop-deck had not taken the edge off her sleep debt. It wasn't a lack of rest per se; Jagdea was sure it was a lagging tension fatigue. Her conversation with Asa Garrant the night before had left her with a strange mix of encouragement and doubt. Fourteen days, and she could be out of it, but a razor-wire noose of guilt and responsibility had now been hooked around her.

Her Voss felt tired too; sullen and dull, as though the new weight of the heavy autocannons and accompanying ammo drums under its wings was a load it resented.

However hard he had partied in the chantry, Lopard was showing no signs of impairment. His ghost-pale Bolt led the way through the dead hive's lethal obstacle course with alarming eagerness, taking tight turns and choosing risky path options that she would have thought twice about. It was the first time she'd winged him, and it was taking every ounce of her concentration to keep pace.

She didn't know Lopard. She didn't know any of them enough to *know* them. But from what she had learned about him, during their brief but interesting encounters, she somehow doubted he'd slept at all. Maybe he was still buzzed and riding the fumes of his excesses, which might explain his headlong rate. Maybe he always flew like this.

She thought of the wafer he had given her, now stashed in her billet. She was dying to go over it. Go-ready since waking, there hadn't been an opportunity.

Four minutes out from the Campanile, Badler jockeyed ahead of her on a wide turn-out where she had lingered too cautiously, and stole the second slot in their racing line.

'Keep it tight, Driver,' she heard him chide over the vox.

She kept her response to herself. Now she was chasing both of them: Lopard's snow-white Bolt and Badler's black Voss. Though Harlot's headlong racing continued to be relentless, Exec seemed intent to pass him too. Jagdea imagined Exec Badler had little time for Harlot and his devil-may-care affect. It was telling to be in a chase position where she could observe them both. Badler was a fine pilot, finer than her already decent impressions. His driving was surgically precise, exacting and true on turns, sharp and efficient on every line. His touch was minimal, never bleeding power, never over-gunning, a superb economy of control that pushed the line but left plenty in reserve.

Lopard was something else. The word 'flamboyant' came to mind, but that was unfair. Harlot wasn't showing off for anyone, except perhaps himself. Every manoeuvre displayed a nimble grace and refinement lacking from Badler's superb precision. Where Badler banked around a tower or obstruction with a meticulous wingtip lean, prudently conserving power and angle with the utmost discipline, Lopard would sweep his Bolt around in a lithe vector-nudged roll that made the turn tighter, and spoke to incredible finesse. It was the difference between technical excellence and art. Maybe Lopard's prowess came from his experience and his Glavian heritage and hardwiring, or maybe she was just witnessing a reckless streak of luck that had yet to run out. She knew which of them she'd rather wing: Badler, because of his rigour and fidelity. She also knew who was the better pilot. But Harlot's flying, with its indelible signature of a natural genius, came with the unpredictable whim of any artist. And she'd seen the inevitable end of that kind of talent too many times.

Hive central, an immense and rising summit of spires and habitat structures, was coming up fast. This was her first sortie into the central zone, and she'd been advised that much of it would be in-structure flight due to the scale of the formation. The thought did not appeal. They were climbing hard, zagging up the lower shoulders of the city-peak in the titanic shadow it cast, as though they were running an intruder op up the blindside of a mountain range. Dense forests of masts and antennae sang and shivered as they burned over. Banks of black smoke from long-standing internal burns swathed the flanks like high-altitude weather. Hazards like vent pylons, bulk docking gantries and headless defence towers whipped past. They ran in under the enormous span of high-tension structural cables, steel tubes thirty feet in diameter and twenty miles long. There was a steady blizzard of rust flakes. Harlot was starting to bank west.

'Harlot, copy?' she heard Exec call.

'The Gullet,' Harlot responded.

Jagdea heard Badler object.

'It'll snip four minutes plus off intercept,' Harlot responded.

Badler objected again, but Harlot was already committed. Whatever his reservations, Badler, like any good wingman, stayed with him. Jagdea followed them both.

The Gullet was a thermal vent. Jagdea flinched as she saw Harlot turn in under the lip of the overhanging hive-plate and burn directly into the throat of the industrial chute. Exec rolled in after him. Cursing them both, Jagdea sticked over onto their tails.

She flew into the darkness, chasing the firefly glow of their engines up ahead. The chute was as broad as a carrier's main deck, but it felt far too tight at high rate. It ran straight, but began to curl away down into the depths of the hive-core.

Gusts of rust and fibre-litter kept coming at her, exhaled by the wind-trap of the vent system. Her airframe shook, and she jarred in her seat. She could hear the grit pattering off the nose and canopy. She kept the stick true.

'Hard hard left,' Badler instructed.

Lopard hadn't bothered with a courtesy warning. In the whipping darkness ahead, both tail burns suddenly vanished. She executed hard, and left the main vent into a snaking side chute that ran west.

It was smaller. It was tighter. A pipe rather than a main vent. But it was lit. Evidently, some sections of the central hive mass were still powered by energy leaking out of abandoned reactors. The chute was illuminated by lighting ribs every fifty yards. They shone with an electric blue that was almost neon. At her speed, they strobed past. She narrowed her eyes at the acute visual disturbance, and appreciated how much she'd been enjoying the reduced distraction of the tape-masked headache.

Now she could visualise Lopard and Badler. They were tail-chasing hard ahead of her, extending their lead. The pipe undulated gently, forcing her to concentrate on its dips and rises, as a firm line would risk chipping the Voss' belly or clipping the tunnel's arch. In places, the chute had been punctured, and cables and housing debris dangled from above. Most were visible and avoidable. She saw Lopard suddenly bank hard, and Badler do the same a moment later. She followed suit, tipping wings vertical, in time to avoid a cluster of girders that had speared down and bisected the entire pipe. Far too close. No room for error.

Beyond the girders, the chute was unlit for a good distance where the lighting ribs had failed. Then they hit a powered section again, and the strobing returned, more fiercely than before. The scream of her ram was bottled up in the throat of the chute, howling around her so fiercely it felt as though she was being carried by noise and not a fightbird.

On the vox, she heard Badler issue a brief instruct.

'Gets tight,' was all he said.

It did. Harlot and Exec banked wings-vertical in order to fit. Jagdea did the same. The pipe's diameter remained the same, but the chute itself was partially filled by a long run of heat exchanger vanes that were stepped out along the bottom of the tube, reducing available space to a keyhole shape. They were now running on their sides with their lower wings slotting the top of the keyhole's bar. A moment's lapse, a moment out of true, and they would make passing contact, shear off the wing, and end up fireballing past the strobing lights.

The shred oozed into her lungs and guts, chuckling.

Then they were clear. They swung level into another section of unlit pipe, and pale daylight yawned ahead. Lopard lit full burn.

Jagdea hammered out of the pipe into the wide open space of the hive-block interior. Harlot and Exec were already plunging into a burning dive. The three fightbirds came off the pipe-end as though they were shooting off the top of a vast waterfall into the chasm below. It felt roomy suddenly, but it wasn't. The thick hive-shell was behind them, veined with pipework, and a soaring habitat structure, burned out, rose like a granite cliff ahead. High above, the ceiling was enclosed by the extending slope of the hive-shell, where huge, heavy-ribbed plasglass panels had been installed to draw natural light down into the levels beneath. The plasglass was soot-caked, and the light it was admitting was a dirty brown. They fell through the slanting beams of light towards the floor of the canyon where the clustered spires had made their roots.

'Track,' Lopard voxed.

His run down the Gullet had cut their response time impressively. They were entering the central zones ahead of the tracked hostiles. Jagdea craned around, and spotted two bats rating hard far below to the east.

'Be alert for lag formations,' Badler voxed. There was every chance the Archenemy would be employing their new tactics of bait and catch. Lopard was already committing, slicing down on top of the hostiles. Badler peeled away after him. Jagdea applied a bootful of rudder and rolled onto her back in pursuit.

The bats made them, and turned away into a deep air gulf, skimming over an iron jungle of pipes and ducts. Lopard adjusted and gave chase, continuing his descent, with Badler stuck to his tail. Jagdea followed, but started scanning wildly. The bats' turn made no sense. Why were they staying low? In their position, aware as they evidently were of an intercept dropping on their heads, Jagdea would have climbed hard, either to increase the evasion options or proactively engage.

'Bait,' she snarled. 'They're bait.'

No one replied. She could see Lopard kick burn as he pushed in for lock range.

A glint. Up at her high ten. Two, no three more bats diving in.

'Bats, bats!' she rasped. 'High ten, descending.'

She turned hard out of her dive to meet them, first pulling savage g-crush, then inverting and hanging in her straps. She climbed nose-on to the attack. The lead bat, a Hell Blade, running well ahead of its wingmen, ripped straight past her, gunning for Badler and Lopard below. The other two broke wide. She went after the one that had split left, banking tightly. It spiralled into a dive to get off her nose. The other, a silver Razor, pulled a tight loop to try to sit on her tail. It came in at her nine.

Forgetting her quarry, Jagdea turned hard left to meet it and present it with significant closure and angle problems. The instant she turned in, she saw a launch flash and realised it had loosed a missile at her. She stayed nose-on to keep the heat of her efflux away from its seeker system. She glimpsed the black heater as it rushed past wide.

The Razor, exploiting the power advantage of its dive, rolled out of her line and swung in on her right. The Razor was going for a fly through. She could tell that from its high crossing rate before she even heard the warning tone. She turned hard left, and rolled on her back to prosecute the fly through, but it didn't snap out past her and into her firing envelope. Jerking her head left, then right, she saw it diving away to join its fellow hunters instead.

She rolled into a pursuit dive.

Far below, there was no sign of Lopard. Jagdea was certain that he was still intently chasing the original duo of bats along the chasm floor. Badler, like any decent wingman, had broken off and begun a steep climb out of the ditch to meet the other bats coming down. The Blade had pulled wide to avoid this confrontation, but Badler was rising head-on to meet the bat that Jagdea had forced to split left. It was another Razor, dull grey like pewter. She could see the coughs of smoke it was trailing as it opened its cannons at Badler. He peeled off, but spat a missile off his rails as he bent away. Head-on, he must have had a perfect murderlock, because the pewter bat ate the heater nose-first, and became a ragged cloud of flame and debris that rained down into the trench below.

There was no time to compliment him. Jagdea had no idea what the dense pipework in the floor of the ditch was carrying, but it was highly flammable, and sparked off the moment the burning mess of the Razor spattered into it. There was an initial blink as pipes ruptured and gas or liquid ignited, then a rolling, pulsing flutter of conflagration as the blast kicked off down the bed of the ditch, burning and chasing along pipes and sump-heads. It was as though a wave of fire was washing down the gulf, ripping through the jungle of pipes and turning it into a blazing sea. Jagdea saw jets of flame squirting a hundred yards or more into the air and large pieces of pipe debris flung much higher. Badler's Voss stumbled in its climb as superheated air and blast-wash, focused upwards by the trench of the ditch, caught him with the shockwave. He continued to ascend, riding the wave. The silver Razor, stooping towards him, turned out hard and curved away towards a neighbouring habiculum block.

Jagdea pushed the throttle and racked her bird around to pursue it. Then she saw the Hell Blade again. It was crossing below her at high speed, coming in on Badler's nine. Despite the glare of fire below, it was side-on to her now, and she could see that it was banded black and silver.

She stamped the rudder and corkscrewed to go for it instead. The snap roll was brutal, putting a huge load on both her and the Voss' stabilisers. But she was fangs-out. It wasn't that the Blade was indisputably the bat that had killed Sorrentine. It was the fact that it was muscling for Badler. She was Badler's wingman. It wasn't even a question of target choice.

'Break! Exec, break!' she growled as the snap roll crushed

the air out of her. Badler started to curl out across the firefields below, but the Blade curved with him. The roll had cost her power. At Hessenville, the Phantine aviators had been taught to enter a turn using stick followed by rudder, but life had taught her to go hard in with rudder because it tightened the turn considerably. She had a decent angle, but no lock, because both Badler and the bat were outpacing her.

Jagdea kicked the burner to close the space differential. The Blade had flopped onto Badler's tail. Badler was trying to force a lateral separation and get it on his outside. She hammered down and leased off her guns in an effort to scare the bat off his back. It would not be put off. Badler executed a roll-out that must have red-lined him, but which managed to shoot the bat past him. She saw Exec's Voss fall away in what looked like an unhappy stall or an outright departure.

She stayed on the bat as it started to climb away, using her diving speed to boost her ascent. She had a poor trail position and it was changing heading rapidly in an effort to dump her.

The banded Blade swung low and began to haul away down the gulf. Below, the inferno was continuing to propagate down the base of the ditch as fire caught. It had to be some kind of refinery or processing plant, Jagdea guessed, and the whole thing was progressively igniting. She dropped down in pursuit, into the raging glare, feeling the thermal upwash of the massive burn rock and tremble her airframe. Geysers of feathery white flame spewed up around her, filling the air with clouds of sparks. The Blade up ahead suddenly veered off left, heading for the blackened wall of the industrial trench. She saw what it was running for. The open mouth of another ventilation chute.

She clipped off a burst with both las and the heavy hard guns, but her angle was bad. The Blade vanished into the chute. Briefly doubting her own sanity, she powered in behind it.

The vent chute was another pipe similar to the final section of the Gullet that Lopard had run them through. It was lit by illuminated ribs, but their neon light was a deep red, perhaps a hazard signifier automatically triggered by the raging conflagration outside. The air was dense with filmy smoke. The Blade was dead ahead, its afterburner dancing in front of her. There was no room in the pipe for evasion. It has no choice but to run.

Tone ping. She had immediate murderlock. The Blade was trapped in her firing envelope. Her finger instinctively flexed on the FIRE stud.

Then common sense overcame the hungry lust of the shred. If she splashed the bat – and she could, easily – she'd splash herself. At current velocity, she'd race right into the exploding Blade or be struck by back-flung wreckage. There was also a high chance that the Blade would bring down the pipe if she bounced it.

She took her finger off the stud. The Archenemy pilot must have read the dilemma. By boxing her into the pipe behind him, he had essentially disarmed her. She didn't dare fire. All she could do was stick to his six and chase.

Jagdea also realised that she had been assuming the Blade knew where it was going. Lopard had flown them through the Gullet because he'd flown it before and knew it led somewhere. Where did this chute lead? Did the bat pilot even know? Were they accelerating towards a sealed iris shutter or a section of collapsed pipe? The former seemed most likely. The vent system might have automatically sealed in response to the firestorm in the trench.

She was tempted to drop speed, or bring the Voss to a hover stop, swing around, and go back. The red neon ribs continued to flicker past. How far was she prepared to push it? Her hand was on the vector control, ready to crank it to the hover stop, or click past that to full brake. Maybe that was the answer? Brake stop, and *then* fire. Kill the bat without the risk of running into its death-blast. But at the rate the bat was moving, there'd be no time to execute a hard stop *and* fire. The bat would be out of gun range. She registered the bitter irony that missiles would have been a more workable option.

Abruptly, they ran out of pipe anyway. The narrow chute opened into a large pumping chamber. She clipped off another burst of fire as the bat turned wide, but only managed to kill the top of a heat exchanger. The bat lifted. She ran low under a series of gantry walkways, and then turned up. There was another chute mouth in the chamber's ceiling. The bat went straight up into it in a vertical burn. She pulled around and went with it.

Now they were climbing hard, blue rib lights strobing past. The bat's burners lit bright and then dimmed rapidly. She knew it was dropping speed to make an execute of some kind. Then it vanished, pulling a hard right into a connecting chute. She managed to match the turn. Now they were running horizontally again, back towards the trench. At least, she assumed so. The speed and the conditions were making it impossible to focus on much except staying on its tail.

The Blade jinked in the pipe ahead. Jagdea rolled hard to avoid the same loops of fallen cable it had narrowly dodged. Then they were out, in the open, above the blazing trench again. The bat rolled left, again trying to dump her and push her in front. She saw the gambit coming, and muscled back, fighting adverse yaw. Then she swung in.

Tone ping. *Murderlock.*

Someone howled her name. She flinched. Lopard's white Bolt suddenly filled her canopy, crossing her nose on at full burn. She rolled out frantically in order to avoid collision.

What the f–?

She didn't understand what was happening for a second. Then las-bolts ripped past her from behind, and the silver Razor shot by her right shoulder. It must've picked her up as she emerged from the chute, and she hadn't seen it because she'd been too intent on the banded Blade. If Harlot hadn't crossed and forced her out of line, she'd be dead.

Why hadn't he fired? Head-on, that close, the Razor would have been right in his envelope. Why hadn't Harlot just killed it instead of barging her into an emergency evade with his whole frigging bird?

She applied opposite stick to counter the violent roll. The Voss coughed and stumbled, but came level. The banded Blade had vanished into the smoke coming off the burning trench, but the silver Razor was dead ahead, trying to yank right to get off her nose. It was so close, she could see its ducts rotate as it went for a hard brake to spit her out.

There was no beating that. She didn't even try. She burned instead, and hammered the Voss into a hard loop, levelling her wings as she came over the top and out of the bottom, right behind it again.

Tone ping, instantly. She ripped off the wing cannons and watched, as though time had stopped, the huge punctures deform the silver Razor's fuselage. It fell apart in the air, shedding tangled debris as it became a spear of flame that streaked down into the fire below.

'Kill,' she snarled.

Refectory, Intercept 66, Vesperus, 16:01

Lopard got up on the chair, chalk in hand. A slow handclap was already building around the room. He marked a tally stroke beside the name EXEC – for the pewter Razor – and the clapping intensified. Then he marked two strokes beside HARLOT. Lopard had splashed both of the bats he'd chased down that gulf trench.

There was cheering. A few of the aviators in the refectory had got to their feet. Gangster had a shot-glass raised high, and was yelling Lopard's name. Some of the crowd had put their hands on their heads, the hands-clear signal of touch-down compliance repurposed as a gesture of respect and submission. Lopard turned to look at them, and bowed his head politely, affecting modest appreciation. Then the showman in him took over. He made to put the chalk down, then hesitated, as though remembering something at the last minute. He turned back to the wall and triumphantly marked the first tally beside DRIVER.

He looked down at Jagdea as the whoops and cheers rose.

'One of us now,' he said, grinning.

'That's enough,' said Jagdea. She didn't like the fuss. 'I could have marked it myself.'

'It's the privilege and honour of a wingman to score up his partner's first kill,' Lopard replied as he stepped off the chair. 'Squadron tradition.'

'Is it?'

'No idea, but let's pretend.'

They walked to the food line and piled their trays.

On their way to a table, pilots rose to congratulate Harlot. A few shot Jagdea approving nods too. As they sat down, Gangster, Rockcrete and Camo slid into chairs around them. Rockcrete slammed a bottle of joiliq on the table, and went to fill their glasses.

'I don't think so,' Lopard said with a disapproving wag of his finger. He pulled a bottle of vintage amasec out of his flying coat.

'Special occasion,' he said.

'You carry that around all the time?' Jagdea asked wryly.

'I got it from my locker,' he replied, as though reluctantly explaining a card trick. He filled their glasses. 'Special occasion. You never forget your first time.'

She stared at the glass he'd filled for her.

'This isn't my first time,' she said.

Yesof grinned. 'Damn right,' she said.

Jagdea shot her a warning glance.

'First time here,' said Lopard. He raised his glass. 'To special occasions,' he said.

They all toasted and drank. Rockcrete, either already pissed or still drunk from the night before, thumped the table repeatedly with his palm.

'I mean, of course,' Lopard added, 'my solo double kill.'

Camo and Yesof laughed.

'Seriously,' said Lopard. He looked at Jagdea. She ignored him and tucked into her food. 'Seriously, Jagdea. That was a good kill. That loop?'

He looked at the others. They were eager for a glory story.

'She was in tight on this Razor,' Lopard told them. 'It tried to heave her through, so she let it, looped, and killed it from the six.' He pinched his fingers to his lips and kissed them. 'A piece of work,' he said. 'You could learn something from her.'

'I think that's the idea,' said Camo.

'You turned a spit-out into a loop, and reacquired?' Yesof asked, clearly trying to imagine it.

'It was instinct,' said Jagdea, trying to chew an especially stringy piece of slab.

'It was frigging beautiful,' said Lopard. 'And beautifully insane.'

'Speaking of,' said Jagdea, sitting back, 'what the hell was that pass? Nose-on? It would have been polite just to shoot it off my arse.'

'It was polite not to let you die,' Lopard replied casually. 'I was black on ammo and stores. I'd used everything taking the two bats in the trench.'

'So you flew at me?'

'I put myself between you and the Razor to turn you out of line and prevent it from killing you,' Lopard said solemnly. 'That's what wingmen do, isn't it? Watch your back? We had an understanding.'

'Yeah,' admitted Jagdea.

'Trust.'

'I get it. And I appreciate the effort, even though it nearly killed us both.'

'If it doesn't nearly kill you,' said Lopard, refilling the glasses, 'it's hardly worth doing now, is it?'

Wash block, Intercept 66, Vesperus, 16:57

The torrential storms had refilled the Campanile's tanks and reserves. Water rationing had been suspended. Jagdea left the refectory to get the first shower she'd been able to snag since arriving at Intercept 66. It wasn't much; about two minutes of a weak, gritty flow that smelled of rust and sterilising agents, but it felt like luxury.

The wash block was a grubby stone chamber with cracked plasterwork that had been outfitted with a row of curtained stalls by the Munitorum. The plastek curtains were filthy and spotted with mould, and the water wasn't even warm. A pull-chain activated a gravity flow that doused you in a portion of water. Lopard had told her how to twist the chain to fool the gravity system and steal an extra thirty or forty seconds of water. It had sounded too complicated.

'Easier if I show you,' he'd suggested with a wink.

'I'm good,' she had told him.

'But we agreed to wash each other's backs,' he said.

'You just said "wash" when you know you meant "watch",' she said, closing him down.

The shower rattled to a drip. Water gurgled away down the drain plate dug into the cracked tiled floor. Jagdea wiped her face, and pulled back the curtain.

Sister Meredith stood facing her.

'Throne's sake!' Jagdea exclaimed, and grabbed the ragged, grey sheet of fibrecloth that passed for a towel.

Merry Death didn't move or apologise. Her face was stern and her gaze unwavering. She towered over Jagdea, dressed in her full black habit and starched head dress.

'The frig are you doing?' Jagdea asked, struggling to wrap the cloth around her dripping body.

'You made a kill,' said Meredith.

'What? Yes.'

'You will be spared,' said Meredith.

'What do you mean?' Jagdea asked.

Meredith continued to stare at her for a moment, oblivious to her discomfort.

'You will be spared,' the Sister repeated.

'I don't know what that means,' said Jagdea.

Meredith raised her right hand sharply. Her fingers were black with fireplace soot. Before Jagdea could stop her or fend her off, the Sister had pressed them to Jagdea's forehead and drawn some kind of mark.

'Frig's sake, I've just showered!' Jagdea cried, recoiling.

'You will be spared,' Meredith repeated. She turned and strode out of the wash block.

'What does that mean?' Jagdea yelled after her. 'What the frig does that even mean?'

* * *

Billet, Intercept 66, Vesperus, 22:05

There were eight this time: Wilzar, Camo, Tantrum, Nosedive, and four new smokes Jagdea didn't know. She'd called them to her billet, because she hadn't expected many, and she wanted to do right by Garrant and keep the whole thing on the quiet. There was barely space in her small room, even with her cot pushed back. They crushed in, and sat on the floor, except for Nosedive and one of the newbies, who leant against the wall either side of the door. When Gumm arrived, he had to squeeze in to join Jagdea, and ended up perched on the head of her cot.

'More like it,' he murmured.

Jagdea shrugged.

'News of a kill gets around,' he said. 'Good for you, by the way.'

'I think it's other news getting around,' she replied.

Gumm didn't ask what. He gestured gently at Jagdea's face.

'You got, uhm–' he began.

'I know,' she said. She'd looked at herself in a mirror. Merry Death's fingers had left a mark on her forehead, a sooty smudge that may or may not have been in the shape of an aquila. She didn't want to wipe it off until she understood what it was. But that made her as superstitious as the worst of them, and she didn't like that either.

Jagdea started off walking them through the basics of the so-called J-turn again. She didn't like the term, but it had clearly stuck with them. She'd had time to go through relevant parts of the Voss book, and was able to expand her ideas with citations from it. Steeley, Glick and Wilzar took careful notes. Two of the newbies didn't even fly Vosses: Blowout, a young male, said he drove a Twin, and Dummy, an older female with hair shaved as short as Jagdea's, flew a Bolt. But all of the newbies listened intently. Kinny 'Camo' Inthimal just sat cross-legged and stared at Jagdea with a dopey, almost infatuated gaze.

'Something on my face?' Jagdea asked her suddenly, mid-brief.

Camo sniggered, blithely unaware that Jagdea was trying to stop her wide-eyed staring.

'Just the blessing of the Saint,' she replied.

'That's a good thing?' Jagdea asked.

'Merry Death doesn't give it to just anyone,' said Glick.

'The Sister don't give it much to no one,' Blowout added.

Jagdea resumed, about to hand over to Gumm so he could talk about the potential advantages of overriding the target lock default, when someone tried to push the door open to enter. Glick and Wilzar stood aside. The door opened, and Gangster peered in. Rockcrete and Slumbag were behind her.

'You started?' Gangster said. 'We didn't know where to find you.'

Jagdea was surprised. 'There isn't much room,' she began.

'We'll crowd in, no issue,' said Gangster. 'Close up formation, smokes.'

The young aviators shuffled around and made room for the three new-comers to squeeze in. The billet was almost laughably packed, and combined body heat was making it sweaty.

There was an awkward silence.

'I'm not sure if I have anything to say that will interest you three,' Jagdea said to Gangster and her boys. She had a feeling she knew what this was. Word had got around, and Gangster and her gunfighter crew had decided it would be funny to roll up, intimidate the smokes, and generally disrupt and piss-take.

Disa Yesof took her aback with the directness of her response.

'We all gotta learn,' she said. 'Every day. I got kills, but they won't count for shit if I bite it, and the day I say I know all there is to know is the day I start biting.'

'True thing,' snarled Rockcrete, and smacked palms with Gangster directly above the flinching head of Tantrum.

'So you all listen up, smokes,' said Slumbag. 'Listen up good.'

'These are just…' Jagdea began, 'just some observations I've made. I don't claim to know–'

'Nah,' said Gangster. 'You're Jagdea. Bree Jagdea of the Zoph. So we listen when you talk.'

She locked Jagdea with a look so fierce that it felt like there should be a heater ready to follow it in. Though more aggressive, it was somehow more rapt than Camo's crush-stare.

'All right,' said Jagdea. 'Gumm's going to talk about sighting defaults. I'd like to get the veterans' perspective on that, since you're here. Then I'll introduce you all to the benefits of hose tape.'

'You gonna talk J-turns, though, right?' Rockcrete asked.

'We did that,' said Glick.

'Well, *we* weren't here, Tantrum,' Rockcrete growled at him.

'I can circle back to that subject,' said Jagdea. 'Or you can stay after.'

'And I want to know how you turn a spit-out into a loop-and-kill,' said Gangster.

The informal huddle lasted over two hours. There were lots of questions, and some genuine debate.

'Same time tomorrow,' Jagdea said as the aviators filed out. 'But I'll find somewhere bigger, so listen out.'

'Stand you a drink?' Gangster asked.

'I'll see you in the refectory,' Jagdea replied with a nod.

When they were gone, the billet was overheated and stank of perspiration. Gumm propped the door open.

'So,' he said.

'That went better than I thought it would,' she replied, gathering up the pages of the Voss book.

'What she said,' he muttered. 'Yesof. I've heard the same from others. It true?'

'About me?'

'Yes.'

Jagdea nodded. 'I didn't put it out there,' she said. 'I don't want to carry a rep any more than you do.'

'Well, it's out,' Gumm replied.

He looked at her, his small blue eyes unblinking, his porcelain face unreadable.

'Zophonian Sea, eh? That's some glory story.'

'Long time ago, Gumm,' she said. 'I'm not that person any more.'

'You are to them,' he replied. 'Never thought I'd see Yesof show up and admit fallibility. Maybe a rep has some use after all.'

'Maybe,' she said, pondering. 'Thinking about using yours?'

'I'm just a driver from the reserve pool,' he said.

'All right,' she said, half-smiling.

He sighed. 'I–' he began.

'What?'

'I keep my rep tight,' he said, his voice more fur-soft than ever, 'because the glory story that it comes with ends like this.'

He tapped the hard ceramic of his cheek with his index finger. It was a hollow, inorganic clack.

'Then don't tell it,' she said. 'Ever. I won't ask again. All I know is, now you know more about me than I know about you, and that's an asymmetric payload. And if it's pain that keeps your story inside you, telling it to a friend might help. I'm just saying.'

'We didn't join the Aeronautica to make friends,' he replied.

'And yet...?' she said with a grin.

'And yet.' Gumm shrugged. 'I appreciate the offer. I mean it. Maybe one of these days.'

'If we have enough left,' she said.

'Indeed.'

'You coming to the refectory?' she asked. 'Apparently, the drinks are on Yesof.'

He shook his head. 'I'm going to turn in. And I don't drink. You know that.'

'I do know that about you,' she agreed. 'So that's one thing at least.'

DAY 93

Intercept 66, Vesperus, 04:45

She woke early, deliberately, and went up to Campanile Control before the morning alert-ready call got everything too busy.

She'd taken a look at the wafer Lopard had given her, but it was a huge data-block that exceeded the capacity of any slate she could lay her hands on. She needed a significant cogitator to review it properly.

It was quiet, even in Six-Six Control. The high-vaulted belfry chamber was manned by three operators, all reaching the weary end of the overnight shift. Jagdea peered in through the doors. There was no sign of Badler or Dampier. The veteran pilot known as Jongleur was acting as duty exec. Jagdea wanted to keep her activities lo-res to keep the heat off Garrant for as long as possible. But Control was the only place in the war deck where there was a cogitator of sufficient power.

She walked in, bold.

'Help you, Driver?' Jongleur asked, looking up.

'I need to review some data,' she replied, acting like there was nothing off at all. 'Can I snag a spare station?'

Jongleur scratched his bearded chin. He was too tired to care.

'High watch is free,' he replied, gesturing to a console at the far end.

Jagdea nodded her thanks, and went over to the desk. Jongleur turned his attention back to the strategium table.

She slotted in the wafer and waited for the data to load. It took a while. Under the bell yokes and headstocks, the repurposed chamber was almost silent, apart from the voltaic hum, and the occasional murmur of voices or the squeak of a chair. But the shred was here. Sitting in the blue gloom, waiting for the data to process, she could feel it. Control was the nest where the shred dwelt. It was the secret lair from which it made its sudden sorties into the hearts and guts of every aviator. At any moment, a screen could light up and threat tones ping. No wonder Jongleur and his warfare officers looked so frayed. An overnight shift in this lingering menace would drain anyone.

Her screen blinked. Data began to unfold. Leaning forward, she played with the aspect dial to make sense of it. Tri-D holo-lithic mapping, which she could rotate to any orientation, showed her Vesperus as it had been in life. Parts of it. She zoomed out, appreciating how big the data-block was and, in consequence, how very big the hive was. She saw, as wire-frame models, streets and avenues she had flown along, towers she had circled, urban chasms she had run at high burn. She looked for overlay options, unfamiliar with the console layout, found what she was looking for, and entered her requested function. A second map of bright red and amber lines superimposed itself on the hive map like an impossibly complex, impossibly dense cobweb. The routes and links of the hive's vast public transport system, banded into altitudes and frequencies, colour-coded for priority and connection.

It was everything she had–

'What the hell is this?' a voice asked at her shoulder.

It was Senior Deck Dampier.

Leader's office, Intercept 66, Vesperus, 05:11

'You sanctioned it?' Dampier asked.

Garrant sat down at his desk. He looked tired and angry.

'Deck,' he said, 'I don't have time for this.'

'None of us have time for it, Lead,' Badler said. He was standing by the window shutters, arms folded, glaring at Jagdea. 'But Driver's making us make the time.'

'I intended no–' Jagdea began.

'You can shut up completely,' Dampier snapped at her. Head up, hands behind her back, Jagdea stiffened and tried not to catch Garrant's eye.

'You sanctioned this?' Dampier asked Garrant again.

'I gave Jagdea an unofficial nod to proceed with some informal flight instruction, Deck,' said Garrant.

'We know about her huddles, Lead,' said Badler. 'I've seen one.'

'Then why the frig have you pulled me in to talk about it?' Garrant asked, mainly to Dampier. 'I should be briefing–'

'Why keep it unofficial?' Dampier asked.

'Because you could never permit it to be otherwise, Julett,' Garrant told her. 'You're Prefectus. If you don't officially know about it, you can deny it. I didn't want you compromised. Either of you.'

'Because the combat techniques Driver is circulating are non-standard and contrary to Aeronautica regulations,' said Badler. It wasn't a question.

'You know they are,' said Garrant. 'They may also save lives and improve our performance, in this particular theatre, which is why I turned a blind eye. I turned a blind eye so that neither of you would have to.'

'Lead Garrant was not–' Jagdea began.

'I said shut up,' said Dampier. 'Pretty convinced I meant it.'

'It's your job to run this deck to code, Dampier,' said Garrant, 'and you are scrupulous, which is why I am glad to have you. It's my job to prosecute this frigging war and meet the lord militant's requirements. Sometimes those objectives do not overlap. This is one of those times.'

'I fully support your–' Dampier started to object.

'You can't fully support me!' Garrant snarled. 'Not where I'm going. Not where I'm obliged to go. For frig's sake, Julett. What are you going to do? Approve the masking of cockpit instruments? Approve pilots to reject stores if they feel like it? Approve the tasking of fightbirds in unauthorised performance? You can't have things like that on your official transcript and not expect the service to gut you when this tour is up.'

'I think that should be my choice, Lead,' said Dampier. 'What goes on my record and what doesn't. My choice.'

'Well, I was making the choice for you, so you didn't get burned,' said Garrant. 'You've seen the stats. We're stopping one in five. We need that up to three at least to meet the threshold. We are letting too many through, and the south-east 'plex is getting pounded.'

'A few non-standard tricks is one thing,' said Dampier. 'But this is something else entirely.'

She held up the wafer.

'Restricted Administratum data,' she said. 'Critical strategic data, accessed without authority on a Control station.'

Garrant opened his mouth to speak, then closed it, and shook his head.

'Lead Garrant knew nothing about it,' said Jagdea.

'Last warning, pilot,' said Dampier.

'Where did the data come from?' Badler asked.

At attention, Jagdea flexed uneasily. She thought of Lopard, of trust...

'I'll repeat that question,' said Dampier.

'I'm not prepared to say, Deck,' said Jagdea.

'I'm pretty sure I know,' said Dampier.

'Then why are you asking me?' Jagdea snapped. She dropped her hands to her sides, and turned to Dampier. 'What is the point of this conversation?' she asked.

'Resume position and shut up!' Dampier growled.

Jagdea glanced at Garrant. He was frowning, as though fighting a sudden, knifing migraine.

'Permission to speak, sir,' she said.

'Granted,' sighed Garrant.

Jagdea looked at Dampier and the glaring Badler.

'Lead knew nothing about the data,' she said. 'Nothing. I had an idea, a hunch, and I was playing it to see if it had any utility. And I think it does. But I acknowledge the data is restricted, illicitly obtained, reviewed without any auth, and without Lead's knowledge or approval. He's mad at me, not you.'

She glanced at Garrant.

'I'm sorry I've dropped you in this,' she said.

He scowled. 'I don't need this shit, Jagdea,' he replied. He turned his gaze towards Dampier. 'But if you're charging her, you're charging me too. This data may be news to me, but I consider its acquisition and examination to be part of the free hand I gave to Jagdea.'

'Don't–' Jagdea whispered.

'Oh, Asa,' said Dampier. 'How frigging difficult do you want to make this?'

'File your report, Dampier,' Garrant said.

'No,' said Jagdea. 'This entire discussion is arse-about-face! You're so concerned about the data's auth level and origin! You're not even asking the obvious questions!'

'Which are?' asked Dampier.

'Why the frig didn't you have it already?' said Jagdea. 'And why aren't you using it?'

'I haven't begun to review the data,' said Dampier.

'It's transit system maps for the entire hive,' said Jagdea. 'Every flight level and route, every obstruction and structure logged. A complete navigation brief for flying this city.'

'It will be out of date,' said Badler. 'The damage–'

'Parts of it, yes,' said Jagdea. 'Big parts. But even if only some of it is valid, it will save lives. Pilots can focus on bat-hunting rather than just trying to miss this frigging city at every turn. Why haven't we been running this since day one?'

There was a pause. Dampier glanced at Garrant.

'No one knew it still existed,' said Dampier.

'Did anyone even ask?' said Jagdea.

'Watch your tone–'

'It took me, what, two days to find it,' said Jagdea. 'All right, I got it from an illegal source, and maybe most hive data has been burned or wiped. But I bet there's a copy of this in the databanks at Orison 'plex. Why is no one thinking? Why is no one asking these questions?'

Nobody spoke. She knew the answers anyway. Everyone was too shredded. There was no time to think. It was the same with everything. Minute-to-minute survival obscured any big-picture thinking. And, as ever, the chain of command, so remote and theoretical, was not considering practical applications at the sharp end. No one had supplied Six-Six with the data for the same reason they kept sending Six-Six Voss Strikes. Wrong tool, wrong job. Somebody high in the chain had ordered that something got done, and the grunts at the bottom had to find a way to do it.

'The data's too big,' said Badler after a moment.

'What?'

'Too big to load onto a fightbird's onboard.'

'Agreed,' said Jagdea. 'So we packet it by district, and issue packets to match sorties.'

'That's a lot of work,' said Badler.

Jagdea nodded. 'And we don't have any time to waste,' she said. 'I know. But you put two or three competent pilots on this for a week or two, sorting, subdividing, packeting, you would extend everyone's sortie time. It's just basic warfare economics. Fewer pilots in the sky now, but more birds in the sky for longer lifetimes. Fewer losses, more kills.'

Badler looked at Garrant.

'With due respect to whatever frigging legend Driver may have once been,' he said, 'we can't spare–'

'She's not wrong, Ricou,' said Garrant.

There was a knock at the door, and it opened without a wait for permission.

'Multiple shouts, Lead,' Jongleur reported, sticking his head around. 'Inbound tracks.'

Garrant rose immediately.

'Get to it,' he said. 'We'll revisit this later. Deck, get that data analysed for feasibility.'

'You're on report, pending,' Dampier said to Jagdea. She looked at Garrant. 'Lead, you are also–'

'Whatever,' said Garrant.

Sixth drop, Intercept 66, Vesperus, 05:55

The war sky was waiting for them. A stagnant sunrise bled across the hive, filling the streets with smudged light and long, blotchy shadows. It was a busy morning already.

Jagdea dead dropped off the spire with Tantrum and Smoke,

the fourth intercept to go in as many minutes. They were tasked to a track coming in through Vanitas. It was Wilzar's first time back in the air since his collision, and Jagdea could tell he was applying himself, flying his repaired Strike with assertive authority. She didn't know if the huddles had improved his attitude, or if he was just determined not to screw up again.

But Tantrum was sticking with confidence too. She didn't have to make allowances for either of them. She had the lead spot. She lit the coals and led them on a tag-chase between towers and over roofs.

The track turned into nothing; either a false read, or the bats were already long gone. Jagdea voxed control, reporting intention to return, but was instructed to perch instead. The promised fuel load was due to arrive from Intercept 43 that day, but until it did, conservation regs were in place. Now they were out, they would stay out rather than burn fuel getting back to the Campanile only to burn more when they were scrambled again.

They found a roost high in the eaves of a habitat tower just south of Vanitas, dug their landing claws into the buckled plating, and shut down.

The sun rose, shifting the angle of light across the skyline. It was a sickly, bloodshot radiance. Dust clouds and reactor smoke threaded the streets far below. A light breeze creaked and shifted their perched birds. Wilzar and Glick, roosting either side of her, chatted quietly over cockpit comms. Jagdea sat back, rolling through the combat channels with her fingertip, trying not to think about the mess she'd dropped herself and Garrant into. Dampier might remove him from command. She had the authority. She was hard to read, but she seemed the epitome of the dedicated Prefectus officer. Jagdea admired that as much as she loathed it.

She rolled her finger across the frequency selector. There were several intercepts underway. Harlot had engaged bats near Centimel.

It seemed Merry Death had chalked up a kill already. Somewhere out near Machinko, Longlas, Gangster and Slumbag were committed in pursuit. Reaper and Blindside reported contact near the Treves Shelf. After a few minutes, Blindside reported two splashed, one by Reaper, one by Dummy.

Jagdea smiled. That was most likely Dummy's first kill of the tour. She'd told Jagdea she'd done tours out in the Eastern Boxes, and was proud of her tally there. She'd earned the name 'Dummy' after an ill-advised attempt at fake-out evasion during her first drop in Vesperus. She had struggled, like all of them, to understand the combat dynamics of the new war sky.

The vox crackled. Mischief was declaring contact with hostiles crossing east along Union, but expressing concern they were bait. Jagdea heard Badler verify his flight was dropping inbound to support.

Then she heard Garrant reporting an urgent engage in the vicinity of Zado. Jagdea didn't hear much of his chatter, because Control immediately cut in with an order for her to drop in support. Her instruments were already receiving the track routing.

'Driver, instruct copy. Dropping.'

She released her claws and fell with a jolt. Tantrum and Wilzar dropped on her tail. Flakes of rusted plating shook loose and fell with them, obliterated seconds later by their efflux as they fired and lit. They pulled up steeply and began their chase down a deeply shadowed canyon of ruin.

'Arm, live,' she voxed.

'Tantrum, copy.'

'Smoke, copy.'

'Hard left left, Zado West,' she said. She dropped her visor, watched the combat data start to flow, then braced into grip as they took the turn and the G-load that went with it. 'Lead, Lead, Driver. Inbound in three.'

'Copy, Driver.'

'Sit-rep, Lead?'

She half-heard Garrant reply, but his words were mashed by static.

'Vox check, Lead. Say again.'

They cornered high into Zado South, viciously tight. A bat, a Talon, she thought, went past them high, trailing smoke. She wanted to look back and see where it had gone, but at the G-load they were pulling, a turn of the head would scramble her inner ear. She kept her grip tight, face front.

They immediately ran through the middle of a turning fight. Garrant, Gumm and Slipstream, knifing across the wide Heliocet Plaza with three or four bats. They were past it before they'd even seen it.

Jagdea calmly levelled wings, preparing to loop and reset.

'Stay with me,' she told her wingmen. 'High turn to re-engage.'

'Negative, negative,' Wilzar voxed. *'Bats, bats.'*

She saw them. Hostiles moving east, low. A glint of sunlight on glass.

Venoms. Hell Venoms, at least three of them.

'Climb and push over,' she voxed. They raced up the mountainous flank of an Administratum pyramid, then rolled in series through a gaping blast hole in its superstructure and began to drop towards the contacts far below. Venoms. Big multi-engine fighter-bombers, bigger than Talons. Biggest bats she'd seen in the hive-grave, biggest she'd even heard reported. Garrant's flight had engaged their top cover, but the heavies were still running.

Rapid stutters of tracer came up at them as they made their dive. The Venoms had rear and spinal turrets, and they were raking the air to keep the fightbirds off. Huge, dense streamers of shots whipped across them. She felt the thump of a glancing hit.

Tone lock. She loosed a spray of cannon fire that stitched

across the back of the tailender, then fell in behind the Venom it was following. She could no longer see or hear Tantrum or Smoke. The Venoms were moving in convoy, which limited the envelopes of their nose guns and aft turrets. Snuggled between them, they couldn't hit her without the risk of hitting each other. The Hell Venoms were huge, glossy black beasts mottled with toxic-yellow blob patterning. They were also blocked: they were too big to yank an evasion into adjoining thoroughfares. They seemed to fill the immense breadth of Zado Avenue. Jagdea could hear the volcanic rumble of their engines.

The Venom ahead of her decided to fire anyway. Tail turrets traversed and ripped at her. She dipped, then pitched left, and let off a burst of fire from both nose and underwing mounts, disintegrating the left aft turret in a spray of debris, and then rupturing the Venom's port engine. It began a ferocious burn almost at once, pluming fuel-rich smoke and flames in its wake. For a second, the plume engulfed her Voss completely. She rolled right, came level, and began pounding the starboard side with her hard cannons. She missed the starboard aft turret, but sent her fire straight into the efflux of the starboard engine, a blaze of heat painting bright red on her visor display. The engine suffered a critical failure instantly. The Venom faltered, then rose abruptly, spewing a vast fan of black smoke from its port side and dazzling splinter-clouds of debris from its starboard. She dipped hard to avoid collision, and shot under it as it climbed askew, like a wounded animal making one last attempt to bolt. Then it ploughed into the face of the hab-blocks on the left side of the Avenue. The Venom kept going for some distance after impact, some two or three hundred yards, disintegrating against the city structure and gutting the habs so that the facade collapsed like a slow, rolling avalanche onto the street below. Dust, lurid pink, blossomed in huge sheets, choking the light.

The Venom behind her loomed out of the dust, firing its nose guns. She was low, so she stayed low, hugging the street at light-pole level. It started to pass over her, ponderous and heavy.

She eased back the power, intending to jump up on its tail.

'Driver, chase out,' she heard Tantrum bark.

She didn't question it. She advanced power hard and shot out from under the big machine, sprinting ahead of it again. Tantrum was somewhere high behind her. She heard Glick yell something, something gleeful and inarticulate. He had just loosed his heaters into the Venom from its six.

The Venom went up in a flash, bursting like a balloon of flame, scorching the buildings around them. Jagdea rode the flame-rush, gunning out of its radius and shock-pulse to chase the third Venom, now way ahead. Wilzar rolled in beside her. The Venom was drawing on the huge power of its engines to accelerate, and it was raking Zado Avenue with everything its stern-chasing turrets could fire.

'Break, break!' she heard Glick yell, away behind them.

She rolled out left, climbing. Wilzar rolled out right. A pair of Razors shot through between them at full burn. Climbing, she saw Wilzar's Voss bank to avoid the bat that was looping back for him. He'd pulled too wide. He was going to clip the corner of a thirty-storey structure.

Wilzar J-turned. It wasn't perfect, but it was good enough, and besides, the turn was insanely imperfect at the best of times. He threw his Voss around, letting control depart, letting logis compensate for choke and intake momentum drag.

He missed the building, and the ground. He flopped over, regaining stick, and dropped right onto the tail of the Razor as it overshot him. She saw him fire, and saw the Razor buck, fold in half, and disassemble in a cloud of sparks.

'Kill!' Wilzar crowed triumphantly. *'Four-A!'*

He banked hard out of the smoke wash and turned to rejoin her.

'Concentrate,' she warned. The other Razor had dropped right back, trying to heave her through and then drive her off the tail of the remaining Venom. She wanted to drop too, but a gantry arch was coming up, and she needed power to tuck in under it. She throttled up, and shot under the gantry. The Razor's burst went wide. She gripped hard and started to climb. G-crush. The Razor stayed with her, at her seven. Bastard was good. They went up the face of an Administratum block together, pulling vertical. She rolled out of the climb, vision coned, legs heavy. Threat lock. She rolled. Threat lock again.

Shots striped past her port wing.

The Administratum block had lost almost all of its windows in the upper levels. It was a skeletal frame from the waist up. Taking hits, she banked through it. There was zero clearance. Torn pipework, spooled cables and rockcrete columns slapped past. The Razor rated in after her. Las-fire blew out a column to her left. She jagged hard right, then harder left to avoid the remains of an elevator assembly. She came out of the other side of the structure, banked as hard as she could, and went back in through a higher floor as the Razor shot out of the ruin below her.

She burned through the ruined interior again. Her left wing tore through a skein of dead cables. Gunfire. The Razor wasn't just good, it was persistent. It had turned and followed her back through the tower.

Threat lock. There was nowhere to evade. She'd hoped the second pass would shake the bastard off her, but he was not letting her go.

Las-fire caught her across the right wing plating and the nose, then hammered into her right flank. The bird shook. Her canopy exploded, half-torn away. Damage conditions started bleating, their sound oddly shrill with the canopy gone, and the wind rush and engine roar blasting in.

She exited the tower and dropped into a steep dive. She knew she was trailing smoke. An engine burn? The stick was not happy, and the bleating would not quit.

She tasted blood in her mouth.

The Razor was diving after her. She could hear Wilzar and Glick yelling over the vox. Threat lock.

She J-turned herself. It seemed the only way to shake the bat. She trusted her airframe and logis systems were intact enough to recover her. G-crush nearly punched her unconscious. The Voss went into a nasty tumble, then settled with a snap, pushing the chasing Razor down past her. Without thinking, she rolled after it, ignoring the damage advisories and the wind whistling in her ears and freezing the blood on her face.

Murderlock. The Razor jinked out of her crosshairs. She jinked to match, and slid it right back in again. Nose guns, sustained. The heavy K68s drummed out streams of las-fire. The Razor veered away. It looked like a frantic evasion, but it was already dead and its mangled flight surfaces were simply throwing it headlong in a wild spin. She saw it fragment in a puff of metal, and its power plant torch-off in a bright flash that turned into a comet arcing towards the streets below.

'Go frig yourself,' she snarled, spitting blood.

She banked. Her Voss was leaving a lot of smoke in the sky behind her. She could just hear Tantrum over the wind-noise, reporting her situation to Control: *'Driver hit. Visible damage, making smoke.'*

She shook her head to clear her vision. There. It hadn't been a mistake. From her current altitude, she could see the remaining Venom gunning east, low, moving onto the Magistry Processional.

She banked and blew in after it, ignoring the squeals of vox protest from her wingmen and Campanile Control, and the icy blast of the wind. She dropped five hundred feet and turned past the tower of Saint Angelos to orientate and line up. None of the birds from her flight or Garrant's were close enough to catch the Venom now. She was the only thing left between it and the east 'plex.

'Driver, Driver,' the vox crackled. It was Garrant. *'If you are still flyable, divert to Six-Six for recovery immediate. Respond.'*

'Instruct, copy,' she replied.

'Gain height. Do not engage.'

Screw that. She advanced power. The Voss coughed. It was now punctuating its stream of smoke with donuts of greasy black soot. Ahead and below, the Venom lit up its turrets, striping the air with tracers. She dropped lower and accelerated onto its six. Her K's were out, power expended. She gave the big bat everything she had left in the canisters of her wing cannons, and flew over the Venom as it fireballed, leaving a gouge in the street-level rockcrete a mile long.

Intercept 66, Vesperus, 07:58

Garrant's Twin rolled in beside her as she staggered towards the Campanile.

'Hell was that?' he voxed. *'I gave you an instruct.'*

'Copy,' she said. She wasn't in a position to argue. The Voss was barely hanging in the air and she was losing power. Airstream battered her through the smashed canopy.

Garrant, no matter his temper, understood.

'You're making smoke,' he voxed more gently. *'You need some height.'*

'Working on that, Lead,' she replied.

'Can you make hard arrest, or do we clear a top deck?' he asked.

The Voss shook.

'Driver, respond. Can you make hard arrest?'

'Uncertain. Stand by.'

She checked her instruments, peeling off some tape where necessary.

'CAD says I still have ducts,' she replied. 'I think hard arrest is viable.'

The Campanile, rising above the roofline of Orundo, still seemed a long way off.

She heard Garrant confer with Control on the vox. A quick, urgent exchange.

'Driver, Control instructs a top-deck down for optimal outcome,' said Garrant.

'Not sure if I have the lift, Lead,' she responded.

'Let's try. Prep for autotrack.'

She understood the odds. Putting a wounded bird down in a landing box left no margin for error or malfunction. There was more space on the roof decks they used for launch. But the roof decks were much higher up.

Her logis-engine responded as it received the autotrack instruct. On her visor, the autotrack display pulsed towards launch deck four on the west side of the spire. The ground crews were clearing everything off it that they could.

She nursed the engine to gain a little height. The Voss, hurt, didn't like it.

'Driver, lift,' Garrant voxed, riding off her right wing.

'Copy,' she replied. She wasn't getting much positive feel from the stick, and every time she nudged the throttle, there was a grating clatter from somewhere below her.

The bell tower was now dead ahead, its pyramidal spire soaring above her. This was not going to work. She was nearing stall speed, and way too low.

'Lead, it's going to have to be the box or nothing,' she voxed.

'Copy,' was all Garrant replied.

A pause. The autotrack flickered, vanished, and then recomposed, indicating the landing box where she had put in when she first arrived. She'd been recovered back into it after every sortie since then, and had never thought about it twice after the stress of the first time.

This was different.

It felt too tight again. The Voss began to cough and stumble badly. She pumped the rudder to maintain control, and eased the stick. The logis-engine was screaming data at her across her instrumentation and visor. Some of it had been corrupted by malfunction.

'Driver, easy in, and prep for hard arrest.'

'Copy, Control,' she replied, one hand on the stick, the other on the vector thrust in an effort to soothe the stumble. Almost at the hover stop, on an engine that seemed likely to fail at any moment.

'Driver, hard in. Hard in now.'

'Copy.'

'Steady, hold that line.'

She felt the gyroscopic effect of the struggling engine pulling her nose. She soothed the rudder.

Then she was into shadow, crossed the lip into the slot. Over steel, the Voss bucked in a spasm. She threw everything to the brake stop and, as she had seen Bloodspot do what seemed like years before, dropped her fightbird like a rock.

Hard arrest.

Jagdea exhaled, and killed the turboram and the power.

'Driver down,' she reported. In the box outside, she could see Tarr and Boa running up, leading the ground crew forward. Some of them carried suppression canisters. Two of them were lugging a stretcher.

She sat back and put her hands on her head.

* * *

Infirmary, Intercept 66, Vesperus, 10:03

'I can only presume that was some kind of declaration of intent,' said Lopard. 'Marking your territory.'

Jagdea tried to glance aside at him.

'Head still,' the medicae warned.

She kept her eyes front, sitting on the edge of the surgical bench as Stanslaf, the deck medicae, washed and sealed her wounds. She'd taken cuts to her forehead, neck and shoulder from flying canopy plex. Superficial but bloody. There was suspected concussion, but she'd refused a head scan. She perched on the edge of the cot with her dirty flightsuit peeled down around her shoulders like a ball-gown as the medicae worked on her. Her ears were still ringing.

'What is that, now?' Lopard mused, dragging up a stool to sit on. 'Four in two days? Three in one sortie? Two of those after you'd taken enough damage to force you into recovery?'

'It was a busy sky,' said Jagdea.

'It's almost as if you had something to prove,' remarked Lopard.

Now she shot him a look. 'Like what?'

'Head still!' the medicae snapped.

Lopard smiled.

'Like you know what you're talking about so people should listen to you,' he suggested.

'It wasn't like that,' said Jagdea.

'Doesn't matter,' said Lopard. 'That's how it looks. Three in one sortie is, I believe, a Six-Six record. Not to mention that three of your proteges finally got on the wall the same day.'

'They're not my proteges.'

'Whatever they are... those are outcomes no one can ignore.'

'Is this professional jealousy?' she asked.

'Hell, no!' Lopard exclaimed, looking surprised. 'I came to congratulate you. Frigging Four-A, Jagdea.'

He produced a bottle of amasec from his coat pocket.

'She's on pain meds,' objected Stanslaf, frowning at the bottle Lopard was unstoppering.

'I haven't taken any yet,' said Jagdea, and thrust her hand towards Lopard. He put the bottle in it. Stanslaf stepped back, forceps raised, while she swigged.

She swallowed, breathed hard, then passed the bottle to the medicae. He sighed, took a sip, and handed the bottle back to Lopard.

'Good flying,' Stanslaf muttered, as he leaned in to resume suturing.

'Good flying indeed,' agreed Lopard, raising the bottle to toast her. 'May you return to deck, in relatively one piece, before the bats know you're up.'

Jagdea remained solemn. Her ears were still ringing, and her face seemed numb from the cold and the wind, as if it would never thaw. There were four people in the war deck's scrappy little sickbay, and one of them was the shred. It was still with her. It had clung to her through the fight, licked the blood off her neck, and followed her all the way home, its hand on the stick over hers. It had slithered from the hangar to the sickbay at her heels. Now it was reclining in the corner, like a bloated predator sleeping off a meal. Its smile was bigger and more insufferable than Lopard's.

'Three in one drop,' Lopard was saying. 'Best I've done is two, though I have done five in the same day. Separate drops, though. I've clearly got to raise my game. Maybe I should come to your classes?'

'One bat,' said Jagdea, letting Med Stanslaf tilt her head to get better access. 'Two were heavies. They don't really count.'

'Oh, I assure you, everything counts, Jagdea,' said Lopard. He was about to say something else, but Garrant had walked in, still suited, dirty and sweaty from flight. Lopard stood.

'Give us the room, Reno,' Garrant said to him.

'Of course, Lead,' said Lopard, and walked out, casting a 'pretend scared' grimace at Jagdea. Garrant looked at Jagdea's cheek and neck.

'You too, Doc,' he said to Stanslaf. 'Finish later.'

The medicae nodded, and also withdrew.

'What the hell's wrong with you?' Garrant asked.

'Just superficial,' said Jagdea. 'Shards of plas-glass–'

'Don't be clever,' said Garrant. 'I gave you a clear instruct to go for recovery. Which you confirmed. Your bird was in no state for dancing. But you went in hot, on a target that was almost out of the kill box anyway.'

'It was right there.'

'That's your answer?'

'No one else was in a position to stop it. It was...'

'What?'

'It was on my way home.'

Garrant scowled. 'This funny to you?' he asked.

'No, Lead.'

'A Voss Strike is a valuable asset. Tail Four-Four was badly knocked. Plating, some flight surfaces, some ram defects. It'll be grounded for several days. You had an obligation to bring it home so it could remain in service, but you muscled it around instead. You didn't know how bad the damage was. Adverse g-load could have folded it up under you.'

She didn't reply.

'I'm not just talking about the bird, Jagdea.'

'I sort of got that, Lead.'

He frowned at her, fuming. 'I've got an uphill climb to keep Badler and Dampier calm over this data thing,' he said. 'I'm not even sure I can smooth it out–'

'And I apologise, Lead. I never meant to pull you into–'

'Not the point,' he said. 'It's sticky, and there's likely to be blowback. You disobeying a direct instruct from me, and risking yourself and a bird unnecessarily, is not going to help convince them that we should trust you or your judgement.'

'Then transfer me out,' she said.

'Really? That's what this was about?'

'No,' she said, shaking her head. The movement pulled at her sutures, and reminded her how tender her neck and shoulder were. 'No, not at all. But it's an option. So is the idea that actions speak louder than words.'

He stared at her, trying to read her.

'I never took you for that kind of gunfighter,' he said. 'Not a swaggerer like Harlot or Yesof.'

'I'm not,' she replied. 'But Lopard just pointed out that this will be spun however people want to spin it. What I actually did, and why, is not the point. For you, today's drop could be definitive evidence that I am high value, and Badler and Deck Dampier will have to suck it up. End of discussion, end of any disciplinary.'

'Is that why you did it?' he asked. 'To remind everyone you were the hero of the Zoph, and that regs don't apply to you? A three-kill drop. And three of the smokes got off the blocks this morning, no small thanks to you, I imagine.'

'Again, no,' she said. 'That's not why I did it. Tantrum, Smoke and Dummy may just have had good days. I'm saying, if that's what it looks like, use it. Get Dampier in line. Boost damn morale. Whatever. I don't frigging care. Prosecuting a war sky is ninety-nine per cent mental game. Mindset, attitude, confidence. You know that. Think right, and the rest is vapour. I'm an asset. I'm a pilot in your squadron. You get to use that asset to your best advantage.'

'I can't believe you think that clinically,' he said.

'I can't believe I'm even coherent right now,' she replied.

Garrant studied her for another moment.

'Why *did* you do it?' he asked.

'I did it because I'm Aeronautica,' she replied. 'I was in a target-rich war sky with a mandate to intercept and kill bats. I saw opportunities, and I took them. I didn't do it for glory, or rep, or to honour the God-Emperor, or to prove some kind of point. I did it because it was my job. I did it because it was the job *you* gave me.'

Hangar bay, Intercept 66, Vesperus, 13:07

She stood on the WALK ONLY and stared down into the empty cockpit of Tail 044. The fightbird seemed so heavy and so dead, just an inert tonnage of cold metal. She found it hard to imagine it even moving, let alone flying. How did this ever leave the ground? How did it move with such violent liberty, with her as its beating heart?

The Voss was utterly extinct. No trace of power, no residual heat. She could smell the musty odours of its carcass – the oil, the metal, the fyceline, the leather, the fuel – but there was no trace of life. The only movements were the steady drips of prom and other fluids leaking from the underside onto the hangar's steel flooring.

She looked at the furrows in the wing plate, like the wakes of invisible ships frozen in water, where the bat's heavy las-bolts had clawed her. The fuselage plates below and behind the cockpit on the right side were staved in around blackened craters that armour had barely stopped. She traced a fingertip around the sharp, raw metal of the punctures. Any of those behind the cockpit should have sheared off her tail assembly or blown up the ram. Those below the sill, any one of them could have punched through and atomised her in her seat. The remains of the canopy had already been removed. Tarr had told her the repairs would take at least three days. She would be assigned another aircraft in the meantime, if she was cleared to fly. She stared down at the litter of canopy fragments on the seat and in the footwell, the spots of her blood on the leather and half-taped instruments.

It made her think of something that she didn't want in her head. Not death, not dying in combat. Not luck, or how close she'd come. Something that, like the shred, lurked between those things. Something else that was far more unpleasant.

'Busy day for you,' said Gumm.

He was standing on the deck below, looking up at her.

'Looks that way,' she agreed.

'Everyone is talking.'

'Everyone can shut up.'

She climbed down to join him. Her face and neck no longer hurt, but her right arm and ribs were sore. Referred concussion trauma, she thought.

'Three kills,' he said. 'Showing us all how it's done?'

'Don't you start,' she snapped, too harsh. She raised a hand in apology. 'Sorry,' she said. 'I've had it from Harlot and Lead. The remarks. The insinuations.'

'Of?'

'Showboating,' she said. 'Hot-sticking. Territorial demarcation.'

'Then I apologise,' said Gumm. 'I was only teasing. I presume you were just doing what had to be done.' He glanced at the Voss' damage. 'By the skin of your teeth,' he added.

'You should see the other guy,' she said.

'Are you all right?' he asked.

Jagdea nodded.

'Are you grounded?' he asked.

'I'll be given another bird,' she said. 'Until Four-Four is patched. Whatever Tarr can find in the Tomb.'

'A Voss?'

Jagdea shrugged. 'So how was your day, dear?' she asked, making her face smile.

'Well, the resupply from Four-Three came in earlier, so that's something,' he said. 'Keep us all in the air a little longer. And I got one. Talon. Pales in insignificance, of course. Apparently anyone can bag one these days. Even smokes.'

'They had a good day,' she agreed.

'Should we be proud of that?' he wondered.

'They did it, not us. But it feels like something worthwhile is beginning to take place. I don't think we've taught them anything, Gumm. It would be arrogant to think so, and we've barely had time. But maybe... maybe just having someone make the effort has flash-started them before they hit the ground.'

'That would be more than enough for me,' he said. 'Speaking of, are you well enough for a huddle tonight?'

'Yes.'

'Thoughts on venue? Your billet wasn't really adequate yesterday, and I have a feeling there will be more tonight.'

She hadn't thought of that. Notoriety, bringing in a crowd. It made her flush cold.

'I don't know,' she said. She thought about the chantry, and then wondered if that was just taunting Dampier and Badler.

'Can I suggest hangar three?' he said. 'I was speaking to Slipstream when we got back, and he said that he and Mischief wanted to sit in. Of course, they can't come to us...'

'Sounds fine to me,' she said. She frowned. 'Really? Slipstream and Mischief?'

'If Gangster can come of her own volition, nothing surprises me,' said Gumm.

He looked at her with those sharp little blue eyes.

'Are you all right?' he asked.

'You've asked me that already.'

'No, are *you* all right?'

She scratched at the sutures on her cheek. They were starting to itch.

'I did my job,' she said.

'Yes.'

'Just my job,' she said. 'Whatever Harlot thinks, Garrant... whatever motives they want to attribute. I was just doing my best.'

'I believe you,' he said. 'Why does that sound like it's a problem?'

She looked at him.

'It was stupid,' she said. 'I pushed too far. I was so fired up, I ignored regs and a bird that was dying under me. I pushed past the limit and took chances I should never have taken, and I flew better than I have flown in years.'

'So...?'

'I thought that person was dead, Gumm,' she said quietly. 'Long dead and left behind. I thought I was me now, just Reserve Driver Jagdea, but I'm not. She came back. I was her again, fangs out, and I liked it far too much.'

'I think...' he said. He seemed unsure what to say. 'I mean, isn't that to be expected? Welcomed, even? The only way to survive here is to fly your best, and if your best is coming back to you, then that's like a natural threat response. Adaptive. A survival tactic. I'm saying, it's a good thing.'

'You don't understand,' she said. 'My best was crazy. Dangerous. Lethal. I don't want my best back. I don't want to be her any more, because it will kill me. Or worse.'

'Worse?' he asked.

'I liked it,' she said. 'I'm afraid that if I start being her again, I won't be able to stop. Ever.'

Gumm nodded. 'I understand,' he replied. 'I believe I understand. I'm sorry, I wish I could offer you advice.'

His voice trailed off. He turned to walk away, then stopped.

'I understand,' he said, standing with his back to her. 'I…'

'What?' she asked.

He turned to look at her.

'All right,' he said, with odd resignation. 'All right.'

'All right *what*?'

'Come with me,' he said.

Refectory, Intercept 66, Vesperus, 13:45

A crowd had gathered around Wilzar and Dummy, whooping and clapping as they retold their glory stories. Glick sat nearby, watching them, beaming, and clearly very drunk.

Everyone started cheering and put their hands on their heads when they saw Jagdea walk in with Gumm.

'Glory stories later,' he called out cheerfully, and led her to an empty corner away from the fuss.

'Sit,' he said, and walked away.

She sat. Her hands were trembling. She looked at the fireplace, and saw the fresh marks on the wall, beside SMOKE and TANTRUM and DUMMY, beside DOLLFACE and REAPER, HARLOT, MERRY DEATH…

So many. It had been a good day for the Circus. Someone, and she guessed Lopard, had chalked up her kills for her.

Gumm returned. He flapped out his coat, sat facing her, and plonked a bottle of joiliq and two glasses on the table.

'What are we doing?' she asked.

'Celebrating,' he said.

He uncorked the bottle and filled the glasses.

'You don't drink, Gumm.'

He ignored her.

'Sagittarius Gumm,' he said, without preamble, his silky voice barely above a whisper, 'was a multi-ace. Served as flight leader with the Twenty-Second Furies in the Khulan Wars, then as squadron lead with Hundred-and-First Fleet Intercept in the anti-piracy campaigns along the Sabbat Flank early in the crusade. We weren't assigned to the main crusade force, because we were Battlefleet Khulan, but we were running interference along the spinward edge. The drukhari were trying to take advantage of the instability caused by Slaydo's advance. Saw action at Banzier, Ansara, Ansara Quad, the Metalus Tract. Would have made wing commander, but I was head-hunted by Red Deck.'

She looked at the brimful glasses, then at him.

'*The* Red Deck?'

'You will have heard of them, I imagine.'

She had. Of course she had. Red Deck was an elite squadron, a prestige squadron, the best of the best. Like the Apostles and Blackhammer Flight, they were invite-only. To be offered a place was to be acknowledged as the very finest gunslinger.

'Sagittarius Gumm flew with Red Deck for eight tours,' he said, still lapsing oddly into the third person as though he wished to create some distance. 'Eight tours, six and a half years. Anti-piracy in the Newfound Trailing, then precision work at San Sargo, Kazin II, Urus and the Bethan Halo. By then, we'd been folded into the crusade fleet, running rearguard operations on the supply lines. It was an adventure every day. High shred. Big kills. There's not enough chalk in this room.'

'You don't have to tell me this, Gumm,' she said. 'You don't have to tell me any of this.'

But he kept going.

'Sagittarius Gumm was good,' he said. 'I was good. I didn't need the exaggeration of glory stories. I was the best. Like you said in the hangar, I liked it, Jagdea. I delighted in it. I revelled in my talent. I held the deck's leading stats for two years. But you know what that's like, don't you? There's only so high you can fly, and only so long you can stay there.'

'But while you're *up* there...' she whispered.

'Oh, while you're *up* there,' he agreed. He slid his hand towards the glass in front of him. 'The way you described it, Jagdea. Like an addiction. It needs to be fed, or it eats you. You want to stop, because you know where it's taking you, but you can't bear the thought of letting it go.'

He looked at her.

'How could you begin to live without it?' he said. 'Isn't that what you asked yourself?'

'Too many times,' she said.

'The shred was unbearable,' he said. 'Every second, every day. It was just inside me all the time. Inside all of us. I couldn't slow down. I couldn't decel. I couldn't shake it off my six. It was part of the delight, the addiction I couldn't quit. We all... we all found ways to alleviate it, to block it, just like here at Six-Six. Narcotics. Stimms. Drink. Idiot risk-taking. Transgressive behaviour. Things I have no wish to remember.'

'Gumm, you can stop. I said you don't have to tell me–'

'I can't,' he said. 'Not now I've started. So listen. I think we ran riot because we wanted to get stood down. Disgraced. Rotated out. Even if we didn't know that's what we were doing. But they wouldn't let us go. Because we were too good. We were valuable assets.'

He looked down at the drink beside his hand.

'Drink was my thing,' he said. 'Stimms had little appeal for me, but drink. That numbed me. I used one addiction to mask another. To hide it. Drink was my hose tape.'

She waited for the rest. She knew what was coming. Not the precise specifics, but the general shape of the hole it would leave.

'A bat got me,' he said. 'Bethan Halo. Actually, no. It wasn't the bat. The drink got me. I'd been drinking too hard for too long. I was sloppy and careless, and far too sure of myself. Crashed and burned. Literally. I should have died. They had to sew me back together from what was left, and replace the pieces that were missing. They gave me a new face. This one. A fine piece of work, better than I deserved, but Red Deck was very good to its casualties. We were the favourites of – let me get this right – the son of the niece of the Khulan Sector governor, so noble purse strings would always open to provide benefits and pensions, and the finest augmetics. You know, I actually believe they thought I would come back once I had my new face?'

'But you walked?'

'Resigned my papers, took a transfer ticket to the reserve pool. I wanted to fly, but not like that. I have been driving cargo ever since.'

He sighed, as though he was finally letting go of something he'd held in for too long.

'So… now you've heard my glory story, Jagdea.'

'They're all the same, in the end,' she said. 'A rather formulaic structure. Hard climb. Fangs out. A nice big finish. No sequel.'

'Indeed,' said Gumm.

'I'm sorry I ever pressed you to hear it,' she said. 'You didn't have to tell it.'

'And I doubt I'll ever tell it again,' he said. 'But after what you said in the hangar, I felt I had to. The least I could do for a friend. Drink up.'

She picked up her glass.

'You don't have to–' she began.

'I'm not going to,' he said. 'That's sort of the point of all this.'

His hands were flat on the table. He stared at his glass and the bottle.

'If I can sit here,' he said, 'with that in front of me, and not touch it, then I've landed safe. I'm not Sagittarius Gumm. I'm me, in a regrettable situation. I can't change who I am, but I can stop being who I was. Drink's not your thing, Jagdea, I know that, but I think the analogy is fair. You've had the experience. You know the dangers to avoid. Just like we tell the smokes. If you don't want to be the hero of the Zophonian Sea again, you know what to fly around. Don't hide from it. Don't pretend it wasn't you. Put it on the table where you can see it, and stare at it.'

She knocked her drink back.

'Good flying,' she said.

He nodded back.

Hangar 3, Intercept 66, Vesperus, 22:10

More had come, just as Gumm predicted. Nearly thirty, including Gangster and her boys and, to Jagdea's surprise, Reaper, Jongleur and Blindside. Wilzar looked the worst for wear. Only Tantrum had not reappeared. Jagdea imagined Glick was asleep somewhere.

They had set up near the dark green Bolt and silver Cypra M belonging to Mischief and Slipstream. The bio-linked pilots had pulled their cots up as close as their umbilicals would allow, and were lounging like nobility viewing some amusement.

Jagdea was about to start when she saw Sister Merry Death walk in. The Sister knelt, rigid, as though praying, at the back of the sprawled huddle. Her eyes were locked on Jagdea.

'Shall we start with a blessing?' Jagdea suggested. There were groans from the less devout, but she was determined not to let Meredith's hawk-stare put her off. 'Sister?'

'Kill sinners,' said Merry Death.

'Good enough,' said Jagdea. 'Gumm's got a few words to say about weight-to-lift ratios and turn angles. The stuff we were all taught barely applies in Vesperus, so listen to what he's got to share.'

Steeley pulled out his notebook, and Reaper had brought a slate, but Jagdea could feel the impatience in the group.

'Before that,' she said, 'I want to say I'm pleased to see so many here. And I know why. It's not the quality of our advice, which is dubious at best. You want to hear about today.'

Gumm glanced at her, surprised. There was a volley of applause, a few whoops, a few sets of hands placed on heads in deference. 'Three kills!' Gangster cried, snake-arming cross-legged in the middle row.

'Thanks, thank you,' said Jagdea, hands raised. 'Damp audio. I know you won't settle until you hear it, so let's get it out of the way. I dropped. I killed three bats. Bite me.'

More laughter, uproar.

'I took chances,' she said, as the noise died down. 'I took chances. I took too many. The first kill was legit. The second, survival. The third, I shouldn't even have been there. I ignored an instruct. Never ignore a frigging instruct, no matter how good the glory story you're going to get to tell. I was frigging Four-A this morning, fangs out, hair on fire. And I was stupid. There's taking chances and there's "taking chances".'

They were quiet now.

'Could you go a bit slower,' asked Steeley, looking up from his pad, 'because I appear to have written the same phrase twice.'

'We all take chances,' said Jagdea. 'It's part of the spec. We take chances from the moment we drop. Every second of every sortie is an opportunity to eat it. The hive is trying to kill you more than the bats are. I've encouraged you to be confident. You have to be. So take those chances. I'm talking about calculated risk. Will my bird fit through that gap? Will I miss that wall? Lack of confidence will kill you. So trust your gut, and be bold.'

She cleared her throat.

'But uncalculated risk will kill you too,' she said. 'That's what I took today. Yeah, I got three kills, but I was dumb. The second kill was questionable, though I can excuse it by necessity. The third? Just frigging greedy. I should have left it. I knew exactly what I was doing, I knew exactly what my situation was, and I knew exactly what I had to do, which was follow instruct and go for recovery. I was so fired up, I ignored what I knew and everything I had ever been taught. Three kills. Big whoop. I could just as easily have had the bird die under me, and cost the Circus a Voss and a driver. So, disappointing as it will be to hear, my thing tonight is cognitive approach. Be bold enough to do what you know you can do, but be smart enough to avoid the things you can't. Brains before balls. There's a fine line.'

'How will we know it?' asked Blowout.

'You know it already. All of you know it, because you're trained Aeronautica,' said Jagdea. 'You just have to remember that you know it. Here's a hint. We're not here for personal glory. We're here to fight a war. If you're doing the first thing, then you've crossed the line.'

'So, be bold but not too bold?' asked Camo. 'Push it but don't push it?'

'Uh huh.'

'This from the pilot who taught us you need to depart control to pull a J-turn?' asked Slumbag.

'I never claimed to be consistent,' said Jagdea.

'So, too much caution, or too little?' said Steeley. 'Everything's going to kill us?'

'Yes,' said Jagdea. 'You're all going to die.'

There was silence.

'I'm sorry,' she said, 'does that come as news? You're all going to die. I'm going to die. All of us. Death is inevitable. The only say you get is how long you keep flying until it happens. Calculated risk versus uncalculated risk.'

'I don't want to die!' said Camo, involuntarily. It was more a blurted whisper, and it surprised even her.

'I know,' said Jagdea. 'Neither do I, Kinny.'

'Death in the service of the God-Emperor is a service to the God-Emperor,' said Sister Meredith in cold, clear terms.

'The Sister makes a good point,' said Jagdea, 'so there's consolation in that. Also, death is easy. It's fine. It's nothing to be afraid of. Death is not the worst part.'

'What is?' asked Mischief.

'Dying,' said Jagdea. 'That's the part that you should avoid.'

The huddle broke up, and everyone filed out, talking. No one seemed downcast or scornful. Gumm had made some valuable points, stuff that even Jagdea hadn't considered, so they hadn't wasted anybody's time.

'That was good,' Mischief called out to Jagdea and Gumm as they started to leave.

She got up off her cot, pale and sickly, dragging her umbilical around like the train of a dress.

'It was good,' she said. 'Valuable. Good to hear you say it. No one talks about those things.'

'The tricks?' Jagdea asked.

'The tricks, and all the other things you said.'

'It's a waste,' muttered Slipstream. He hadn't risen from his cot.

'A waste?' asked Gumm.

Slipstream looked up at them, bleached out and haggard.

'I suppose I admire your initiative,' Slipstream said, 'but screw them all.'

'Who?'

'The smokes. Screw 'em. They can learn this shit for themselves. The hard way. Like we did.'

Gumm took a step forward. Jagdea put a hand on his arm.

'Is that why you invited us down here?' Gumm asked. 'To pick it apart?'

'We just wanted the company, really,' said Mischief wistfully. 'I liked it. I liked what you said.'

'I didn't pick at nothing,' said Slipstream quietly. 'I didn't interrupt. I could've. I didn't. You go ahead and tell 'em what you want to tell 'em. But I say to hell with 'em.'

He rose slowly to his feet as though his muscles were wasted and weak.

'Look at me,' he said. 'I gave my life to the Aeronautica. To the God-Emperor. My actual life. Not in theory. For real. I let them make me into this... vampire. You want to see dying, Driver? It looks like this. This is me for the rest of my days. What did those smokes ever do? What did they ever sacrifice? You're trying to make things easy for them. They should learn the hard way.

'Besides,' he added, as an afterthought, 'you can't save 'em all. Ask Dicebag.'

Dicebag was a smoke Jagdea hadn't even met. What with her exploits, the day's big tally, and the fuel resupply from Intercept 43, things had been so busy she'd missed the news that Dicebag had been lost on an afternoon sortie, splashed by an unseen bat.

DAY 94

Seventh drop, Intercept 66, Vesperus, 10:11

Wilzar's second kill was such a fine execute, the sight of it almost took Jagdea's mind off her new bird.

They'd dead dropped into fine rain and fretting mist, and turned south towards Helot Bay on the scent of a track. Her, Wilzar and Gumm. Jagdea had been assigned Tail 011, the only flyable bird Tarr could drag out of the Tomb. It was a Voss Strike. The Tomb was the sub-hangar where recovered machines were stored. Most were wrecks, slowly skeletonised for parts and spares, but a few were intact enough for reconditioning. Tail 011 had been patched, strip-serviced, and fitted with a recycled ram. It was Sorrentine's bird, the bone-white Voss he had died in.

When she first saw it, Jagdea had almost refused it. It felt unseemly to touch it or make it fly again. But by then, it was already tail-up in dead drop position on the platform lip, and they were go-ready.

'Best I could do,' Tarr had said, seeing the expression on Jagdea's face. Jagdea had climbed in, the fitters clearing away the hoses. Tail 011 was in all respects identical to Four-Four, yet it seemed utterly unfamiliar. It was more worn and scuffed, and there had been no time to tape-mask any of the instruments, or adjust anything to Jagdea's preferences. Jagdea had started to walk the parish quickly, making refinements. The cockpit stank of counterseptic wash and cleaning gel, which only seemed to enhance an underlying scent of stale sweat and organic residue. The seat had been crudely reupholstered.

'Checks Four-A,' Tarr had said. 'All prime, but the ram's a recyc, and the burner has a cranky take-up lag I can't iron out. Some good news, though. Look.'

Jagdea had flipped on the voltaics. Tarr was pointing proudly at the hydraulics indicator. It was green.

'You're racking stores,' Tarr added.

Jagdea hadn't even looked.

'Relax,' said Tarr. 'Intercept Four-Three brought some actual Skystrikes with the fuel, so I've racked you two.'

Jagdea had nodded. She went to arm the seat.

'No seat,' Tarr reminded her.

Bloodspot's Voss, like all the bio-impulse birds, had been stripped of its ejection system to make room for the wet-link system's plasma reservoirs. They'd been removed, but there had been nothing to put in their place. Jagdea could see the redundant, capped valves for the neuroreactive feeds below and beside her position in the seat box.

'Done this before?' Tarr had asked.

'Not willingly,' said Jagdea.

'That's the spirit,' Tarr had replied, and latched the canopy.

They came through the hive structure at high rate, nose-to-tail, and dropped into the rockcrete outflow canyon that ran along the inside of Helot Bay's massive seawall. The seawall girdled the southern edge of the hive, a barrier half a mile high to keep the ocean out. But it had been breached in several places along its two hundred mile run during the hive-death. This was the main source of the hive's sub-level flooding. The outflow trench was a mirror of black water dotted with emerging debris and prismatic slicks, like the foetid moat of some wizard's castle. Every time they zipped past a major breach in the seawall, Jagdea glimpsed the bleak, grey emptiness of the Western Ocean beyond.

The hostiles had either turned back to meet them, or Jagdea's flight had come up on the trap part of their bait-and-trap formation first. Two bats, both Talons, had rolled into the trench to greet them.

She reminded herself of the advice she'd given the huddle the previous night. Cognitive approach. No matter how much she might want to use Sorrentine's bird to stake a little payback for him, she wasn't going to let the old gunfighter take over. By the regs. Note enemy state – altitude, airspeed, direction of attack. Guns live, lock running.

'Driver, split left,' Gumm voxed.

'Copy, in hot.'

The Talons were approaching for a head-on pass down the trench. One was so low it was kicking a wake in the dead water. Jagdea broke line wide, gunning for the higher bat. Gumm and Wilzar stayed low.

Chief Tarr had warned her about One-One's burn delay, but the hesitation at the top of the throttle still surprised her and spoiled what should have been a perfect set up. By the time she fired, climbing, the bat had kissed through her envelope.

Jagdea gripped and pulled into a loop, the trench and its stagnant waterway swinging over her head. Her prey, a black Talon, was inverting too. Just from its lithe turn, she knew it was a hunter. It wasn't payloading anything that required a low-G tolerance.

But it wasn't coming for her. It cut past her again, diving back on Wilzar and Gumm, who had just crossed and exchanged with the second bat and were peeling up for round two.

'Break, break,' she called. The second bat had just rated below her, entering a climb. She pushed over onto its heels rather than bleeding performance to scissor around after the black Talon.

Behind her, the black Talon was now hounding Gumm, having tried to bounce him from above. Gumm rolled out, knowing not to hold a heading or position for more than four seconds. Wilzar was racing up at the Talon's eight, trying to get inside the pursuit curve.

She lost sight of them. The second Talon, scarlet and silver, had her full attention. It banked out of the trench space and back into the hive. She gave chase, determined not to lose it. They bulleted under a processional arch, over a powerduct, then through the gutted superstructure of a free trader embassy. It was a dark volume, with only the main rockcrete verticals still standing inside the building's shell. She was visor only. She went for guns, but the rockcrete dust they were raising with their ramwash was as thick as chaff and denied her lock.

Exit. Sunlight. Hard left. The Talon cranked down, trying to lose her in a freight wharf that led back towards the sea. She bent onto it, gripping into negative g, eyelids closing like heavy shutters, trying to avoid full red-out. Blood pushed into her head. It felt like her sutures were about to pop.

The scarlet Talon managed to dump her.

She lost sight of it. She levelled, cursing herself.

'Lose the sight, lose the fight' was pretty much a day one basic. She was almost back at the seawall, knowing she must already be past its turn point. It was somewhere behind her now, about to recover her quickly.

She flashed back into the trench, turning to run it. Gumm zipped past her at once, trailing a ragged, torn curl of plating from his port wing. The black Talon was on his six, firing, but the separation was poor, and the las-bolts were passing off Gumm's starboard flank. Both Gumm and the Talon were moving faster than her, so she let both go by and then flopped deftly onto the Talon's back end and throttled up.

Tone lock. Slippy, but enough. She toggled to stores, awaiting a hard heat-lock on the bat's efflux plume. It tried to shake her.

'Dollface, break high in three,' she voxed.

'Copy.'

'Two, one–'

Gumm turned high to avoid secondary heat lock. The bat rolled left, but her lock was positive. The Skystrike thumped off her starboard rail with a shriek and a release bang that rattled her airframe. The bat rolled harder, but the running heater had him and would not let go. The detonation splashed a flower of fire across the inside of the seawall.

There was no time to call the kill. The scarlet bat was suddenly on her six, and firing. Jagdea flat-planed One-One, trying to pull the bat through between her legs, but the Talon matched her, making a big speed brake out of its belly. The Talons seemed more agile than the rapid Blades. More agile than the Voss. She had reversed heading but was still being chased.

Threat lock. Missile alarm.

She couldn't even see the heater it had sent after her. She rolled high, dispensing countermeasures, sowing a dazzling trail of decoys for the heater to sniff. The sun came out briefly behind her head, and her bird rocked.

The scarlet Talon blew past her port side, confident it had killed her. When it realised it hadn't, it broke away inland, darting under the rotting vanes of a coastal wind turbine. Wilzar, coming the other way out of nowhere, J-turned perfectly onto it, air-skidding around the turbine's huge mast.

The turbine was the first of thirty that were spaced down a rockcrete berm which bent inland, away from the seawall, like giant flowers in a titanic cultivation trough. The Talon wound back and forth between the massive stems, trying to use them for cover as it scrammed. Wilzar did the same, but at higher speed, to keep on it. Jagdea, well behind them, followed the inside curve of the turbine row. She saw the Talon and Wilzar's Voss criss-cross around the masts as though they were threading bootlaces, their tracks describing an insane double helix. The Talon was good, but nothing like as fast as Smoke. It was magnificent flying from Wilzar. Jagdea was stunned by his kick-and-change rate of weave and twist. He was gaining.

The Talon tried to peel out and run. Wilzar somehow J-turned out of the mast line, then *reverse* J-turned in a tight S to reacquire. At that point, the Talon stood zero chance.

A burst from Wilzar's cannons. Nothing excessive. Just sufficiently plenty. Hit, shedding debris, engine and one wing on fire, the Talon spat into a mad climb, out of control, leaving a long ripple of combustion behind it. It went straight up and hit the fan of the last turbine mast dead centre. The Talon exploded, taking the fan with it, burning segments of vane the size of a Firmament's wing falling like petals.

'Four-A,' Jagdea voxed.

Wilzar turned high. Ignited debris from the turbine scattered into the sea wind. The top of the mast, headless now, was ablaze and lifting black smoke, like a beacon fire on an ancient watchtower.

'Bats, bats.' It was Gumm. He'd scared up the bait that the two Talons had been covering, and was chasing them down the trench. Jagdea and Wilzar rolled out together to join him.

As they dropped into the outflow, black water twinkling below them, she heard it again.

'Bats, bats.'

It wasn't Gumm this time. It was Harlot.

'Driver copies, Harlot,' she replied. 'More, please.'

'Six bats inbound, seawall trench,' she heard Lopard say. His voice sounded tight, like he was pulling a g-load. *'In pursuit. On you in ten.'*

'Copy.'

Harlot's flight, with Lopard leading Slipstream and the Sister, had dropped ten minutes before Jagdea's after a possible track in the Pallisades. Jagdea's gut told her that those hostiles had changed heading to support the bats her pack was hunting.

It suddenly got very busy over the seawall zone. The bats – four Blades and two Razors – appeared at high rate, in hard pursuit of Gumm, who was several miles ahead, chasing the bait-portion of the original hostile formation: two Talons and a Venom laden with ordnance for the south 'plex. Jagdea voxed Gumm to warn him and advise a breakaway, but he waved her off. He was closing, in hot, and adamant he wasn't going to let the bombers get away.

Jagdea and Wilzar gunned up the moment the enemy hunters went over, high and fast. Jagdea pushed back her concern that Gumm was out on his own, and her deeper worry that Gumm, in his determination, had sounded too much like the old Sagittarius Gumm she'd got to know the day before. The risk-taking gunslinger, hell-bent on success.

Harlot's flight came up on their six just seconds after Jagdea and Wilzar had extended in pursuit. Slipstream, in his green Bolt, and Merry Death, in her chequered black Bolt, seemed especially eager to burn past Driver and Smoke to reach the hostiles. They'd been chasing them for nearly forty miles.

'Intercept, ease back,' Jagdea voxed. 'They've seen us.'

The bats had. They'd been aware of Harlot's strenuous pursuit, but now they had five interceptors running the seawall after them. Jagdea knew they wouldn't like those odds, and would undoubtedly break, at least some of them. If the Six-Six fight-birds were maxing when that happened, they'd go under the scattering bats and be forced to turn before they could engage.

'Copy, Driver,' Harlot responded, no idiot.

Instantly, the bats broke as predicted. One Blade kept going after Gumm. The others umbrellaed into high turns above the trench. Though she had warned them, Slipstream and the Sister overshot the manoeuvre, running too hard. Jagdea, Harlot and Wilzar, exercising cool restraint, pulled up out of the trench to greet the scatter.

The war sky, damp and pale with a stiff crosswind, was more open above the seawall and the coastal zone. There were far fewer structural obstructions. Eight machines met in a whirling dog-fight, belatedly joined by Merry Death and Slipstream to make it ten. It was the first proper turning knife-fight Jagdea had known since arriving in Vesperus. The first she had known in years.

The brawl was messy, bewildering, spilling its improvised dance down through the sky. Gripping, inverted, after a Blade, Jagdea was almost hit by Slipstream crossing high. A Razor shot past, spewing fuel burn. It was all a blur. The G-load chop was so fierce, her vision coned and then greyed out into mono-chrome. She got a lock, lost it. Tracers speared past. The world revolved, sky, trench, the expanse of the ocean with a nearly vertical horizon.

She got on a Blade, pulling g so strong she felt her cheek sutures part and blood weep down her face. She achieved a lock, but then a threat warning sounded, and she pulled tight to evade. She passed a bat and then the Sister nose-on, too close, and banked into a dive. Below, in the trench, Wilzar was chasing a Blade.

Threat lock. The bat was still on her. Or another one was. It was impossible to tell. She dipped into the outflow trench, came up again hard, and saw las-fire stripe past her. The bat had levelled out, still on her six. There was no way to turn and spot it, not pulling this load. Looking over her shoulder would clamp blood vessels, and somatogravics would fox her inner ear, and disorientate her into thinking she was travelling in a direction that she wasn't.

Grip position. Discipline. Focus. Instruments. When the threat lock sounded again, she popped a flurry of flares, and banked out of the trench through one of the ragged holes where the seawall had collapsed.

She was out over water, over half-submerged lines of rusting transport barges, over white crinkles of waves, over Helot Bay.

She swung wide. The sun was playing for her side. She could glimpse the flickering shadow of the bat behind her on the water to her left.

Hard right. High rolling rate. Hard right. She spat the bat out. She saw it, a green Blade, at her eleven, lifting to turn. Hard roll. Harder. Almost inverted, the horizon line sweeping up to midnight like the second hand of a timer. The Blade bent around over the sea in a broad curve and began to burn back towards the seawall.

Murderlock. Heat track. Missile selected, and away with a jolt.

It was a long walk for the heater. It seemed to take forever. She chased the Skystrike's motor plume as it sliced the air, jinking and snatching to stay on-heat as the Blade tried to lose it. At the last gasp, the bat kicked out some kind of countermeasures, a flurry of lurid violet cinders. Whatever they did, they did it. The Skystrike detonated short.

But it was too late anyway. The shockwave of the near-miss airburst slapped the green Blade's tail, kicked it askew, and sent it into a crazy, spasmodic tumble. It tried to recover, failed, and screwed into the seawall with a bang of fire.

Jagdea lifted her nose and hopped back over the wall. In the trench, she saw a burning fuel slick and a litter of floating debris. No clue as to friend or foe. She started to call for a check-in and regroup.

Harlot cut her off with a bellow of, *'Splash!'*

His call was then also truncated by Wilzar triumphantly proclaiming his second kill of the day.

Then the vox rasped. A sharp burst of electromag distortion. Someone was screaming.

Wilzar's bird shot past over her left shoulder. Tail 035's entire back end was missing. It had been replaced by a cloud of flame. He'd either taken a heater to the tail, or a direct burst of cannon into the engine.

There was no hope. The bird was gone. She heard the screaming and knew it was Wilzar.

'Eject! Eject! Eject!' she yelled.

Tail 035 was already falling. She saw a flash of canopy, the creased banner of a deploying 'chute. Then it was all behind her, and the burning Voss was exploding in the trench bottom below.

'Wilzar! Copy! Wilzar!'

She thought she heard him screaming again, just for a second. But there was no chance of that being real.

Infirmary, Intercept 66, Vesperus, 13:00

As it turned out, there was.

'Jagdea,' Garrant growled, in both warning and compassion. He blocked her way.

'He's alive?' she asked.

'Recovery Valks just brought him in.'

'Step aside, Asa.'

'You don't want to see him, Jagdea,' Garrant said calmly. His face looked as though it couldn't withstand many more losses before collapsing like a rockslide. 'Stanslaf's still working on him anyway.'

'I want to see him.'

'No,' said Garrant. He put a hand against her shoulder. She looked past him, and saw the trail of blood spatters leading up the corridor to the infirmary door, the blood-wet splats of soaked, discarded dressings.

'Status?' she asked, looking Garrant in the eye, and not liking what she found there.

'Wilzar banged out,' Garrant said. 'It was low. You know that. But he ejected. Jagdea, Wilzar is tall.'

He stopped talking. She knew what that meant.

'Both?' she asked.

'Both, above the knee.'

She turned away, so there was only the empty hallway and the shred to see her face.

'He was getting it,' she said.

'I know.'

'I mean really,' she said. 'Two kills today.'

'I know.'

'The first was one of the best I've ever seen. Just… good flying. He was listening. He was learning.'

'Jagdea…'

She wouldn't look at him.

'It was good flying,' said Garrant. 'Another good sortie. A full bag.'

'I don't want to hear it, Asa.'

'Well, I need you to hear it, pilot officer. I want you to put it in perspective. This is the loss of a promising pilot. I despise these moments. You have to think about the gains, or you won't get past it. None of the bats got through. Wilzar took two. You took two. The Sister took two. One each for Harlot and Slipstream. Gumm matched the record you set yesterday. Three in the trench. No one got away.'

She turned, and looked at him. She could feel the tightness of her cheek where the blood from her burst sutures had dried.

'You got the job done,' Garrant said. 'But the job costs.'

She heard footsteps. Gumm hurried down the hall to them.

'Did he die?' he asked simply.

'No,' said Garrant.

'Lead means not yet,' said Jagdea. 'Wilzar punched out. The canopy frame took both of his legs off.'

Gumm swore.

'I don't know what other injuries he took,' said Jagdea. 'Some, I'll bet. And I don't know how long he was in the water.'

She glanced at Garrant. She still had a coal of hope inside her.

'Ninety minutes,' he replied.

'So if blood loss and shock-trauma don't get him,' said Jagdea, as the coal sputtered out, 'infection probably will.'

Refectory, Intercept 66, Vesperus, 13:30

They sat in the refectory, and ate food they didn't want. The tallies had been chalked up, but the place had emptied since then, taking any celebration with it. Other shouts had come up.

'It's getting busier,' said Jagdea. 'More raids.'

'More intensive,' Gumm agreed. 'Suggesting increased desperation on the part of the enemy.'

'You matched my record,' she observed.

'I don't really care about that,' he replied.

'You didn't really like Wilzar,' she said. 'He wasn't your friend.'

'You didn't much like him either,' said Gumm. 'That doesn't matter. He had begun to stick well. What I saw today, superb. I never thought he'd be the kind to learn. And anyway, whether we liked him or not, he was a person.'

Jagdea pushed her plate aside.

'You matched my record,' she said.

'Shut up about that…'

'No, Gumm,' she said firmly. 'I'm returning the favour. Yesterday, you watched my back. Reminded me how not to be the hero of the Zoph again. My turn, *Sagittarius*.'

'You're mistaken, Jagdea,' he replied. 'My performance today–'

'You upped your game,' she insisted. 'Ran solo after three bats. Splashed them all. It was reckless, given the coverage. Besides, I could hear it in your voice.'

'Really?' he said.

'Definitely. The bottle's on the table, Gumm. You're still staring at it, but your hand is a little closer.'

He sat back and folded his arms.

'This is your opinion?' he asked.

'This is my observation,' she replied. 'Offered without malice. That's what friends do.'

Gumm hesitated.

'Copy instruct,' he said.

They looked up as Steeley approached their table.

'Lead said to tell you that Wilzar's awake,' he said.

Infirmary, Intercept 66, Vesperus, 13:50

The sheet-covered shape on the surgical gurney didn't seem to represent enough to be Wilzar, even with the covers tented above his amputated legs. His head was bandaged and gel-packed, and his splinted arms were raised and tubed to portable life-sustain units.

Garrant ushered them in. Dampier was present too. The little infirmary, pungent at the best of times, reeked of blood, chemicals and bio-waste.

Med Stanslaf glanced at Jagdea with professional concern.

'I'll need to re-dress that cheek,' he said.

'Just tell me how he is,' she said.

'Stable,' said Stanslaf. 'Critical. Both legs severed by canopy collision. Considerable loss of blood volume. I've debrided and cleaned the stumps, but I can't do more for now. Breaks to arms and ribs. Head trauma. I'm watching for pollution-triggered sepsis, which is inevitable, because both skin and open wounds were in the water. The next thirty-six hours are critical. If he survives those, I strongly recommend medical evac to Orison at the first possible opportunity. We really don't have the apparatus to support personnel so seriously injured here. And we certainly don't have recuperation programmes or access to augmetic rebuild, which should be applied as early as possible if he's going to have any quality of life.'

Jagdea looked at Garrant.

'So, a place on the next transport out,' she said. 'What's that? Twelve days from now?'

'Four,' said Garrant quietly. 'They brought it up.'

Jagdea nodded.

'Four,' she echoed.

She moved past the medicae, and looked down at Wilzar. She didn't recognise him. His head was too swathed in dressings, and his face too swollen and blood-bruised.

'You did better,' she told him, even though she was certain he couldn't hear her.

'Let's clear the room, I think,' said Stanslaf.

'Agreed,' said Dampier. 'Everyone out.'

Jagdea stared at Wilzar for a final moment.

'I didn't even see it, Smoke,' she said. 'I'm sorry. I didn't even see the bat that got you.'

She flinched as the swollen mask below opened the one eye that would still open. The cornea was bright red. The puffed slot that used to be his mouth moved.

'Did he say something?' asked Gumm.

'Come on, everybody out,' Dampier insisted.

Jagdea leaned in close, close enough to smell the stink of meat and putrid breath, close enough to hear the slow, sucking purl of respiration.

'Wilzar?' she whispered.

'Not,' he gurgled.

'Not? Did you say not?'

'Not... bat...' the gurgle answered, so very far away and drowning in its own mucus. 'Fight... bird...'

BACK FROM THE DEAD

VESPERUS

IMPERIAL YEAR 795.M41, DAY 94 – DAY 103

DAY 94

Intercept 66, Vesperus, 16:41

'You must have misheard,' said Gumm.

'You were there,' Jagdea replied.

'I didn't hear him,' said Gumm. 'You must have misheard.'

He'd come to find her in the hangar. She was sitting in One-One's open cockpit, painstakingly masking the instruments with hose tape. Gumm leant against the fuselage below, arms folded.

'I know what he said,' she said.

'Fightbird?'

'Right.'

'So you think Wilzar was telling you that he was splashed by one of us?' asked Gumm.

'By someone,' she said, tearing off another strip of tape with her teeth. 'By a friendly. One of us, Aeronautica... I don't know. Not the Archenemy, is my point. Wilzar was splashed by someone he should have been able to trust.'

Gumm thought about it.

'He was delirious,' he said.

'Yes,' said Jagdea. 'And now Stanslaf's put him in an induced coma, so we can't ask again. But he got four words out. Took a huge effort. It wasn't raving, Gumm. It was something he needed to say.'

Gumm remained silent for a while.

'Well,' he said finally, 'it happens. It's ugly, but it happens. Friend-on-friend. Especially in a turning knife-fight like that one. It's unavoidable. A situational hazard. You must have seen it?'

'Of course,' she said. 'Too many times, even at the highest discipline. Tragic, accidental, terrible. I often think it's worse for the shooter. To have to live with it, afterwards.'

She smoothed down a piece of tape, then tossed the roll onto the top of the headache's casing.

'But I've never known anybody not put their hand up to it,' she said, staring at the dead control panels.

She got up, and swung out of the cockpit. He was looking up at her.

'Never,' she said. 'Pilots always step up, even when an incident isn't witnessed. That's just the code. Service honour. You admit it, you confess it, you take the consequences.'

'True,' he said.

'We own our mistakes and failures, no matter the shame or ignominy,' she said.

'Unless a pilot doesn't know they've done it,' Gumm offered. 'Loose fire. A stray heater that locks the wrong plume. If a pilot doesn't see–'

'Wilzar was splashed by direct fire from the rear,' said Jagdea. 'Whoever took that shot knew all about it. But no one's come forward.'

'Out of shame? Guilt? Fear?'

'Maybe,' she said. She jumped down to the stand beside him. 'Or something else.'

She started to wipe her hands on a rag. She looked around and saw him staring at her.

'I had a hunch this was where you were going with it,' Gumm said wearily. 'A white crow?'

'It could be a white crow,' said Jagdea.

'It could not be a white crow!' he exclaimed. 'White crows are myths! Just scuttlebutt. All these years, I've never even heard of one, let alone encountered one–'

'Neither have I,' she agreed. 'But there have been some.'

'In the whole history of the service?' he asked. 'Yes, all right. I'm sure. A few. One or two psychos or freaks, one or two traitors or heretics. But in actual, real life, it's groxshit. Made up, just like glory stories. Creepy rec room tales to scare the smokes.'

'Like they're not scared enough already,' she said.

'You think that a pilot from this squadron deliberately tried to murder Wilzar?'

'From this squadron, or maybe one of the other Intercepts covering Vesperus.'

'Why would they?' Gumm asked.

'Any number of reasons,' said Jagdea, tossing the rag aside. 'Mental illness? The corruption of the warp? Personal grudge? To serve some secret agenda, perhaps because they're a traitor to the Throne? To feed some psychopathic urge? Or just for frigging kicks?'

'Oh, come on,' he said. 'Six-Six is Aeronautica. High levels of–'

'Six-Six is full of drunks, stimm-heads, and pilots burned clean through by shred. There are plenty of psychos.'

'Yeah? What about zealot fury, Jagdea?' asked Gumm sarcastically. 'It could be someone on some personal holy crusade to purge the weak. We've got plenty of hellfire here too!'

'Yep,' she nodded. 'Could well be that instead.'

He shook his head. 'I have great respect for you, Jagdea,' he said, 'but I am not having this conversation. Poor Wilzar was wrong, or delirious. It wasn't any of us.'

'Well, it wasn't you or me,' said Jagdea.

'Really? You're making a suspect list? *Really*?'

'Starting from the centre, scene of crime, moving outwards,' she said. 'Opportunity and motive. You or me? No. Harlot–'

'Harlot?' Gumm exclaimed.

'Drunk. Stimm abuser. Risk-taker. A predator in every other aspect of his life. Desperate for a new challenge and a new high–'

'Drop it,' growled Gumm, dead serious.

'Slipstream,' she went on. 'Dying painfully, bitter. Despises smokes, almost eager to see them suffer because he has to suffer.'

'Jagdea–'

'You were there when he said it. Sister Merry Death. Fire-breathing zealot who wants to kill sinners, and seems to think the label "sinner" applies to everybody–'

'No!' Gumm barked, so suddenly it made her start. 'Stop it, Jagdea. I'm not listening to this. I'm walking away.'

'All right,' she said.

He strode past her, heading down the stand towards the exit.

'But watch your back,' she added.

He stopped. He turned back.

'I'm walking away,' he said.

'So you said,' she replied.

'No, I mean...' His voice had softened. 'Not just from this stupid conversation,' he said. 'I'm walking away. Garrant said the resupply was coming in four days. I had a private word with him. He said he was prepared to honour the informal agreement he made with me. With both of us. He'll let us leave if we want to. Emergency retention over.'

'He said that?'

'I asked him directly. He'll let us go in four days. So I'm going.'

Jagdea exhaled. She nodded.

'I'm sorry,' he said.

'For what?'

'For leaving you in the lurch. For abandoning you. Unless you're coming too?'

'Of course I am,' she said. 'I've been trying to get out of this since we arrived.'

'Good,' he said. 'That's good. I was worried. I had this feeling that you might have wanted to stay. I was worried you might hate me for quitting on you.'

'We both want out, Gumm,' she said.

'Yes, but Six-Six needs us,' he said. 'And you have a startling sense of responsibility. So I thought you might resent my reason for quitting.'

'What reason, Gumm?'

'You,' he said. 'You were right, Jagdea. My hand is inching too close to that bottle. I can feel it. I can feel Sagittarius Gumm, back from the dead and riding in the seat behind me, about to snatch the controls. If I stay any longer, I'll never go back. So I'm going while I still can.'

DAY 95

Refectory, Intercept 66, Vesperus, 05:20

Jagdea gathered in with the other alert-ready aviators as Garrant led the morning huddle. Breakfast was being fried and stewed in the food carts behind them. The huddle formed in front of the fireplace, with the roll call and tally board above them.

Garrant began with the usual: atmospherics, projected conditions, ROP reports, flight rotas. Jagdea listened attentively, but found her gaze wandering. She studied Sister Meredith, who stood with her eyes down, as though in meditation. As ever, there was no clue as to what might be going on in the preacher's mind. Why would there be? Jagdea had no idea what kind of tell she fancied she might pick up. How do you detect a killer in a room full of killers? How do you detect a killer when you are a killer?

Nearby, Lopard. He looked sick that morning, tired and drained, the tell-tale wear of excessive drinking or stimm-use. Or too much empty sex instead of sleep. Or whatever else Lopard had numbed his downtime with. He was fiddling with his silver lho-stick case. Lopard clearly wanted to smoke, but he couldn't in the middle of Garrant's huddle. The silver case was like a set of worry beads in his red-gloved hands, something to fidget with to soothe... to soothe what? Anxiety? The urge to smoke? Shred? No, Jagdea decided.

She could see Lopard's hands were trembling. A red flag for narcotic abuse. He was playing with the case to disguise the tremor.

Garrant moved from brief basics to a blessing, thanking the God-Emperor for the previous day's vital fuel resupply from Four-Three, and then reciting one of the Benedictions of Saint Kiodrus, which he clearly knew by heart. Jagdea looked up from her study of Lopard, and saw Gumm watching her. His face said nothing, but she understood his disapproval. Maybe he was right. Maybe the shred of the Six-Six tour was pushing her into paranoia and mania. It wouldn't be the first time non-stop rotations had done that. It made her smile. She couldn't read much in Lopard, or anything in the Sister, but Gumm could tell exactly what Jagdea had been thinking.

The instruction session the night before had gone well enough. Jagdea had feared no one would show because Wilzar's inevitable fate had demonstrated the sheer folly of her efforts. But only to her, it seemed. There had been even more in attendance than the night before, more smokes, more veterans. Maybe Wilzar's fate had done the opposite, and motivated more of them to seek new tricks that could keep them alive. What had saddened her was that no one mentioned Wilzar at all, not once. No one seemed to care. He was a smoke, and smokes were just bags and toe-tags waiting to happen. Everyone had forgotten him already.

Like hell the Aeronautica remembers, she thought.

But the session had gone well enough. Even Slipstream, watching from his cot alongside Mischief, had kept his resentment to himself.

Garrant finished with a prayer. They all lowered their heads.

'Good flying,' Garrant said, as the huddle broke up. 'Driver? With me.'

She walked beside him down the hall, heading for Campanile Control.

'Problem, Lead?' she asked.

'Not a new one, Jagdea,' he replied. 'I need you for something.'

At the foot of the stairs, he paused and looked at her.

'Before we go in,' he said.

'Lead?'

'Wilzar,' he said. 'What Wilzar said. You sure it was "fightbird"?'

Control, Intercept 66, Vesperus, 05:37

Dampier and Badler were waiting for them in Campanile Control. The stations were already busy, ROP traffic coming in, Garrant led the three of them into his office and closed the door.

'Am I in trouble?' asked Jagdea.

Badler sneered at her.

'I have reviewed the wafer,' said Dampier. 'Begun to, at least. There's a lot of it. Your instinct was correct, Pilot Officer Jagdea. The data contains full route mapping for Vesperus, multi-level. It's not foolproof, obviously, because aspects of the hive structure have changed since it was compiled, but if we use it, I estimate it might reduce accidental collision losses by as much as a third.'

'And improve performance stats?' asked Badler.

Dampier nodded. 'Response times, catch ratios, kill rates,' she said. 'So my recommendation is that we use it.'

'And I have approved that,' said Garrant.

Badler looked annoyed. Jagdea doubted the exec had any problem with improved performance. He just seemed to begrudge the fact that the idea had come from her.

'There will be considerable logistical difficulties implementing the data,' said Dampier. 'As discussed, we need to divide it into packets, and distribute the packets according to sortie. I will detail a working party to begin that process. And pilots will need to be trained to use it.'

'Maybe Driver could run the training?' said Badler. 'She fancies herself as a mentor, after all.'

'I'm not a mentor, Badler,' Jagdea said.

'What would you call it, then?' the exec asked with disdain.

'An instigator,' she replied.

'Enough, you two,' said Dampier. 'It could be a month before a mapping programme is running comprehensively. We need it slam-checked and reliable before we fully commit.'

'A month,' murmured Garrant. 'If we're still running intercepts by then...'

'Why wouldn't we be?' asked Jagdea.

'Rumblings from high command,' Garrant said. 'A possible shift of strategy coming down the track.'

'A shift to what?' asked Jagdea.

'That's outside of this conversation and your need to know, pilot officer,' said Dampier. 'My point is, we'll implement the mapping on a trial basis to see how it works in practice. Shake it down. See what refinements we need to make.'

'When?' asked Jagdea.

'Today,' said Dampier. 'With you.'

Badler chuckled.

'And you, exec,' Dampier added.

Eighth drop, Intercept 66, Vesperus, 07:12

Rain was bleating in across the launch platform. From the top of the Campanile, the hive was a malicious rumour lurking behind polluted cloud. Jagdea walked out with Badler, who went over immediately to the fitters setting up the three birds. Gangster was waiting, sheltering from the rain under the blast shields.

'What is this?' she asked Jagdea.

'We're trying out some new mapping,' said Jagdea.

Gangster explained in anatomical detail what new mapping could do with itself.

'Think of it as a new trick,' said Jagdea.

'Yeah?'

'One of mine, actually,' said Jagdea. 'I'm surprised they even went for it.'

This seemed to make the whole thing more agreeable to Disa Yesof.

They waited while Badler talked to the ground crew and the preset was completed. Boa, shrouded in a bright yellow plastek rainslicker, backed the cargo-8 tractor away from the stands, its tyres hissing on the wet deck. As usual, the servitor swung the lifter around in fast, swerving lines, even up on the open platform, oblivious to the sheer drop on three sides. The thought of hurling a truck like that around like that, so high up, on a comparatively small deck with no proper barrier rail, made Jagdea go cold.

'He looks like a pile of groxshit under a tarp,' Gangster snorted.

'Boa?'

'Doesn't he?'

'I wouldn't let him hear you say that,' said Jagdea.

Gangster fiddled with her helmet straps, and glanced sidelong at Jagdea. It was painfully furtive body language.

'So,' she asked, 'it true?'

'What?'

'What Smoke said?'

Jagdea stiffened. 'And what did Smoke say?'

'You know,' said Gangster. 'He said "fightbird", right?'

'Where's this coming from?' Jagdea asked.

'It true or not?' Gangster asked. 'Smoke got splashed by a fightbird?'

Jagdea hesitated. No way Gumm would have told her. Definitely not Dampier or Garrant.

'Med Stanslaf's got a big mouth,' she said.

'And a drawer full of spare stimms, if you play nice with him,' Gangster said, grinning. 'And I *do*.'

'I don't know what Wilzar said, Yesof,' said Jagdea. 'He was half-dead and rambling. So don't go spreading stuff around.'

'It's spread already, Driver,' Gangster replied, amused. 'Like a fire.'

Jagdea said nothing.

'So, which gak done him?' Gangster asked.

'I don't know. What have you heard?'

Gangster shrugged, an expressive movement that was almost her sway-armed victory dance for a moment.

'Nothing,' she said. A long pause followed. 'You think we got a white crow?'

'Do *you* think we've got a white crow?'

'I think anything is possible in this shithole,' Gangster replied.

'White crows aren't real, Yesof.'

'Nuh-huh,' she said, shaking her head emphatically. 'There were white crows in Vervunhive. At the end of the siege. This is actual true fact. Didn't call 'em white crows, but. And not pilots, maybe, but soldiers on the ground. Scratch troops. Citizens too. People who were killing just for the buzz of killing. Crazy gaks. And there was so much killing, no one noticed till too late. You hide murder with murder, right? Like hose tape.'

'Well…'

'I'm saying, if soldiers and what not can do it, why not gun-slingers? This place is psycho. No regs, no rules. Who would notice?'

'Why would you say this, Yesof?' Jagdea asked.

But Badler was calling their names and waving at them impatiently.

''Cause Smoke weren't the first,' Gangster replied as she hurried away.

Jagdea mounted One-One, forcing herself to focus on the task at hand. Tarr's team was unlatching the hoses. Jagdea saw two Skystrikes on One-One's rails.

'Checks Four-A,' Tarr said. 'The blower lag will be an old friend of yours by now. So, this mapping packet thing, it's gonna load direct from Control via the autotrack system. I've cleaned that off for you, no need to thank me, all part of the service.'

Jagdea saw where the hose tape had been peeled off the autotrack display and the auspex, leaving little outlines of sticky adhesive.

'It'll show like a track,' Tarr continued, 'and run via logis on your auspex and visor. Right?'

'Copy. Active logis control?'

'No, unless you want it, in which case you select the routing on the autotrack, then throw the 8/10 and 8/12 switches to approve.'

She leaned into the cockpit to point and demonstrate.

'Then logis will go auto-stick,' she said. 'But that's off as a default. Right now, it'll show you routing options for any track you steer onto or select. Then threat warning will ping if you deviate.'

'Threat warning?' asked Jagdea.

'Not ideal, I know,' agreed Tarr. 'I avoided missile threat lock and threat lock, because you'll want to know those for real, and if they keep going off, they'll scare you empty, and I ain't washing your seat off when you get back. So I enabled hydraulics warning instead. It's a higher "ping-ping".'

'I am familiar.'

Tarr looked pleased with herself.

'And the hydraulics indicator will show red,' said Tarr. 'For a reason, this time, but not the usual one.'

The patch of tape had also been removed from the hydraulics indicator. It glowed green. Jagdea sighed.

'I thought you'd enjoy that,' said Tarr.

'What if there's an actual hydraulics issue?' asked Jagdea.

'Oh, then you're screwed,' said Tarr, 'because you won't know nothing about it. I hear this was all your idea.'

'It seemed like a good one when I had it,' said Jagdea.

'Lidding you up,' said Tarr. She looked at Jagdea. 'Done this before?' she asked.

'Obviously not,' said Jagdea.

'First time for everything,' said Tarr and latched the canopy.

Jagdea began walking the parish.

'Vox check,' Badler crackled over the comms.

'Vox check, Driver receiving.'

'Check check, Gangster.'

Jagdea went to arm her seat, remembered there was no point, then continued her steady slam-check.

'This is Exec, deconflict auspex. Control reports shout from ROP Four-Zero. Power plant noise, Pallisades West. Stand by for route packet.'

'Copy,' said Jagdea. She waited. The Pallisades packet had been the first one prepared, and their flight had been held go-ready until a shout came in from that zone. The autotrack flickered as the data loaded, then the auspex came up with a lo-res map that indicated a path in red. It wasn't the usual flat mapping. It was a tri-D wireframe projection.

'Packet received,' Jagdea said.

'What is *this gak…?'* Gangster crackled.

'Gangster, clear vox,' Exec responded. *'Go for start. Go for start, immediate release.'*

They went off the bell tower, down Orundo, then turned onto Shurac Processional, Badler leading, then Jagdea, then Gangster, expressing full military power. Using the map-track took a while to get used to. The interface was unfamiliar, and none of them had trusted auspex or modar since arriving in Vesperus. Deviation advisory kept pinging.

The routes close to the Campanile were habitual, the opening stretch of many sorties, but the track was taking them ways they wouldn't have risked, or at heights they wouldn't have tried. At Shurac, the map confidently led them through a transit conduit beneath the vast Mercantile Palace, a path no pilot at Six-Six had attempted before.

As they turned out and climbed, they were already eight seconds in front of the intercept estimate. The map knew the hive in ways that they didn't, and couldn't possibly have put in the hours to learn. A straight line under the powerducts at Sacristy, previously regarded as no-go. A high transit at Trinity Subspire that no one knew existed. A guided low bend onto Calisto that avoided the huge skyway that always took everybody by surprise, and had killed two smokes.

The real gains were in second-by-second stick response. Jagdea's situational awareness remained high, but she was making far, far fewer micro-corrections to dodge and avoid. The map guided her through places without the need for constant assessment and correction. It knew where to go.

They were flying fast. They were flying low. They were making hard turns. But it all seemed calm, as though they were simply cruising at high-alt on a firm heading. No exhausting hyper-vigilance, dodging, avoiding, jerking the stick.

It was so smooth, it seemed wrong. Jagdea realised it wasn't the map-track she was trying to get used to, it was the shift in the psychology of her flight approach. Only a couple of times did they force a sudden execute in a flurry of pings to avoid obstructions where war damage had changed the contours of the city.

As they sharp-steered around a collapsed skyway on Horatio, Jagdea reflected that on every previous sortie she'd flown, she would have already executed two dozen moves like that, all at the last moment, in high shred. And not to avoid damage. Just to avoid the city.

It was almost exactly like flying.

On comms, Badler made no comment of approval, but Jagdea hadn't expected any. Yesof, meanwhile, kept chuckling and uttering gleeful 'woo-hoo's.

They rolled out over Pallisades West two minutes ahead of projection, and measurably less shred-fatigued. Below, through the low vapour, three bats were running south-west. Two Blades and a Talon. The Six-Six fightbirds overbanked to visually confirm target, then tipped over from their perch to bounce them from above.

They took one each.

Hangar bay, Intercept 66, Vesperus, 09:01

'A few knots to work out,' said Badler grudgingly, 'but it's promising.'

Garrant nodded.

'It makes things real nice and smooth,' said Gangster.

'It's the implementation that's going to give us the biggest headache,' said Garrant. 'There's a lot of work to do preparing the packets, and then squirting the right packets to the right birds in a fast shout. But that makes it a dispersal issue, and a problem for Control, not a flying issue.'

'Agreed,' said Jagdea, 'but we mustn't forget the complacency issue.'

'Meaning?' asked Garrant.

'She means it feels real easy,' said Gangster. 'We could get lazy quick. Right?' She looked at Jagdea for confirmation.

'Exactly that,' said Jagdea. 'Use of the pathfinder programme will give us appreciable benefits. It's going to be a vital tool. But Yesof is right. It makes it feel easy. In contrast to what we've been experiencing, it is. But Vesperus is not easy. There is a risk of reliance, and thus complacency. Pilots must maintain rigid situational awareness or the hive is still going to kill them. The map's an enhancement upgrade and a great support tool, but it's not omniscient. It can't be allowed to replace what we're already doing. It just eases the strain a little.'

'Noted,' said Garrant. 'So we instruct to fly as rigorously as always, with the mapping as an extra trick in our arsenal. All right, stand down, and get food and hydration.'

'Yesof? A moment,' said Jagdea as they turned away.

Leader's office, Intercept 66, Vesperus, 11:12

'You said this was informal,' said Garrant, 'but you've closed the door.'

'Informal, but private,' replied Jagdea.

He sat at his desk and offered her the chair opposite.

'Our conversation earlier, about Wilzar,' she said. 'I haven't mentioned it to anyone. But it's already out there.'

Garrant had been about to go through some reports while she talked, but he put them aside. He looked at her, and raised his eyebrows in a long-suffering lack of surprise.

'Of course it is,' he said. 'Let me guess–'

'Doesn't matter who leaked it,' she said. 'Everyone talks here. Stories are currency. A pilot brought it to me. I remained non-committal, but the pilot gave me to understand it wasn't a big surprise.

'Which part?' asked Garrant.

'The idea that we might have a white crow.'

'Well, we don't,' said Garrant. 'Why would they think this?'

'Several losses over the last few weeks, all smokes, where the circumstances are not clear,' said Jagdea.

'Not clear?'

'Not definitive.'

'We have a high rate of losses–' Garrant began.

'Yes,' she replied. 'But many are demonstrably pilot error, and others verified enemy kills. There are a number where actual cause of loss is not definitive.'

'It's hard to be definitive about a lot of things in Vesperus,' said Garrant.

'Some names were mentioned,' said Jagdea. 'Incidents. The rumour's not new, Asa. Wilzar was just the latest example. Is that why you were evasive when I asked if Dampier was investigating? You already know there's a problem?'

'You know what a white crow is, Jagdea?' he asked.

'Of course,' she said. 'It's the Aeronautica term for a rogue or renegade who uses the confusion of war to kill, for whatever psychological reason. Breakdown, latent psychopathy, derangement… a white crow commits atrocities outside the legal remit of war, often against his or her own comrades.'

Garrant smiled a humourless, patient smile.

'I'm sorry,' he said. 'I meant, do you know why we use the term "white crow"?'

She realised she didn't.

'It's because they don't exist,' said Garrant. 'All crows are black. To prove that statement false, one does not have to find all the black crows in existence, merely one white crow. The single anomaly disproves the rule. No white crow has ever been found.'

'That's just pedantry, surely?' she replied. 'Asa, forget the term. There are many archived examples of rogue combatants in every branch of the Imperial military, including the service. Traitors, heretics, spies, deserters, psychotics–'

'Agreed,' he said. 'But this specific idea of a serial hunter, an assassin, a predator, dwelling secretly among us and picking us off under cover of combat circumstance. There's never been a recorded instance. That's what you're talking about.'

'When Wilzar said what he said,' she replied, 'I thought we were looking at a friend-on-friend accident to which no one had confessed. But *now* that's what I'm talking about.'

'No one in Six-Six–'

'Then maybe a neighbouring Intercept?' she said.

'Jagdea–'

'Is this being investigated as a potential white crow?' she asked. 'Is this why you're being so evasive?'

'I asked you to keep a lid on it,' he said, 'because this place talks. You just said it yourself. Shit gets said. Stories are currency. The matter of your rep, for example. Given that, don't you think someone would have said something at some point? Some accidental remark. Not a confession, but something that seemed off?'

'I don't think a white crow is going to admit killing their own to anyone,' she said.

'No,' he said. 'But just a slip. Something behavioural. This place is tight, and it talks. If there was a killer operating, there'd be a suspect or two by now.'

She couldn't bring herself to admit she had a few suspects in mind already.

'Look,' he said. 'If this is what you're thinking, why didn't you bring it to Deck Dampier?'

'Because I don't know what to make of her,' Jagdea replied. 'And if I took it to her, it would become formal really quickly. I don't feel she's ready for yet more trouble from me. So I'm here, informally, privately.'

For a moment, he didn't reply.

'Jagdea,' he said, after the pause had become uncomfortably long, 'I appreciate you coming to me quietly. I want you to put this aside and focus on your duties. Consider me aware of your concerns. Know, please, that I do not think we have a white crow.'

'All right,' she said. She rose to her feet. 'But think about this. If white crows don't exist, why does the Aeronautica have a term for them?'

Dead zone, Intercept 66, Vesperus, 22:57

Another storm had come in, early in what passed for evening, pelting the Campanile with rain. It didn't ease back, and after an hour was joined by lurid pink lightning that sizzled across the hive-scape and boomed like artillery.

The night's huddle, held in hangar three once more, had been well-attended and lively, despite the fact that Gumm had seemed subdued. The group, the largest so far, had discussed angles of deflection and boresight shooting. Jagdea had wanted to mention the pathfinder programme, so that pilots could be prepared when their turn came to try it. But it hadn't been made official, and she didn't want to talk out of turn.

'Are you all right?' she had asked Gumm when the meeting broke up.

'Fine,' he had replied. 'Just tired.'

He wouldn't be drawn further, and she didn't press it. He seemed off with her, and she was sure it was because he knew what was on her mind.

Thundercracks, now sounding catastrophic, shook the stonework of the old templum as she made her way out into the dead zones alone. She followed the route that Lopard had shown her, out through the chantry and the non-secure chamber beyond, picking her way by flashlight.

Twice, she thought she'd taken a wrong turn.

As she approached what had once been the High Ecclesiarch's

private sanctum, she heard music over the hammering rain outside. A harpsichord, some melancholy cantata.

On a velvet upholstered sofa just inside the door, she found Camo asleep under a pile of blankets. The girl's clothes were strewn on the floor beside her boots, along with someone else's discarded clothing. Kinny stirred, restlessly, but didn't wake. Jagdea turned off her flashlight. She could smell the lingering residue of stimms.

In the main chamber, Lopard was playing the harpsichord by the light of a candelabrum. Lopard was naked except for the shorts of his flightsuit. A bottle of amasec, full and sealed, sat on the top of the instrument beside the candelabrum. Jagdea could see the old scars notching his muscled back, the patches of blue fibreweave graft at the base of his spine. The mosaic floor shone in the candlelight. The boarded windows rattled at the onslaught outside.

He stopped playing.

'Coming up at my six?' he asked, without turning his head.

'Just hunting for the good stuff,' she replied.

He turned to face her, and grinned.

'Well, you know where to find it,' he said.

'And someone to share it with,' she said. 'Though you seem to have that covered.' She gestured over her shoulder at the girl comatose in the far corner.

Lopard wiped the air with a dismissive hand.

'She's asleep,' he said. He reached for the bottle. His movements were slightly clumsy. He seemed half-cut already, though the amasec was untouched. Jagdea saw stimm canisters discarded on the floor under the harpsichord.

'Heavy night?' she asked.

Lopard snorted, and pulled the cork from the bottle.

'Just another day,' he said. He handed her the bottle without taking a sip or getting up. She took it, raised it in a casual toast, and swigged.

'So,' he said, leaning back against the keys, which plunked slightly under his elbows. 'To what do I owe the pleasure? Have you changed your mind?'

Jagdea scowled. 'No, Reno,' she said. 'And even if I had, you're occupied.'

'Kinny won't mind,' he said. 'Kinny can be very friendly and inclusive.'

'Still no,' she said.

'Still can't believe her name is Kinny,' he responded.

He held out his hand. She gave him the bottle.

'So if it wasn't the promise of my company...' he said.

'Just a drink,' she said.

'Well, Driver,' he said. His left eye twitched, and he rubbed it and blinked. 'I thought we had a trust.'

'Meaning?'

'You didn't come down here for a drink.'

'*And* conversation,' she said.

'About?'

Jagdea hesitated. Now she was here, she regretted it. Stupid. She had no idea what she was hoping to achieve.

'Relax,' he said. 'You look tense, Driver.' He took a drink, then handed the bottle back to her. Then he got up and padded across the mosaic floor to the clothes scattered beside Camo's make-shift bed. Thunder roared like a Medusa outside.

'I think I know what this is about,' he said.

'Do you?' she replied.

He bent down, and rummaged around in his clothes, rifling pockets. When he rose again, he had his silver case and his igniter.

'Do you ever take those off?' she asked as he wandered back to join her, fishing a lho-stick from his case and lighting it.

Lopard looked down at his undershorts and smirked.

'The gloves,' she said.

'Oh,' he said. He regarded his gloves as though bemused to find that he was still wearing them. They were short, stopping just below the wrist, short enough for her to glimpse where his dark skin ended and the glint of microdermal circuitry began.

'Not if I can help it,' he said. 'It's a Glavian thing, a custom. Besides, I'd feel naked without them.'

'And how does Kinny feel about that?'

'I didn't hear her complain,' he said. 'Although she was very vocal–'

'Enough,' said Jagdea. 'Go on, then. Why do you think I'm here?'

'White crow!' he said, dramatically, hands thrown wide like a compere presenting the next act.

'So talk about that,' she said.

'Why not?' he replied. 'Everybody else is.'

He held the silver case open and offered it to her.

'No thanks,' she said.

He closed it with a snap, and put it and the igniter down on the harpsichord. He gazed up at the painted ceiling reflectively, as though seeing it for the first time.

'Word has it,' he said, exhaling smoke, 'we have a white crow. Did for your Wilzar.'

'Wilzar's not dead,' she said.

'Might as well be, though. Poor child. Anyway, the whisper goes he's not the first. There's been gossip for weeks. And I supposed that gossip has now reached you, because of Wilzar and what Wilzar allegedly said, and *you*, manifesting the crippling responsibility for *everything* that you seem to carry like a permanent yoke, have decided to look into it.'

He glanced at her.

'How right am I so far?'

'Not bad,' she said.

'So, what's your thinking?' he asked. 'Personally, I think it's all groxshit, but if we do have a crow, my money's on one of the observants. A Throne-devoted zealot.'

'Really?'

'All that damnation and punishment?' he asked. 'That obsession with sinners? I wouldn't put it past them.'

'So you suspect–'

'No, Jagdea, not really,' he interrupted, sarcastically. 'Faith may be fierce, but it's not sociopathic. Not here, anyway. I was just making conversation.'

She took a sip of amasec.

'Conversation is good,' she said. 'But so's honesty.'

'How am I not being honest?' he asked.

Jagdea glanced towards the sleeping Camo.

'You said you never brought anyone down here,' she said. 'Said it was your sanctuary.'

'You're so naive,' he replied, his tone testy. 'Yes, all right. I lie. Sometimes. Especially where women are concerned. You weren't the first I brought down here, and Kinny won't be the last. So what? Where are you going with this?'

'This rumour's been around for a while, like you said,' she murmured, 'since before I arrived. There are certain losses that seem to fit a pattern. All downed without cause verification. Wilzar. Dicebag. Tailend. Voxback...'

Lopard suddenly looked at her sharply. Some odd, slightly hazy change came over his face, as though he had rapidly sobered up.

'Wait,' he said. 'Now just *wait*...'

'Lopard–'

'Now I get it,' he said. 'Now I understand the conversation you want to have. Screw you. Screw you, Jagdea. You think it's me.'

'I just–'

'Oh, for frig's sake!' He had become edgy, and she could smell his anger, as though it was triggering a chemical response from the stimms he'd taken. 'You think it's me. You came here... frig's *sake*... you came here to ask me to my face!'

'I don't know what I'm asking you,' she replied.

Lopard started to pace, agitated. He tossed aside his lho-stick stub, and immediately lit another. She was suddenly aware of how large and powerful he was, and how unpredictable the stimms might have made him.

'Because of Voxback?' he asked. 'Voxback and Tailend? Because I was in the air when...' He trailed off and stared at her with sudden focus. 'No, no,' he said. 'It's not that, is it? It's what I said to you. About killing them in their sleep. About putting them out of their misery. It's *that*, isn't it?'

'It seemed a strange thing to say,' she said. 'And you've said it more than once.'

'I've *confided*,' he corrected her bitterly. 'Shit. I thought we were wingmen. Friends. But Bree Jagdea, hero of the Zoph, she thinks I'm the white crow!'

She didn't answer. She stared at him, warily meeting his furious glare.

There was scorn in his face. Anger. And something else. Was it fear? He seemed to be battling to choose his next words and locate the right thing to say, and the right emotion to go with it. When he settled on it, it was defiance.

'Well, I am,' he said. 'I confess. I killed them *all*, every last one of them. I put the little bastards down. Why? Because I was bored. Because the bats no longer offered enough of a challenge. Because war has made me hungry for blood, and I cannot keep my murderous impulses at bay.'

He took a step towards her.

'Well done, Jagdea,' he hissed. 'Well done. You caught me. But stupid, too. You've come down here alone. No one knows you're here. I doubt you've got a weapon. What do you think will happen now? You, alone, unarmed? Me, a homicidal killer? No one will know what you've figured out, because no one will ever find you. What a colossal frigging error of judgement.'

'You have no idea who I've told,' she replied quickly. She tried not to back away, but he was getting closer. She'd never been issued with a sidearm. She'd left her utility knife in her locker. She wondered how effective the amasec bottle would be as a weapon. Or the heavy flashlight in her pocket. 'I might have told someone, I–'

She stopped. Lopard was suddenly laughing. He was laughing so hard he was almost bent double, helpless.

'What?' she asked.

'Your face!' he gasped. 'Throne above, your face! Priceless! Such a picture! You actually believed me!'

'Lopard–'

'I had no idea I was such a fine actor!' he snorted, wiping tears from his eyes. 'I should have *really* disappointed my family and taken to the stage! "A *pilot*, Lady Lopard Delevane? In the *Aeronautica*? The shame!" "Alas no, *much* worse! My son is a *thespian*!" Oh my goodness, the look on your face!'

'All right,' she said.

'You actually believed–'

'All right, enough!' she said. 'You frigging idiot! That wasn't funny!'

'Quite the contrary, my dear,' he replied, 'it was hysterical. And your reputation will be dented when I tell the story.'

'You won't tell the story–'

'I certainly will! Letting me tell the story is the *least* you can do to make this up to me!'

'Shut up, Lopard,' she snapped. She had seldom felt quite so embarrassed and mortified. She took a swig of amasec.

'You really thought it was me?' he asked.

'Frig off.'

'And you really thought I would just *tell* you it was me?'

'Shut up.'

He laughed some more, then sat down on the harpsichord stool.

'I suppose I understand,' he sighed. 'Not your half-arsed approach. That was laughably terrible. But your suspicion. I *have* said some things.'

'Yes, you have.'

He looked at her. His smile had flatlined. His eyes, abruptly, were painfully sad.

'Stupid things,' he said, 'said by a stupid man who is drunk most of the time. Drunk, or otherwise numbed, in a hopeless effort to blot out the sheer frigging misery of this place and all the poor souls caught up in it. It breaks my heart, Jagdea, it breaks it! To see them all come here, so bright-eyed and keen, and then watch them die, one by one, pointlessly and miserably. It's so futile.'

He gazed down at the floor.

'I *would* spare them,' he said softly. 'It was a stupid thing to say, I realise. I couldn't kill them. I shouldn't have said it, though. I didn't mean it. It was just a dramatic pronouncement to impress you. I was showing off again. But if there was any way I could spare them, I would. I mean it.'

'You could help me,' she suggested. 'You could instruct. A pilot as good as you–'

'You are just prolonging their agony,' he snarled, looking up at her. 'Why can't you see that? You're not sparing anyone. You're just making it worse. Giving them nothing but false hope and a few more days…'

'We will agree to differ,' she said.

He shrugged. 'I said what I said about smothering them in their sleep because it was a way to vent the fury I feel,' he said. 'I thought I was safe saying it to you, because you'd understand that.'

'I'm sorry,' she said. 'I'm sorry I accused you.'

He stood up without warning and reached for her. Jagdea flinched.

'Just the bottle,' he said.

She handed it to him. He took a long swig.

'I've probably ruined any trust between us,' she said.

'No,' he said. He shook his head emphatically. 'No, Jagdea. In this situation? In this hell-pit? It would take more than that. Friends are few, Bree. I will excuse a moment of stupidity if it means I keep a friend.'

'That's generous of you,' she said. 'Do you… do you think there is a crow at all, or was that just part of your performance?'

He cleared his throat.

'Yeah, I think there is,' he said. 'I've thought so for a long time. But not here at Six-Six.'

'No?'

'No,' said Lopard. 'I think it's another deck. I thought Four-Three for a while. They're even more of a feral mess than we are. But I'm starting to think it's a gunslinger out of Five-Two.'

'Why?'

'Gut,' he said. 'Just gut. I've got no evidence, or I'd have spoken to Dampier. But Five-Two is coming apart at the seams, and there are a couple of real bastards flying there. Animals. I heard from an ROP spotter that there's a lot of in-fighting at Five-Two. Brawls. The shred's got to them badly. Their area intersects ours, and we often pick up the strays that outrun them. So a white crow from Five-Two would have range to slip into our part of the war sky. And, as you know, we can't verify the track on anything in this place. They could come and go, and we'd read it as auspex clutter.'

'Have you mentioned this, even informally?'

'No,' he said. 'No proof. And Dampier will not budge unless she has something solid to bite. Besides, I am well-known as an awful reprobate and liar. She'd kick me out for stirring up trouble.'

Thunder rolled. A particularly ferocious squall of rain drove at the shutters, and wind whistled in through the cracks between the boards. The flames of the candelabrum flickered.

'Then how do we find out?' Jagdea asked. 'How–'

'What's going on?' asked a voice.

Camo had woken up. She was wandering towards them, Lopard's flying coat pulled around her to affect some degree of modesty. Her hair, undone, was tangled loose. She looked baffled and sleepy.

'We were just having a chat,' Lopard told her gently.

'Has something happened?' Camo asked, bleary.

'No,' said Jagdea.

'Go back to sleep,' Lopard told her.

'Yeah,' said Camo, rubbing her eyes. 'Can I–?'

She pointed to Lopard's silver case.

'Help yourself,' said Lopard.

Camo picked up the case and the igniter, fumbled out a lho-stick with clumsy fingers, and lit it. She sat down on the harpsichord stool.

Jagdea and Lopard looked at her. Camo stared glassily at the floor, smoking with a trembling hand.

'I'll go,' said Jagdea. Lopard nodded.

'We'll talk tomorrow,' said Jagdea. He nodded again, then followed her as she walked across the sanctum to the door.

At the doorway, they glanced back at Camo. She was still

sitting with her back to the harpsichord, huddled in the coat, gazing glassily at nothing from under the hood of her messy hair. The burning lho-stick dangled, half-forgotten, from her fingers.

'I'm sorry,' Jagdea said quietly.

'Don't,' he said. 'Don't do that. Forget it.'

'I don't know what I was thinking, really,' she confessed.

'That much was obvious,' he replied with a grin. 'Besides, Jagdea, that's not how it would have gone down.'

'What do you mean?'

'If I *had* been the white crow,' he chuckled, 'that ridiculous little charade is not how our confrontation would have played out.'

'Is that so?'

He nodded. 'Of course not,' he said, still amused. 'You would have confronted me, properly. And then we would have settled it like gunfighters. Pilot-to-pilot. Glavian and Phantine. Voss and Bolt. Skill against skill, in the air where we belong.'

'A duel, Lopard?'

'The greatest ever,' he said. 'You and me, testing against each other, as the God-Emperor intended. That's how it should have gone down.'

'Like the big finish of some glory story?' she asked.

'If you like.' He smiled. 'That would have been appropriate. Respectful of our reputations. Epic. A fitting end to the story.'

'In this scenario,' she said, 'you realise you're the killer? The monster? Why would I give you a fair chance?'

'Because that's what friends do,' he said.

'I see,' she said. 'Well, *in this scenario*, I fancy you'd like that to be the case because you're confident you'd win.'

'Well, of course. I mean, you're good, Jagdea. You'd have a chance. But, in the end...'

'It wouldn't be a satisfying glory story if the killer got away unpunished, would it?' she asked.

'No?'

'They're very formulaic,' she said. 'Glory stories. They always have a triumphant and uplifting ending. A white crow escaping to kill again would not be considered an agreeable finale.'

'Even if the duel was magnificent?' Lopard asked. 'A true test of the finest fightbird talent?'

'Not even then,' she said. She shot him a thin smile.

'I see,' he said. 'Well then, the hero of the Zoph had better be Four-A and at the top of her game. *In this scenario.*'

'Good night,' she said.

DAY 96

Ninth drop, Intercept 66, Vesperus, 06:03

Claw release. Off the drop. Into the dark. Ram lit.

Tail 011 felt tetchy and slow, as though it had slept badly. The blower lag was particularly pronounced. Jagdea adjusted the ad-mix and fought to keep up with Merry Death and Slipstream.

The shout had come in fast and early, an alert put through by ROP 27 reporting engine noise out past Harquin. It was barely daybreak, and what little light the pre-dawn had brought was stained with dust raised by the overnight storm.

No pathfinder packet had yet been prepared for Harquin District, so they were flying what Tarr was already calling 'Six-Six Standard bare-knuckle'. Two other flights were go-ready on deck, with packets prepared, respectively, for Pallisades and West Vanitas, regular hunting grounds, though Jagdea knew Garrant would loft them 'bare-knuckle' to other areas if the need arose. Lead wanted to stress-test the pathfinder programme as thoroughly as possible, but not if it meant ignoring shouts.

The air was thick and dark, and the hive shadows sliced at her. Jagdea focused, sharp as a boot-knife and as quick as a las, even if her bird wasn't. The shred, lurking at her shoulder and dripping black thoughts like an oil leak, seemed especially entertained by the identities of her wingmen. Slipstream and the Sister, Jagdea's two key suspects. Of *course* she'd end up winging them after the previous day's paranoia. Fate's wheel was cruel, irony's rails were racked with hi-ex stores, and the shred was almost giggling in anticipation.

At least, Jagdea thought, she didn't have to worry about either of them sneaking onto her six. One-One was so sluggish she could barely hold on to their coat tails.

Two and a half minutes into the intercept run, Jagdea heard Campanile Control order out two more drops, one to Pallisades, the other to Machinko. Nine birds up, and not even sunrise. It was going to be busy. Her hunch that Great Haven was ramping up its operations seemed on the money.

Harquin was a relatively low-rise district under the immense bowl of the primary mid-hive dome. As they flew in, a thousand feet below the curve of the vast steel roof, visibility dropped even further. It was a ghost realm of shadow, like flying into a deep cavern where the stalagmites were the towers and spires of the ruin below. Jagdea dropped her visor and switched to low-light enhance and optical boost a few seconds before Slipstream voxed exactly that instruct, followed by a terse, 'Keep the hell up, Driver.'

They stayed high, hunting. The darkness was so still and heavy, she could almost smell it.

'Sinners!' Merry Death suddenly voxed, and immediately rolled out. Jagdea saw the orange glow of her engine in the gloom ahead as it swung and dropped away south.

'Bats, bats,' Slipstream said a split second later, making the contact call a little more formal. *'Low, south, six miles. Fangs out.'*

He rolled out too, burning his green Bolt down after the Sister. Jagdea followed, executing a snap roll that put a load on One-One's vertical stabilisers. They had a good setup. A high perch, then a tip over into a hard dive to bounce the hostiles from above.

But the bats, three Blades, were already climbing to meet them, as though they had seen them minutes earlier.

Jagdea switched guns hot and armed her stores. Closure in three seconds. The bats were rising fast. She heard a sharp threat warning ping, and knew that she was being locked, and that the Sister and Slipstream were probably hearing the same.

But she could not get a clean lock herself. Modar and targeters were refusing to grasp the specks, ascending fast, that she could see with her own eyes.

She remembered Supervision Officer Brodie, a lifetime before. *The Archenemy uses the night well. They bring the darkness with them, screw with our auspex.*

'Split break!' she voxed. 'Split break now!'

She rolled hard out of the attack dive. Slipstream, arriving at the same grim conclusion, did the same. Spears of bright pearl and venomous amber seared past them. She felt the jolt of a hit on a rear surface. The world rotated hard. The dim steel roof turned past her, then the dark ruins of the streets. In grip, she tried to get level and burn out. Threat warning was still shrilling. She'd lost all visual on Slipstream and Merry Death.

She started to pull true. Blower take-up was delayed again as she tried to hit it. A plane shot by, ascending vertically past her nose. Just a glimpse, but even in the gloom she made the shape of a Blade, and saw the silver-and-black banding. The same bat that had escaped her in hive central on her fifth drop, the same bat that had claimed Sorrentine on her third.

It had killed Tail 011 before. She was damned if it was going to do it again.

But it had vanished. The darkness seemed to have seeped into everything, and foxed all her range and target systems.

Threat tone again. She rolled out. A crimson Blade rushed past her on the left, climbing. She tried to close on it. One-One was so damn sluggish.

Then the missile warning screamed at her. She tumbled into a blind evasive, thumping out flares. Something flashed bright in the air behind her. She was falling, her spin almost beyond her ability to correct. She saw Merry Death's Bolt race by below, rating hard with a Blade on her six. The spin continued, and got uglier, dome ceiling, grey streets, dome ceiling, grey streets...

The shred chortled, and licked her neck. She felt panic clamp in her chest and throat.

Jagdea fought the stick and got One-One stable. The shred's eager sniggering incentivised her efforts. Anything to spoil its fun, even if she had to break her arms on the stick.

Proximity and collision alerts began to scream. She had tumbled low, far lower than she'd realised, in among the ruined towers and habs of Harquin. She barely avoided a steeple and a powerduct, and almost clipped a ridgeline. For a second, One-One's sluggish performance played to her advantage. If she'd been pulling any higher thrust, she'd have piled clean into the obstructions.

Low, slow, she fought to get her bearings. Sticking the mangled street trench and avoiding terrain collision required immaculate focus. She tried to climb to gain some clear wing-space, but las-fire ripped past from a Blade slicing across the rooftops, like a sniper trying to pick off a lasman who had been foolish enough to raise his head from a trench.

She dropped low again, hugged the street, leaning onto a wingtip to make a corner between light-poles. The damaged faces of buildings strobed past in the gloom. Then the Blade flashed overhead, crossing the street at roof height. She didn't have the power to climb after it. She turned hard right into a shadowed processional, the regal statues lining each side of the avenue zipping past. Ahead, the avenue ended at the skeletal corpse of the Harquin Terminus.

There was still nothing on the scope. Where was the bat? It had to have seen her, and it had to be circling back. She twisted her head to see, but there was nothing but shadow enfolding her, and she couldn't afford to take her eyes off the course for more than a second.

Then she heard Slipstream yelling for an assist over the vox. Jagdea couldn't ignore that, and there was zero response from the Sister. Maybe Merry Death was already splashed.

Hand on the throttle, Jagdea prepared to burn up in an effort to locate Slipstream. She braced for the inevitable lag.

The instant before she advanced power and lit the burner, the bat reappeared. It was coming down the avenue towards her, head-on, firing.

Face to face. The crimson Blade was right there, coming straight at her, but she still had no murderlock and nothing on her scopes. She felt hits on her front plating, and her canopy cracked sharply–

Instinct took over. Madness, perhaps. She completed her intended execute, lighting the burner and climbing hard out of the processional, but as she did so, she launched all four of her heaters.

One-One shook hard, from the hits she was taking, from the bump of the stores releasing, and from the delayed pick-up of the afterburner. As she burned up out of the avenue, above roof level, her missiles streaked away below. They were unguided, with no lock, but there was nothing in front of them except the straight, open run of the grand street and the oncoming Blade.

She didn't see if it tried to evade. Probably. Any sane pilot would if they saw four missiles racing towards them. She was gripped, and climbing by then. The processional below and behind her went up in a dazzling thump of flame that washed out through the buildings on either side, and demolished statues that had stood for centuries. Nothing could fly through that, no matter how hard it was starting to lift.

'Slipstream, copy,' she snapped, ascending hard. 'Slipstream, copy.'

Dead air. Visibility under the dome was still as poor as a moonless night.

'Slipstream, Driver. Do you copy?'

Nothing, except a faint crackle of vox. A sob of static. A little slice of voice, cut off. She feared they were both dead. That idea cut deeper than the thought of how intensely alone that left her.

She banked north, dropping power and trying for some flicker of visual acquisition. Now One-One's blower lagged the other way, taking its own sweet time to cut the burn once she'd throttled back.

Still nothing. It was like she was alone in the darkness under the vast dome.

'Slipstream, copy. Merry Death, copy.'

Another sob of static. Something tickled her peripheral vision. She turned her head, and saw a flurry of tiny sparks, four miles out, to the south. Las-fire. Bird guns.

She banked and throttled up to give chase. There was still nothing on the vox, and the auspex was cycling an empty pattern, not even tracing the cityscape below. The cloying darkness was in everything – auspex, modar, target scope, heads-up, even her eyes.

Jagdea maintained rate. She saw another flurry of sparks, and judged them now to be two miles out. She adjusted course.

There. Another burst of gunfire, now lower and off to starboard. She banked in, and finally resolved the birds, but only when she was less than a quarter mile distant.

It was Slipstream, with the banded Blade chasing his six.

There was enough empty space under the dome at Harquin for a proper turning fight, and Slipstream was throwing his Bolt around to shake the bat, banking, bending, climbing, rolling, diving. The Blade was stuck to him, mirroring every manoeuvre, leasing off brief bursts of las. Slipstream's port wing was already tattered and trailing smoke.

He attempted a hard, rolling dive. They were close to the southern edge of the dome, and he was trying to make a run for the huge blast holes in the rim and escape the suffocating murk. Improved visibility would boost his chances of surviving the tangle. Jagdea saw the Bolt's burner light, though it seemed pale and weak in the black air. The Blade was staying on him, effortlessly.

She tore in, coming over in a high sweep. She still couldn't raise Slipstream on the vox, and with her scopes dead, any shots she took would be boresight only. But she hoped, at least, she could discourage the bat, or push him out of his chase position.

Jagdea raked in, and squeezed off a burst that went wide of the bat. It was almost a clean hit, but the bat was already twisting out, a neat, pre-emptive evasion, as though it had sensed her coming in. It went up high, right over her.

Slipstream was still running for the exit. Jagdea knew she had a choice. She could follow him out, hopefully into a clearer war sky where their instruments would function, or she could turn and attempt to stay on the bat. If she stayed, she'd be playing to the bat's strengths in the bat's darkness, but she'd buy Slipstream vital seconds. If she went with the Bolt, conditions would improve, but the bat would be behind them both.

She opted for the latter, even though it would give the bat the positional advantage. She chased Slipstream out through a tattered rent in the dome.

Outside, they raced into the hive-rise density of Valis Industrial, the manufacturing zone that bordered Harquin. The sun had risen while they'd been prowling the darkness under the dome. It was a poor, thin light, but it felt shockingly bright and clear by comparison. Her scopes immediately lit up, their blindfold removed.

Slipstream, bleeding smoke, tore out across Valis straight and level. The dirty blocks and smokestacks of Valis towered around them, a forest of potential collisions. Proximity alerts were already sounding. Immediately on exit, Jagdea pulled a steep climb, heading for the sky, and turned the ascent into a wide loop that skimmed her down across the edge of the dome in time to see the banded bat exiting below and ahead of her. It was trying to reacquire Slipstream, and it had the speed to do it. Slipstream, for reasons she couldn't fully fathom, was sticking to his straight-and-level course. Perhaps he'd taken so much damage he couldn't risk loading his airframe with a strong manoeuvre.

'Slipstream! Bat at your six, closing, copy!' she announced.

She heard some chopped burble of response, and saw Slipstream's Bolt begin to turn, but it was a half-hearted, weary effort.

She was already slicing down on the bat's tail, rich with power and diving speed from the downward portion of her loop.

Tone lock. Murderlock.

She lit off two quick bursts from her guns. The second clipped the bat across its port wing-assembly and produced a puff of micro-debris. The Blade jinked, and twisted out of line, heaving out of her envelope and away to starboard. She turned with it. They were in among the filthy chimneys and vent derricks of Valis, dodging and veering. She wasn't going to let it go, but the constant, violent shifts of heading to avoid collision prevented a gun lock. She tried to get in closer. They raked through the arch of an immense powerduct, under the span of a processional bridge, then turned around a cluster of huge storage tanks, and snapped either side of a towering chimney stack. The bat executed a brutally hard turn, and screeched away to the east, almost doubling back. Jagdea turned wider and higher, passed between two manufactory blocks with frig-all clearance, and throttled after it.

It had about a six-second lead on her. They were chasing down parallel thoroughfares, the bat burning ultra-low along a wide rockcrete causeway between silos, Jagdea following a transit road to its right. She had a partial track of it on her scopes, and she kept glimpsing it flash between silos. It was trying to extend and escape. She was running out of transit road.

Hard left, in grip. She chopped between two of the rusting drum-silos, then banked onto the causeway on its tail. It had an eight-second lead now. She tried to coax more thrust out of One-One's ram, foolish amounts of thrust for such low-level, inter-urban conditions. They were coming up on the last mile of the causeway, and it was criss-crossed by girderwork and heavy power lines.

The banded bat screamed in under those obstructions, dropping even more height but maintaining speed. Cynically observing her own madness, Jagdea followed it. Girderwork and stanchions chopped by over her head, and she felt as though she was scraping her belly on the rockcrete. They were both raising clouds of dust and grit in their wakes.

The bat broke hard right and vanished into the gaping maw of a derelict warehouse barn. Jagdea managed to execute the same move without losing a wingtip to the girders on her turn. The interior of the huge barn was dust and shadow. The roof was peppered with holes and partial collapses. They filled the enclosed space with their howling engine noise. Daylight ahead.

A long, covered loading dock. She leaned out left to avoid the extended run of support pillars. The bat, significantly narrower than her Voss in span, stayed inside the pillars, and ran the cargo space between the pillars and the dock's rear wall. It reached the yawning mouth of the exit at the far end, three seconds before she did.

It chopped out through the exit. Committed, she did the same. She wasn't sure she was going to fit. She did, somehow.

Outside, it was like flying off the edge of a cliff. Valis bordered Machinko, looming over it on an artificial plateau. They were dropped towards the streets of Machinko.

And straight into a knife-fight.

There were at least eight bats and six birds from Six-Six wrangling in a clumsy dogfight swarm. The vox went live with shouts and warnings. At their high rate, both Jagdea and her prey blew through the middle of the spiralling fight formation. Immediately, she got a lock warning. Something had picked her up. She deceled and evaded, almost colliding with Reaper as she came across her nose. More shouts.

Tracers sliced in from behind her. The scope showed a Talon at her seven. She stooped into a dive to shake it off. She'd lost visual on the banded bat. The Talon tried to tap her again, now on her five. A tracer scorched her wing. She dragged in the throttle and tried to throw the bat out past her, but it countered and flopped directly onto her tail.

Threat warning.

She pulled hard right, barely avoided a yellow Razor coming the other way, and then missed Tantrum and Blindside by an even smaller margin. She heard Tantrum yelp in shock as she ripped past his tail.

The Talon had managed to stay on her. Lock warning sang, and she rolled left, but that threw her across the stream of fire

Camo was loosing at a Blade she was chasing. Hard rounds punched through Jagdea's fuselage, and One-One rocked into a stagger that threatened to become a spin. Damage warnings lit up on the headache.

Jagdea wrestled to right her bird. Mischief raked under her, gunning for a Razor that was already fluttering a streamer of smoke.

Threat warning.

The damn Talon, *still.*

'Driver, immediate break right.'

It was Garrant. She didn't hesitate. She broke. Garrant's blue Cypra screamed past her port wing, belly cannon thumping. The Talon vanished from her scope.

A second later, as she banked around, she saw it, tumbling end over end towards the streets of Machinko below in a halo of burning fuel.

There was no time for gratitude. She was no longer feeling anything except the vice of extreme focus and the toxic squeeze of prolonged shred. Garrant looped and raced out ahead of her, chasing a yellow Razor that was streaking across the sky perpendicular to them both.

Garrant banked and entered a seamless turn to snap in on its six. Jagdea advanced throttle to wing him, but again the ram laboured and lagged.

The banded Blade came up like a rocket from somewhere far below.

'Lead, break! Break!' she yelled.

The Blade was already firing. Its shots unstitched the belly of the electric-blue Cypra, and blew off part of the tail assembly. Garrant was starting to spin, on fire, when the Blade shot past him vertically and continued to climb.

The Cypra plunged like a stone, three-quarters ablaze, spinning wildly like a top.

'Lead, eject!' she yelled. 'Eject!'

She saw something. A chute? Or just out-flung debris as the burning Cypra fell apart in the air?

'Garrant! Respond!'

No, it was a chute. She saw it. Deployed and full, but very low. Too low. There was a flash of fire from the ground as the burning Cypra met Machinko. Smoke rose. She could just see the open chute still, drifting hard, dangerously low. She was already banking and diving to track it. Crossfire chopped past her. A bird crossed under her. A Talon shot over her.

She ignored them. She was determined to keep visual on the chute. If Garrant was hurt or unconscious, and she was certain he was both, she needed to track the ditch point to guide the Campanile's Medivalks in as fast as possible.

Then she saw the banded Blade. It was tearing in low across the roofscape, heading directly for the lonely, drifting chute.

'Bastard!' she snarled.

That was not going to happen. That was *absolutely frigging not going to happen*. She hit the burner. There was a nasty bump of lag, but the fierce thrust spat One-One forward and propelled it directly into the bat's path, squarely across its firing envelope.

It was on her six. She had *put* it on her six. But she was between it and the descending chute.

Threat warning sounded at once. She felt the first hits. One-One lurched and thrashed. Damage buzzers and alerts screamed. The banded Blade, deterred by her reckless intervention, broke high and sharp, passed over her and soared away.

She'd lost sight of the chute. One-One was rattling and yawing. The CAD was a mass of blinking red, failures and errors. She could smell smoke in the cockpit. She could hear the ram grinding and clattering, the howl of a wounded engine.

'Driver, copy! Driver, do you copy?'

It was Lopard. The vox was so disrupted, it sounded like he was shouting at her down a drainpipe.

'Driver copies, Harlot,' she replied, fighting with a stick that felt loose and rubbery.

'Driver, do you copy?' he repeated. Her vox was clearly no longer trans-mitting.

'Driver, you're dragging smoke. You've got an engine fire. Eject now, copy.'

Yeah, not an option. There was no point saying it. He couldn't hear her anyway. He knew One-One had no seat. Harlot sounded frantic. He wasn't thinking.

'Driver! Do you copy?'

She was scanning for a possible site to set down. A plaza. A broad rooftop. A hard-down was her only hope, provided she had enough control left to pull it off.

There was nothing. The horizon was tipped at an angle. The streets of Machinko were too dense, too narrow, too obstructed. She was already too low, and she couldn't see anything remotely big enough to glide a dying bird onto.

'Driver, this is Harlot. You're too low. There's a fabricatory shed two miles west. Flat roof. Lift your nose.'

She could hear the concern in his voice, despite the lousy quality of the vox. It sounded so genuine, so agonised, it almost brought tears to her eyes. The voice of a friend, desperate, pleading.

'Driver! Two miles west. Get your nose up! Duct now, or burn some thrust to climb before your engine dies under you! Driver!'

Two miles. Might as well be a hundred. She couldn't even see the structure he was yelling about, but she trusted him. He knew the dead hive better than she did. If he said she was too low, she was too low.

The ducts were non-responsive. She yanked the stick full back, and locked her elbow around it to hold it there. She advanced the throttle, but it was loose too. The engine sputtered and banged. She had reached rooftop height. There would be no sticking around these towers and blocks. One-One was going into terminal shutdown, controls dead, barely gliding.

Harlot's voice had reduced to angry static.

One last try to buy some height. Throttle full forward. Burner on.

The ram coughed, choked, a death rattle. This wasn't One-One's petulant blower lag. This was full-on engine failure. She–

Jagdea was mashed back in her seat. The burner lit, suddenly full burn. She was accelerating wildly, punched backwards by sudden, accumulating G-force. Only the crook of her elbow around the stick held it back. The nose was coming up.

She missed a roofline by about two yards. She continued to climb, accelerating hard at maximum boost. There was no control. It was all she could do to keep the stick back and straight. Her eyes were squashed back into their sockets. Her head weighed ten times its actual weight, her limbs–

Everything was vibrating. The ram was howling. She was climbing at forty-five degrees and still accelerating. G-force flattened her.

Sometimes, the God-Emperor remembered your name. Offered you a second chance. Brought you back from the dead. She had some height now, more every second. Where the hell was this roof Harlot had been yelling about? Maybe she could make it. Maybe she could hard-down after all–

Vision coning, she saw something ahead. A big building, oblong, flat-topped. One chance. She had the lift now, viable height. Her left hand fought multiple gravities to reach the throttle and snuff the burner.

She got a grip on it. She dragged it back, cutting thrust and killing the burner.

But the thrust did not die back.

It wasn't the damn lag. The engine was redlining. Having coaxed the shot-up, damaged ram back to life, she now had it jammed at max burn.

It was firing her across the dead hive like a missile.

DAY –

Location unknown, time unknown

She woke up, in total quiet and stillness, in soft sunlight.

Her head was lolling. There was a taste in her mouth. Something. Copper. Blood.

Everything was so quiet.

Jagdea raised her head slowly. She'd blacked out, for sure. Extreme, sustained g-crush had forced the blood out of her head, and loss of consciousness had followed. She recognised the distinctive hot-wire throb in the base and centre of her skull, the aftermath of cerebral hypoxia.

Befuddled, she thought for a moment that she was dead. The soft sunlight was part of a dream she couldn't remember. It wasn't sunlight, it was the eternal radiance of the Throne. The misfiring ram had thrown her from one side of the sky to the other, ploughed her into some wall or tower, disintegrated her, and now she was waking on the other side of Eternity's Gate, at the foot of the Golden Throne where she had fallen, awaiting His final sanctity.

Except she didn't believe in that shit. Not that literal Word of the Truth shit the zealots spouted. This was literally sunlight.

She stirred, trying to slacken her harness straps. Everything hurt, every bone, every joint, every tendon. She felt like she'd been beaten with a meat-tenderiser. The bruising was head to toe.

She... she'd somehow missed everything. One-One, redlining far past maximum output, with her unconscious at the stick, had managed to miss every possible collision and obstruction the hive-grave could present, and then brought her to the ground intact.

It was beyond belief. Beyond luck. Beyond any possible permutation of probability. A miracle, the sort of miracle that got people beatified. She had survived the unsurvivable, saved by something, some power, some higher–

She became aware of a sound. A voice.

What was it saying? It was so quiet. A whisper.

It didn't matter. She sat back and closed her eyes. She could feel the soft sunlight on her face. She could feel the pooled blood stinging its way back into her numbed extremities, her feet, her calves, her wrists and hands, her ears...

Her mouth was dry, her throat raw. She swallowed. Relieved of pressure, her ears popped and cleared.

The voice was suddenly quite distinct.

Pull up... Pull up... Pull up...

Her eyes snapped open.

She was still in the frigging air.

Now she could sense the gentle, silent swim of the Voss, the tremble of air currents. The uncontrolled burn had launched her through the air. She had no idea how many miles she had covered, but the ram had cut once the fuel was exhausted. The engine was dead. No power. She was gliding, drifting, descending.

Eyes wide, she grabbed the stick, and felt its slackness. The rudder was ominously soft. The CAD was all but dead, with only a few red runes winking menacingly.

Pull up... Pull up... Pull up...

She peered out of the canopy. She was still over Vesperus, over some mangled, bomb-pummelled quarter she didn't recognise. She could only gauge by eye, but it looked like she was about three hundred feet up, sinking steadily. Ground speed about a hundred twenty, a hundred fifty...

She had no means to develop lift, and no way to execute any significant manoeuvres. All she had were the flaps and control surfaces, unless they had seized, or been shot away. The ground was coming up; blown-out habitats, warehousing, a cold, dead reactor tower. She worked stick and rudder, trying to trim, trying to regain some fraction of control, enough to tilt, enough to pull heading by a degree or two. She still had hydraulics for the flaps.

Here came the ground, faster, rushing at her. Everything down there was going to kill her. Everything was a collision impact. There was no space for a cold-down or a sliding run-out. Ahead, a manufactory, a row of smokestacks, a line of warehouses. She was going to auger into the side of the first one. Negative lift. She worked at the rudder and flaps. *Turn, turn, turn!*

Almost. *Almost*. She cleared the warehouse, but grazed her port wingtip along its side wall. Broken stonework sprayed. The tip of the wing sheared off. Rocked by the glancing impact, the bird began to tremble and yaw out of its gentle, floating descent.

But she'd cleared the warehouse. Beyond it, nothing but darkness. She was plunging down into the shadowed well of the hive floor, leaving the sunlit level. Below her, pitch blackness. The glint of a mirror. No, water. A flooded street deep in the shade.

She had no choice.

The black mirror raced under her, glinting. She could no more force the Voss down than she could make it rise. She switched off master voltaics, and rode the long, shallow decline until the bird's belly kissed the water.

Which felt like solid rockcrete. The Voss shook wildly, skipped, hit again, and resumed its furious vibration. She could hear the belly plate shredding. Spray kicked up over the wings in frothy plumes, washing the cracked canopy into a blur. It wasn't going to end. The roaring, the tearing, the shaking… the water was going to rip her airframe apart.

Then it stopped, or at least decreased. She was sliding, skating, casting up spray. Just when she thought she'd made it, and aced a belly-ditch, something snagged the right wing. The impact was violent. It threw her forward in her straps. It wrenched the whole Voss around to the right. Most of the starboard wing tore away with a bitter shriek of metal.

Then a jerk, a lurch, and she was no longer moving. The nose began to dip. Black water gurgled and frothed up over the gun mounts and the cowling. She was sinking, snout-down.

If you go down, don't ditch in the water, Lopard had told her.

The floodwater was washing up to the canopy line. It was suddenly pouring into the cockpit footwell. She could smell the stagnant reek of it.

She punched her fast-release buckle, struggled out of the harness, and got up on her seat in a crouch, braced against the bird's forward tilt. The canopy had distorted on impact and wouldn't unlatch. She cursed, thumping the lever with the ball of her fist, her head and shoulders hunched against the canopy glass. The floodwater was sloshing up the sides of her seat. The stick was half submerged.

'Come! Free! You! Bastard!' she snarled, every word a spit of rage as she punched at the lever.

The canopy released. She hoisted it up. She could smell the river, the rotting stink. There was nothing to see except darkness.

She reached back down into the cockpit. The emergency pack was strapped to the struts beside the seat. She pulled it free.

Water was now bubbling up over the edge of the seat and the toes of her boots. The pack, lightweight, had a torch strapped to the case. She detached it, hung the pack over her shoulder, and played the torch beam around. Water, like black glass, caught her light. She saw weed, floating debris. A mossy rockcrete stump.

She raised the beam. She'd come down beside some sort of loading dock which the floodwater had turned into a wharf. Her right wing had caught against the rockcrete pilings. The impact had torn some of the wing off, but it had also swung the Voss nose-in against the dock. She scrambled out of the cockpit, onto what little of the broken wing remained above water. The angle was steep. She had to pocket her torch and clamber with her hands, kicking for footholds.

The water was about to swallow the Voss. Jagdea rose, arms extended for balance, teetered, and then leapt across onto the rockcrete piling. Her foot slipped on the wet moss as she landed, and she went down, but she managed to cling on and haul herself up the broken pilings, then up onto the dock.

She removed her helmet, and peeled off her gloves. The left one was bloody.

Panting, exhausted, she flopped onto her back and lay there, staring up at the darkness where the sky had once been.

Location unknown, time unknown

She'd fallen asleep without meaning to. She woke with a start, felt the cold rockcrete under her and the ache of her body, and remembered where she was.

Something had woken her, some sound. She listened, and heard nothing but the lap of invisible water in the darkness.

She sat up, which hurt, then stood up, which hurt more. She was cold and her body was clumsy and stiff. She'd turned off the torch to conserve power, and her eyes were slowly adapting to the darkness. She could make out shapes: pale shapes against the pitchy shadows. The shape of the rockcrete dock, the row of support pillars that ran along it, the heavy overhang of the building above. Some glimmer of light was filtering down into the hive-depth, a sickly green cast that contrasted with the shadow.

She had no idea where she was, or how long she'd been there. Her left sleeve was ripped, her forearm gashed, though the blood had crusted, and her chron had been torn off at some point. Methodically, she checked herself from head to foot for other injuries. Extensive bruising and joint pain. Concussion, probably. The painful debt that followed hypoxia. She felt sick and weak. She didn't want to think about the rad levels at the hive floor, the bacteria, the contaminants. Everything was polluted, even the dust.

Towards the end of her body-check, she found a sliver of fuselage aluminoid about the length of her index finger sticking out of her right calf. She pulled it out, teeth gritted. The wound started to bleed profusely, and she dressed it using the medicae kit in the emergency pack.

She checked the rest of the pack. Two vacuum-packed ration bars, a pack of dextrose tablets, a bundle of small stick flares, two stimms of powerful analgesics, four chemical hand-warmers, a tightly folded foil blanket, a small, and empty, water bottle and some purification tablets. One loop in the pack was empty. There was no tracer beacon.

It took her hurting brain a moment to puzzle that out. The emergency pack was usually strapped to the ejection chute, so it would stay with the pilot if they bailed. On the ground, the pilot could detach the pack, and activate the tracer so that recovery elements could find them.

But Tail 011 had been Sorrentine's bird. No ejection system. So the pack had been strapped to the cabin wall instead. If a bio-linked pilot went down, they would have no choice but to stay with their bird... assuming they and their bird had survived impact. They couldn't wander clear of the crash site and find shelter, so no tracer had been issued. Stores were in such short supply at Six-Six, why waste a piece of kit that wouldn't be used? Chief Tarr was thorough and methodical, but she hadn't remembered to add a tracer to the pack when Jagdea inherited One-One.

Jagdea sat back. She didn't know whether to laugh or cry. It seemed likely both of those things might happen at once. She was never going to be found. It would take weeks or months of recovery sweeps to locate the crash site. It wasn't visible from the air. Her ram-ride had been so wild and unpredictable, Six-Six probably didn't even know which part of the hive to begin searching. They didn't have weeks or months to waste sweeping for one pilot who was probably dead anyway.

She didn't have weeks or months.

She sat in the silence and the darkness for a while, shivering, until the cold of the rockcrete dock began to make her hips ache. She got up. She got up, draped the foil blanket around her shoulders, and used one of the hand-warmers. She could start walking. How far would she get? She didn't even know which direction to head in. The nearest Intercept or ROP might be close by, for all she knew. But without knowing where exactly, she could end up trekking in the opposite direction.

'Get a grip,' she told herself, out loud. Her voice sounded odd against the silence. She had to be methodical, logical.

She fished out the torch, lit it, and started to wander around the dock area. One-One was just a buckled tail and the remains of the trailing wing edges jutting out of the water. The dock was dank, decaying, and littered with debris that had fallen through the building levels above. She hoped she could find some sort of sign, a wall-plate, a serial code, a stencil… something that could identify her location. The street, perhaps, the block, even just the district.

She'd been doing that for a while when her tired mind recognised the logic flaw. Even if she found a name or serial code, she had no charts.

There were no paper charts or tearsheets in her thigh pouch, and none back in the flooded cockpit. All Six-Six sorties were directed by autotrack, using target-specific data squirted by Campanile Control. The only 'map' she had was whatever Control had loaded into One-One's CAD that morning.

That morning? Or the morning before?

It didn't matter. The onboard data covered Harquin and its vicinity, not the whole hive. Even if it had showed the whole of Vesperus, no Intercepts or ROPs were marked for security reasons, in case the enemy recovered them. And the onboard data was held in One-One's logis-engine and instrument block, which was now half-submerged in toxic water and undoubtedly unrecoverable.

Jagdea turned off her torch, and stared at the darkness.

'It's like you're trying to kill me,' she said to the hive.

The hive replied.

A noise. A skitter of pebbles. A creak of debris.

Jagdea froze. The shred had survived the crash too. It hunkered in the shadows beside her, delighted by the situation.

There was something out there, something nearby, moving furtively in the gloom. Along with warnings about infection, radiation and toxic floodwater, refectory horror stories had often been filled with tales of scavengers and animals still living in the black depths of the hive-grave. Scavengers, or worse. Vermin, predators, mutants, survivors of the hive-war driven insane, cannibals...

Jagdea had paid them no attention. She had never planned to visit the hive floor.

She had no sidearm. She'd never been issued with one. She stooped down slowly and drew her utility knife from her ankle pouch. It was sharp, strong, serrated on one edge, but it was not long. It wasn't a combat weapon, it was a survival tool.

She listened. The silence filled her ears until she could hear her own pulse. Nothing moved.

That didn't mean there was nothing there.

Location unknown, time unknown

When nothing appeared, she returned to the edge of the dock, and to logic and first principles. She was tired, but didn't dare sleep. She was hungry, and if she portioned out the ration bars, she could make them last two or three days. She was thirsty, but the only water was the black soup of the floodwater, and she knew her purification tablets would never render that safe.

If she stayed put, she would be dead. If she started walking without a proper heading, she would be lost and dead. She had no beacon, so she would never be found.

It started to rain. The sound, inexplicable, made her jump at first. She thought it was the whatever-it-was, come back. But it was rain. She could hear it splashing on the floodwater. It was falling down through the hive, through whatever slots and apertures it could find, and hitting what had once been open streets in the base levels. How many miles down was she? How many miles of hive-rise and structure stood over her, climbing to the sky and blocking out the light?

She went to the edge of the dock, and looked out. Her torch

picked out the ripples where raindrops were hitting the still, black water. She looked up, and her torch beam briefly lit the falling drops white against the murk above her.

Above her. Finally, logic was prevailing. If she walked away from the crash site, going horizontally was futile. But going vertically? She had to climb up, as high as she could get. She had to go up through the hive. If she made it to a rooftop, or a platform, she might be seen. She could light a fire, maybe. Maybe, above the darkness, she might spot a landmark, a structure she recognised, and get her bearings.

It would be hard going. But it was something, and all she'd had until then was nothing.

She picked up her emergency pack, tucked her gloves into her belt, and clipped her helmet to the pack by the chin strap. She wondered if there was anything helpful she could salvage from One-One before she abandoned it. The bird was nose-down in the water beside the dock, its ruined tail raised. She couldn't think of anything useful it might contain, and just getting back onto it would be hazardous.

Sucking on a dextrose tablet, she started to explore the dock again by torchlight. She felt some confidence kindled, either because she had a plan, or because of the blood sugar rush. The dank rockcrete loading dock was about sixty yards long and thirty wide. It was entirely overhung by the floor above, which was supported on massive 'crete pillars. One long side was the water where One-One rested. The other long side was the back wall of the dock. There was a rusted vent grille that she couldn't lever off, and a large open archway that led into what had once been a staircase. But it was choked by masonry rubble and dust that had fallen from above. Peering up, she could see that nothing of the staircase remained, except the empty well, and she couldn't even make out where entrances to other floors might be. That was not an option.

Most of the dock space around the pillars was scattered with debris too, lumps of rockcrete, broken rebar, loose stones and other detritus caked in moss and wet dirt. The ceiling around the top of the pillars had buckled and caved, but not enough for her to crawl through, even if she'd been able to reach it.

One of the dock's shorter sides was open, and had once overlooked an adjoining street. Now, that too was flooded, a tributary joining the street she'd ditched in. The water was black, scummy and noxious. Her torch beam picked out the far side, another rubble-strewn, overhung shelf of pavement, but it was too far away. Too far to leap, and there was nothing she could fashion a bridge or ladder from. She wasn't going to swim it.

The opposite short side was another wall, forming an 'L' shape with the dock's back wall. There was an access hatch in it, solid and sealed, the surface peeled and scorched. She could make out the remains of a stencil, but couldn't read what it said.

The hatch control, as she expected, was dead. There was no power down here. She tried to force the hatch, but it was either locked, too heavy, or fallen debris on the other side had blocked it and buckled it into its frame.

Frustrated, she repeated her methodical tour. There had to be a way off the rancid dock that didn't involve water. The only possible option seemed to be the staircase, but that seemed unlikely. She'd have to clear rubble out of the way, which would tire her even more, and then climb, somehow, using whatever handholds she could find. She had no rope.

Her energy and confidence ebbed.

She heard a sound. It was a hollow, metallic knocking. It was sporadic, a thump every few seconds. Sometimes two came in quick succession, then nothing for over a minute.

The shred licked its lips and smiled. Controlling her breathing, she played the torch beam around. She couldn't tell where the sound was coming from. It seemed close, but the overhang of the structure above her muffled the sound and confused its origin. Was it coming from the waterside? Was it coming from her imagination?

She crept back to the edge of the dock. The rain had ceased, and the black, oily flood was as still as glass. There was a stink of vegetation, mildew and putrescence. She crouched down, and panned the torch. The main thoroughfare where she had ditched One-One was much wider than the side street at the far end. She could barely pick out the opposite bank. There appeared to be another shelf of pavement, or the top of a platform rising clear of the water. Above that, darkness, and the hint of a crumbling wall, an overhang, pipework, skeins of torn wire dangling like creepers.

She heard the knock again. It was so close, it made her jump. It had come from the pilings right beside her. She rose, her knife in one hand, and searched with her torch.

Tail 011 had moved. It was still nose-down in the water, but it had rotated silently so that the raised tail was now facing the dock. Somewhere, a tide had risen or fallen, or some deep current of the permanent floodwater had ebbed. The undertow had quietly moved One-One in the water, turning the drowned, floating corpse of the Voss through one hundred and eighty degrees. The edge of the ragged tail assembly was bumping against the dock and the pilings every time the invisible tide stirred it.

Jagdea exhaled. She almost laughed. She had been so tense.

'Screw you,' she told the shred.

Click-click-click, the shred replied.

Jagdea tensed again. It wasn't the shred. The shred wasn't real. The sound was. A tapping, a scuttle. Feet, heavy feet, padding quietly, disturbing grit. The click of claws or nails tapping rockcrete with each furtive step. Something was breathing.

She snatched the torch up, and aimed it across the water at the far bank. For a second, just for a second, the beam of light showed her the monster staring back at her.

Then it was gone.

Location unknown, time unknown

She tried not to think about the monster's eyes. Yellow eyes, baleful and dead, thick scars knotting the heavy brow and massive snout.

'Just shut the hell up,' she told the shred.

She'd been working hard, with almost feverish intent. Hours had passed. She didn't know how many. With One-One's tail turned against the dock by the current, the rear end of the Voss was now just in reach. She'd leaned out, braced, and used the utility knife to pry broken struts and plating from the tail assembly. Most were too buckled for use, but once they were out of the way, she could get at the taileron and rear control surfaces, and strip out the effector rods, internal slats, and some heavy-duty voltaic trunking, thinking that maybe she could fashion a ladder. She'd worn her gloves at first, but they were thick and robbed her of dexterity. Now her fingertips and knuckles were scraped and bloody. She paused to use another of the hand-warmers to get her fingers working, but it didn't help much.

She tried not to think about the monster's eyes. Yellow eyes, baleful and dead, the scar-knotted brow and huge snout. The snuffle of its breath. The drip of saliva. The teeth.

It took constant concentration to strip out the tail. She was working, awkwardly, at full stretch, and any lapse could slip her off the slimy pilings into the water. She used a rudder slat as a pry-bar to extend her reach, and once she'd pulled out a decent length of voltaic cabling, she used it to lash her utility knife to the end of an aluminoid tail spar. Now she had a spear, of sorts. Now her extended reach had a bite on the end.

She tried not to think about the monster's eyes. Yellow, baleful, dead. The teeth. One thick tusk of a canine, broken. The enormous hunch of shoulders. A sheer bulk that her torch had merely suggested before it vanished.

She freed a longer length of thicker trunking, dragged it out of the bird's carcass hand-over-hand until it spooled on the dock at her feet. Then she wrenched out another, panting as she yanked it a bit at a time out of the tail, as though she was stripping intestines or major tendons out of an animal kill. She tested the trunking for flex and pliability. It was too heavy to serve as a rope to help her scale the blocked stairwell, but she tied one length into a noose, threw it around the top of the tail assembly, cinched it tight, and then tied the other end off around the tallest of the pilings. Now One-One couldn't rotate or drift away when the tide turned.

She tried as hard as she could not to think about the monster's eyes. Its snout, its snuffle, its scar-tissue face. Its bulk. A quadruped. Its solid mass had definitely outweighed her significantly.

The eyes, so dead, so completely lifeless.

'Shut your frigging mouth,' she told the shred.

The plates covering the countermeasures system had torn away on one side of the tail, exposing the launch slot and mechanism, and some of the little mag-phos decoy flares. She'd dispensed a batch during combat, but some of the little metal drums remained, tightly packed in the compression hopper, like budding teeth in a gumline. Leaning out as far as she dared, she managed to push three out. The fourth slipped from her bloody fingers, fell into the water with a plop, and sank like a stone. The hopper's compression spring was supposed to advance the flares as they were dispensed, pushing each one rapidly into the ejector, but with power dead, the compression mechanism was stuck. She'd freed the ones she could reach, but the rest didn't advance, and remained tantalisingly beyond her fingertips. She wondered if she should attempt to clamber back into the cockpit and throw the master voltaic back on, but the only route was via the tail, and she didn't fancy her chances of either getting there, or making it back, without taking a toxic dunk. Or of electrocuting herself if live cables were trailing in the water.

She tried not to think about the monster's dead eyes.

She examined the three flares she had retrieved. They were familiar, of course, but only as tactical kit. She'd never really had to load or handle them. They were small, and quite heavy despite their aluminoid casing. There was a serrated metal tear-band around the rim of each one. When the rear-facing compressor pumped, it fired the decoys via the ejector at high velocity, and simultaneously stripped the tear-band off each one, which both opened and ignited them. Slipstream effect did the rest. The flares were packed with extremely volatile mag-phos powder, which burned very bright and very hot. She gingerly unscrewed one of the flares, smelled the pungent powder inside, and then screwed it tight again.

She tried not to think about the monster. The shred, reclining on the dock nearby, oozed out some more of its unsolicited black notions, and reminded her that she had to. It had been real, not her imagination. It had gone, but it would come back.

She crouched down, surveying the tail to see if there was anything else worth stripping out. There was a sheaf of wiring that looked as though it had potential. Teased out, it would bind her knife to the spar more securely. It was out of reach. She tried to hook her spear onto the tail, and steer the bird around, but even supported by water it was far too heavy.

Then she saw the light. A tiny green light, blinking on and off behind a wiring loom inside the tail cavity.

Power was off. She tried to think what the hell it could be. She tried not to think about the monster.

But the monster had come back anyway.

Location unknown, time unknown

She heard it snuffle and growl. It wasn't on the far bank this time. It was much closer. It was on the other side of the flooded side street at the end of the dock. She heard the pad-click of its paws as it moved. She smelled a new smell, the stink of diseased meat.

She got up, gripping her spear, and moved to the end of the dock. She switched on her torch and aimed it. Nothing on the far side, nothing on the slimy pavement.

Then there it was.

It stared at her out of the gloom, just shy of her light. When she tried to get the beam directly on it, it turned and vanished into the shadows. Whatever it was, it was big. Three feet or more at the shoulder. A hundred and fifty pounds at least.

She waited. Nothing moved. She was about to switch off her torch when she heard it again. Heavy, rapid footfalls. It was running.

The monster thundered out onto the pavement, right into her light. It was powering into a leap, to clear the water and reach her. At the last second, perhaps confused by her beam, it changed its mind, and skidded to a halt. It stood there, gazing at her with its dead eyes, panting and snuffling.

It was a dog. The biggest canid she'd ever seen. A war-dog. A vat-bred mastiff, gene-modified for bulk, power and aggression. Its short coat was almost black with mange and dirt, and its immense head was a hideous mass of scar tissue. One ear was missing, and its jowls were frayed by old wounds. Jagdea could see the outline of its ribs. It was starved. It was mad with hunger. It glared at her with its lifeless eyes. Drool wept from its muzzle. A deep, phlegmy growl rumbled out of its throat.

It stooped its huge head, sniffed the edge of the pavement and the water beyond. Then it began to pace up and down the pavement, prowling the brink, keeping its eyes on her. Side-on, she could see the burned-out cybernetic implants fused into the meat of its shoulders like a collar, and the brand tattoos on its matted flanks. Magistratum. It was an Adeptus Arbites cyber-mastiff, an attack dog from hive enforcement. Hive enforcement was as long dead as the hive itself. The dog was feral, its obedience implants broken and fried.

It vanished into the shadows again. Jagdea knew it was coming back. She could hear the galloping slap of its paws. It was taking another run-up.

She stumbled backwards in terror. The canid burst back into the light, and launched itself off the pavement at full stretch. An immense bound, driven by the power of its thickly muscled legs.

It almost made it. Its forepaws hit the dock, but its hind legs slipped short and struck the water. It began to slide backwards, snarling, spraying water with its thrashing hind legs. But it had a grip, and it was monstrously strong. It began to haul its bulk up onto the dock on her side.

Jagdea ran at it. Once it was on the dock, she was finished. She had one moment of advantage. She ran at it, and jammed her spear into its chest before it could get its back legs on the rockcrete.

She felt bone crack as the blade went in. The animal howled, and lunged at her, snapping at her with its massive jaws, spraying her with spittle. She kept the spear wedged in place to hold it off, but it was so powerful, it was actually shoving her backwards and bending the spar.

It kept snapping, biting chunks out of the air. She could hear and feel the bear-trap thump of its jaws slamming shut, the clack of its teeth clashing. She was assailed by its putrid breath, and every time its maw opened, she could see straight down the red-raw, pulsing cavern of its mouth and gullet.

It shook hard, pushing her back. It swung its head from side to side, and tried to gnaw at the spar impaling its chest. She snatched her fingers back before it could chew on them too. The spar was short, and now bent. She only had a grip on the very end of it.

She yelled in fury, and rammed even harder. She felt something break. The canid struggled furiously for another second, then its entire bulk slipped backwards off the dock into the water. Her makeshift spear, wedged fast in its breastbone, went with it.

She backed off. It was thrashing in the water, churning spray, trying to paddle, trying to float. The mirror-black water around it began to discolour and cloud. Then, almost abruptly, it sank out of sight, leaving nothing but glugging bubbles and red froth.

She waited for a long time to see if it would resurface. She expected it to at any moment. She expected it to explode back out of the flood with vengeful wrath.

But it didn't. After what she reckoned was an hour, she went back to work.

Location unknown, time unknown

The little green light was still blinking at her. She had finally worked out what it was.

Six-Six hadn't put a beacon in Sorrentine's emergency pack, because he was bonded to his bird and couldn't eject. But if he went down and survived the impact, they'd need to locate him. So they'd fitted the tracer beacon to his Voss, because he and his Voss would remain in the same place.

It was running off its own voltaic cell. It had been transmitting since the crash, automatically triggered, no doubt, by registered impact.

She wasn't dead after all. Not quite so dead, anyway. If they were up looking for her, they had a tracer to follow. Provided it had sufficient range, given the distance she must have travelled. Provided the depth to which she had fallen, and the sheer density of the structural levels above her, weren't masking its pulse. Provided the beacon had enough power to maintain signal.

She sat down on the dock, and stared at the blinking light. Now she had a glimmer of hope, a little, green, winking glimmer. She knew it wouldn't be much longer before fatigue, hunger, cold and thirst began to seriously incapacitate her. Another day, perhaps? Then another day to slip away and die?

How long was a day down here?

She reviewed her plan to make for a higher level. If she had started down that route earlier, she would have unwittingly left behind the only hope of anyone finding her. Which meant, conversely, she was now stuck here. She couldn't move away from the tracer.

Unless she could take it with her.

She crawled to the edge of the dock, and peered into the tail cavity. The tracer was well out of reach. Even if she got up on the tail, she wouldn't be able to reach down to it. There was a chance she could reach it if she turned the tail in closer to the dock, but she no longer had her spear, and she hadn't been able to move One-One with it anyway. If she got in the water and swam out–

She wasn't getting in the water.

She got up, and tried hauling on the trunking line she'd tied to the tail. Her bloody hands kept slipping, and the trunking bit grooves in her palms. One-One didn't budge. Ten and three-quarter tons of ramp weight. What was she even thinking?

She got the other length of trunking, and fashioned a second noose. It took about a dozen casts, but she finally managed to throw it out, and catch it around the torn end of the port wing. Then she dug in her heels and began to drag on it, using both arms and her whole body weight. She leaned into each heave, trying to use the tail line as a pivot to swing One-One around.

She tried for a long time until, hyperventilating and weeping with frustration, she accepted it was impossible.

She sat down. Then she lay down. Then–

Location unknown, time unknown

She woke up. Exhaustion had just shut her down. She was even colder now. She rummaged in her pack for the last of the dextrose tablets and a piece of ration bar. Her hands were shaking.

Kneeling on the rockcrete, she stuffed a chunk of bar into her mouth, and started chewing. Then, recklessly, another, even though she knew it had to last. Why? Why did it have to last? She wasn't going to. She was so hungry. It was probably thirst more than hunger, but she was so hungry. Like a dog. Like a famished dog, scavenging the ruins for bones.

She stopped chewing. Something had woken her up. She realised that now. Something had woken her up. A sound. Something. Not the knocking of One-One's tail against the pilings. Not the rain.

She stood up, swallowing her mouthful. She fished out her torch. What was out there now? She walked the length of the dock and back, playing her torch. No part of the nightmare had changed. Darkness. Rubble. Mould. Slime.

She stopped at the far end of the dock, where she had killed the mastiff. Had it come back... back from the dead? Like the shred had wanted her to imagine?

She ran her light across the water, then along the edge of the dock. The torch flickered, and went out briefly. When it came back on, its light was not as strong. Its cells were getting low.

She raised her arm, and aimed the torch across the water at the opposite pavement, where the mastiff had prowled, watching her. There was something there, a shape. A lump. A sack. Something that hadn't been there the last time she looked.

It was the canid. Or what was left of it. It was lying on its side. She could make out the head, the wet and matted fur, the front legs. But from the chest down, most of it was gone. She could see bare ribs, bloody meat. Its guts and thighs had been stripped of meat and eaten. Parts of its head, snout and lips had been gnawed away, exposing teeth and gums in a permanent leer. Something had dragged it out of the water onto the bank and fed on it. It was definitely the same animal. Her makeshift spear was still wedged in its chest.

'What the hell could do that?' she whispered. The hive didn't answer. The shred moaned in delight, excited to find out.

The torch flickered, and went out. Jagdea flicked it on and off, shook it. It relit briefly, then died for good.

She stood in the darkness for a moment. One-One's tail bumped softly. Now the light had gone, she could hear something moving. Things.

Sniffing. Scratching. Scrabbling. A sharp crack of bone.

She reached into her pocket and took out one of the stick flares. She tore the pull-tab off, and lit it. The flare fizzled and started to burn, casting a red glow around her. She held it up. The wavering light didn't really reach to the far bank. There was something there, though.

She threw the flare, underarm, as far as she could. It landed in the water near the far side, and floated, hissing, still burning, throwing its red glare up across the opposite pavement.

There they were. She saw the mirror-glint of retinas first. More dogs. A pack of them. She could see eight or nine at least. All were as filthy and emaciated as the cyber-mastiff. Some were relatively small. At least two were larger than the monster she had barely killed.

They had been feasting on the corpse. Their faces and snouts were plastered masks of gore. They had all raised their heads to stare at the light and, through that light, at her.

They started to stir, to yip and growl. Some trotted to the edge of the pavement, and leaned out, peering across the flood at her, sniffing. Some hurried up and down the edge, excitedly. One of the largest padded forward and snarled at her. It shook out its brawny shoulders, flapping its jowls and grinding its jaws.

Then it turned away. She knew where it was going. It was going to take a run-up and launch itself at the opposite side. She had no doubt it would make it. The mastiff almost had, and this brute was significantly bigger and more powerful.

She had nothing, not even her knife. She had to get off the dock, even if it meant leaving the tracer, her only lifeline, behind. She grabbed her pack and started to run. Behind her, two of the smaller canids leapt off the bank into the water, and started to thrash across, paddling, heads held up. The others started to growl and bay, their agitation increasing. She could hear the big dog coming, paws pounding.

She reached the archway, and started to scramble up the mound of rubble piled on the stairs. She kept slipping and sliding back. She could hear the sound of baying rising behind her. She scrabbled harder, clawing her way up into the darkness until she reached the top of the heap and met the scarred wall of the stairwell. The air was dank. She groped for a handhold. She couldn't see anything.

She took out another stick flare, lit it, and tossed it onto the rubble. By its quivering red glow, she re-examined the walls. The remains of a step offered a crude foothold. Higher up, a missing stone allowed her fingers to grip at full stretch. Now what? Old pipework, out of reach and impossible to grip anyway. A dangling power cable.

She reached for that, missed, and tried again.

A yowling canid burst into the stairwell below, and began to skitter and paw up the rubble after her. Another came in right behind it. She'd almost grasped the hanging cable when the first dog reached the top of the mound and began to leap up, snapping at her, clattering its paws against the wall as it fell back to try again. She tried to reach the cable. The canid leapt again, and she kicked out at it to keep it at bay. The second one arrived at the top of the rubble, and tried to claw itself up the wall to get at her. Its ears were back, its eyes wild, its teeth bared as it bit at the air.

The first one leapt again. Jagdea yelled as she felt its bite close around her ankle. It was hanging off her, writhing, shaking its muzzle. If it hadn't been for the metal inserts in her flight kit boots, it would have bitten through to bone. She tried to shake it off. It would not let go. Its weight and frenzy were going to drag her off the wall. Her fingers were slipping.

With her free hand, she released her helmet from the strap of her pack, gripped it by the visor, and used it as a club to beat at the canid's skull. Just the effort of doing that threatened to throw her off the wall. The canid was a swinging weight, pulling her over. It felt as though it was going to bite her foot off.

The helmet connected with an ugly crack. The dog let go, and dropped away. It tumbled, yelping, down the rubble. The other hound started leaping at her too, its jaws closing with a snap at the summit of every jump.

She hurled the helmet at it, caught it across the muzzle, and knocked it aside.

More of the feral pack were bounding up onto the rubble. Their coats were wet. Some were biting and savaging each other to get to her first. The snarling and yelping seemed to fill the empty shaft.

She reached for the cable, caught it, and then jerked on it to test how secure it was. It slipped slightly, then held. She let go with her other hand, and threw herself sideways onto the cable. She got it with both hands, arms burning with effort, toe-tips against the wall.

Below her, the gore-faced canids were baying, leaping and snapping.

Jagdea didn't look down.

The flare went out anyway.

Location unknown, time unknown

In pitch darkness, she rolled off the cable and onto a rockcrete slab. She had no idea how high she'd climbed. The desperate baying of the hounds echoed from below.

She could barely move, her limbs on fire and locked with effort. She was panting, unable to draw enough breath. She had climbed as far as she could, way past the point her hands and legs had threatened to give out, high enough to find a ledge to transfer to.

Now she had even less idea where she was. She rolled upright, feeling the floor around her. Stone or 'crete. She was dizzy, and her head wouldn't clear. She fumbled out another stick flare. Her fingers, bleeding and stiff, wouldn't work properly. She got it lit.

She looked around in the crimson glow. She was on a higher floor, a level above the loading dock. It was empty, filthy, abandoned and bombed out. Glass litter lay under every blind window. The ledge she was sitting on was the mouth of the doorway that had once opened onto the stairs, when there had been stairs.

She got up, unsteady. She almost fell. She braced against the wall with one hand, flare raised in the other. The wall was coated with sooty grime. She edged her way along, testing the floor at every step. There were holes in it in several places, where cave-ins from above had cascaded down and punched through. Water dripped. Her throat was so dry she couldn't swallow.

She could still hear the dogs baying. They refused to let food escape.

She needed to get higher. She wondered if there were any stairs intact. She couldn't climb like that again.

She found a room lined with decayed bunks. The bedding had rotted and disintegrated. Beyond that, a room containing the desk and chair of some supervising intendant. Everything was caked in dust. Filing cartons were full of mulch. There was a voxcaster, a cogitator and other apparatus. She didn't even try them. She could see how split and dead they were.

She followed the hallway, testing the floor. A large section had fallen in, so she had to turn back. She followed another hallway, which brought her to a small administration annex. The chamber was circular, and the systems around the walls and in the central console were burned out. A human skeleton sat in the single chair, staring at her.

Her flare went out.

She lit another.

The skeleton was still there. She had almost expected it to have moved. It had been burned in its seat. Fire had gutted the chamber, and the corridor beyond, which was littered with debris and a few large human bones that the blaze had not consumed.

She stopped and leaned against a wall to rest. She could still hear the dogs in the distance. She thought about the tracer she had left behind, the green light blinking. Survival had forced her to leave hope behind, or was it the other way around?

There was no way out. She would never be found.

She limped on.

She found another stairwell, but that had collapsed too. There were no others, but she kept looking anyway. Just off the next hall, she found a hatch standing open, rusted in place. It led onto a walkway bridge.

She looked out. She was three storeys up. The flooded side street was directly below her, and the bridge crossed it, linking one structure with its neighbour across the street. Above her, there was nothing but darkness.

She edged across the bridge. The metalwork creaked, but it was secure. She got to the other side, into the other structure through a hatch that appeared to have been cut off its frame. More dust, more bones.

And, eventually, a staircase.

It was intact. It led down into the depths below, and up into the shadows. She started to shuffle her way up it. The metal handrail collapsed and fell with a clatter. She stuck to the wall instead, fumbling her way.

Another flare died out.

She didn't have many left. She decided to wait for a few minutes, to get her breath back, and allow her eyes to adjust. She would keep going without flares for a while, if she could, to conserve them.

Her night vision slowly settled. She moved on upwards, feeling the wall. All she could see was a ghost of shapes, darkness against darkness, blackness of different intensities placed against each other. After a while, she became aware of a glow. Faint, green, the thin remnant of upper daylight filtering down through the depths, just as she had seen down on the dock.

She kept going. Another flight. Another. Her foot slipped on something. She was pretty sure it was a human femur that rolled out under her sole. She almost fell, but managed to catch herself. The femur, or whatever it was, rattled away down the steps.

She stopped to rest again, and ate the last pieces of the ration bar. She didn't know if she could keep going. She had no strength. She felt so weak, and everything she was carrying seemed so heavy. She wondered what she could get rid of. Not the stick flares. Perhaps the decoy flares. It had felt like they might have a use at the time. She decided to keep them. She tossed her gloves, the useless purification tablets, the empty, mocking water bottle, the last of the hand-warmers, and the blanket. She knew she was probably being tired and stupid, but none of them seemed worth carrying. She looked at the medicae kit. It was rudimentary at best. If she picked up another injury now, it was academic. She was dying. She thought about redressing the wound in her calf before casting the kit aside. The effort seemed like too much.

But the wound was starting to hurt. She picked up the analgesic stimms. They were strong, designed to numb serious trauma. In her weary state, would they just put her to sleep? Maybe it would be better that way.

She popped one, and stuck it in the meat of her leg before she could think about it further. She tossed the empty stimm aside and sat back. Slowly, very slowly, a lazy warmth crept through her. She didn't feel better, but she felt less pain, and as her pain was just about everywhere, it felt like a win.

She felt like she could move. As though she had a little fire left.

She ditched the medicae kit, and the emergency pack. She

stuffed the decoy flares into one of her suit pockets, and the stick flares into the other, along with the last stimm shot.

She got up and resumed her climb, step by step. There would be a top, and she was going to reach it.

And die there, the shred reminded her. *And die there.*

'Shut your damn mouth,' she whispered.

Another flight of steps. Another. She stopped. She could hear a whining sound echoing through the blown-out building below. A distant wail.

The dogs. The feral packs of the hive floor moved through the darkness and the ruins with greater facility than she could. They could squeeze through gaps, leap walls, and thrash through water that she was not prepared to touch. They were driven by a ravening hunger that was all they understood.

They had her scent.

Location unknown, time unknown

There seemed to be more light. The dusty air was streaked with a chemical green. Either that, or her eyes were becoming truly nocturnal.

But the whining had increased. It came and went, and it was echoing and muffled, but it was getting closer. Occasionally, she thought she heard the skitter of paws, a yap, or a bark. Something trotting along a floor below her, sniffing for spore.

She had no idea how many flights she'd climbed. From windows, she could see nothing below to gauge distance, and nothing above. But the darkness above her seemed thinner than the darkness below.

That's what she told herself. The shred confidently disagreed.

The brief sense of wellbeing from the stimm shot was beginning to wear off. Aches and pains were returning. She thought about using the last one, but decided to save it until she really hurt.

She continued to plod up the stairs. Everything was desolate and empty. She had expected to find some scraps, some litter, maybe even more bones or personal effects. But there was nothing except dust and ash. Firestorms had scoured the building back to the bare structure, and it was amazing it was still standing.

Or it was being held up by the buildings around it.

She day-dreamed of amasec, the good stuff. Or lousy joiliq. Or just chemical-tinged water from a chipped jug in the refectory. She day-dreamed of her cot, in her billet room. Of talking with Gumm. Of laughing with Lopard. Of arguing with Badler. Of flying. Flying free. The brutal reality of operational life at Six-Six seemed like heaven now, brighter and warmer than the radiance of any golden throne.

'I'll make a deal,' she said to the hive, much to the shred's amusement. 'I'll take it. I'll stick to it. Just give it back to me. Forget Orison. Forget driving cargo. Forget a ride home on a replenishment carry. I'll take it. I'll accept it, fangs out, guns hot. Just give it back to me.'

The hive did not reply.

'No?' she said, clumping up the steps. 'Then I'll plead to the Saint. You know the one. Sabbat? Yeah. To her. In supplication. I'll commit. To her, to the God-Emperor. I'll embrace that truth, because it's better than this. I'll be His gunslinger, avowed and faithful, and make it my duty to fly for Him, until the ground comes up to meet me.'

Don't you do that already? the shred wondered.

'Shut your frigging mouth,' she said.

That's not how duty works, the shred suggested, laconic. *That's not how gods work.*

'Shut up.' She didn't want to listen. She felt as though she was losing her mind. Or worse, that something was stealing it. But the shred wouldn't be quiet.

You live, or you die. That's down to you. Gods don't make deals. They simply exist so you can fear them. Like me.

'Shut *up*.'

She could hear the whining again from below. The baying of hounds. On the next scorched flight of stairs, she felt a breeze lift the dust. Cold air on her face. She started to hurry, almost stumbling.

Jagdea limped out onto a platform. A wide, wide platform. A landing pad for lifters and service vehicles. A passenger dock. The mangled portico of the dock shelter adjoined the stair exit. She could feel the hive wind blowing in, stale and cold. She could feel the spatter of rain.

She was outside. The roof of the structure.

She sank to her knees. She could see nothing. Burned-out hab-blocks and hive-rise structures rose all around her, blocking any view of distance, and any hope of spotting a landmark. They rose high above the roof she was standing on, some standing thousands of feet taller, derelict, windows blown, obscuring the sky itself, except for a small patch of pale green cloud directly above.

She started to weep. She was so dehydrated, no tears came. Her shoulders shook. She coughed and gagged.

The whining was louder now, a persistent wail, the lingering scream of wolves. She got up, and walked directly to the edge of the platform. All fear of heights had gone, or been rendered inconsequential. You could only fear the drop if you didn't want to fall.

It was a long way down. A long way. So far, she couldn't even see the bottom. The darkness down there made it look like the drop went on forever.

A dead drop. She wouldn't let the dogs have her. Of all the deaths her life could bring her to, being torn apart by a pack of feral canids would not be the one. She would rather make the decision herself, not leave it to animals.

It was a long way down. It would almost be like flying.

She took a deep breath, and a step forward, right to the lip. The wind tugged at her. She could hear the whining and the baying from the building below.

Then she realised that the shred had vanished. It had gone completely, dissolved like dirt in the rain. Now she was at the brink, there was nothing left to fear. It couldn't grip her any more, it couldn't choke her or wind its coils around her. Fear had no meaning. It had nothing left to threaten her with.

She tipped her head back. She felt free for the first time in her entire life. If this is what the end looked like, what it felt like, why had she been running from it for so long? It was empty, and meaningless. Death was nothing. Dying was the hard part.

And not even that. Living was the hard part. The pain, the mess, the sheer bloody fight of it, full of effort and aspiration, despair and hope. Life was a war, and in war there was always a chance of victory. Death was just defeat.

Fight. Fight until you can't. Fight life, weapons hot, fangs out, hair on fire.

Fight like you mean it.

She ran back across the platform to the top of the stairwell. Edging a few steps down, she could clearly hear the baying as it echoed up the stairs. The wailing. The whining. The heavy slap of paws on rockcrete.

Jagdea went back up, and backed away across the platform. She stopped, ten yards from the staircase door. She took one of the countermeasure decoys out of her pocket, and set it down. She took out another, the one she had previously unsealed, and unscrewed the top. The mag-phos powder inside was dense and heavy. She trailed out a curving line of it, twelve yards long, on either side of the first decoy, facing the door. A little lifted away in the light breeze, but not much. Then she carefully tipped out the rest of it in a straight line, starting at the first decoy and stretching back across the platform. There was enough for another three, nearly four yards. She tapped out the empty canister and tossed it away. She could hear the dogs on the stairs, scrambling up, claws raking and scraping. She could smell them. She could hear their yap and whine and snarl.

She took three steps back. Four. Five, to be safe. She took out a stick flare and held it ready, her fingers on the tab.

The canids burst onto the roof, scrambling and sliding in their urgency. They barked and snapped. She saw clouded eyes and torn ears, the blotched marbling of old burns and scars, black lips loose with spit and chests flecked with foam, pelts stiffened with dried blood. There were half a dozen, and more behind them. The biggest beasts were the largest she'd yet seen. Monsters. Wild monsters from the depths of the shred. They didn't hesitate. They bolted towards her, rapacious, jaws open to seize and clamp.

She pulled the tab on the flare. It tore off. Cursing her stiff fingers, she threw the dud flare away and snatched another from her pocket. She jerked the tab. The stick flare lit in a hissing cloud of red. She tossed it onto the end of the mag-phos trail.

It missed by half a yard, and lay sputtering on the platform.

Holy Throne, what's wrong with you? Your hands are useless. Your aim is shot! You stupid–

She took a hasty step forward to kick the flare into the powder trail. But a red, windblown spark had already spat into the mag-phos.

It went up. It went up with even greater fury than she was braced for. The flash was blinding, bright white like a star, and the heat a sudden wall. She cried out, and fell over backwards, shielding her face, scrambling away.

The powder trail combusted, a bright, rolling surge of incandescent fire. It raced back to the planted decoy, and then rushed out along the powder trails on either side until it felt like the entire platform was on fire. The charging animals were caught in the inferno as it sprang up. Some were engulfed entirely. Others staggered, coats ablaze, rolling and thrashing. One, its back on fire, ran clean off the edge of the platform in its panic to escape. Those still behind the white-hot wall whimpered and howled, and cringed back.

Then the planted decoy cooked off. It detonated like a bomb in a vicious starburst, a blast big enough and hot enough to betray a racing heat-seeker.

She saw dogs lifted into the air, seared by flame. The whining became shrill, a terrible scream.

But though mag-phos burned ultra-hot and ultra-fierce, it also burned fast. The bright white fury died away in seconds. The platform was littered with burned carcasses, and crawling, half-scorched things. In the stairwell doorway, the canids that had been driven back in fear began to pad forward again. They sniffed and growled at the scorch marks and the lifting smoke. A couple began to devour one of the roasted corpses. The others began to wander forward, yapping, their dead eyes fixed on her.

Jagdea took out the last decoy. She peeled back a little of the serrated tear-band, but there was no way to throw it and yank the strip off at the same time. The hounds were approaching, their whining intolerable. She jammed a stick flare into the decoy's broken seal, tip-first, her tired, locked hands fumbling, then pulled the tab on the other end and threw the whole thing as the stick flare lit.

It landed among the leading dogs, distracting them. They slowed, and hesitated, eyeing the throbbing red glare suspiciously.

But it wasn't hot. Stick flares didn't burn very hot. There was nothing to be afraid of.

But it was hot enough. The last decoy blew. Another giant starburst, so cruelly bright it hurt her eyes. It showered incendiary mag-phos on the brutes, blowing two over, igniting others.

'Get away from me!' Jagdea yelled. 'Get the frig away from me! There's more where that came from!'

She was lying. The surviving dogs, milling in panic and anger, didn't know that. They didn't understand her. To them, she was just noisy meat.

The light of the last countermeasure died away, leaving a dribble of flame, a haze of smoke and a reek of charred flesh.

The canids, and there were still about a dozen, resumed their advance. They were wary now, hackles up. They didn't like pain, or heat, and the light hurt their eyes. But they liked food.

The whining grew in intensity. Jagdea wasn't sure how the remaining monsters could be making such a loud, continuous noise. She knew she'd played it bravely, but played it wrong. She should've torched the stairwell, and caught the entire pack in it, but she hadn't wanted to annihilate her only way back down. She couldn't trap herself on the roof platform.

Except, that's how it had ended up anyway.

She turned her back on the dogs, their whining in her ears, and began to walk towards the edge. Her last dogfight. It had been far too literal and not at all what she had ever expected. It had not ended the way she had hoped.

The wind rose, and blew up in her face, almost driving her backwards. Jagdea covered her face. The true source of the whining slowly rose into view beyond the lip of the platform.

It was Saint Sabbat Beati.

Saint Sabbat Beati, clad in golden plate and selpic-blue robes, wielding a flaming sword.

Saint Sabbat Beati, painted on the nose shield of an Aeronautica Imperialis Avenger Strike Fighter, right above the immense, under-snout rotator cannon.

The hook-winged, twin-engined brute rose vertically, its ducts screaming. The scream of wolves. Jagdea stared at it in absolute astonishment.

A voice boomed over the speaker.

'Get the frig down!'

She dropped into a ball, on her knees with her arms wrapped over her head. The bolt cannon kicked off above her, a roaring, drilling, cycling howl that rattled her skull, her bones, and seemed to quake the entire platform. She felt the heat of a massive muzzle flash. She felt the platform shudder as the hail of explosive rounds raked across it.

The firing ceased. The rotating drum squealed to a halt. The world stopped vibrating. The air was thick with fyceline discharge. She was half-deaf, but she could still hear the ducts whining.

She raised her head, and looked behind her. The top of the stairwell was gone, along with the derelict portico of the passenger dock shelter that had adjoined it. The entire structure, along with the portion of the platform around it, was chewed away, a smoking, cratered ruin. The dogs had vanished, atomised, except for a few hanks of smouldering flesh.

She turned from the devastation and looked up. The Avenger had risen a little higher, sliding sideways on its shrieking ducts. The downdraught was so fierce, she could barely look at it.

'Pilot Officer Jagdea?' the speaker blared.

'Yes,' she said. Then she raised her hand, because there was no way the crew could hear her.

'Stay put,' the speaker boomed. *'Stay on-site. Your location is marked. Medivalk recovery inbound, four minutes out. Do you understand?'*

She raised her hand again.

'Copy that,' the speaker echoed. *'The Emperor protects.'*

The whining increased in pitch. The ground-attack bird rose higher, tilted, and began to pull away, climbing towards the patch of sky.

Jagdea eased herself to the deck, and sat cross-legged, head bowed.

'Well, someone does,' she said.

DAY –

Medivalk, time unknown

'What day is it?' she asked.

The medicae corpsman triaging her was hooking up another hydration pack. He glanced down at her.

'What day?' she repeated.

He told her.

'Three days,' she murmured. She'd been gone three days.

The corpsman started to clean and dress her hands, which had stiffened into bloody claws. He'd told her his name, but she'd forgotten. His green flightsuit had patches woven onto it. Aeronautica. Intercept 52. Same as the recovery Valk she was riding in. Same as the Avenger that had found her.

The corpsman said something as he applied orange counterseptic wash with a sponge. She couldn't hear him over the drone of the Valk's engines.

'What?' she asked. She was woozy. He'd given her shots.

'I said, you were lucky, pilot officer,' he said, preparing a wrap of synth-flesh.

She was. She knew it. An odd, unfriendly luck that took as much as it gave. She felt the Valkyrie banking steadily. It was running fast. Daylight was flickering through the compartment ports, but she couldn't see out because she was strapped back on the deck-clamped gurney. All she could see was the low ceiling, and his helmet and glare visor as he worked over her. The visor was a black mirror, like floodwater.

'Where am I?' she asked.

'Safe,' he said. 'In flight.'

'Where was I?' she asked.

The corpsman was busy with her hands. 'Try to stay quiet,' he said.

'Where was I?' she asked.

'Vobiscum,' he said.

Vobiscum... Vobiscum... that was a district way out to the north-east reach of Vesperus. Way out. One forty, one fifty miles east of Machinko. Probably two hundred north-east of the Campanile. So far. The ram-ride had carried her so far.

'So far,' she murmured.

The corpsman nodded.

'How did you find me?' she asked.

'I really need you to shut up and rest,' he said. 'You're banged about, extremely fatigued, dangerously dehydrated–'

'And lucky,' she said.

'And that. So just stop talking and rest.'

'Then tell me,' she said. 'Please. Then I can stop asking.'

'We picked up the signal from your beacon,' he said, calibrating a handheld imager. 'We'd been running sweeps, wider and wider. One of our Avengers picked it up in the end. Tail Forty. You weren't at the down site, but then the Avenger crew saw a flare. A mag-phos burn. They found you, and called us in.'

He started to run the imager over her head.

'No one thought you'd made it,' he said, 'but no one was giving up. You've had recovery sweeps from just about every Intercept up looking for you these last few days. Six-Six put out the call. Everyone put birds up. But you were a long way out, well outside the range projection. It was luck in the end. Just luck Tail Forty picked up the chirp.'

'So far…' she murmured.

'That's right,' he said. 'A long way. Everyone thought you were lost. They should have scaled back the search, really. But there wasn't a deck officer in Vesperus who wanted to make that call.'

'Why?'

'And risk leaving the hero of the Zoph to die? Seriously?'

Jagdea shut her eyes, and shook her head weakly.

'We're running you straight back to Six-Six,' the corpsman told her. 'Direct. You understand? You're going home.'

She nodded.

'Tail Forty,' she said.

'Say again?'

'Tail Forty? The Avenger?'

'Tail Forty,' he said. '*Beautiful Beati*. That's who found you. Pilot Officer Omar Omarti and Warfare Officer Olga Hodd.'

'Thank them for me.'

'I will.'

'You run Avengers out of Five-Two?'

'We run anything and everything they send us,' the corpsman said, checking the imager's data. 'Avengers aren't really fit for purpose out here, but the crews have evolved practices. Hunting in the low hive for surface advances. And operating as ambush predators. They stay low, then pop up when the bats come through. Surprisingly effective. It's mostly street-level operation. Probably why they found you.'

Jagdea sighed. Her breathing was thready and short. Finding ways to use whatever ill-suited tools they send us, she thought. Learning and adapting. Where have I heard that before?

'How are things at Five-Two?' she asked.

He shrugged, and braced his hand on a stanchion as the Valk banked again.

'Business as usual,' he said.

'What about… what about stats? Losses?'

'Average. By which I mean, high and nasty. You know how it is out here, pilot officer.'

'I mean… unusual losses. Unexplained losses.'

His glare visor was down, but she could tell he was frowning. 'I don't know what you mean,' he said.

She didn't know how to ask the question. She didn't even know how he was supposed to reply, even if he knew the answer.

'I heard things were bad at Five-Two,' she said. 'Someone said. Bad mood. Low morale. Ugly.'

'This is Vesperus,' he replied. 'It's like that everywhere, isn't it? Now I really need you to stop talking and rest. Your vitals are low, and I need to push more fluids.'

He moved out of her direct vision. She realised he was starting to cut her out of her filthy compression suit.

'Don't do that!' she said, jerking up against the gurney restraints.

'Relax. I need to get this off you.'

'I might need it!' she cried.

He laughed. 'Let's hope so,' he said. 'But not now. When the time comes, someone will find you another one.'

'But–'

'Please.'

She lay back and let him work.

'How are things at Six-Six?' she asked.

'I don't have any information on that,' she heard him say.

'Did Lead Garrant–'

The corpsman moved back into view.

'You really need to rest,' he said, with greater emphasis. 'All this talking. You're coming back from a long way out.'

She saw him prepping an injector shot.

'What's that?' she asked.

'Just relax.'

'Don't–'

The injector pushed in.

DAY 101

Infirmary, Intercept 66, Vesperus, time unknown

She woke, briefly, several times. Once on a gurney as it bumped and rattled. Then under moving ceiling lamps. Then in an unfamiliar place that seemed familiar all the same. She drifted in and out, but most of the time she was out.

She woke, and heard monitors beeping, and saw the Six-Six infirmary and Med Stanslaf.

'There you are,' he said.

She tried to speak, but her mouth was gummed up. He supported the back of her head, and helped her sip from a spouted flask.

'We kept you under,' he told her. 'Just to get you stable and rehydrated. Pull those vitals back up. You're going to feel shit for a few days at least. Concussion, exposure. But good news... no major injury or infection. You were lucky, Driver.'

'So they keep telling me,' she slurred.

'I mean, really lucky,' he said. 'Frigging miracle Five-Two picked you up after all that time. And I swear by the Throne I have no idea how you walked away from that down.'

'The Emperor protects,' she said.

'What?' he asked.

'I made a deal,' she said.

Stanslaf frowned. 'Let's... get you resting so you can clear your head,' he said. He picked up an injector.

'Don't,' she said.

'It's just–'

'Don't put me under again. Just let me lie here.'

'All right,' he said, and put the injector on the tray. 'But I'm maintaining fluids, and I'm going to give you something for the pain. Just to take the edge off. Your good luck continues.' He picked up a pharm carton and shook it proudly. 'Fresh supplies. Not expired shit.'

Jagdea blinked.

'The replenishment carry came in,' she said.

'Finally,' he said, nodding. 'Three days ago. Fuel load, munitions, consumables, everything.'

'Has it gone again?' she asked.

'Of course. Overnight turnaround.'

'I was supposed to leave on it. I was supposed to leave on it with Gumm.'

'Nothing we can do about that,' he said.

She turned her head and looked around. The other cots in the infirmary were empty.

'They took Wilzar?' she asked.

'Yes, Driver. They took Wilzar. He's back in the hive-plex. They'll take good care of him.'

'Was he awake before he left? Did he say anything?'

Stanslaf shook his head. 'Induced coma. Smoke wasn't talking at all.'

She heard the door open. Badler approached her cot. There was an odd look on his thin face. Deck Dampier stood at his eight.

'It's good to see you back,' said Badler. It actually sounded like he meant it.

Jagdea hoisted herself up on her elbows. Stanslaf started to protest, and then gave up and helped her settle on her pillows in a raised position.

'The carry came in,' said Jagdea.

'Yes,' said Badler.

'I was supposed to leave on that,' said Jagdea. 'Me and Gumm. Back to Orison. We had a deal with Garrant.'

'We couldn't hold it here,' said Dampier.

'And you were missing,' said Badler. 'Driver... operational profiles have shifted a little. You wouldn't have been going back anyway.'

'What do you mean?' she asked.

'We need pilots,' said Dampier. 'I'm sorry, Driver, but that's the way it is. As soon as you're rated fit again. We're down several sticks–'

'I had an agreement with Garrant,' said Jagdea.

'And Six-Six have new instructs,' said Badler.

'I want to talk to Garrant,' she said.

Badler hesitated. He looked uncomfortably at Dampier. Her face remained set.

'Asa didn't make it,' Dampier said.

'What... What do you mean, he didn't make it?' asked Jagdea.

'Lead Garrant didn't survive the scrap at Machinko,' said Badler.

'I saw him eject!' said Jagdea. 'I saw the chute!'

'He ejected,' said Badler, 'but...'

'Recovery found him,' said Dampier. 'Impact with a building after bail-out. Severe trauma. Broken neck. It was probably quick.'

'I saw the chute...' Jagdea whispered.

'Badler is now acting lead of Six-Six,' said Dampier.

'Congratulations,' said Jagdea. 'I had an agreement with Garrant.'

Badler cleared his throat.

'I'm sorry, pilot officer,' he said. 'I'm not in a position to honour any informal agreement you may or may not have had with Lead Garrant. Even if you'd been here when the replenishment arrived, I would not have authorised your release. That's just the way it is. I need sticks.'

Jagdea stared at him until he was forced to look away.

'It doesn't matter,' she said. 'It really doesn't matter. I had decided to stay anyway. It would have been a courtesy to get a choice in it, Badler. But I had already decided to stay. I made a deal.'

'With... Lead Garrant?'

'No, *Lead Badler*,' she said. 'Another deal. A *different* deal.'

'Then it's all worked out,' remarked Dampier curtly. 'We'll leave you to rest.'

'Who else?' Jagdea asked as they made for the door.

'What?' asked Badler.

'You said you were down several sticks,' she said. 'Who else? Who else have we lost?'

'We'll let you rest,' said Dampier.

Infirmary, Intercept 66, Vesperus, 15:03

Sometimes, the God-Emperor remembered your name. Offered you a second chance. Brought you back from the dead.

Only a fool would ignore that. A fool, or someone eager to join the shrieking hosts of the damned. You took the deal. You didn't question it, or negotiate the terms. You took it, even if you didn't understand what it would entail, or where you would end up.

She lay there for a few hours, but sleep wasn't going to happen. When Med Stanslaf left the infirmary, she got out of bed and detached her monitors. She had a limp, she discovered. The wound in her leg throbbed. She borrowed Stanslaf's coat, which was hanging on the back of the door, and put it on over the paper smock she was wearing. It was a clumsy business doing it with bandaged hands.

The hallway outside was empty and quiet. She limped along, one hand against the polished rockcrete wall for support, heading for the central staircase. She'd got quite a long way when she heard footsteps, and saw Tantrum and Nosedive strolling towards her. They stopped dead when they saw her.

'Are you sure you should be up?' Glick asked, his face furrowed in concern.

'Who died?' Jagdea asked.

'What?' asked Steeley.

'No one will tell me anything,' she said. 'Who died? Who have we lost since I… since I went down?'

Glick and Steeley glanced nervously at each other. Steeley said something that Jagdea didn't catch, and Tantrum hurried away with a nod.

'Where's he going?' Jagdea asked, irritated. 'Glick?'

'You really shouldn't be up, Driver,' said Steeley gently. He took a step forward, reaching out.

'I really shouldn't be alive,' she replied, brushing off his hand. 'Answer the question. Who died? Who else have we lost, Steeley?'

'Garrant,' he said solemnly. 'You know about Garrant?'

'I know about Garrant. Who else?'

She saw him think about it for a second, and realised death was such a daily routine at Six-Six, all the losses blurred into one.

'Blowout,' he said. 'We lost Blowout, the day before last. Longlas the same day. No, day before. Jongleur and Shovel, same day as Garrant. And Fancy, last night.'

'Fancy?'

'Smoke,' said Steeley. 'He arrived on the replenishment.'

'So he lasted two days?' said Jagdea.

Steeley nodded. The smoke had come and gone in two days, without her even knowing him.

'Did Slipstream make it back?' she asked. 'The day I went down? And Merry Death?'

Steeley nodded again.

'Yes, they both came home,' said a voice behind her.

Jagdea shuffled around. Glick had returned. He'd brought Gumm.

'What are you doing here?' she asked.

'That should be my question,' said Gumm softly. He reached out to take her arm.

'You shouldn't be here!' Jagdea snapped. 'You should be in Orison. You should've gone back with Wilzar.'

'Well, I didn't,' he replied. He glanced at Glick and Steeley. 'Off you go,' he told them. 'I've got this.'

The younger pilots hesitated, then walked away.

'Did Badler rescind your release too?' she asked.

'Yes,' said Gumm. 'Well, he would have done. I didn't give him the chance. I told him I wasn't going back.'

'Why the hell would you do that?'

'Because I wasn't going anywhere until they'd found you,' he replied.

Refectory, Intercept 66, Vesperus, 16:54

'I could've been dead,' Jagdea said.

'I thought you were,' said Gumm. 'But I stayed to find out. I wasn't going to just up and leave.'

'That's stupid,' she said.

'That's what friends do,' he replied.

She took a sip of water from a chipped glass. She hadn't touched much of her food.

'That's why we don't make them,' she said. 'It makes you do stupid things. Like not leave when you get the chance.'

'Get over yourself,' he replied. 'It's not as noble as it sounds. Badler wouldn't have let me go anyway.'

She looked up at the board over the fireplace. She was aware that people at the tables nearby were still looking at her. The aviators and crews in the refectory had made a fuss when Gumm first walked her in, until he'd quietened them down.

There were so many more names struck through on the board than the last time she'd been there. New tallies too. Two more marks beside DOLLFACE.

'You've been busy in my absence,' she said.

'We all have,' said Gumm. 'The raids are escalating.'

'What's this "shift in operational profile"?' she asked.

'Don't know,' he replied. 'Badler hasn't told us yet. Apparently, it's been coming for a while. An initiative from high command.'

'Fancy was a smoke,' she said. 'Blowout and Shovel too. Who were up with them?'

Gumm sighed. 'Are you still on about that?' he asked. 'I had hoped you might have let it go, what with–'

'I haven't,' she said. 'There's a white crow somewhere.'

'Jagdea...'

'There is, Gumm.'

He sat back. 'Well, neither Blowout nor Fancy were definitive.'

'And who was up with them?'

'Everyone,' he replied. 'It's been a busy time. Multiple intercepts in the air, right through the day. Look, Bree... it feels like you're obsessing.'

'I think it's more alarming that you're not,' she said.

'You nearly died–'

'I had a lot of time to think,' she said. 'Out there, in the depths. A lot of time.'

'About what?'

'Life and death. The usual. And I made a deal.'

'With who?' he asked.

'Doesn't matter. Myself.'

'A deal about what?'

'That doesn't matter either, Gumm,' she said. 'But I made a commitment.'

'To?'

'This place,' she said. 'These people. Pretty similar to the decision you made when the carry-flight came in, I should think. A commitment to stay. To fight. And that includes fighting anything that's trying to kill us.'

'All right,' he said. 'I think you're wrong.'

'Just wing me if I need it,' she said.

He nodded. She got to her feet.

'I need to see some people,' she said.

'Dressed like that?' he asked.

She looked down. She was still wearing the surgical smock and Stanslaf's coat.

'I'll go to stores first,' she said. 'Then I've got to see some people.'

'You should make sure Camo is one of them,' he said.

'Why?'

'She's been a mess since you went missing. She thinks she was the one who shot you down.'

'What? She didn't.'

'That day, over Machinko,' said Gumm. 'She hit your bird.'

Jagdea frowned. She remembered it now, just one piece of the blur. The wild tangle.

'She didn't shoot me down,' she said. 'I was evading. It was an accident. I flew through her envelope.'

'I'm sure,' said Gumm. 'But she's been beside herself ever since. Came back and reported it to Dampier immediately.'

'I'll talk to her,' said Jagdea. She looked at Gumm. 'You see what I mean, though? Accidents happen. Pilots report it. To hell with guilt or blame, they report it. They don't cover it up.'

The chapel, Intercept 66, Vesperus, 18:30

It turned out the Campanile had a chapel. Jagdea had never seen it, or even heard about it. She thought that the squadron's shrines were the fireplace of the refectory, and the altar in the dead zone chantry.

But there was an actual chapel, for service use, on the floor below Control.

It was small and clean, better swept and cared for than any room in the station, including the infirmary. Tapers burned softly below a gleaming mosaic of the God-Emperor. He was flanked by the saints of the Sabbat Worlds. Kiodrus bore the Emperor's sword. Sabbat herself carried fire in her hands.

Jagdea stood in the cool silence for a moment, breathing the scent of incense and floor polish. She'd drawn clothes from stores: black boots, grey trousers, a white vest and a black leather flight jacket, all donated by their previous owners. Jagdea had asked the quartermaster to return Stanslaf's coat to him.

Sister Meredith was kneeling in prayer at the altar. The quartermaster had said that Jagdea could probably find Merry Death in the chapel, and then he'd had to explain where the chapel was.

Jagdea waited, out of respect, for the Sister to finish her devotions. As she waited, she gazed at the mosaic. She lingered on the saint with fire in her hands. For a moment, she could hear the scream of wolves.

Her own hands felt like they were full of fire too. She looked down at the bandages. The pain meds were wearing off.

Meredith rose, bowed, and turned to leave. She saw Jagdea.

'You returned,' she said.

'Back from the dead,' said Jagdea.

'Prayers offered were not in vain,' replied the Sister. She lowered her gaze, and began to walk to the door.

'I was spared,' said Jagdea.

The Sister stopped, and glanced at her.

'What did you mean by that, Meredith?' Jagdea asked. 'You came to find me. You said, "You will be spared." You blessed me with a mark.'

'The holy aquila,' said Meredith.

'What did you mean?'

'I have no answer for you,' said Meredith. 'Meaning belongs to the God-Emperor, not to a–'

'No,' said Jagdea. 'I'm not going to have that kind of conversation with you. You say very little.'

'My actions speak for me.'

'Then I'll be direct. You kill sinners, Sister. It seems this place is full of sinners. Are you killing them?'

'I don't understand,' said Meredith. It was the first time Jagdea had seen the Sister's face register anything beyond disapproval or contempt.

'There's a white crow,' said Jagdea. 'Is it you? Tell me now. The Emperor is watching. The Emperor and His saints. They'll know if you're lying, and so will I.'

'I would never do that,' said Meredith. Her voice had become very small. Jagdea could see the shock and confusion in her eyes.

'No?'

'You are asking me if I have slain my own brothers and sisters?' asked Meredith. 'By treachery? By deceit?'

'That's what a white crow does. You've heard the stories, then?'

'Idle lies. Rumours.'

'Is it you?'

'I could not do it,' said Meredith. She took a step towards Jagdea. 'The God-Emperor would bind my hands and strike me dead if I turned against His children.'

'Then why did you tell me I would be spared?'

'You are an effective pilot,' said Meredith. 'This unit needs you. I have tried to keep you in my prayers, so that the Emperor might spare you.'

'So I can kill more sinners?'

'Of course,' said the Sister. 'And I know that you are blessed.'

'How do you know that?'

'Because I know who you are. It is spoken of. You are Bree Jagdea of Phantine. You are but one removed from the Saint herself.'

'How?'

'You served at Cirenholm,' said Meredith. 'I have read this. You served in the presence of Ibram Gaunt. He was the one who brought the Saint back to us. Saved her and raised her up. Now he stands at her side as Lord Executor, like Kiodrus reborn. You knew him. Met him. The sanctity of the Beati is thus imparted to you through that lineage.'

'That's... that's backwards,' said Jagdea. 'I served with him briefly, a long time ago. Before any of that happened. He was nobody then, just an officer with promise. I never met the Saint.'

'Sanctity cares nothing for time, or causal order,' said the Sister. 'Ibram Gaunt was chosen by the God-Emperor to find and restore the Beati. You walked with him on the road that took him there. You were part of his holy duty, thus a measure of her grace is transmitted to you. The Beati has returned to save us all, but you have come closer to her than many.'

Jagdea wanted to scoff, to laugh at Meredith's superstitious folly. But the Sister's sincerity felt genuine, and her hands hurt like fire.

'So I, in turn, pass a little of that grace to you?' she asked.

'If the God-Emperor wills it,' Meredith replied with a nod. 'I pray that it is so, that you bring a little of her to us. I could not lie to you, Jagdea, any more than I could lie to her. He would see it. I am not this killer you speak of. I would hunt this sinner with you, for they stand in opposition to our faith in the Throne.'

'Then tell me if you hear anything,' said Jagdea. 'The slightest thing. Come to me directly. I'm not so concerned with faith, Sister, for faith can look after itself. But I am concerned with the lives of the men and women in Six-Six.'

'I will,' said Meredith. 'The Emperor protects.'

'He protects through us,' Jagdea replied. 'Through our actions. Just like He protected the Beati through Gaunt. Don't forget that. He can't protect us if we don't let Him act through us.'

Meredith nodded, and walked away towards the door.

Then she stopped, and looked back.

'I think you are wrong, Jagdea,' she said.

'Wrong?'

'You say you have never met the Saint. But I think you have.'

Hangar bay, Intercept 66, Vesperus, 20:14

'I heard you'd come back,' said Slipstream. He sat up on his cot as Jagdea walked up. Mischief was asleep on her cot, under the wing of her bird nearby.

'Back from the dead,' said Jagdea.

Slipstream nodded. 'We all do that every day,' he said, 'every time we go out. But you came back a little further than most.'

Jagdea stood for a moment, looking up at Slipstream's fight-bird, her bandaged hands stuffed in her jacket pockets.

'Did you want something, Driver?' Slipstream asked.

'Yeah,' she said.

His eyes narrowed. He looked sicker than ever.

'Wait,' he said. 'You want me to thank you?'

'For what?' she asked.

'Covering my tail that day at Harquin. Is that why you're here?'

'No,' she said.

'Well, good,' said Slipstream. He sat back, and took a swig of something from a plastek bottle. 'I mean, it's not that I didn't appreciate it. But asking for thanks, that's an arsehole move. You don't *ask* for thanks–'

'I'm not asking for thanks,' she said.

'Then what do you want?'

'The white crow.'

Slipstream's face pulled into an ugly sneer.

'That?' he said. 'That's just glory story bullshit.'

'Is it?'

'Glory story bullshit,' he repeated emphatically, looking her dead in the eyes.

'I don't think so,' she replied. 'You've heard the chatter, then?'

'Yeah.' He shrugged. 'Smoke rumours. Scuttlebutt. The usual whispers. Someone's always got to make up some shit in the refectory. I'm surprised at you. I heard you had experience. You should know better than to listen to nonsense.'

'Maybe,' she said.

'So why did that bring you here?' he asked.

'Do you know anything?' she asked back.

'Hard to know anything about something that isn't real,' he replied.

'But if it is real,' she said, studying his face for reaction, or some kind of tell. 'If it is real, this white crow... it would have to be a pilot who was pretty frigging bleak in outlook, right? Someone who'd lost the will. Who didn't care.'

'I guess...'

'Someone who didn't really value life, and thought that smokes should learn by their own mistakes.'

She let that hang. It didn't take long.

'Frig you, Jagdea,' Slipstream said. It was quiet, barely a hiss, but it cut the air like a bolt-round. He was on his feet suddenly, faster than she'd expected, faster and angrier.

'You frig!' he snarled. 'You piece of shit! Really? Me? You're accusing me?'

'I'm asking you,' she said.

He came towards her, moving with power and intent, the fat loops of his umbilical feeds playing out behind him.

'And I'm telling you,' he growled. 'Frig you. And frig you for even asking. You come here and ask me that? Accuse me? To my frigging face?'

'What's going on?' Mischief mumbled, woken by the raised voices and sitting up. 'What's happened?'

'This bitch just asked me if I was the white crow!' Slipstream exclaimed. 'Accused me! To my face!'

'There isn't a white crow,' Mischief mumbled, not fully awake.

'Oh, that doesn't matter!' Slipstream yelled. 'The frigging accusation is what matters! Bree Jagdea, hero of the Zoph, thinks she can come in here, bold as frigging brass, and say that to me! To me!'

'We need to find the white crow,' Jagdea said, staying as calm as she could. 'I need to ask.'

'You need a frigging slap is what!' Slipstream shouted. He was right in her face, pulling at the limit of his umbilicals. Rage had made the puffy flesh of his face pale and blotchy.

'Calm down,' said Jagdea. 'Calm down and–'

He swung for her. His fist would have knocked her down, but she wrenched back, and the taut umbilicals denied Slipstream full reach. He staggered, then came back again, still swinging.

Jagdea stepped away so he couldn't get at her. He was screaming her name, calling her every obscenity he could think of. Mischief had got to her feet, and was yelling insults at Jagdea too.

Then they both stopped suddenly.

'What's the meaning of this?' Dampier asked, striding across the rockcrete towards them.

'Just a little disagreement, Deck,' said Slipstream, still seething but trying to hide it.

'That altercation was not "just a little disagreement", pilot officer,' said Dampier.

'Driver accused Slip of being the crow,' said Mischief.

'Did she?' said Dampier. She turned and looked at Jagdea. 'Come with me,' she said. 'Right frigging now.'

Office of the Senior Deck, Intercept 66, Vesperus, 20:27

'Stand there,' said Dampier, pointing at a patch of threadbare carpet in front of her desk. She closed the office door.

Jagdea hadn't been in the deck's office before. It was a small chamber on the other side of the control chamber from the lead's office. There was a singular lack of personal effects, a faint background smell of stale lho-smoke. Jagdea doubted that anyone would have the temerity to smoke in front of Dampier, so she presumed the senior deck took the edge off her own nerves when she was alone with the door shut.

'I'm going to cut you a little slack, pilot officer,' Dampier said, 'because of what you've been through these last few days. But just this much.'

She was standing behind her desk. She had pinched her thumb and index finger together, with barely any visible space between them. Jagdea said nothing, and stood facing her, her hands behind her back.

'I will not have you going around, throwing accusations at my pilots,' said Dampier.

'I'm one of your pilots,' said Jagdea.

'Yes, you are.'

'As one of your pilots, I have grave concerns regarding the presence of a white crow,' said Jagdea.

'So you decided to handle it yourself?'

'Garrant said it was being investigated, but I've seen no sign of that,' said Jagdea. 'Pilots are still dying in non-definitive incidents. Garrant–'

'Did Lead Garrant tell you he thought there was a white crow?'

Jagdea shook her head. 'But there was a subtext,' she added. 'Garrant–'

'Lead Garrant is gone. Lead Badler is in command now, and this is my deck. I decide how things get done. Not you.'

'I understand,' said Jagdea. 'I have a list of potential victims...'

'And a list of potential suspects, no doubt?' said Dampier.

'Yes,' said Jagdea.

'Slipstream being one of them?'

'Yes. I had three. I've discounted two of them. I considered Slipstream because of a nihilistic attitude I've observed in him. Given the nature of his response, I'm disinclined to believe it's him.'

'Because?'

'His outrage was genuine,' said Jagdea. 'Hard to put on. But I could be wrong.'

'In so very many ways, pilot officer,' said Dampier. She sat down at her desk. 'So you've confronted two other aviators about this?'

'Yes.'

'Names?'

Jagdea hesitated.

'Harlot, and Merry Death. I found their reactions both credible and genuine, so I–'

'Oh, shut up, Jagdea,' said Dampier wearily. 'You've accused three of my best pilots of an abhorrent crime. Morale in this Throne-forsaken deck is shaky at best, and you seem determined to further undermine it. I should have you thrown in the coop for inflammatory behaviour. Scratch that. I should have you thrown in the coop for being an absolutely shitty investigator. Just go up and ask people? You think that's how it works?'

'I find a direct approach often brings surprising results.'

'Yes, you do, don't you?' said Dampier. 'Since the day you got here, you've freely spoken your mind and undertaken all manner of... of unilateral activities. The mentoring. The modifications. The classified data. All without instruct or authority.'

'And all with a degree of success, Deck,' said Jagdea. 'Permission to speak openly?'

Dampier snorted. 'I wasn't aware you needed permission,' she replied.

'We're at full stretch and hanging on by our fingertips,' said Jagdea. 'I say this as no slur on your efforts or anybody's. There isn't time to do all the things we need to do, or should do, to keep Six-Six running. It's all we can do to survive, and we're barely doing that. Garrant said as much.'

'Garrant's dead.'

'You're making my point for me,' said Jagdea. 'I'm just doing what I can, doing things that I can see need to be done–'

'Because you have some complex, some fetish for responsibility?'

'Because I'm Aeronautica.'

Dampier frowned.

'I'll take whatever reprimand or punishment you see fit, Deck,' said Jagdea. 'But I don't feel guilty, and I'm not going to apologise.'

Jagdea took a breath.

'One last thing,' she said.

'Go on, *please*.'

'I notice that at no point in this conversation have you denied the presence of a white crow.'

Dampier glared at her. Then she pursed her lips, and pointed to the ragged armchair facing her desk.

'Sit.'

Jagdea sat down.

'Despite my first impressions, Jagdea,' said Dampier quietly, 'I was beginning to like you. No, "like" is too strong. Admire you. Appreciate you. You have achieved things since your arrival, despite your attitude. You've improved a few things, and you've flown well, well enough for me to regard you as a genuine asset. Enough of an asset to outweigh your bullish affect and the non-standard manner in which you've done the things you've done.'

She looked at Jagdea.

'I trust almost nobody, Jagdea,' she said.

'Is that the nature of your role, or an aspect of your personality?' asked Jagdea.

'Both,' said Dampier. 'My personality is why I'm in this role, and vice versa. Prefectus discipline requires a degree of suspicion and distance, of mistrust, if you will, or it is compromised. I trust very few people. I trusted Lungrim. I trusted Asa. Ricou Badler may win my trust, but he's young and untested.'

She paused.

'I believe there is a white crow operational at Six-Six,' she said.

'Is that you telling me you trust me?' asked Jagdea.

'Not really,' Dampier replied. 'Trust has different values, and it has to be earned. Some people get a small measure of mine. Not complete, but a little. You mentioned Lopard just now. I don't trust Reno, because he's inherently untrustworthy. But I understand him. I have his measure, so a degree of trust can be extended. I have a feeling the same can be given to you.'

'I'm flattered,' said Jagdea.

'Don't be. I've been aware of the potential white crow for several weeks. Garrant wasn't lying to you, it is being investigated. The fact that you weren't aware of that investigation is because it is being conducted discreetly. Unlike your ham-fisted efforts.'

'And?' asked Jagdea.

'And what?'

'Your conclusions so far?'

Dampier looked down at her desk and didn't respond. Then she sighed, and opened her desk drawer. She took out two tins of Munitorum-issue boot polish. From one, she removed a lho-stick and an igniter. The other, she opened as a makeshift ashtray. As an afterthought, she offered the tin of lho-sticks to Jagdea.

'No, thank you.'

'I feel confident you won't speak of my habit with anyone,' said Dampier.

'Of course.'

Dampier lit her lho-stick and inhaled deeply.

'There's definitely a predator at work,' she said softly. 'The three individuals you named were all on my list, despite their abilities at the stick. I have discounted them all, for different reasons. I have suspected everybody, and worked backwards. I have also examined the idea that the crow is an aviator from another Intercept, hunting on our turf. I can find no evidence to support that.'

'So?'

'So I think we're looking for someone who has been burned through by shred. Burned through to the point of sociopathic or psychopathic urges, just as a way of easing their torment. Or sharing their pain. I don't know. Almost any of the smokes here fit that template.'

Jagdea shook her head. 'It's not a smoke,' she said.

'Because?' asked Dampier.

'Because none of the smokes are good enough sticks,' she replied. 'Don't get me wrong, they'd be decent in a different war sky, and they're learning. But they don't have the chops here. The crow is fast, discreet and ultra-precise. The kills have been brutally clean. The crow has got experience and confidence. He or she is a hot stick.'

Dampier frowned. She didn't like it, but she didn't argue.

'Do you have any suspects left, Deck?'

'A few,' said Dampier. 'I'm not going to disclose their names. My faith in what you might say or not say... or who you might confront... stretches only so far.'

'That's fair, I suppose,' admitted Jagdea.

'You're damn right it is,' said Dampier. 'I'm taking you into my confidence because you're alert to this situation. And I know you won't leave it alone, either. If you hear anything, see anything, or even get a hunch, you bring it to me. You don't take any action yourself. You bring it to me. That's a direct instruct. Are we clear, pilot officer?'

'Absolutely Four-A,' said Jagdea.

DAY 102

Hangar bay, Intercept 66, Vesperus, 05:01

Badler had called a full-squad huddle, attendance mandatory. He'd summoned everyone to the hangar so that the wet-linked pilots could be part of it too. Aviators and ground staff assembled, many carrying cups of caff from the refectory.

When Jagdea walked in, she got greeting smiles and a few welcomes, but also plenty of surprised reactions at the sight of her alert-ready in full flight gear. Despite his strenuous objections, Med Stanslaf had rated her fit to fly, but only after she had carefully explained to him how bad things might get if Dampier somehow found out he was supplying med stimms to pilots on the quiet.

She was wearing her black leather jacket over a red compression suit she'd signed out of the stores, and she carried a gleaming black Ultris-pattern helmet. The helmet and suit were new, brought in on the replenishment. She was their first owner. No one had yet painted a name on her helmet's visor plate.

'Back from the dead,' Lopard murmured to her with a smile as she passed. 'How was it?'

'Overrated,' she replied.

Yesof grinned at Jagdea, and raised her hand to exchange a

palm-slap. Jagdea obliged, and masked the pain that throbbed in her hand afterwards. Under her flight gloves, her hands were still wrapped in synth-flesh and dressings.

Jagdea took a place beside Gumm.

'Should you be here?' Gumm asked.

'Where else would I be?' she replied.

She looked around. Through the gathering crowd, she saw Slipstream and Mischief standing beside their cots. Both were glaring at her. She ignored the looks. She was hunting for Camo. She hadn't been able to find the girl the night before. There, on the far side of the gathering, between Dummy and Slumbag. Camo looked tense, and pointedly avoided any eye contact.

Badler and Dampier walked to the front, and stood under the nose of Mischief's bird.

'Attention, Six-Six!' Dampier called out, silencing the chatter. She stepped back behind Badler, and stood tall and solemn.

'Starting today, we've got a shift in mission profile,' said Badler.

There were a few groans and grumbles.

'Pay attention,' Dampier barked.

'We'll still be running intercept operations as before,' Badler said. 'Check the ready-board for assignments. Most of you will be go-ready, bareknuckle, but some drops will stand by for pathfinder packets. Follow the instructs.'

Nobody questioned this, and Jagdea understood that pathfinder sorties had been formally phased in during her absence.

'As for the new profile,' Badler continued, 'we've had instructs from Air Command. Some of you will be running recon–'

The murmurings of discontent welled back, louder.

'Quiet!' Dampier snapped. 'Lead Badler is talking.'

'The instructs have been personally authorised by Lord Militant Jahkel,' said Badler, 'so this is not optional. The lord militant is dissatisfied with the Vesperus catch-rates. We're not stopping enough.'

'We're not, Lead?' asked Blindside.

'None of the Intercepts in Vesperus are,' replied Badler. 'This isn't just us, and we won't be the only station running recon.'

'Recon of what?' asked Gangster.

'The north-east sectors of the hive sprawl,' replied Badler. 'In the last few weeks, it's become clear to all of us that the Archenemy has stepped up its game. They've moved from solo and duo runs to groups to improve their ratios. Staggered groups, with fightbat escort. We've all seen it. They've also started running bigger bats. Dedicated bombers.'

'That means they're desperate,' said Dampier. 'They're pushing harder for a faster result. It'll be rainy season in a month, and when that hits, it'll make a ground assault much less viable. Great Haven clearly wants the south 'plex softened up and broken before then, ready for a full-scale armour push. If that doesn't happen before the rains come, they'll probably have to postpone until the spring. We're all aware how busy this bat-run is getting. The lord militant wants it choked off.'

'For months now,' said Badler, 'the Archenemy sorties have been coming through long range, at tank-limit, probably from fields in the north, like Caeran and Zigmus. But the levels of raid saturation and fast turnaround we've been seeing recently suggests they're now operating out of forward bases to reduce operational range, especially for their bigger, slower multis. Intel suggests they have established advance decks in the north-eastern zones of Vesperus. These will have steady fuel reserves and ordnance stocks, reducing their flight-time on raids, and increasing frequency. Orison Command wants those forward operating decks located and identified, so they can be targeted by long-range bomber formations.'

'And we've got to look for them?' asked Rockcrete.

'We have,' said Badler.

'Can we take a pop when we find them?' asked Gangster.

'Negative,' said Dampier. 'Locate and report only. Our fight-birds don't carry enough punch to take out a deck.'

'I dunno,' said Gangster, 'We could ruin their day a whole lot.' There were murmurs of approval, and Gangster exchanged high-slaps with Rockcrete and Slumbag.

'Locate and report only,' Badler insisted. 'That's the instruct.'

Jagdea could see the tension in Badler. He was hiding it well, but the stress of the lead role had wired him tight. He was too young. Garrant had been right: Badler would make a fine squadron lead one day, but that day was a few years off yet. The shred was in him, writhing in his chest.

She thought about the crow. She'd drawn a blank, and so had Dampier. But the profile remained valid. Someone stricken with shred, burned out to the point of psychopathy. But still, someone who masked that and presented as functional. And someone who was a hot stick.

Badler met all those criteria. What had Dampier said? *Ricou Badler may win my trust, but he's young and untested.*

Jagdea thought about it. She didn't like what she was thinking.

'We're lofting two recon flights today,' Badler was saying. He checked his data-slate. 'Recon one... Slipstream, Reaper and–'

Dampier cut in, and whispered in his ear. Jagdea saw Dampier shoot a look in her direction. Badler nodded.

'All right,' he said, making an alteration on his slate. 'Recon one is Slipstream, Reaper and Rockcrete. Recon two... Driver and Gangster, with me.'

Sister Meredith led the blessing, and then Badler dismissed the huddle. Jagdea looked around as the crowd dispersed, and spotted Camo leaving the hangar by the west hatch. She ran and caught up with her in the corridor outside.

'Kinny?'

Camo turned, saw Jagdea, and almost immediately burst into tears.

'I'm sorry!' she gasped.

'You didn't do anything,' said Jagdea.

'I did! I caught your bird!' Camo put her face in her hands and started to rock. Her pink-lensed glasses fell off. 'I wanted to come and find you, but I didn't know what to say–'

Jagdea picked up her glasses, and stood there awkwardly, a hand on the girl's shoulder as she sobbed.

'You didn't do anything,' said Jagdea. 'I've come to tell you, you didn't.'

'But–'

'Cut it out, Kinny,' said Jagdea.

The girl stopped sobbing, and raised her face, sniffing.

'Yes, you clipped me,' said Jagdea. 'That was entirely on me, and it happens in a knife-fight. I was splashed by a bat. I put myself in its envelope.'

'W-why?'

'I was trying to save Garrant,' said Jagdea. 'You didn't do anything wrong. In fact, you did it all right. You reported it on return. It was an accident, and you owned it.' She handed the shades back to Camo. 'Stop torturing yourself, for frig's sake,' Jagdea told her. 'You've got to fly today, and you don't need that kind of mental baggage.'

'Do you forgive me?' Camo asked, wiping her eyes.

'I don't have to,' said Jagdea. 'Nothing to forgive.'

'Just say you forgive me,' said Camo. 'I want to hear you say it.'

'All right. I forgive you.'

Camo sucked in a deep breath and nodded, trying to smile. 'Good. Thank you,' she said. 'I couldn't bear it. I owe you.'

'You don't owe me anything,' said Jagdea.

'I nearly killed you,' said Camo, quiet but fierce. 'Let me owe you. A favour. A serious favour. Something, I don't know. I'll think of something.'

'You can buy me a drink tonight.'

'Something better than that. I–'

'Will you watch my back? If we're up together?'

'O-of course!'

'Then that's favour enough,' said Jagdea.

'And I'll stand you a drink anyway!' said Camo.

Jagdea sighed. The girl needed penance. She had to give her something.

'Just get me a good bottle of amasec from Reno,' she said. 'Oh, and a pack of sticks. Then we'll call it even.'

Camo nodded eagerly. 'You don't smoke,' she added, with a frown.

'Lho is currency,' said Jagdea. 'Always handy to have a pack in your pocket.'

Especially if you were having a private conversation with Deck Dampier and wanted to get on her good side, she thought.

'All right!' said Camo, and smiled.

'Good flying,' said Jagdea.

Tenth drop (recon), Intercept 66, Vesperus, 07:41

Tail 044 was waiting for her on the launch deck. The enginseers had run full repairs while Jagdea had been out. Four-Four was nose-down, tail raised at an angle of seventy degrees to the platform lip. It was also now matt-black. The forest green and pale underside were gone.

The day was wet and overcast, and the Vesperus skyline stewed in the vapour. As Jagdea walked out onto the deck, she realised, with a degree of surprise, that she was alone. The crews were still working around the three birds, Boa was reversing the tractor towards the ramp, and Badler was standing in conversation with Yesof. But Jagdea was alone. The shred had not followed her up from the billet. In fact, now she thought about it, the shred had found somewhere else to crash the night before. Its absence felt odd, not the relief she might have expected. She hated the shred, but she knew a pilot needed a taste of it, at least, to keep sharp. She wondered how she would cope without it. She had a feeling she'd left it somewhere on the edge of a roof in Vobiscum.

'Are you sure you're fit?' Badler asked her bluntly as she walked up.

Jagdea nodded.

He looked doubtful. 'If you're not Four-A, I won't have you flying,' he said.

'I'm Four-A,' she replied.

'You were slated to go up with recon one,' Badler said. He looked displeased. 'But Deck Dampier said there was some issue between you and Slipstream, and advised against it.'

'We had words,' said Jagdea. 'It'll blow over.'

'What occurred?' asked Badler.

'I was my usual self,' she said.

Badler didn't look surprised, but he seemed satisfied.

'We'll be sweeping Box Four-Five-Three,' he said. She could hear the edge back in his voice. 'That's Errico District. Autotrack and mapping is loaded. We'll be low-level, looking for... whatever we can see.'

'And if we find something?' Gangster asked.

'We locate and report,' said Badler.

'Nah,' said Gangster. 'You're not following me. I'm saying, if we find a bat nest, they'll see us. They'll have bat-cover over any deck. Interceptors.'

'We'll deal with whatever we find,' said Badler. It didn't sound as convincing as he meant it to be. 'If they lift anything out there, ROP Nine-Nine will pick acoustic tracks and alert us with plenty of warning.'

Gangster didn't look reassured.

'If we do find a deck out there,' said Jagdea, 'and it's wide open, it'll feel wrong just leaving it.'

Badler glanced at them both conspiratorially.

'I agree,' he said. 'Instruct is locate and report, but if we do find an open nest and we don't scare anything up, it's too good an opportunity. Under those circumstances... and *only* those circumstances, Dampier's given me approval to call in a ground strike from Five-Two. They're the nearest, with territorial overlap. And they lift Avengers.'

'Which could mess up a deck pretty completely,' agreed Jagdea.

'But it's my call, Driver,' said Badler. 'Are you clear on that?'

Jagdea nodded.

Badler stared at her for a moment, then lowered his head to begin the blessing, a short prayer to the Beati. Jagdea had heard it enough times to say the words along with him, even though she'd never consciously committed the lines to memory. Pain smouldered in her hands.

'Let's go,' said Badler. 'Anything else?'

'You chosen your exec yet, Lead?' Gangster asked him with a cheeky grin.

'I'm considering several candidates, Yesof,' he replied. Jagdea knew the role would probably have gone to Jongleur, if Jongleur had still been around.

'But exec?' said Gangster, pushing hard with a wink. 'That's gotta come with a pay-bump? Right? Right?'

'Shut up and mount up,' said Badler.

A stern enginseer had anointed her Voss, and the ground crew was withdrawing. Jagdea climbed in.

'I guess we just can't get rid of you,' said Chief Tarr.

'But you clearly prepped for my funeral,' replied Jagdea. 'What's with the paint?'

'Didn't have any green to match,' said Tarr. 'No belly-blue, neither. And there were a lot of patches to cover, so. It was black, or black.'

'I see you went with black,' said Jagdea.

'Plus side,' said Tarr, patting the cockpit side wall affectionately, 'nice clean flank to paint your tally on.'

'I don't do that,' said Jagdea.

'So I've noticed,' said Tarr.

Jagdea settled in and locked her straps. The dials of the headache had been neatly and freshly masked as per her preferences, except for the auspex secondary.

'Checks Four-A,' Tarr said. 'All prime. Had a full strip down and rebuild. The throttle's gonna be stiffer than you remember. Just so you know, the hydraulics indicator has a new bulb, and is showing green. Not that you'll see that through the tape.'

Jagdea glanced at her. 'The auspex there?' she asked, pointing.

'You've got an auspex booster package under your nose, with forward and down-angled picters. Shouldn't affect drag in any way. That stud on your stick below guns, see? Tap that, and the picters will burst-fire in sync with the booster, which will record a precise logis-lock on image location. Auspex secondary records that data for analysis, and also squirts it back to Control automatically on sub-vox. Don't want to be losing recon data if you, you know, crash again.'

'How many shots?' asked Jagdea.

'Thirty multi-frame high-res bursts, so wait until they smile, huh? Lidding you up.'

'Wait,' said Jagdea.

'I ain't sight-checking your surfaces, Driver,' said Tarr with a scowl.

'I know,' said Jagdea. 'I want to ask you a question. Just between us.'

Tarr frowned, and scratched the electoo on her cheek. Vox was off, and no one else was close enough to hear them. The pre-flight sign-off between a pilot and her fitter was about the most intimate and private conversation possible on a war deck.

'What do you know about white crows?' Jagdea asked.

Tarr squinted at her. 'Not much,' she replied. 'Except one thing.'

'What?'

'White crows are very seldom white,' she said.

Jagdea wanted to ask a follow-up, but Tarr already had her hands on the lid.

'You looking for trouble?' Tarr asked.

'It seems to find me all by itself,' said Jagdea.

'Good flying,' said Tarr, and latched the canopy.

Jagdea flipped the voltaic master and began her slam-check. She walked the parish from the left: vector thrust secondaries to preset, auspex and modar, starter, pump, ad-mix. Verification of target system, guns on. The starter compressor began to spool up. She armed countermeasures.

'Vox check,' Badler crackled over the comms.

'Vox check, Lead. Driver receiving.'

'Copy, Driver.'

'Vox check, Lead, Gangster copies.'

'Copy, Gangster.'

Jagdea armed her seat. At least she had one this time.

'This is Lead, deconflict auspex.'

'Copy,' she replied. She adjusted the auspex, then blinked a test pattern through auspex secondary and activated the booster package.

'Control to wings. Go for start. Go for start.'

'Copy, Control,' she heard Badler reply. *'Lead to wings. Dead drop now.'*

Jagdea released her landing claws.

Engine primed but unstarted, she fell nose-first down the side of the Campanile.

Errico District was over thirty-five minutes out from Six-Six, a mangled north-eastern district in the war-torn edges of the hive-grave. The three birds passed ROP 99, and banked east through blocks of mid-rise habs and ransacked manufactory areas. They were moving low at about five hundred in chase formation, Gangster's pink Voss in the lead, followed by the two black Strikes, Badler's, then Jagdea's. The overcast was heavy, and the cloud low. Vapour trailed across the rooftops and streets, veiling the route, and they kept hitting pockets of squally rain. Box 453 lit up on Jagdea's auspex, a luminous patch slowly tracking towards her, an area of about sixty square miles.

Badler had instructed a standard break-sweep. They would split up as they entered the designated recon area, and scope a portion each. They could hunt the box faster through a division of labour.

'Break in ten,' Badler voxed.

'Copy, Lead,' said Jagdea.

'Gangster copies.'

Badler gave the instruct, and Jagdea saw the two fightbirds ahead of her peel off, Badler to the left, Gangster to the right. They quickly vanished from sight. Jagdea maintained course, dipping even lower. The ruins were dense and close-packed, rising high above her on either side. The space was lanced with shadows and bars of thin daylight. Below, where the daylight touched, she glimpsed the glitter of water in the flooded streets.

She started to quarter the streets, moving systematically. Past Quire Point, the air and light took on a rusty, orange glow from the hot pollutants leaking from a nearby reactor hub.

Mapping was only showing the rudimentary layout of the district, and, as ever, primary auspex was jammed with clutter and next to useless. She turned under the skeletal arches of the Errico Bridge, leaning to avoid dangling girders, and swept onto the Claudian Processional. She was searching by eye, dipping the wings to study the structures she passed and the surface below. It was hard to specify what she was looking for, but she knew she'd know it when she saw it. Buildings that showed signs of recent conversion or reinforcement. Cleared patches of rubble. Equipment stores under netting. Blocked roads that had been reopened. Maybe even hints of personnel or machines on the ground.

At the end of Claudian, she circled back, and fired off two pict-bursts as she circled an old Missionaria complex. The place was a ruin, and evidenced no sign of life, but some of the windows showed traces of makeshift armour panelling. There was no way to tell if this was recent, or work done during the war that killed Vesperus, but she marked it carefully, and then banked away.

Less than a minute later, she passed over a vast sea of loose rubble where an immense tower had collapsed. She noticed oddly regular marks in the brick scree that seemed like vehicle tracks or areas cleared for vehicle use. She made two passes, using the picter and recording a logis-lock on the location. The small display of the auspex secondary rotated an icon as it stored the data.

She pulled clear, cautiously rounded a tower that had remained upright when all its neighbours had been levelled, and then rolled away north following the Noctis Skyway. Rain bleated across her.

Below, the skyway was a river of rockcrete segments, cracked and pock-marked. She got the sudden impression of movement, and turned back, running low along the elevated sections. Some slabs of the skyway had dropped off their elevated pilings and shattered, so that the route looked like a badly derailed train sculpted in 'crete. Ungoverned weeds, mainly thick wirebush and bindthorn, were growing in thickets from cracks in the skyway. They were nodding and shifting in the low wind, the source of the movement she'd picked up in her peripheral vision.

Jagdea raised her nose, climbed out, and turned wide around a gutted hab-block. Then she started flying north again, back down the line of the skyway, and banked west onto the Pharioc Processional. Sparking clouds of ash billowed across her path as she crossed the smoke-plume of the abandoned reactor. Ahead were three bulk processing depots. The hive-rise structures to her left rose to more than fifteen hundred feet, a dead-eyed cliff.

If there was a hostile deck out in Errico, Jagdea was sure it would be concealed. The Aeronautica Intercepts were. If she came up on one, unwittingly, would her presence scare up a response, or would a bat nest lock down and hide until she was gone? The Campanile, and the other stations, tended to avoid detection, but the Archenemy thought differently and behaved differently. They were, in her experience, generally more impulsive and less inclined towards strategic discretion.

The depots were vast precincts, skirted by security walls, with a row of squat generator towers along the western end. She went in low, skimming the rooftops of the bulk barns and flaking silos, then turned out for another pass. The transit ways, for loading and supply, were fairly clear, threading between the barns. She saw cargo vehicles, little yellow specks, but they were burned out. She glimpsed what looked like weapon batteries.

She climbed out high, rolled over, and returned for a third

pass. Nothing on the scopes, no heat tracks or acoustics, but the scopes were jittery with junk images anyway.

Definitely gun emplacements. She went over low, firing the picter. But as she passed over, she saw them for what they were: derelict, the remains of old Imperial fortifications.

She checked fuel and range. Another twenty minutes, and they'd need to pull out of Errico for the homeward run.

Something chirruped on the vox, a brief crackle.

'Driver to flight, say again.'

The hiss of dead air.

'Flight, this is Driver. Lead, Gangster, copy back.'

Still nothing. Then a brief, incoherent burble.

'Driver. Recon elements, respond.'

She waited. Still no response. Then, an abrupt explosion of sound and static for about five seconds.

There was a voice hidden inside that noise. Jagdea wasn't able to make out words, but the voice had been Gangster's.

Jagdea banked around to the east and gunned up.

'Gangster, Gangster, respond. This is Driver. Report position and situation, over.'

Another chop of noise. It sounded desperate. She couldn't get a vox-fix.

'Driver to Lead. Gangster's in trouble, respond.'

Nothing. Where the hell was Badler? Was he in trouble too?

She gained height and kicked off a little burn to increase her rate. Gangster had been sweeping the box portion to her east. She headed that way in the hope of picking up a visual. She alerted Control to her situation, but they had nothing. ROP 99 had nothing showing either.

'ROP Nine-Nine, confirm no power plant track, over.'

The observation post confirmed.

Jagdea raced into Gangster's area along the Valentire Processional, maxing situational awareness. The shred wasn't back in the cockpit with her, but she could smell it on the wind.

'Gangster, Gangster, copy back.'

Where the frig are you, Yesof?

She saw a column of smoke to her north, and rolled towards it, passing between two shattered spires and along a deep avenue. She whipped out under the arch of a primary powerduct and saw a patch of waste ground ahead. Thick smoke was boiling up from the rubble. A fuel burn. A crash site. Something had gone down hard and disintegrated on impact.

She circled. It was impossible to tell what had augered in.

'Gangster, Gangster, do you copy?'

There was a monolithic range of buildings at the north end of the waste ground, an Adeptus Mechanicus palace, twelve hundred feet high. Beyond them, a significant habiculum complex.

A bat crossed her, burning hard. Jagdea had no idea where it could have come from. She got a glimpse of its yellow fuselage as it went by. Jagdea slammed up into a turn to give chase, but before she could complete the execute, a second bat, a blue Razor, ripped past on the tail of the first. She was now coming around behind two of them.

The blue Razor fumbled in the air, jerked, and then shredded into a travelling fireball. Jagdea saw beads of spitting las-fire. Gangster's pink Voss blurred past her in a high-speed travelling roll, still firing as it went for the other bat.

Jagdea's turn put her behind Gangster, and she throttled up to stay close. Gangster's wings and hull showed signs of damage and scoring. Yesof had been through something, and it had been bad.

'Gangster, respond. Gangster, respond.'

Gangster throttled back out of her pursuit, and swam in alongside Jagdea's bird. Jagdea could see Yesof in the cockpit. Yesof was gesturing urgently. A throat-cut gesture. Vox down. Jamming probably. That explained a lot. Jagdea signed an acknowledgement. Gangster circled her hand to indicate a rapid exit instruct.

Shit. What–

Yesof glared at her and aimed one finger up, fiercely.

Jagdea looked up.

Bats were peeling off the roofline of the Ad-Mech palace structure. Dozens of them. They were dead dropping from the parapet. No wonder there had been no acoustic track or power plant signature.

Gangster burned away hard. Jagdea slotted the throttle and raced after her. The whole zone was lousy with roosting bats, and they were cold-starting on their heels in what felt like swarms. They were coming from everywhere, tumbling off high ledges, and plunging like dislodged gargoyles until their plants lit and they lifted, or fluttering like flocks of carrion birds out of windows and off tall perches.

The yellow bat Gangster had been chasing had vanished. Jagdea stuck to Gangster's seven, gripping hard as they tore back towards her plot area far too fast. They skipped and kinked to avoid collision obstacles, running to get clear. Running for their lives. They were hitting rates that were too rapid for these conditions, even by Gangster's reckless standards.

But there was a full-on bat swarm behind them. Jagdea's unreliable scope showed fifty-plus contacts on their heels. Even allowing for ghosting and clutter, there had to be twenty minimum.

The first shots rinsed past her. She heard threat warning, and shifted out to break it. More passing shots, the glimmer of las. Gangster cranked a hard left onto a manufactory approach. Jagdea went with her.

'Control, this is Driver. Contact, contact. Multiple hostiles.'

No response. How far would they have to go to exit the enemy's jamming cone?

More passing shots. A thump against her rear plate that rocked Four-Four.

Then Gangster's pink fightbird suddenly broke into a hard vertical. What the hell was she–

Jagdea knew *exactly* what Yesof was doing. They weren't going to outrun the bat swarm. They simply weren't. Gangster had pulled a hard loop to turn and face them.

Verghast strong. And Verghast *insane*.

Jagdea waited a moment longer.

'Screw it,' she said, and flat-planed her bird. Full-speed breaks, hard g, rolling out into an inversion. Her vision coned briefly. She was not going to let Yesof do it on her own. Besides, she'd made a deal.

Levelling, she hit the burner, and punched clean through the heart of the pursuing swarm pattern. Max-rating bats blew past her on either side. Reaction time was down to hundredths of a second. She saw a green bat coming head-on, and opened up her guns before murderlock even sounded.

The bat went up, a dazzle of debris that passed under her belly. She rolled hard into a steep, banking climb, and instantly picked up a purple Talon. She was on its heels. Brief murderlock, but it tried to break. She chopped off a portion of its tail, but it stayed flying and tried to execute a hard-out left. She rocked into its turn, right on its inside, and let go with the wing cannons. The tracers hosed in the air, bent by the fierce g, and pummelled the Talon across the centre mass. Debris spalled off it, then a wing tore loose and went whickering backwards like a spinning scythe. Sheeting fire, the Talon dropped in a sickening, uncontrolled dive.

Threat warning. Jagdea rolled out, then killed her thrust, spitting a Blade out into her envelope. The Blade tried to scram vertically. She fired her nose guns and missed, but the near-hit scared the Blade into a hasty overcorrect, and smack into the stone piers of an aqueduct that neither of them had seen coming.

The Blade became a fireball to her right. Jagdea almost fireballed with it, but somehow managed to skin Four-Four under the arch instead of into it.

Threat lock. At least two hostiles behind her, and two more coming head-to-head. Jagdea's body screamed from the G punishment and the grip stress. Her mind was frighteningly clear.

The clarity was extraordinary. No shred. Total biopathic control. Her skin, wrapped tight in her new red suit, was drenched in sweat, but it felt like she had all the time in the world. The odds against her and Yesof were so great it wasn't even funny, but they were *so* great, there was nothing left to lose. In these few lethal seconds, she was taking chances she'd never have considered risking in the Vesperus war sky, chances she'd have rejected even twenty years before in her prime, when she was making her own glory stories.

There was no room for doubt or fear. With nothing to lose, and hope wiped from her scope, there was only space left for the gunfighter. The bat-killer. Fangs bared, claws out, hair on fire, screw them all.

She J-turned out of a nose-on collision, shook one of the bats off her tail, then looped into a clean murderlock on a turning Razor that she pulped with an audacious fly-through. Her angle of deflection was pure instinct. Then she was climbing hard. Shots ripped passed her. Gangster slammed by, chasing one bat, chased by another.

Jagdea twisted over into a barrel roll. Missile lock sounded. She popped flares, and banked right, diving down the face of an Administratum keep. The heater detonated in her wake. Bats flocked after her, mobbing her like crows as they chased her down into the hive canyon. A closing Talon misjudged the space completely and sheared itself in two on a high-tension cable that split it like a hot wire. She took another glancing hit. She was diving into the gloom, street-level, hive floor, the Vesperus abyss. Bat-fire rippled past her and sprayed up filthy water from the flooded floor as she pulled level. Bats behind her, closing fast. Threat warning. Threat warning.

Obstacle ahead. A landslip of rockcrete half-choked the trench. She lifted her nose and cleared it by inches. At least one bat behind her didn't. Hard left into a side street. There was a bat dead ahead, coming the other way. They crossed, barely missing each other. Jagdea saw its banded hull as it whipped past her canopy.

The banded Blade. Sorrentine's killer.

She wanted to loop out and give chase, but the idea was stupid, and there was no room to pull that kind of execute anyway. She burned Four-Four out along a swamped drainage gulley, under a footbridge, and then into a climb.

A bat picked her up as she turned clear into the next shadowed avenue. Threat warning. She couldn't see it, and she couldn't shake it. She yanked hard right through the roofless ruin of a manufactory, and then entered a blown-out Administratum block through a gaping hole on its sixtieth floor. She was counting on the block being gutted, but there was too much debris, and too much of the original structure intact. Bulkhead walls loomed ahead.

The bat followed her inside, dropping its rate cautiously. It found her as she was turning to meet it. She was at hover-stop on screaming ducts, swinging her tail towards the wall behind her. The bat braked hard, but her guns were already firing. Four-Four's airframe shook. The combination of vector down-thrust and cannon wash filled the dark cavity with 'crete dust. The bat exploded in a belch of fire.

She advanced the throttle and gunned forward out of her hover, back the way she had come, through the flame-wash of her kill and into the open.

As Jagdea accelerated down the gloomy avenue, she spotted Gangster far ahead, caught in a rolling brawl with at least four bats. She advanced power to close and cut in, determined to give Yesof backup, but two Talons immediately rushed over her, descending fast. They'd been bearing down on Gangster, and Jagdea had appeared out of nowhere in front of them. The Talons were moving at a high rate, and had overshot her, but now they were both braking back deeply to get on her. For a moment, Four-Four meshed with them, as though all three aircraft were locking into a formation pattern. Jagdea deceled to yank them past. One of the Talons shot ahead of her. The other stayed on her wing. She glanced over, and saw the Talon sitting right alongside her. She couldn't see the pilot, because of the bat's tinted canopy. She could feel the menace.

She had tone lock on the Talon ahead. It was trying to split out of her envelope. The one beside her was pulse-ducting to ease onto her tail. She lit off a squirt of cannons, smacked the Talon ahead, and then tried to brake back to keep its partner at bay. It wasn't having it. They jockeyed, each trying to nudge the other out in front.

Suddenly they were draped in black smoke. The Talon up ahead, limping and trying to lift out, had started to burn. Her cannon burst had started a fire in its engine. Fuel-burn smoke was trailing back across Jagdea and the Talon she was racing with.

The stricken Talon shivered and bucked as it suffered a catastrophic engine blow-out. It came apart in the air, scattering debris. The airframe disintegrated so thoroughly, Jagdea actually glimpsed the rag-doll figure of the pilot spill out and cartwheel past.

She jinked to avoid impact with the tumbling debris. The Talon beside her did the same. They came back together, almost side by side again, but the bat was nosing her ahead. She glanced aside again. She still couldn't see the pilot, but she gave him the finger anyway, and ripped into a savage barrel roll to port.

As she rolled back up, the Talon sliced over her. It had no idea where she'd gone, but it clearly had a nasty feeling, because it was deceling even harder. She tried to break and rise onto its six. It wasn't having that either.

They shot past Gangster coming the other way. She'd splashed one bat, but the others were hounding her tail. Jagdea decided to lock into a loop and let the Talon go. Gangster was going to get bit any second.

Threat warning. Lock warning.

Something had dropped in on her tail. It was tight, and she couldn't see it. There was a causeway bridge ahead. No space to flip. The Talon shot under the bridge, then Jagdea, then whatever was on Jagdea's heels. On the far side of the bridge, they raced down the length of a large habitat block. Some of its windows were intact. She got a flash of their reflections in the filthy glass, reflections that jumped and flickered. The Talon, Four-Four, and then another aircraft on her tail.

A fightbird. A Voss Strike. A black one.

It had to be Badler. It had to be Badler, smack on her six. Threat lock screamed in her ears. Missile lock warning. What the hell was he doing?

White crows are very seldom white.

The Talon started to extend, burners lit, trying to outrun her. Badler's Voss suddenly popped up behind her, guns roaring, and took the Talon with an absolutely clean kill. Badler's black Voss shot over her head, accelerating into a strong climb and turn.

Jagdea climbed after him, and turned tighter. She was trying to get a fix on Gangster. Off her left wing, Badler's black Voss still seemed as hostile as the multitude of angry bats criss-crossing the airspace.

Before she could decide whether to lock him or wing him, there was a shriek, a squeal of noise, the scream of wolves ringing in her headset.

It was the vox. They had flown clear of the Archenemy's jamming field, and it had woken back up with a howl.

'Driver, this is Lead. Do you copy?' Badler's voice, grated into strips, came through the blitz of static.

'Driver copies.'

'Stay tight. We're going back for Gangster.'

'Copy that,' Jagdea snapped. She wanted to ask what the hell he'd been playing at. Why had he locked her? But there was zero time for questions, and she was gripping so tight she could barely breathe anyway.

They soared back down the shadowed avenue, Jagdea at Badler's right wing four. The air was still thick with bats. There was no room for anything besides maximum aggressive flying. Two Razors crossed them trying to turn. A stream of las-fire spat between them from somewhere above. Jagdea could hear Badler on the vox, reporting the situation to Control and requesting assist. A Blade came burning at them through the deep shadows, head-on. Badler didn't flinch. He raised a wing and banged off a missile. The streaking heater erupted in the crook of the Blade's starboard wing and blew it in half. The forward half of the burning airframe maintained course in a wild tumble, spewing fire and machine parts, and Badler and Jagdea had to split and tilt to let it pass between them without collision. As Badler came level and powered ahead of her, she saw he had only one heater left on his rails.

They were low on stores, and guns. Range level also told Jagdea she was fuel light. She was betting Badler was the same. She'd been approaching range limit before the fight even began, and the fuel-cost of high-burn combat meant she now had nothing like enough in the tanks to return to the Campanile.

That was a problem that would have to wait. The vox had dropped out again. They were back inside the enemy's jamming cone. Bats were mobbing them from all sides. The sheer number of hostile machines in the airspace was almost an advantage: crowding compromised the Archenemy's angles of attack and fields of fire. Even so, it was just a grim countdown to the inevitable. What were they going to run out of first? Fuel? Ammo? Sky?

Luck?

Jagdea shook off another threat warning. Shots puffed past her. She spotted Gangster's pink Voss, crossing low and fast between fabrication plants. It was trailing a thin ribbon of smoke and there were two Razors behind it.

There was no way to know if Badler had seen Yesof, and no vox to tell him. Jagdea stamped the rudder, leaned on the stick, and peeled out, hoping that Badler would read her lead and follow it.

She lost sight of him. There was the bright flash from a near-miss heater, and Four-Four shook like a child's rattle. She tightened her turn, lungs crushed, and slotted the throttle up as she ran down into a broad freight dock. The air was orange from the burning reactor, the depths below a toxic green shadow. There were gantries to avoid, the dark skeletons of crane derricks and hoist assemblies. Las-shots and tracers dotted the darkness like fireflies.

A Razor was coming up at her on a hard burn. They both lit off bursts as they passed at high rate, neither of them hitting. Threat warning. She rolled over, and another Blade, this one a dusty tan, lurched past her, trying to correct its haste. She nudged her ducts and speed brakes, letting the bat flop, and then raked its back end with her las as it swung into her firing envelope and murderlock shrilled. The Razor seemed unharmed for a second, then it twitched and dropped like a stone into the darkness below.

There was Gangster, passing the rockcrete revetment at the end of the dock, trying to climb out between two slabby habiculum towers. She had a Razor and a Blade on her heels, and a Talon cutting down from a high angle. Jagdea pulled hard left to set up her position, then hard right to pull down on the chasers. She figured Yesof had a better chance of engaging the diving Talon.

She kept her focus on the chasers. Both were climbing hard. The Razor was an almost fluorescent blue. The Blade was the banded bat.

Modarlock acquired the Razor neatly. She leased off a burst, but the bat pitched away in a frantic evasion, and disappeared. Jagdea ignored it, and pulled over onto the Blade. It was chipping off quick shots at Gangster's eight. Gangster was rocking and switching to shake it, but her climb was fierce, and it was bleeding her performance.

Jagdea got a quick murderlock tone, and opened up. There was a negative thump, and a rune lit on the CAD. The powercells of her nose guns were drained. She toggled to cannons, but the banded bat had now seen her and veered out of her line. Split-second decision: roll over on it for the sake of payback, or stay on Gangster?

Not really a choice. A gut one, perhaps, but not an Aeronautica one. She chose Yesof, and pulsed the blower to stay with her. Gangster was rolling high in an almost lazy, lingering slump, her Voss winded. The Talon stooped past her, turning wide to reacquire. Jagdea didn't waste rounds trying to take a crack at it. It had already sliced past her. But the blue Razor had reappeared, accompanied by a grey Blade. They knifed towards Gangster in formation. Jagdea banked hard and went for them, coming from their ten. She got a lock on the Razor and ripped off with her wing cannons before she lost it again. The blue Razor convulsed, veered wildly, and clipped its wingman as it went into a death dive. As the Razor plunged nose-first to its doom, the grey Blade staggered to port, trailing cables and part of a wing, then began to spin as it lost control entirely. It chopped below Four-Four on a downward trajectory, end over end.

The Talon had re-entered the tangle. Or a different Talon had joined. It was becoming hard to tell one machine from another. G-force was needling Jagdea's vision. She stomped around, but Yesof had already seen the Talon coming, and banked onto it. Her cannon fire sliced off its canopy and the upper skin of its fuselage. It started to break up in the air, and probably would have disintegrated entirely had it not met the north face of one of the habiculum towers first.

Jagdea pulled clear of the towers through the smoke drag. Gangster pushed past her, then dropped in on her right wing, bleeding dirty vapour from her efflux. They exchanged quick hand signals while they still had line of sight.

Yes, Disa, it's definitely time to go.

Her ammo counts were nearly zeroed, and fuel load alerts were blinking. There was no more fight left in either of them. Yesof's belligerent attitude didn't count for anything any more. Their birds were spent.

Time to go. Not that the bat-swarm would see it that way.

Jagdea advanced power. There were hostile machines massing behind them in pursuit, and more approaching rapidly from their eight. They would show no mercy, nor extend any respect towards valiant rivals who had counter-attacked with such vigour. The Archenemy didn't work that way. If anything, the enemy's hunger would be greater, enraged by the damage the pair of them had wrought. She and Gangster were right back where they had started, caught in an ambush and outgunned. Except now they had no combat ability. This, thought Jagdea, is what it's like to survive a last stand. This hollow stillness. It felt oddly unreal. When she had first cranked back with Yesof, she realised, neither of them had expected to live. They had turned to fight to the death, rather than wait to be splashed, to take as many down as they could, until they got bit. Like the laughable ending of one of Klay Menomar's glory stories.

Life wasn't anything like so neat and clean. No bright flash and quick ending. They had survived the death they had chosen, and traded it for a slow and helpless doom. These last minutes, last seconds, were just the inevitable tick-down of dying. The ugly part. The hard part.

She tried to spot Badler. There was no sign of him. She saw bats ahead now, two miles out, rising from the hive floor and bearing in to block off any viable exit.

Badler shot under them and pulled out ahead. His port wing was shot up, and he too was trailing smoke.

The vox squawked and rasped. Then she heard his voice.

'Recon, Recon. This is Lead. Burn now.'

'Lead, this is Driver. Nowhere to burn.'

Had he even seen the bats ahead of them?

'–frigging all over us!' Gangster was yelling.

'This is Lead, Recon. Follow the damn instruct. Burn now. Five-Two has got us covered.'

They weren't bats. The specks approaching dead ahead were birds. Three V-formation trios. Avengers from Five-Two.

As they shot past the Six-Six fightbirds, Jagdea heard wolves again, just for a second.

* * *

Intercept 52, Vesperus, 08:59

There was no way to reach Six-Six. Jagdea put Four-Four down on a rooftop deck, standard duct arrest. As she powered down, she saw ground crews running out to Gangster's Voss on the deck nearby. It was broiling smoke from its underside, and the teams were spraying it with foam.

Intercept 52 occupied the upper storeys of a ragged Munitorum storehouse. The main deck was far bigger than any at the Campanile, and ran open all the way to blast shelters at the west end. It was sleeting rain.

She put her hands on her head until she couldn't keep them there any more, then unplugged, popped the canopy and almost fell out. She couldn't breathe. Her compression suit had cinched so tight, for so long, that even now the bladders were deflating, her lungs refused to fill and her ribs refused to move.

She sank to her knees, and dragged off her helmet and flight cap with numb, shaking hands. She sucked in cold, wet air and spat out blood. There were people crowding around her. She heard voices. None of them made any sense. The deck was sloping like a ship at sea. Someone got her to her feet. She pulled off her flight gloves. Bandages and shreds of synth-flesh came with them. He hands were gore-slick and clawed.

'You're down,' someone was saying. 'Breathe. You're down.'

She heard laughter. Familiar laughter. Gangster was pushing through the throng of bodies to reach her. She was laughing in glee, like a child, even though her face was drenched in grease and sweat.

'How many? How many?' Yesof yelled.

Jagdea couldn't speak.

'I got eight!' Yesof yelled. 'Eight! That was something! Hey, talk to me! Driver?'

'Ten,' murmured Jagdea. 'I think... ten.'

'Ten?'

'Not all gun-kills, but...'

'Ten?' Yesof howled. 'You bat-killing bitch!'

She hugged Jagdea as tight as any compression suit.

'You were meant to go,' Yesof exclaimed, right in her ear. 'I told you to go.'

'You turned back...'

'Yes, so *you* could go, you frigging gak!'

'Couldn't just...'

Gangster grabbed her by the face with both hands and glared jubilantly into Jagdea's blurry eyes.

'Four-A!' she cried. 'That was Four-A! That was a real frigging thing!'

It was something, all right.

There was a howl as Badler's Voss went over, pulling down for duct arrest.

'Are you two claiming eighteen kills between you?' someone asked. 'Is that what I'm hearing?'

A tall, grey-haired man was looking at them. Jagdea blinked to clear her vision and made sense of his pins. She started to salute.

'Forget that,' the man said with a brush of his hand. 'Welcome to Five-Two.'

His name was Bastine, senior deck at Intercept 52. In the Intercept's rec room, a fairly handsome and refined space, he poured them drinks. Even Badler took one.

'Some show,' Bastine remarked. He had a dry voice that sounded rusty or smoke-damaged.

'We appreciate the assist, Deck,' said Badler. He was putting on a decent show of civility, but Jagdea could see his shakes and tremors.

'Happy to oblige,' said Bastine. 'That was a significant nest.

It's marked and plotted. Orison Command will be running raids by tonight.'

'It won't be the only one,' said Jagdea quietly.

'You know that how?' asked Bastine.

'The numbers, sir,' replied Jagdea. 'A big nest, as you said. The enemy's moved into the hive. They won't have put everything in one place. So a nest that big speaks to significant supply lines and other big nests. We'll all be running recon for weeks.'

'Well, one's a good start,' said Bastine.

'Yes.'

'And on your first sweep.'

'We got lucky,' said Jagdea.

'Is that how you'd describe it?' Bastine asked, with a wry smile.

'It's the only word that comes to mind, sir,' said Jagdea.

'I suppose so,' said Bastine. 'Against those numbers. Eighteen, eh?'

'Estimated,' said Jagdea.

'For definite,' said Gangster.

'And you, Lead?' Bastine asked.

'Just six, sir,' said Badler.

That made Bastine laugh. 'That's Zoph Sea numbers,' he said, with a glance at Jagdea.

She didn't reply. Bastine got to his feet, finished his drink, and set the glass aside.

'Clean up,' he said. 'I'll see to refuelling and temp repairs on your birds. Get you back to Six-Six this afternoon. Lead Badler, make sure you pass on my regards to Julett Dampier.'

Once he'd gone, they sat in silence for a moment. The light from the old glow-globes was almost sepia. There were picts tacked to the wall, flight crews, pilots. Jagdea gazed at them for a while. She sipped her drink. Blood from her fingers had smeared the glass.

'You locked me up,' she said at last.

'What?' asked Gangster.

'Badler,' said Jagdea. 'Locked me up.'

Badler had been staring into space. He twitched, as though waking up.

'On my tail,' said Jagdea. 'Hard lock.'

'Did you?' asked Gangster, turning on the sofa to look at Badler.

'No,' he said. 'I thought... I thought you'd get it. That you'd understand. I was trying to get you to spit ahead so I could get a clear heater-lock on that bat. You wouldn't budge, Jagdea.'

'Ah,' said Jagdea. She sighed.

'You were in my line,' said Badler. 'Vox was out. I just wanted you to run out so–'

'I get it now.'

'I thought you'd read my–'

'I get it.'

Gangster sniggered. 'She thought you was the crow, Badler,' she chuckled.

'I realise,' said Badler tightly.

'I did,' said Jagdea. 'Just for a second. But not now. Not after that.'

She looked at Badler, and raised her glass.

'Sorry,' she said. 'For thinking it. Six-Six, Lead Badler.'

'Six-Six,' he responded. She could tell he was trying really hard not to cry.

'Six-Six!' Gangster cried, over-loud, and went to help herself to more amasec.

The Saint was there. Just as Jagdea remembered, though she seemed smaller and paler in the gloom of the hangar. *Beautiful Beati*. Jagdea stood and stared at the Avenger's nose art for a while. From behind her came the sounds of power-drivers, and the shouts of fitters at work.

'Help you?'

Jagdea looked around. A burly woman with dark skin and a bleached-blonde buzz-cut was staring at her. An aviator in full flight gear. She had the heavy chain-mail gauntlets of a gunner.

'I'm looking for...' Jagdea said, trying to remember names. 'Omarti and Hodd. Tail Forty.'

'I'm Hodd,' said the woman. 'Who are you now?'

'Jagdea,' said Jagdea.

The woman frowned for a moment. 'Oh, right,' she said.

'I just wanted to express my thanks in person,' said Jagdea.

'No need for that,' said Hodd.

'I feel I owe you–'

'Yeah? Then tell me the story.'

'What... story?'

'That scrap today. Walk me through it.'

Reliving that was the last thing Jagdea felt like. But it was the least she could do.

Who are you, now? That's what Hodd had asked. Yes. That was the real question.

Refectory, Intercept 66, Vesperus, 20:23

They could hear the thunder before they were even in the room. Hands banging tabletops, feet drumming. A menacing crescendo.

As they entered, the drumming almost stopped completely because everybody present put their hands on their heads. A vocal assault of yells and whoops replaced the thunder.

Yesof grinned. She stepped forward and executed a low bow, arms spread like back-raked wings, accepting the adulation. Then she rose, and gestured like a showman to Jagdea, and to Badler, who was standing slightly shell-shocked behind Jagdea.

Lopard stepped forward, clapping and smiling. He dragged over a chair, and held out a stick of chalk to Jagdea.

Jagdea took it and stared at it, the din ringing in her ears. Then she handed it to Yesof.

'I think it's Lead's turn,' Yesof yelled over the shouting. She turned to Badler, and offered the chalk. Badler shook his head. He actually looked scared.

'Frigging do it, Bads,' said Yesof.

Badler took the chalk, and accepted Yesof's hand to get him up on the chair. He looked awkward and precarious. He quickly scratched up six marks beside his name, then paused and smiled as the shouting and drumming blew up again. Then, with a slightly more dramatic flourish, he marked the eight kills beside GANGSTER. The noise grew louder. Yesof was giving herself a round of applause. Badler leaned out and drew the ten strokes in beside DRIVER.

The tumult was deafening.

'Now you do the dance!' Yesof yelled up at him.

Badler shook his head.

'I'm not... doing that,' he said.

Yesof turned to the hall and did it for him.

DAY 103

Rec room, Intercept 66, Vesperus, 04:47

Lord Militant Jahkel's water-stained features gazed down at her in lofty disdain. Meeting his eyes, Jagdea wondered if the great lord ever thought about the people at the far end of his orders. She doubted it. She'd never encountered a single soul among the upper ranks who spared a moment for the individuals executing their will, except, of course, when it came time to make public speeches with an appropriately solemn air. Compassion tended to stop at deck officer level, and even there, it was in precious short supply. She supposed Jahkel, and his ilk, thought of them only as marker tags on a strategium table, or specks of coloured light on a hololith display, playing pieces on a board to be moved, and squandered, at will.

If they ever thought of them at all.

The musty little rec room was quiet, and she was alone. She sat in a battered armchair, alert-ready in full gear, her black helmet at her feet. She had pulled an early rotation, standard intercept with Gumm and Harlot. After the sustained uproar of the night before, she hadn't felt like facing the refectory's noise and bustle. She waited in silence, regulating her breathing, her hands resting on the arms of the chair to ease the ache and the throb of fresh synth-flesh re-bonding.

Everything ached. Everything, right to the core. She'd numbed the harness burns on her body with neuro-gel and strapped the bruising on her ribs and belly, but nothing could ease the deeper pain. She felt as though she had a piece of shrapnel lodged in her soul, a fragment that turned and tore every time she moved.

The weather was poor. Heavy rain. She heard the clang and thump of lifters and carts from elsewhere in the Campanile as the crews prepped the upper decks. Once or twice, the screaming bang of rams igniting as they fell past the bell tower outside, dead-dropping their way to victory, or something that would look like victory until the last moment.

Footsteps. The door opened.

'There you are,' said Gumm, flight helmet under his arm.

'Here I am,' she agreed.

'Heavy night?' he asked.

'Heavy day. Just fancied a little quiet.'

Gumm nodded. 'I'll leave you alone, then,' he said. 'I was just on my way up.'

'Did we get called?'

'No, but Boa's taken our birds up, and a walk-around never hurts.'

He paused, hesitant in the doorway, like a shade that needed to be invited in.

'You all right?' he asked.

'Yeah,' she said.

'Extraordinary, what you did yesterday. But exhausting.'

'Yes,' she said.

'And hard to get past, I should imagine,' he added. 'To do that, and then have to start again the next day.'

'And the day after, and the day after,' she said.

'We need to talk to Badler,' he said. 'Convince him to honour Garrant's promise and let us go.'

'Never going to happen,' she said. 'We're too valuable.'

'You, certainly. After yesterday.'

'Both of us, Gumm. And Badler's a hardline believer. He won't let a dead man's promises get in the way of service and duty.'

Gumm sighed softly.

'You're thinking about Sagittarius, aren't you?' she said.

'He's not here yet,' said Gumm. 'But another few weeks...'

'Like the old Jagdea,' said Jagdea.

'No, she's already here, I'm sorry to say.'

She looked at him sharply.

'You know it,' he said, his voice fur-soft. 'You may not want to admit it, but you don't do what you did yesterday and not know it, deep down.'

'Not true,' she said. 'I was covering Disa's back–'

'Which is exactly what the hero of the Zoph would do, no matter the odds. The *insane* odds.'

Jagdea got up. 'There's no point pushing at Badler,' she said, 'but I'll work on Dampier.'

'You have an in there?' he asked. He sounded surprised.

'The hint of one,' she replied. 'Just a glimmer. But she's Deck, not Badler. And she was tight with Garrant. If anyone is going to process our papers, it's her.'

'Before it's too late, eh?'

'Before that.'

Gumm nodded. He didn't seem convinced.

'Well, I'll go up,' he said.

'I'll come with you,' she replied.

They crossed the landing and turned to the steps that led up to launch deck one. A cold wind was driving the rain in through the roof hatch, and the spatter was darkening the rockcrete. They heard the scream of distant drop-launches from another deck, probably number four on the far side.

'Driver!'

Jagdea turned, and saw Camo hurrying after them.

'I'll catch you up,' Jagdea told Gumm, and walked back down the steps to meet her.

'Got you this,' said Camo. She pulled a bottle of fine amasec from her jacket. 'It's the good stuff. From Harlot's stash.'

'There was no need, Kinny,' said Jagdea.

'You said we'd be even,' Camo objected. She handed the bottle to Jagdea, and then rummaged in her pocket. 'Wait,' she said, 'this too.'

She pulled out a handful of loose lho-sticks.

'Like you asked,' she said, carefully dribbling them into Jagdea's hand. 'Couldn't get a pack, so I sneaked them out of Harlot's case when he wasn't looking.'

'Thanks,' said Jagdea, and dropped them into her thigh pocket.

'He won't miss them,' she said. 'He's got more. He'll probably think he smoked them.'

Jagdea nodded, and turned to go. But something about the girl's affect made her stop. Camo was grinning, pink shades on, her usual cheerful self, but there was a tension in her.

'Something else?' asked Jagdea.

'You don't mark your tally on your bird,' Camo said.

'I don't,' said Jagdea. 'Not enough room now,' she added, trying to make light of the girl's curious focus.

Camo laughed, but it was just a courtesy giggle.

'Some people do,' she said. 'Some people keep tallies.'

'They do.'

'On the wall,' said Camo, 'on their birds...'

'Yes.'

'Why... why wouldn't a pilot's tallies match?' asked Camo.

'Match?'

'Different tallies,' said Camo. She seemed edgy. 'Different scores. Why would that be?'

'I'm not sure I follow you,' said Jagdea.

Camo shook her head hastily.

'Forget it. Forget it. I want to have your back, Driver, but I don't want to get anyone into trouble. I don't want to say the wrong thing.'

'Kinny?'

'Forget it. I've said too much. I don't want to be the one. It's all about trust, right? You don't betray that. I'm not that person. But I heard what you said that night...'

'Which night? Why don't you relax and tell me–'

'No, no,' said Camo. She forced up a big grin. 'I don't want to say the wrong thing. Just... just think about it.'

'I don't know what I'm supposed to be thinking about,' said Jagdea.

'Forget it,' said Camo. 'Good flying!'

She hurried away.

Jagdea walked up the steps into the wind and driving rain. By the time the squall hit her in the face, she'd put the pieces together.

It was still pre-dawn. The sky was almost as dark as the ruined skyline. The wind had a blade in it, and the fierce rain was glowing like a blizzard of tiny las-bolts where it pelted through the light of the sodium lamps the fitters had rigged up to work by. Voris had deck duty that morning. Jagdea's bird and Harlot's Bolt were already set in drop position on the lip. Jagdea saw Gumm sheltering under the deck awning as Boa trundled Gumm's Voss into place. Jagdea could smell the tractor's exhaust, incense, the wet stone, the background taint of pollution, the stink of prom from detached hoses. Rainbow slicks shone in the sheen of puddles on the scabby deck, barred with the reflected light from the lamps.

She walked out into the rain. A fitter was shouting instructions to Boa as the ogryn wheeled Five-Four into position. Two enginseers passed her on their way back to the steps, their ministrations done. They nodded courteously. She had no smile for them, no nod.

Voris grinned at her as she passed.

'Nice morning for it,' he said.

She glanced at him, and held out the bottle Camo had gifted her. 'I owed you a drink,' she said.

Voris took it, surprised.

'Very decent of you,' he said.

'Don't neck it all at once,' she said.

His smile was full of blackened pegs.

'Can't promise nothing,' he replied.

She kept walking. Lopard was standing under the tail of his crimson-nosed bird, eyeing the underwing stores.

'Ready to smite the foe?' he asked. 'Or did you smite yourself out yesterday?'

'I've got some left,' she said.

'Good,' he said. He took out his silver case, removed a lho-stick, and cupped his hands around his mouth to block the rain as he lit it.

'Spare one?' she asked.

Lopard frowned. 'Didn't think you smoked,' he remarked.

'We all pick up bad habits,' she replied. 'The longer we stay here.'

He shrugged, and handed her the case. She popped it open.

'Dampier's assigned you flight lead today,' he said, exhaling smoke. 'In light of your performance, I imagine. I'm happy to follow you, of course. So don't worry, I'll be right behind you every step of the way.'

'I'm sure you will,' she said.

'I guess you'll be leading us in the blessing, then?' Lopard snorted.

Behind her, on the other side of the deck, a fitter shouted. Boa began to back the tractor away from Gumm's tail-up bird.

'Forty-nine,' said Jagdea.

Lopard glanced at her. 'What?'

She nodded at the flank of his upraised Bolt.

'Forty-nine marks,' she said. 'Your tally. It matches the refectory fireplace.'

Lopard looked perplexed.

'Why do you mark your tallies, Lopard?'

'Oh, you know me,' he said with a wicked smirk.

'I thought I did. Pride, is it? The showmanship? Establishing your dominance?'

'What's the matter with you this morning?' he asked.

'So, pride, then?'

His brow furrowed in annoyance.

'Yes, I'm proud of my kills,' he said. 'You're talking like it's strange to display a tally. I'm sure you've done it in the past. I'm surprised you don't now, except for the self-effacing modesty you seem compelled to adopt at Six-Six. We're killers, Jagdea. Bat-killers. Gunfighters. I'm proud of my accomplishments.'

'And you can't help but commemorate them.'

'Is that a question?'

'No,' she said. 'But this is. Why don't they match?'

'Why don't what match?'

She raised his silver case, open. She hadn't taken a stick. She turned the case over and let the lho-sticks, a dozen or so, tumble out onto the wet deck at her feet.

'What the frig?' he exclaimed in surprise.

'Nine,' she said calmly. 'Just nine.'

She held the case out, open, to show him the interior. The neat row of nine cross marks scratched inside the lid.

'Nine,' she said. 'Not forty-nine. A private tally.'

He stared at her, the rain pouring off their faces and sleeting the air between them. She wasn't sure what she was expecting him to say.

'I don't know what this is,' he said.

What story was he going to tell her? That it was an old case, with the relic tally of another campaign? That it wasn't even his case, just something he'd found in the pocket of a dead man's jacket procured from the stores, with a dead man's tally scratched into the lid?

'Which one is Wilzar?' she asked.

Lopard didn't answer. He stared at her. There was no expression on his face.

'Which one?' she asked.

Lopard let out a sigh. Smoke came with it, pluming from his nostrils in the cold morning air. He took another drag on his lit lho-stick. There was nothing to say. They'd already had the conversation, in theory at least, that night in the High Ecclesiarch's sanctum.

'It's over,' she said. 'It's over now.'

She glanced over at Gumm and the fitter crews on the other side of the deck.

'Get Deck Dampier up here!' she yelled.

She looked back at Lopard.

'This is the end of the story,' she said. 'The dirty, little, underwhelming end.'

'But we agreed,' he said quietly. He even managed a little smile. 'We agreed, Jagdea. The big finish. That's how these stories are supposed to end.'

'This story should never have even begun,' she said.

'I'm getting in my bird now,' said Lopard very calmly. 'You go get in yours.'

'No.'

'That's how this works.'

'No, Lopard. What are you going to do? Run? There's nowhere to run to.'

'I'll find somewhere. Ditch somewhere. You'll have to stop me.'

'I'm not getting in my bird,' she said.

'You'll have to,' he repeated. His service sidearm was in his hand, aimed at her gut. 'Go on,' he smiled. 'Back up. Walk to your bird. You know how this goes down.'

'Lopard–'

'Do it,' he hissed. 'Do it for me. One last test of skill.'

'I'm not doing anything for you.'

A tremor of something, perhaps rage or hatred, rippled across his face. His smile dropped several octaves. He raised the weapon and aimed it at her face. She'd never drawn a sidearm from stores.

'Get in your frigging fightbird,' he hissed, his teeth almost clenched. 'Get in. Drop. For me. It's what friends do. Catch me if you can. Kill me, if you're able. I don't think you are. Do it.'

'I'm not going to do that,' Jagdea replied.

'What the hell?' someone called out. People were coming over, curious, puzzled. Voris and some of the fitters. Gumm, just behind them. Even Boa, at the far side of the deck, had turned in the seat of his tractor to look, the rain drooling off his yellow slicker.

'Back up! Off you go!' Lopard snarled at Jagdea. She took a few steps backwards, her hands half-raised, more to keep him calm than to indicate surrender.

'What the frig's going on?' an approaching fitter exclaimed.

'Piss off, the lot of you!' Lopard yelled. Jagdea heard their muttering confusion, but she didn't look. She kept her eyes on Lopard, on the gun, on the tremble in the hand holding it.

'Joke's over, Harlot!' Voris called out. 'Put that away!'

'Back the frig off!' Lopard yelled. 'I told you!'

He snatched his aim around. The first shot went over their heads and made them scatter for cover behind trolleys and tanker-carts. Somebody bumped into one of the sodium lamps, and it fell over with a clatter.

'Throne of Terra!' Voris barked, and lunged forward. Lopard shot him in the chest. The bottle of good amasec hit the deck, and shattered, a second before Voris fell on his face.

'Back off!' Lopard yelled, firing again, causing the last of them to bolt or duck. Jagdea took a step towards him, but Lopard snapped his aim back at her.

'Get in your bird, Bree Jagdea! I won't tell you again!'

Jagdea retreated a few more steps.

'Drop it, Lopard!' Gumm called out. He was running towards them, drawing his service weapon. Boa had leapt down from his tractor and was lumbering after him.

Lopard turned. He fired a second before Gumm. Gumm's round clipped Lopard's left shoulder and made him yelp. Lopard's round hit Gumm in the face and dropped him on his back. He lay very still, like an empty glove.

Boa roared. Lopard put two rounds through him. The ogryn fell to his knees hard, blood instantly staining his yellow slicker. Jagdea threw herself at Lopard, and tried to grapple with him. He was strong. He slapped her aside with the butt of the pistol.

She tried to get up. The blow had broken a tooth, maybe her actual jaw. Her ears were ringing. Lopard was already clambering into his cockpit. He yelled something, some last provocation or invitation.

Jagdea hauled herself to her feet. Lopard had locked his canopy.

Voltaics on. No time for slam-check or walking the parish. She heard the pale Bolt's compressor starting to spin up. He would be gone in seconds.

She started to run across the pad.

He wanted a fight. He wanted his ending. A blaze of glory, one way or the other. Phantine versus Glavian. Pilot against pilot. The legendary contest. She wasn't going to pander to his arrogant madness.

But she wasn't going to let him go either.

Lopard was reaching for the claw release when the brutal impact rocked his fightbird. He braced himself with a cry as his airframe continued to jolt and shudder. He stared out of the canopy.

She saw him staring out at her, his eyes wild with shock and confusion. Staring at her behind the wheel of Boa's tractor as she slammed the fork-lifter claws into the fuselage of his Thunderbolt. The cargo-8 was hard to steer, and the fork was a pig to manipulate. She tried to clamp, grinding fork-blades against metal, scraping paint, rocking the bird on its claws. She worked the levers, trying to get a better grip. Hydraulics whined. The tractor's fat tyres, hissing on the wet deck, were perilously close to the edge. Jagdea tried not to look. Boa had made this work look easy.

She rammed again. A proper broadside. Metal plating tore. There was a shower of sparks as hydraulic forks gouged against belly panels. Lopard was screaming at her. She couldn't hear him. What was he screaming? Rage that she wasn't playing his game? Fury at her? Disappointment? He had a glory story in mind, and they tended towards formulaic endings. Triumphant and uplifting. The noble duel, the big finish.

Not like this.

Her solutions had always been non-standard.

No, it was terror. She could see it plainly in his eyes, in the silent movement of his mouth behind the canopy plex. Terror that she, in her way, was just as ruthless as him.

She rammed again. Metal squealed. The forks pincered the Bolt's tail, crumpling and crushing. One of the tractor's front wheels dropped over the parapet with an ugly lurch. Lopard's eyes went even wider. The shred was in the cockpit with him. He put his hands on his head to show his submission.

'Not in this scenario,' said Jagdea.

Dead drop. A non-standard dead drop. The Bolt began to scrape over the lip, its dendritic claws torn free. The tractor began to slither with it, clamped to the airframe. Inside the fightbird, Lopard was trying to release his harness and pop the canopy.

Jagdea leapt from the tractor as the vehicles went over the edge. At full stretch, she almost made it. She slammed into the parapet chest-first, an impact that punched the air out of her lungs, and clung on with both arms, her legs kicking and milling. The edge of the deck and the stone lip were rain-slick. She couldn't hold on. Her hands tried to grip, but they hurt too much and the gloves were too heavy. She started to slide. One hand came away and she was suddenly looking down.

Engine primed but unstarted, Lopard's bird was falling nose-first down the side of the Campanile. Free-fall, the face of the bell tower rushing past. The tractor was falling with it, gripping it, the massive bulk of the cargo-8 acting like a counterweight, spinning the Thunderbolt as it dropped.

It was almost exactly like flying.

And then it wasn't any more.

Her other hand slipped loose and her slide accelerated. The long drop was going to take her too. Something jerked her hard, her legs and body smacking into the side of the tower. Her right arm cracked taut like a whip, her shoulder almost dislocated.

The pain was immense. Gumm was on his belly, both arms over the edge, clinging to her right wrist. She saw his blue eyes blazing down at her, the cracked chip across the lower part of his porcelain face where Lopard's shot had struck it.

'Other hand!' Gumm yelled.

She flailed. She couldn't. The strain was so great, she was going to pull him over after her. The shred was hanging on her legs and pulling her.

'Your other frigging hand!' he yelled. She tried to reach up. Her left hand smacked against his arms, but she couldn't grip. Her hands were on fire, the synth-flesh still bonding.

'Let me go–' she gasped.

'No!' Gumm yelled.

Then they were both rising, dragged back over the parapet like a fuel-heavy line. Boa had one huge hand around Gumm's shoulder, and the other locked around Jagdea's right forearm. He hauled them both back on the edge of the deck, and dropped them like empty ready-bags. Then he sat back heavily, the rain diluting the blood soaking the front of his yellow slicker, and bowed his head.

WHO ARE YOU NOW?

VESPERUS

IMPERIAL YEAR 795.M41, DAY 105

DAY 105

Dead zone chantry, Intercept 66, Vesperus, 06:20

She'd come alone, to pay her last respects. She lit a few candle stubs, and then knelt, in the soft yellow light, and set a glass of good amasec among the trophies, bones and shell cases nested on the grisly tribal shrine. Somewhere in the shadows nearby, the Saint was watching.

Jagdea's right shoulder and elbow still ached. Torn ligaments, Stanslaf had said when he bound them. And she could still feel the fire in her hands, though the synth-flesh was bonded and healing. A stimm-shot had dulled the worst of the pain.

She felt as though she should say something. Someone was dead, and never coming back, and someone else was alive. Garrant would have known what to say, but he was dead too. In the end, she resorted to the obvious, the tried and true refectory standard.

'The Emperor protects,' she whispered, 'the Aeronautica remembers.'

Maybe the dead were happier being dead? It was the easy part, after all. The person she had come to mourn was certainly at peace. She got to her feet, stiff and sore. Only then did she notice that Gumm was standing in the chantry doorway.

'Sorry to intrude,' he said.

'Don't be,' she replied.

'It's just that we've been called alert-ready and you–'

'I'm coming. I just had to...'

She didn't quite know how to explain it.

'Say goodbye to someone?' he asked.

She nodded.

He hesitated. No one had found a way to repair the crack in his ceramic face. It somehow gave character to his blankness.

'Not... Lopard, surely?' he asked.

'Throne, no!' She laughed, shaking her head.

'Then...?'

'Logistics Reserve Driver Bree Jagdea,' she said. 'She's never coming back. That life is over.'

'I see,' he said.

'You knew that days ago,' she said. 'This is me, now. I made a deal. I can't back out of it.'

She glanced at the shadows. The Beati was invisible, but Jagdea knew she was there.

'For better, for worse, for whatever,' said Jagdea. 'Combat, until I'm done. It's all right, though. It's Four-A.'

She knew he understood. Neither of them would ever be going home.

'Then I wish you good flying all the way,' he said.

'And you, Sagittarius.'

'Dampier's asking for you,' he said. 'And Badler wants you to check on the day's packets.'

'Why me?'

He handed her one of the two flight helmets he was carrying. It was hers, the gleaming black Ultris-pattern.

'Badler finally made up his mind,' said Gumm.

'Oh, for frig's sake,' Jagdea murmured. She looked at her

helmet. In white paint, across the visor plate, someone had scrawled the word EXEC.

Eleventh drop, Intercept 66, Vesperus, 07:01

Tail 044 was waiting for her on the launch deck. Pathfinder packets had been prepared for Machinko, and they had been loaded. She would be dropping with Gangster and Slipstream.

The day was bleak, and the Vesperus skyline lowered out of the gloom. A green, arsenic glow bathed everything. As Jagdea walked out onto the deck, the crews were still working around the three birds, and the tractor was reversing towards the ramp. One of the fitters was driving it, a little hesitantly. It would be a few days yet before Boa was fit to be back in the saddle.

A shout had just come in from ROP 54. Hostile track, Machinko. There would be no time for a blessing.

Jagdea climbed in and locked her straps.

'Checks Four-A,' Tarr said. 'All prime. So, I hear we have to salute you now, or some shit.'

Jagdea glanced at her. 'I can't see any point in you starting that now,' she replied.

Tarr grinned like a wolf. 'Decent game expected,' she said. 'The Circus will have a busy day.'

'There's a particular banded bat I'm hoping to see,' said Jagdea.

'Make sure you castigate the frig out of him, then,' said Tarr.

'Lid me up,' said Jagdea.

'Anything else I can't help you with?' Tarr asked.

'You already haven't,' said Jagdea.

'Good flying,' said Tarr, and latched the canopy.

Jagdea flipped the voltaic master and began her slam-check. She walked the parish from the left: vector thrust secondaries to preset, auspex and modar, starter, pump, ad-mix. Verification of target system, guns on. The starter compressor began to spool up. She armed countermeasures.

'Vox check,' she requested.

'Vox check, Exec. Gangster receiving.'

'Copy, Gangster.'

'Vox check, Exec, Slipstream copies.'

'Copy, Slipstream.'

Jagdea armed her seat.

'This is Exec, deconflict auspex,' she instructed. The autotrack flickered as the data loaded, then the auspex came up with a lo-res map that indicated the wireframe intercept path in red.

The vox crackled.

'Control to wings. Go for start. Go for start.'

'Copy, Control,' she replied. 'Exec to wings. Dead drop now.'

Jagdea released her landing claws.

Engine primed but unstarted, she fell nose-first down the side of the Campanile.

ABOUT THE AUTHOR

Dan Abnett has written over fifty novels, including the acclaimed Gaunt's Ghosts series and the Ravenor, Eisenhorn and Bequin books. His work for the Horus Heresy includes the first book in the series, *Horus Rising,* and the three-volume-long conclusion, *The End and the Death.* He also wrote several novels in between: *Legion, The Unremembered Empire, Know No Fear, Prospero Burns* and *Saturnine.* He scripted *Macragge's Honour,* the first Horus Heresy graphic novel, as well as numerous Black Library audio dramas. Many of his short stories have been collected into the volume *Lord of the Dark Millennium.* He lives and works in Maidstone, Kent.

YOUR NEXT READ

THE FALL OF CADIA
by Robert Rath

Cadia – a bulwark against the forces of Chaos that reside in the Eye of Terror. This proud world stood defiantly for centuries, until it was targeted for destruction by Abaddon the Despoiler in his Thirteenth Black Crusade.

An extract from
The Fall of Cadia
by Robert Rath

Blood and iron.

Iron and blood.

One lay on the other, and within the other. The slick shine of the iron-rich blood – still warm – on the cold surface of the bell. Two related elements, joined in accidental symbolism.

If records were to be believed, the bell had been forged from blood.

It was said that when Saint Gerstahl – the sacred soldier, favoured patron of the Cadian trooper – fell defending the Gate in the centuries after the Great Heresy, acolytes collected his vitae in a crystal reliquary. There it stayed for centuries, a venerated and lucrative relic on the shrine world christened with his name.

Until, one night, Blessed Gerstahl appeared to the cardinal with a message: he must extract the iron from the tarry, coagulated remnants and forge it into a bell.

A bell that would toll when Cadia was in mortal danger.

The cardinal forged the relic as instructed, then took the bell on a tour of the Cadian Gate, purifying world after world with the vibration of its holy resonance. A fortunate choice, since it escaped destruction when the Despoiler immolated the shrine world – and Gerstahl's incorruptible remains – during the Third Black Crusade.

On Solar Mariatus, two million welcomed the bell. Sobbing crowds parted to make a path for the fifty Battle Sisters of the Order of Our Martyred Lady who formed its vanguard. In the Derades Subsector, it was said that its chime healed the deaf and straightened crooked limbs. And on Laurentix, in the Belis Corona System, the populace wailed in ecstasy when it tolled a dozen times without being touched by human hands.

That was when the Black Legion descended upon it, in the opening raids of the Twelfth Black Crusade.

The vanguard had sworn to die rather than surrender their relic. And they fulfilled that oath. Their bodies now lay beneath the cold iron of the bell, some resting in its shadow. Chest cavities blown open, limbs severed from the impact of traitor bolt-shells, their own vitae splashed onto the blood-forged iron. It ran in frozen rivulets down the engraved surface, turning the scroll-work and decorative psalms into channels of gore.

They had saved it, in a sense.

Their stoic defence had given Trazyn time to lock the bell and its entourage in stasis, then spirit it to the archival vaults of Solemnace.

Now it hung, unmoving and fastened in time, among the relics of Cadia past. Gazed upon by the unseeing eyes of general officers snatched from the battlefield, zigzag trench-lines full of Shock Troops and a rank of Chimera variants bisected to show internal detail.

Overhead, a squad of Night Lords Raptors arced through the vaults above a lit display of human eyes.

All of them, artefacts of the Cadian Gate. The ephemera of Abaddon the Despoiler's twelve Black Crusades.

Darkened exhibits stretched across twenty-five square miles, a private gallery of humans, exquisitely arranged to please the historical and aesthetic tastes of the alien curator who'd imprisoned them.

Nothing in the gallery apart from maintenance scarabs had moved in over a millennium.

Which is why the soft *pat-pat-pat* of fluid echoed as far as it did.

It fell from the iron surface of the bell like the first drops of icicles melting on the eaves of a hab. Drip. Drip-drip.

Jewelled drops met the upturned forehead of a slain Battle Sister and stained her pale skin with splashes of crimson.

Pat. Pat-pat.

More drops. Coalescing on her brow, trickling into her open eyes.

Blood moved on the bell's skin, collecting in beads like rain on a window and falling in defiance of the stasis field.

And the bell, without propulsion or force, began to swing.

A hand's breadth at first. A sway. Its clapper moving in a soft pendulum arc too weak to do more than scrape the sides.

Then, the arc widened, the violent motion of the bell flinging droplets of blood to either side, spattering the faces of stasis-locked Shock Troopers. Sizzling on the protective fields of lasgun displays. Swaying wider until the bell went fully perpendicular and the clapper inside dropped, its hammer striking the iron of the bell.

Clang.

One.

The blackstone floor vibrated. A rank of medals swayed, its stasis field shorting out. An organic clatter filled the chamber, the sound of ten thousand jaws – held shut by hard-light holograms – shaken so hard that the teeth rattled.

Overhead, the flight of Night Lords Raptors tumbled from the vaults and into a trench display, snapping bones and crushing lasgun barrels. Neither Traitor Space Marines nor Guardsmen reacted.

Clang.

Two.

Trazyn, Overlord of Solemnace, Archaeovist of the Prismatic Galleries and He-Who-Is-Called-Infinite, screamed in rage.

'Sannet! What is happening?'

'Unclear,' answered his chief cryptek, his multijointed fingers dancing across phos-glyph panels. 'Unknown resonance. Macroseismic. Cracking the vaults, releasing coolant. We've lost the Ooliac sand sculptures.'

'Call the restoration scarabs.'

'Not responding,' Sannet answered, data-chains flashing across his ocular. 'Our nodal program misinterpreted the vibration as a re-interment signal. The legion has entered radical shutdown. I cannot rouse them.'

Trazyn cursed the very wheel of the cosmos. The interval between shocks had been only seconds apart, and while mental speech between he and Sannet was near instant, they were running out of time before the next tectonic shudder would hit.

'It's not tectonic, lord,' said Sannet. 'It's coming from the gallery.'

'Where?'

'The Black Crusades wing.'

'That's only two levels do–'

Clang.

Three.

The shockwave shook Trazyn apart, his joint servos spasming and dislocating with the intensity of it.

He evacuated the dying body and rushed his spirit-algorithm into the network of data-channels in the walls. Found a waiting lychguard he could use as a surrogate. Melted and reshaped the borrowed body into his accustomed form as he ran towards the gates of the Cadian gallery. Waved a hand at the enormous gates in a gesture of opening.

Clang.

Four.

The doors ahead, twice the size of a monolith, blew off their hinges and toppled down at him. He felt them crumple the necrodermis of his cranium like parchment and burst his central reactor before he transferred to another body, sheltered in the lee of a Baneblade.

He sprinted. Waving hands at display plinths, throwing code-signals from his palm emitters. Trying to restart shielding and repulsors, to protect his delicate artefacts.

'No, no, no, no, no, no–'

Trazyn saw the bell.

Trazyn saw the blood.

He slowed his chronosense to take in the swinging relic and its sheets of ruby spray. It was far more human vitae than had been splashed on its surface.

Almost as if the relic itself were bleeding from the pockmarks and scratches where bolt-shells had marked it.

'Sannet,' Trazyn said, casting his visual senses into the data-stream of Solemnace so his cryptek could run analysis. 'The stasis field has failed. Hard restart.'

'The field is active,' Sannet responded. 'Movement should be impossible.'

'Not impossible, warpcraft.'

Trazyn watched in fascinated horror as the bell completed its arc, the blood-forged metal swinging high as the hammer inside dropped like the great mace of a warmaster.

Clang.

Five.

Across the galaxy, past burning stars, teeming worlds and cold expanses of nothing, lay the blasted world of Eriad VI. The Ark Mechanicus vessel *Iron Revenant* hung in its orbit, casting a cruciform shadow on the surface.

Down, down, through the nuclear-blighted atmosphere and crust overrun with ork ravagers. Down in black tunnels of alien scale and curve, stood Archmagos Dominus Belisarius Cawl.

'Nearly,' he said, stretching the word. His eyes squeezed tight, optic nerves rerouted through the visual lenses of the skull probe he'd guided into the bore-hole. The on-off strobe of its ultraviolet lamp – used to map the worming tunnels within the blackstone – was the only illumination. He sensed a data-stream connection. 'Careful, little one. Rise two skull-lengths. Pivot thirty-five degrees right. Ahead four lengths – now, now, now! All ahead steady and open connection! Op–'

The data flooded in, pasting across his vision, unfamiliar glyphs that slid cold into his mind, chill as the nothing of space.

The servo-skull's vision blasted to static, its auditory ports howling in Cawl's augmented brain.

'Damn it!' he cursed, yanking the skull-jack free from his temple. 'Qvo, another probe!'

No response. His programmable servant – cloned from a long-dead companion – was either not listening, or perhaps had reset due to the flood of data.

'Qvo?' He turned. 'Qvo, are you lis–'

He stopped.

The aeldari standing behind his right shoulder had not triggered a single alert in his sensorium net.

She crouched on a cogitator bank, toes together, knees spread wide – an inverted-triangle pose inhuman in its gravity-defying grace.

'The skeins of fate wind tight about the gate,' Veilwalker said, her egg-like mask nothing but a swirl of smoke. The hues of her motley seemed to blaze in the dark cavern. 'Again, I plea – does thy mind now see?'

'Your rhymes are impenetrable nonsense,' he growled. 'It is a necron world, bombarded by the Despoiler during the Fourth Black Crusade. But why would he bombard an empty planet? I cannot fathom why you insisted I come here.'

'More excavation,' the xenos answered, cocking her head, 'will dispel frustration.'

'To hells with your childish rhymes. Just tell me what you want me to know!'

She shook her head, mask gleaming blue in apology. 'You must play your role – the bell does toll.'

'And what, by the blessed reactor, is that supposed to mean?'

Clang.

Six.

'It started an hour ago, canoness,' said Sister Navarette. Even with her daily training regimen, Genevieve could hear that her Seraphim Superior was out of breath climbing the bell-tower stairs.

They should have taken their jump packs.

The Shrine of St Morrican was a large edifice, and the bell-tower one of the tallest buildings in the Kraf Sector – securing the gateway between Cadia Primus and Cadia Secundus.

For nigh a hundred days it had served as a linchpin of the defence, ensuring that the Archenemy forces of the Thirteenth Black Crusade – which had overrun Kasr Myrak to the north – did not break loose into the Kraf Plain.

'It's ringing?' Genevieve asked. 'Are you certain?'

'Without being touched.'

Genevieve bolted up the last flight, emerging into the vault of the bell-tower. And saw her own face, tight-lipped, looking back at her.

'Canoness Genevieve,' said her twin sister, Eleanor, with a formal bend of her head.

It was every bit like looking in a mirror. Ironic, given how different they were. Twin canonesses in twin suits of armour. Only differing in every other way – and the simple fact that Genevieve's recent ocular augmetic replaced her left eye rather than the right.

But when they faced each other, that only enhanced the feeling of looking in a glass.

'I see you are late,' sneered Arch-Deacon Mendazus. 'As was ever the case.'